SILENT CHILD

by

SARAH A. DENZIL

ISBN: 1542722829
ISBN-13: 978-1542722827

CHAPTER ONE

The day I lost Aiden was the day I realised what it meant to lose control. People talk about losing control of themselves all the time, whether it's from drink, drugs, passion, or anger. But they don't know what it's truly like to lose control, and I'm not talking about my emotions, but about my *life*. I lost control of my life. Everything around me fell apart while I remained the impotent bystander.

I've heard it said that you can only control yourself and how *you* behave in any given setting. You can never control the circumstances around you. You can't control how other people react, only how you, yourself, act. That's the great tragedy of life. One moment everything is perfect and the next it's all in tatters because of the circumstances happening all around you. And what are you supposed to think when your child is taken from you? That it was fate? God? Bad luck? How are you supposed to move on?

When it comes to the birth lottery, I lucked out. I was born in the kind of bucolic loveliness that lulls you into thinking *nothing bad will ever happen to me*. Guns and violence may litter the news, but nothing like that ever happens in Bishoptown-on-Ouse. We were nestled in the sweeping landscape of a John Constable painting, with long stretches of rolling green pastures and dry-stone walls. We were safe. At least I thought we were.

On the twenty-first of June, 2006, at two o'clock in the afternoon I donned a great waterproof coat and a pair of Wellington boots, and stepped out into the worst flash flood that Bishoptown-on-Ouse had seen since 1857. The cottage I shared with my parents and my six-year-old son, Aiden, was set slightly back from the quiet street. As I stepped outside that day, the stream of water took me by surprise with its strength. It splashed up my wellies and spattered across my crotch. My heart had already started to quicken, because I was worried about getting to the school. The teachers had rung around all the parents asking them to collect the children because the rain was getting through the roof at school, and there was danger that the banks of the Ouse would burst. We had known about the torrential rain, but no one had predicted this. It fell in a sheet from above, relentlessly soaking my face and battering the hood of my Karimor jacket.

The Ouse twisted through our tiny village like a

boa constrictor through a sandbox. It was picturesque and pretty, this too-big river in our tiny town. Bishoptown had two pubs, a B&B, a church, a school, and a population of around 400 people. It was the second smallest village in England, and the smallest village in Yorkshire. No one moved out of Bishoptown and no one moved in. If a house went up for sale it was because someone died.

We all knew each other. We grew up together, lived together, raised our children together. So when the phone rang and Amy Perry—a teacher at the primary school and one of my old school friends—told me to pick up Aiden, I knew the situation was bad. Otherwise, Amy would have walked the children back to each and every house in the village. That was how much we trusted each other.

I'd heard the rain drumming on the windows, but I'd been lost in my own world yet again, looking at MySpace photos of my school friends who had been to uni and since gone travelling. I was twenty-four. I'd finished my A-levels with Aiden in my belly and watched my friends leave for university with the world at their feet while I remained in my parents' house. I saw some of them leaving for new pastures as I gazed down at the bus stop from my bedroom window, one hand on my swollen stomach. Since that moment, I had spent more time than was healthy Googling my friends on the internet, opening pictures of Thailand and Paris while I nursed a baby.

There was no way I could drive in this weather, and I was the closest to the school out of my little family, so I decided to walk there. Rob—Aiden's father—was working on a construction site outside York. My parents had their own jobs, too. They would be too far away to help, trapped by the weather. I didn't call any of them right away because I didn't think I needed to. Bishoptown was a small place, and it would only take me ten minutes to walk to the school. But the school building was also on the other side of the Ouse, which did worry me slightly. If the rain was as bad as the news suggested, the river could burst its banks.

I trudged up the road through the rainwater with my heart beating a rapid tattoo against my ribs. The slanting rain made it difficult to keep my eyes open as I walked against it. I lowered my head and gripped the strap of the bag over my shoulder, with my hands already soaked and cold to the bone.

"Emma!"

The voice was only just audible above the hammering of the rain on the tarmac. I turned around to see my friend Josie waving to me as she hurried up the hill in my direction. She was an accountant at the small firm where I was working part-time as a secretary. It jolted me to see her so dishevelled, her hair plastered to her head and make-up running down her face. She had no coat, no umbrella. Her pencil skirt was soaked through.

"Jo! Jesus, get inside."

"Emma, I've just been across the bridge. The banks are breaking. You need to go home."

"Fuck. I have to get Aiden from school."

"They'll keep him safe," she said. "But if the river bursts and you're close to the bridge you could drown." She waved me towards her but I stayed where I was.

"I have to get Aiden," I said, shaking my head. The school was too close to the river for me to feel comfortable leaving my six-year-old son with them. If the rain was already coming in through the roof, what state was the school in?

"Be careful. I heard they're sending help but there's hardly anyone by the river right now, no police or anything, and it looks bad, Em. Don't come back across the bridge, okay? Go to the White Horse or something. At least you can get a Chardonnay there, right?" She grinned at the joke but I could tell it was a nervous smile. She was genuinely shaken up, which wasn't like Josie at all.

"All right. Get home safe. I'll see you at work when this bloody weather has calmed down a bit." I returned the nervous smile, trying to ignore the nest of snakes in my abdomen. My dad had volunteered in the Royal National Lifeboat Institute when he was younger and he had always told me that if there was one thing in life you did not mess with, it was the sea.

Our tiny bit of the sea gushed through Bishoptown today. When I reached the bridge, the sight took my breath away. Josie was right: The Ouse was dangerously close to bursting its banks. Usually tranquil and slow, that day the river surged beneath the bridge, hitting the stone arches in waves. The water seeped up onto the sodden grass banks, and some of it dribbled down the hill towards my parents' cottage. I took a step back and pulled out my mobile phone. There was no answer at the school, which did not assuage my worry. I phoned Dad next.

"Emma, are you all right?" he asked. "I'm at the office and the rain is so bad I think I'll be stuck here."

"Don't try to get home, Dad, the river might burst." Dad worked just outside Bishoptown as a civil engineer for a construction firm. "I'm going to the school to stay with Aiden until help arrives."

"Emma—"

"I'm fine. Just… don't try to come home, okay?"

"Emma, the bridge—"

I eyed the short, stone bridge with trepidation. "I'm already past it. I'm on my way up Acker Lane to the school."

He let out a sigh of relief. "I'll call your mother and tell her to stay at the surgery."

"Okay, Dad. I love you."

"Love you too, kiddo."

It was silly, I know, but my eyes filled with tears as I cancelled the call. The time on my phone said 2:10pm. It had taken me ten minutes to walk just half the way. I needed to hurry up and get to my son. I strode up to the bridge and tried to ignore the water level, hoping that my hurried strides would somehow make it less dangerous.

Water poured across the bridge, almost ankle deep. I didn't know if it was rainwater or water that had come from the river, or a combination of both. The only thing I knew was that I had to hurry up. But as I took the last step down off the bridge, a wave of river water hit the bridge hard and chunks of stone dislodged, crumbling beneath my feet. It sent me off balance and I stumbled forward, dropping my phone into the river. My breath left my body as the freezing cold water hit me side-on, almost knocking me straight into the churning waters. I took a long sidestep like a crab, feeling the current trying to drag me along with it.

But the riverbank was soft and muddy, which allowed me to ram the heel of my wellie deep into the earth. The suction gave enough of a foothold to propel myself forward, clawing my way up the river bed towards the road. My left boot came clean off.

With my sock dangling from my foot I climbed my way up to the road, gasping for air as the rain pounded from above. When I was away from the bridge, I turned around and watched my boot slip under the water. I tried to find my breath, soaked down to my bra. That could have been me, and then who would be there to take Aiden home? No, I wouldn't be bringing Aiden home, not with the river like this. I'd have to stay with him at the school. What an idiot I'd been. I'd ignored my dad's warnings about water. A hard lump formed in my throat as I turned my back on the river. One misstep and I would have fallen into the same water as the stones, my phone, and my Wellington boot. One mistake and I would have been floating beneath the current where the water is calm, with my hair gliding out around me, an ethereal water-nymph who would never breathe again.

Another dead young woman. A statistic in a tragic flooding incident. A selfish woman who left her six-year-old motherless after lying to her father. I shook my head and made my way up Acker Lane like I had just told Dad. The road followed the direction of the river for a mile, before turning left onto the school road. The school road carried on for another half a mile before coming to the carpark of Bishoptown school. I noticed that the water had pooled in the car park, where it was halfway up the tyres of some of the cars. There was little chance of all these people making it home for the night. I turned my attention back to the school—it was my school, too, where I'd carved my name into the floorboards in the assembly hall to impress Jamie Glover; a boy who would later break my heart by kissing Fiona Cater on the rugby pitch in secondary school. By this time, of course, it was my son's school. It was his time to make memories and carve his name into wood using the sharp point of a compass.

It was a small Victorian building, built like a

modest church, with steep gables and old-fashioned leaded windows. There was more than a hint of Gothic about it.

Dragging my soaked sock, I ran to the entrance and let myself in, almost tripping over someone in the doorway. When I straightened up I realised that it was Mrs. Fitzwilliam, the same woman who had been headteacher when I was a child. When she saw me, her face paled, and her gaze moved from my eyes to somewhere above my head. There was something about the change in her countenance that made my stomach drop to my sodden feet.

"What is it?" I asked.

A dribble of rain water trickled down the wall behind Mrs. Fitzwilliam. We'd called her Mrs. Fitz when I was a child. She had always been firm but fair. We were a little afraid of her red hair, but it was almost completely grey now, and her stern expression was softer as she finally met my gaze. The tears in her eyes forced my heart to resume into its tattoo against my ribs. I clutched hold of my chest, trying to calm myself while my heart seemed to have been restarted with defibrillators.

"Ms Price… Emma… I'm so sorry."

I took a step forward and she took a step back. Her expression told me that mine was wild. She put both hands up in front of her as if in surrender.

"We've called the police and they'll be here soon."

"Tell me what happened," I demanded.

"Aiden slipped away. Miss Perry was with the

children in classroom four. She was performing a headcount. We had collected all the children from year two in that classroom because the roof leak wasn't as bad. But somehow Aiden left the classroom. We've searched the premises and we believe he has left the school."

I clutched my chest, as if such a paltry action could alleviate the pain that radiated from my heart. "Why would he leave?"

She shook her head. "I don't know. Perhaps he was curious about the rain."

I crumpled in on myself, folding over like paper. Of course he was curious. Aiden was curious about everything. He was an explorer. He climbed trees in the park, he scurried over five-bar gates into fields filled with cows, he hid in the heather on the moors around Bishoptown, and played hide and seek in the forest. I had nurtured that side of him. I wanted a wild, brave child. I wanted that for him; I wanted him to grow into a strong man with a penchant for exploring. I'd pushed my wanderlust onto him.

But I hadn't wanted *this*. I hadn't wanted him to wander away from safety during the most dangerous flood in over a hundred years.

"You've searched the school?" I asked.

"We're still looking," she said.

"I'll help."

The rest of that day was a blur. I checked each classroom myself, tripping over buckets placed under leaks and snatching open cupboard doors, screaming his name until I scared the other children. It was no use. Aiden was not in the school. I'd searched every nook and cranny of the school, even trudging around the carpark and the football field. Eventually Amy got me to sit down and Mrs Fitzwilliam brought me hot coffee.

The police had shown up hours later, along with search and rescue. Somehow amongst all that I'd been given an extra pair of shoes. No one had found Aiden. There was so much for the authorities to deal with. Search and rescue and the police were stretched so thinly that my boy, my missing boy, stayed just that. Missing.

And now, do I resent that? Do I hate the parents whose children were taken to safety in boats and helicopters as the Ouse finally burst and covered our small village in its murky lifeblood? No. I can't. I can't begrudge the men and women who worked tirelessly to help the living. But as I watched everyone moving around me, watched the rest of the children reunited with their parents, and watched the half-drowned people of my village receive blankets and hot cups of tea, I realised that my life was no longer in my own hands. On that day, when I lost Aiden, I lost all control of my life, and with him gone, I would never get it back.

CHAPTER TWO

All that wasted potential. That was the phrase I heard over and over again when I fell pregnant with Aiden in year thirteen of school. I had just turned eighteen when I pissed on the stick, and had already sent my UCAS application to several universities—universities that I had expected to accept me to their humanities courses. However, Rob, my boyfriend at the time, had not applied to any universities. He was hanging on by a thread, and when I announced my news, the thread finally broke.

Rob was never the kind of boy you took home to your parents. He was in a band at fifteen, tattooed at sixteen, and almost completely gave up on school at seventeen. He had stayed on at Bishoptown School to do his A-Levels, but when I look back on that time now, I wonder if he'd stayed to hang out with me more than anything. We were very much in love but it was young love; passionate and idiotic, full of mistakes and drama. The biggest drama was my pregnancy, which prompted a family meeting between the Prices and the Hartleys to discuss what should be done about the whole ordeal. At one point I wondered whether they might send me away somewhere for nine months to have the baby in secret. It all suddenly seemed like the early twentieth century, not the early twenty-first.

This was a small village of rich, rural people. My mother was the general practitioner for Bishoptown. Rob's family owned the boutique B&B in the village and several holiday cottages outside York. We were supposed to have a future. We were middle-class children whose parents had worked hard for our future, and we'd pissed it all away like I'd pissed on that stick.

I could have had an abortion, and believe me, I considered it. Mum even sat me down and described the procedure in a calm and neutral way. Girls like me often chose that route. It's often what they feel is the best decision for them. But there was something about that little bean I saw on the ultrasound scan that made me wonder whether there was a little magic growing inside me. I had the magic bean forming in my womb and I wanted to see how it would all turn out. Maybe there was some selfishness to my decision. Maybe there is some selfishness to every decision. But that was my choice.

My choice was Aiden.

And I never regretted it.

Not when he split open my skin coming out of me, not when he screamed bloody murder instead of taking a nap, and not when they found his red coat floating in the River Ouse three days after the flood. No, I never regretted my choice, not even seven long years after the flood when I finally, officially, had my son declared legally dead.

"Emma, do you want to open this one next?"

I blinked, and found myself back in the teachers' common room, sat on the not-so 'comfy' chairs that had been arranged around a small coffee table. The left wall was covered by the teachers' pigeonholes, and behind me was a small kitchen area with a few cupboards containing old cereal packets and a sink filled with mugs and teaspoons. How long had I been thinking about Aiden? From the looks on the faces around me, I'd not been paying attention for a while.

"Sure! Sorry, I was miles away." I tucked a strand of loose hair behind my ear and bent my head as I smiled and took the present from Amy's outstretched hand.

Ten years ago, when Aiden died in the flood, I would never have imagined that I'd be working with the woman who allowed my son to wander out of school. But life moves on and people evolve. Despite everything, I forgave Amy for that day. She'd been stretched beyond her capabilities during the flood, and when her back was turned, my son did the improbable: He walked straight out of school, down to the dangerous river, and got caught up in the current and drowned. Those are the cold, hard facts. But whenever I thought of them, I disconnected myself from the reality of them. Sometimes I wondered if I'd disconnected from Aiden's death completely. I wondered if I really believed he was dead, not just living like a wild thing on the Yorkshire moors somewhere, frightening hikers by jumping out from the heather and then scampering off to a cave to live like Stig of the Dump.

I pushed my thumbnail under the Sellotape and slowly peeled open the present on my lap. It was wrapped in a pink ribbon with pink wrapping paper of pretty birds and flowers. The paper was thick and hard to tear. Amy hadn't just nipped to the newsagents on Bishoptown Hill for this, she'd gone to Paperchase or Waterstones for such pretty—and trendy—paper. Beneath the birds was a box with a clear plastic front.

"It's beautiful." I exhaled slowly, holding back the tears pricking at my eyes.

"Is it okay?" she asked, a quaver of anxiety evident in her voice. "I know some mums don't like people getting such girly presents for their babies. But I saw it and it was so gorgeous that I just had to."

I met her watery gaze with my own. I'd known Amy since I was thirteen or fourteen, though we'd never been close. She was someone who would hang around in the same circles as me, but not someone I would call on a Saturday night for a veg out and movie night. She had always been somewhat mousy, and would have been pretty if it hadn't been for the long front teeth that prevented her mouth from closing completely. She had something of a stereotypical librarian demeanour. She was quiet, uneasy and awkward with most people, and I know Aiden's death had weighed heavily on her mind all these years. Eventually, after my crippling grief had slowly faded, I'd ended up feeling sorry for her.

"Oh, it's lovely," cooed Angela, head of year seven.

"Pretty," said Sumaira from the English department.

"I want to go back to being a girl and get one myself," said Tricia, the other school administrator.

I looked down at the doll resting on my lap and tried hard to push the memory of Aiden out of my mind so that for once, just once, I could think about my future.

It'd been hard, this decade, harder than I'd ever imagined life could be, but it had not been completely filled with misery. There had been beautiful moments, like marrying Jake and finding out I was pregnant with his child. This should be another happy moment and I wanted to enjoy it. I wanted to live in the present. So I pushed Aiden out of my mind—while saying a silent apology— and thought of the day I would give this beautiful doll to my daughter. It was porcelain, with delicate pink cheeks and wavy brown hair that fell to its shoulders. It wore a pink tulle dress with daisies stitched along the hem, and a butterfly on the shoulder strap.

"It's perfect, Amy, thank you. Where on earth did you find it?" I asked.

"Well," she said. "There's an online shop that makes them custom to order. But they also had some ready-made and this was one of them. I fell in love with her and just had to buy her for you."

I placed the doll carefully on the coffee table next to the huge, shiny card decorated with tiny baby grows on a washing line, then leaned forward in my chair and wrapped my arms around Amy. She patted me on the back, leaning over my protruding baby bump to embrace me.

"I wish I'd had a bump that neat when I was eight months pregnant," said Sumaira. "I was out here!" She demonstrated with her arms and we all laughed.

"I keep thinking that one day I'll wake up and be the size of a house," I said, laughing with them. I'd been active before the pregnancy. Running had helped me deal with the grief and I'd been at the height of my fitness during the early stages of the pregnancy. I still felt some of that strength in my body. I certainly didn't feel weak or encumbered. I did get some of the classic symptoms of being heavily pregnant, like swollen ankles and needing to pee twice as much, but I was a far cry from the comedic elephant-sized pregnant women you see on the television. Not once had I burst into tears at work—and I'd managed to get through the last eight months without craving pickles, too.

"We're going to miss you around here, Price-Hewitt," Tricia said, pulling me into another hug.

"I'm going to miss you guys, too. Don't get too attached to my replacement because I'll be back before you know it."

"You take your time," Angela said. "Don't rush it. Enjoy your time with the baby."

I nodded, taking in her words. No one mentioned Aiden. No one acknowledged that this was my second child. I bit my lip and fought against the rising tide of guilt threatening to take hold.

"Jake will be waiting for me." I stood a little too fast and felt the blood rushing to my head. My joints ached a little, but the kindness of my colleagues had bolstered my energy levels and I felt strong enough to take on the world. I was ready for the next challenge ahead, especially with Jake waiting for me in the carpark. He had been my rock through the bad times, there with an outstretched hand to catch me when I fell. And believe me, I fell a lot. I had fallen into darkness after Aiden died.

"Call us when the baby is born. We all want to meet her," Amy said. She bit her lip and I could see her mind whirring with thoughts of my lost boy, the one who'd walked away from her and never came back.

"Yes, bring the little one into work, won't you? It's been ages since I had a cuddle with a newborn. My Oliver is nearly three now, if you can believe it," said Tricia, her eyes misty with thoughts of her grandson.

"Of course," I replied. "I can't wait for you all to meet her."

I bundled up the cards and presents into a plastic bag and picked up the large bunch of roses with the price carefully peeled away from the packaging. We stood awkwardly near the door and for the first time, I saw hesitation on their faces. I saw contemplation, and I knew what they were all thinking about.

Amy brushed tears away from her cheeks. We might not have mentioned Aiden's existence. We might have all made the unconscious decision to not utter his name while we celebrated the new baby, but Aiden was close, so close I could almost see him standing in the shadows next to the pigeonholes and the corner table. He was in Amy's tears, and in the knowing smile on Sumaira's face. He was in my heart, buried in my arteries, mixed into my blood and my DNA, and every atom that made me 'me'.

I said my goodbyes and made my way down the steps and out into the carpark, the same carpark I had run through that terrible day when my Wellington boot had sloshed through the rainwater and my sock had hung precariously from my toes. Then I saw the silver Audi, and Jake's smiling face in the driver's seat.

"How did it go?" he asked, as I piled the presents and flowers into the backseat. We'd need to sort the baby seat out soon, I mused. It was only three weeks until my due date and there was much to be done.

"Good. You should see the gorgeous doll Amy bought for Bump."

Jake frowned. "You look wiped out. I was going to suggest we go for some tea to celebrate, but I think you need a warm bath and an early night. Shall we order in from Da Vinci's instead?"

I leaned across the gearstick to plant a soppy kiss on Jake's cheek. "That sounds perfect."

As we pulled out of the carpark, I couldn't help but turn and give the school building one last look. I'd been working there for five years now, and I should've been used to the sight of the old Victorian building by now, yet somehow it brought all those feelings rushing back to the surface. And then, she kicked. I clutched my belly and felt the second kick.

Yes, I know you're there. There's room in my heart for you too.

CHAPTER THREE

Bishoptown School is a primary and secondary school in one. They added a newer building to the back of the old Victorian building about twenty years ago. Kids under eleven are taught in the older building at the front, and the kids from year seven upwards study in the newer block behind. I met Jake when I was one of those kids.

He was my teacher.

It sounds creepy. It isn't.

Jake started at Bishoptown just before I started studying for my GCSEs, but he didn't teach me until I started my A-Levels. He was an art teacher and I was an art student. He was young, only twenty-eight, and had just moved up to Bishoptown from a small town outside Brighton. Of course I noticed he was gorgeous back then. We called him Handsome Hewitt. But I was far too enamoured with my own beau, Rob, to even give my teacher a second glance. And then Aiden came along…

Six years ago I was a mess. I hadn't worked properly since Aiden's death, aside from a part-time job in a supermarket, and I survived solely on the inheritance Mum and Dad left after they died in a car crash. It was Jake who sought me out, who got me a job in the school, who pulled me out of the pit of darkness and showed me that it was possible to turn on a light switch and save my own life. Finding him—or rather, him finding me—convinced me that I wasn't cursed after all, just unfortunate enough to lose my son and parents in less than four years.

I owed Jake all that I had.

As we pulled into the driveway to our house, I glanced across at my husband and let my eyes drink him in. Despite being ten years older than me, he was still attractive in a distinguished way. His wrinkles and greying hair didn't matter so much. It delighted me that he dressed like a typical teacher, with corduroy blazers and patterned ties. On him it looked trendy and sexy, not dowdy like some of the aging geography teachers at the school.

He noticed my searching gaze and flashed me a questioning look. "What is it?"

"Nothing." I shrugged. The stressful afternoon washed away and was replaced by a feeling akin to real happiness. Sure, I'd had glimpses of happiness over the last decade, but they'd never remained, not like the spreading feeling I was getting now.

Could it be that my life was coming together? Was my happiness overtaking my grief for Aiden and my parents? They say that time is a healer, but I never believed them. I considered myself irrevocably broken after the flood. But it seemed that at last, those pieces were binding together.

Or so I thought.

*

Jake carried the presents into the house and I poured water into a vase and trimmed the stems of the roses. The kitchen came alive with the sounds of our movements, and the plastic bags rustled as Jake put the presents on the dining table. He began unpacking them one by one.

"Was Jane there?" he asked.

"No, she's hurt her back."

"Again?" Jake shook his head. "I guess that's what you get when you let yourself get into that state. How did she do it?"

I bristled at his callous remark. Jane was middle-aged and overweight. She'd missed half the previous term with constant health issues. It was hard not to think that most of her problems would disappear if she'd just lose the weight, but Jake had a brain-to-mouth problem sometimes. He said what other people didn't dare to. "She twisted her back putting her bra on."

Jake let out a loud guffaw. "You're kidding!"

"Hey," I said, "it's hard putting a bra on when

your skin's all damp from the shower."

"Yeah, but still." He shook his head and carried on removing the presents from the bag. "So Amy bought you this doll then? And you... like it?" He held up the box with the delicate doll inside.

"Yeah, why?"

"You don't think it's a bit... creepy?" He lifted the package higher as I stood with my hip resting against the kitchen counter, scissors in one hand and a rose in the other. His fingers dug into the plastic and I wanted to tell him to stop squeezing it like that. The plastic crackled as he moved it about, setting my teeth on edge.

When he put it down the tension abated and I managed a laugh. "Are you one of those people who cried when they had a clown at a birthday party?"

Jake pushed his glasses further up his nose and gave a half-smile. "Only psychopaths find clowns funny. It's a fact. Just look at John Wayne Gacy."

I shivered as I plopped the final rose in place and gathered up the wrapping from the flowers, the trimmings caught within the folds.

"Don't forget to wipe the side down," Jake said, nodding towards the slight puddle of water I'd left on the counter.

I rolled my eyes but collected a tea towel from the rack to soak up the mess. It was a running joke that Jake had needed to train me to pick up after myself when we first moved in together. He said he used to coach me with praise and slight nudges in the right direction. If I'd been good he'd take me out for dinner. For the first six months I hardly noticed at all. I'd never been concerned with mopping up a little spilled water or picking up my socks from the night before, not until I shared a living space with a neat-freak like Jake. Perhaps I'd been coddled too much by my parents after Aiden died. After all, I did remain living with them until they died. Then, when things became serious with Jake, I sold my parents' cottage and moved into Jake's luxurious three-bedroom property on Fox Lane, a stone's throw from the school.

It was the opposite of my parents' higgledy-piggledy cottage. My parents' place was as quaint as an English cottage could get, with a thatched roof and narrow stairs filled with piles of books and old pieces of art. Jake's house was colourless and neat. The ceilings were high and airy. My parent's house had been painted in various shades of reds and browns, with low ceilings but plenty of windows to let in light. The kitchen had been filled to the bursting point with cast iron pans hanging from the beams and stacks of letters on top of the fridge. Jake's kitchen was minimalist and stark, with white modern cupboards and a hidden fridge.

I set the roses on the table and took a step back, thinking how it was nice to have some colour in the kitchen for a change. Sometimes I missed the red walls of my old bedroom and the patterned duvets that inevitably lay in a tangled heap at the bottom of my bed. These days I slept—or rather tossed and turned—on crisp Egyptian cotton sheets in either ivory or white.

"Let's go sit on the sofa and watch a box set." Jake wrapped an arm around me and led me gently towards the living room.

"Don't you want to read my card?"

"Oh yeah, of course," he said enthusiastically. "Bring it with you. How have you been today? Any back pain?"

I almost laughed out loud. Of course there was back pain. And ankle pain. And then there was the baby ramming her foot against my internal organs. When I was pregnant with Aiden I'd been really squeamish about the thought of my baby sharing space with my kidneys and intestines and everything else squashed alongside the womb, especially when I learned that the body moves and adapts to make room for the baby. This time around I'd been determined to embrace all the joys of being pregnant. That had lasted until my first bout of morning sickness.

"No more than usual." I settled into the sofa. Despite my bravado, I was tired from all the fuss. It was nice to take the weight off my feet. In fact, I probably wouldn't want get up again now, unless I needed the loo. I passed the card to Jake.

"It makes me sad, reading this," Jake said. He stuck out a lip, imitating a pout.

"Why? I mean, I know John in the history department read the card wrong and wrote 'sympathies' but everyone else is happy for us. I hope he read the card wrong, anyway. Maybe he just feels very strongly about people bringing more children into the world." My little joke turned sour in my mouth as I said the word 'children'. It's still there, that bitterness. For a long time I couldn't look at other people's children. I couldn't even say the word. I stared down at my bump and tried to force those feelings away. It was time to be able to say a joke and enjoy it.

"Because we won't be working together for the next year. I won't be taking you to work and bringing you home. I wish I could take the year off with you. I mean, would it be so crazy? Would it be terrible?"

"It might be if we want to eat," I replied. "You'd have to quit your job completely. They aren't going to let you take the year off. Not both of us, anyway."

"I know. But... what are you going to do all day?"

"Well, I think this one will keep me busy." I laughed and pointed to my baby bump. But when I saw the tense line of his jaw and the way he gripped the card, I leaned across the sofa and held his forearm. "I know there's going to be a lot of change happening in our lives, but it's for a wonderful reason. You and I have created life and we're going to get the opportunity to watch that wonderful life be born and grow up." My voice cracked and I steadied myself before continuing. "This is our new beginning."

Jake let go of the card and wrapped his fingers around my hand. "You're right. Our new life together. I'm sorry I got freaked out."

I shook my head and squeezed his arm. I truly believed every word I said. There was a dark part of me filled with bitterness and grief, I could not deny that, but the rest of me was hopeful and strong, filled with the optimism of a new baby and a new life.

My thoughts were interrupted by the ringing of our house phone.

"Shall I get that?" Jake was half-standing, but I pulled him back onto the sofa and pushed myself onto my feet.

"No, I want to stand up and move around a little. I think I'm getting cramp again." I walked over to the phone and picked up the receiver. "Hello."

"Ms Price. Emma. My name is DCI Stevenson. Carl Stevenson. Do you remember me?"

The sound of his voice burst a bubble inside me and all the air left my body. I deflated, feeling myself double over. The room seemed to collapse around me, narrowing into nothing but the rushing blood in my ears, and the narrow spot of light by the telephone.

"Yes, I remember you." My voice was breathless, only slightly louder than a whisper. Of course I remembered him. I gulped in a breath before I said, "You were DI Stevenson then, though."

My heart beat against my ribs. *Der-dun-der-dun.*

"That's right." He paused. "Emma, you need to come to St Michael's Hospital as soon as you can."

Der-dun-der-dun.

Breathless again. "Why?"

"Because I think we've found Aiden."

CHAPTER FOUR

I've spent my fair share of time disorientated in hospitals. When I was five, I came to visit my dying Granddad and wandered away to find a vending machine. A nurse found me curled in a corner with my arms wrapped around my knees, crying about the scary balloons that everyone carried. They were the fluid bags from their IV drips.

There was Aiden's birth, sixteen years ago. The nurse kept telling me I was lucky to be such a young mum—at least I'd get my figure back. "Try having a kid when you're forty," she kept saying.

Then there was the car accident. Mum was in a coma for a week before passing, but Dad's death had been instantaneous after he flew through the windscreen when the brakes failed on the M1. Their accident had caused a traffic jam of over three hours that day. Twitter had been filled with angry commuters lambasting my father's death because it made them late for work. But I still remember negotiating those twists and turns around the hospital, failing to remember which ward the nurse said, or finding out that they'd moved her to a different ward. The abbreviations made my head spin. ICU. A&E. CPR. DNR.

The truth is that I was relieved when she finally passed. By that point the doctors were uncertain whether she would ever regain her mental faculties after the trauma she had suffered, and I didn't want to be the one to tell her that Dad had died while she slept. At least this way they both slipped away together.

In just one moment, I lost my clever mother and my caring father. Like the moment I lost my curious son.

As I burst through the door into the paediatric ward in St Michael's Hospital, a shiver ran down my spine and I knew in my heart that I had found my son. In one mere moment what had been lost was found again. Moments are what make this life, aren't they? A life is built on moments; seconds passing by. Some seconds are fleeting—part of a silly dream, or chopping up vegetables, taking the rubbish out, trimming our nails. Some are not.

Detective Carl Stevenson sat on a small bench in a tiny room on the right of the ward corridor. He rose to his feet—polystyrene cup in one hand—as I approached, and opened his mouth to speak. I didn't let him.

"Where is he?" I blurted out. "Is it him?"

"Emma," he said, doing away with formalities. "We need to talk. Take a moment and sit down. I want to explain everything to you first."

I regarded his dark brown eyes and salt-and-pepper beard—more salt since the last time we'd met—and wondered how on earth he supposed I could sit down at a moment like this. There was a chance my son was back from the *dead*. God, just thinking about it was insane. This was all insane. And yet...

"Love, think of the baby," Jake said. "He's right. Sit down and listen to the detective."

"I need to know," I said. "I need to see him."

What would a sixteen-year-old Aiden look like? Would he have bum-fluff on his chin like the kids at school? Would he be broad and lanky? Or short and stubby? Would he look like me or Rob? I shut my thoughts down. What if it wasn't him at all? What if this was all some sort of mistake? It was the most logical explanation to everything.

"I know," Stevenson said. "But you need to take a breath. Aiden... the young boy we found... has been through significant trauma and is very sensitive at the moment. The doctor will explain more in a moment but I wanted to talk to you first. I thought you might remember me from the investigation after the flood."

"I do," I said.

After we realised Aiden was missing, search and rescue scoured the surrounding area for him. The River Ouse was searched. The woods were searched. The village was searched. But there was no sign of him. There was no body, either. The experts explained to me that when someone drowns in a flood, they do not float downstream like many people believe. They actually sink underneath the turbulent water where it is calmer, and then they rise to the top very close to where they drowned. But there was no body. Aiden was never found. That was when Detective Stevenson had been assigned, because there was a slim chance that Aiden had not drowned at all.

I sat down on the bench as a group of three nurses walked down the corridor on our left. I thought they were staring at me, possibly wondering if I was here to 'claim' the missing boy. Like a leftover sock after a PE lesson. My hands formed into fists and I clutched at the cotton dress I was wearing. It was damp from the rain outside. I hadn't even put on a coat.

"I'm listening," I said.

"A teenage boy was found wandering along the back road between Bishoptown village and Rough Valley Forest. A couple were heading out of the village and came across him. He was wearing only a pair of jeans. No top or shoes. He was muddy all over. They stopped and asked the boy where he was going. They said he acknowledged their questions but didn't speak. He stopped walking, looked at them, and maintained eye contact, but he did not reply. They managed to get him into their car and drove him to the nearest police station."

I let out a long breath, only at that moment realising that I had been holding my breath at all. The baby adjusted her weight inside me, kicking me as she moved. I placed my palm on the bump, barely registering the movement.

"What happened next?" I asked.

"My colleagues at the station ran through a list of missing persons in the area but the boy didn't match anyone in the system. Then they took a DNA sample." Stevenson paused and ran his hands along his jeans. He'd been called in, I realised. He wasn't in the smart suit I remembered from that horrible week when we searched for Aiden. "Do you remember that we put Aiden's DNA on file after his disappearance?"

"Yes," I replied. I had scraped up as much of his hair as I could, and sent in items of clothing with dried blood on them for the police to use. Aiden was always scraping his knees or picking at a scab, and I had never been particularly good at keeping on top of the washing.

"The boy was clearly distressed. He wouldn't speak to any of my colleagues at the station, so they brought him to the hospital. A DNA test was run yesterday and the analysis came back a few hours ago. The teenage boy in that room is Aiden."

I unclenched my fists, let out a shallow breath, then clenched my hands again. How could this be happening? How? A tingling sensation spread over my body, from my scalp to the bottom of my feet.

"Are you all right, Ms Price? Can I get you

anything?"

I vaguely heard Jake's reply. "It's Mrs Price-Hewitt now. We're married."

"I apologise. Emma, can you hear me?"

"Yes," I whispered. I closed my eyes and leaned against the wall behind me. My thoughts swam with Stevenson's words. *DNA. Teenage boy. Rough Valley Forest.* Was it all real?

I realised Stevenson had been right to take me aside and explain all this to me. I needed to compose myself if I was going to step into that room and face Aiden for the first time in ten years. *I declared you dead.*

"I'm okay," I said. "I'm fine. This is all quite a shock, as you can imagine. Can I see him now? I need to see him."

"I'll check with the doctor." Stevenson offered a taut smile and rose to his feet.

"It can't be true," Jake said after Stevenson had left the room. "It's been ten years. Where has he been? I bet the police have bungled something. They'll have got the DNA test wrong or something."

"What if they haven't?" I said. "What if it really is him? Jake, I'll have my son back."

Jake wrapped his arm around my shoulders and squeezed. "I just don't want you to get your hopes up, love. I'd hate for you to be heartbroken all over again. Remember how long it took you to deal with Aiden's death?"

"I know," I said. And the truth was that my

heart was still closed. I hadn't even realised it. I'd thought I was so open and raw, but I wasn't. I was closed up and shrivelled inside.

I rose to my feet when the doctor came to speak to us, and found myself dwarfed by his height. But the man's kind face and open eyes helped to relieve some of the tension that had built up in my chest.

"Mrs Price-Hewitt, my name is Dr Schaffer. I am the head of the paediatric ward here at St. Michael's. There are a few things I want to mention before you go in to see your son. I've been briefed by DCI Stevenson here so I understand the delicate nature of this situation. Your son, Aiden, has been through some trauma. He is currently still in shock from whatever that trauma is, and for that reason we have not completed a full examination. We're trying to space out each procedure to keep him calm and happy. But right now, we can say that he is healthy. He is smaller than most sixteen-year-olds, and we will need to look into that. He has remained mute since his arrival, but he does understand what we are saying, and he is happy watching cartoons or children's television shows. But please don't feel disheartened if he doesn't react when you first see him."

The blood drained from my face. What if he didn't recognise me? I reached out for Jake's hand and he clasped it with his own.

"Thank you, Dr Schaffer," I said with an unsteady voice.

The doctor smiled and led the way down the

corridor. I followed with shaky steps, trying desperately to walk with my back straight and tall, keeping one hand on my pregnant stomach, attempting to soothe my unborn child and soothe myself at the same time. My heart worked double time, pumping and pounding like a dribbled basketball. The hospital walls closed in on me as claustrophobia seeped into my veins, constricting my chest so that I had to remind myself to take deep breaths. I gripped Jake's fingers so hard that it must have caused him pain, but he didn't flinch or complain.

And then we reached the room. The doctor paused and waited for me to nod. He opened the door. In that most mundane of actions, I had one of those moments, the kind you remember for a lifetime, the kind that slow down and leave a permanent imprint on your mind.

CHAPTER FIVE

There was nothing remarkable about the boy in the hospital room. He was propped up by pillows on the bed, with a pigeon chest poking up inside blue pyjamas. I never found out who bought him those pyjamas, but I suspected it was DCI Stevenson. The boy had straggly brown hair that hung lankly down to the collar of his pyjama top. He sat with his fingers clutching hold of the bed sheets, his gaze fixed on the tiny hospital television. I took a tentative step forward, following the doctor but barely aware of anyone else in the room except the boy in the bed, whose head turned in my direction and stopped my heart.

He had Rob's eyes.

My Aiden—the little boy I nursed as a baby— had also had Rob's eyes. They were chestnut brown with a hint of hazel near the pupil. A multitude of photographs popped into my head. Aiden's first birthday, the time he smeared strawberry mousse all over his hands and face, bath-time, bedtime stories, sitting on Nana's lap with Grandpa pulling faces, jumping up and down in puddles... all with a big grin across his face and those shining chestnut-brown eyes.

"How do we know the DNA test was correct?" I heard Jake say. "How do we know there wasn't some sort of balls-up?"

"There wasn't," I whispered, utterly certain that it was Aiden sitting in front of me.

"It's unlikely," answered DCI Stevenson, "but to be sure I was going to suggest that we test his DNA against Emma's. That way we'll know one hundred per cent that this is Aiden Price."

I buried you, I thought, with my gaze holding my son's. *In my heart I put you to rest. Can you ever forgive me?*

Did I even deserve forgiveness? Mothers are supposed to never give up. In the movies, when the child is missing, the mother *always* knows they are alive. They would feel it if the child were dead. That connection, that magical connection between mother and child would be cut, and there was supposed to be a sensation that came along with it. But I'd seen Aiden's red anorak pulled from the River Ouse and I'd assumed he was dead. I bit my lip to hold back the tears.

"Aiden," I said, stepping towards the bed. "Hello." I smiled at the boy with the dark brown hair and small chin. My old withered heart skipped a beat when it hit me that he was so small—not much bigger than a twelve-year-old—with eyes that seemed too big for his face.

"Don't panic if he doesn't react," said Dr Schaffer. "We believe he's listening and taking everything in, but it will take some time for him to process what has happened to him. Would you like to sit down, Mrs. Price-Hewitt?"

I nodded, and moved my body accordingly as the doctor pulled a chair close to Aiden's bed. But as I was sitting, all I could think about was what had happened to my boy. Where had he been? A decade. Ten years. Wars were fought and lost in a decade. Prime Ministers and Presidents came and went. Important scientific discoveries were made. And all that time, my boy... my child... had been missing from the world. Missing from *my* world, at least.

Nudging the chair forward, I leaned towards him and let my hand hover a centimetre above his. Aiden stared down at my hand, frowned, and pulled his away.

"He's not keen on physical contact at the moment," explained Dr Schaffer.

I tried to ignore the pain those words caused, and withdrew my hand to place it on my lap. Twice I opened my mouth to speak, but twice I closed my mouth again. There was a Transformers cartoon blaring out through the room, interrupting the hanging silence, but even so the atmosphere was electric.

"Aiden, do you remember me?" I said in a croaky voice. "Do you know who I am?"

He blinked. He was so still it was terrifying. The little boy I had known was never still, and even though I knew instantly that this boy with the chestnut brown eyes was my son, I was having difficulty associating the curious six-year-old chatterbox with this soulful, mute young man.

I injected some cheer into my voice in a pathetic attempt to lighten the mood. "I'm your mum. We lost each other for a while but I'm back now and I'm going to make sure you're safe, okay?" I blinked rapidly and took a deep breath, trying desperately to quell the rising tide of emotions threatening to sweep me away. "Once you're feeling better you can come home with me and we can get to know each other again. Does that sound okay?"

There was not even a trace of a smile on his lips. His eyes slowly turned back to the television and I longed to wrap my arms around his narrow shoulders and hold him close to me. I turned to the doctor in a panic.

"I don't... I don't know what to do." Despite my efforts to hold back my tears a sob escaped, breaking through the noisy cartoon and jolting me back to reality. Aiden didn't need to see me break down. He needed me to be strong, not a dithering wreck.

"You're doing great," Dr Schaffer encouraged. "Try to keep talking to him. We want Aiden to hear the sound of his mother's voice."

I took a deep breath and steadied myself. Aiden smelled like disinfectant and eggs. My eyes trailed the small table next to his bed. There was a colouring book but no toys, no presents or flowers. My boy should have gifts. I would come back with gifts and he would be Aiden again. He'd be the bright, colourful, and creative little boy I used to know. I took a deep breath and closed my eyes. There he was, walking up the school carpark on his way to class with a Power Rangers rucksack and his bright red coat. I opened my eyes and pretended I was talking to that same boy.

"Do you like the cartoon, Aiden? I remember when you were little and you had a transformer car. Do you remember that? It was red and it turned into a robot. You used to play games where the robot went to war against your stuffed toys. You'd got a bit too big for your stuffed rabbit and teddy bears. You liked robots and cars and Power Rangers, like most little boys your age. But you liked drawing, too. You used to draw the most wonderful pictures for me. They weren't stick figures either—they were proper, coloured-in, gorgeous pictures of me and Nana and Grandpa. We used to pin them up all around the cottage." I paused. None of those things were there anymore. No Nana. No Grandpa. No cottage. Suddenly my mouth felt very dry. "You might not like those things anymore but that's okay. A lot has changed. We can figure out what we like together, eh? We'll go to the shops and you can pick out anything you want. Anything." I let out a nervous laugh and leaned back in my chair. "And in a few weeks you'll get to meet your sister. We don't know her name yet. Maybe you can help me choose it. I would like that a lot." There was nothing. No reaction from him at all. "You grew into your ears! I always wondered if you would." I clutched one hand with the other to stop myself turning into a manic, rambling idiot.

As Aiden continued to watch the television, I felt as though I were in a dream. Was I really talking to my son? Was this pasty young man the boy I'd thought had drowned all those years ago? My head was light but my heart was heavy with the implications of everything that had happened. I found myself unable to think of anything else to say.

Luckily, Dr Schaffer noticed my distress and came to my rescue. "Perhaps we could all go for a quick cup of tea while Aiden has a little rest. Then we can talk about what happens next. We would love to draw a little blood from you, Emma, and then we can establish a DNA match to corroborate the DNA test from yesterday. We also need to talk about what happens next. Someone from social services will need to speak to you."

"I will be able to take him home, won't I?" I asked. A fist of ice gripped my heart.

"It might just take a bit of time," DCI Stevenson added. "With Aiden not talking we've no idea where he's been for the last ten years and who he's been with."

Who. That word hit me like a truck. *Who.* Who had he been with? What did they want from him? Nausea rose to my throat, threatening to spill out onto the hospital floor. My fingers wrapped around the armrest of the chair as I attempted to compose myself.

"Where do you suspect he's been?" I asked, saying the words slowly and carefully.

Both the doctor and the detective glanced across at Aiden and then back to me.

"I think it's best we talk about that in private," said DCI Stevenson.

CHAPTER SIX

Of course, after Aiden's apparent drowning, I suffered from recurring nightmares. There were two images that haunted me as I tossed and twisted myself into the sheets at night. The first was the sight of Aiden's red coat being pulled from the river. It was the image that the press ate up and regurgitated on the front page of every newspaper. Innocence lost. The contrast of a tiny red coat against a murky dark background, mould and dirt on the sleeves. It was a perfect image for selling newspapers. It hinted at a parent's worst fear without being so gratuitous that they couldn't print it.

Does anything sell newspapers better than death? Maybe sex can sell more, given the right story, but the death of a child is the very apex of morbid curiosity. In a tower of sex scandals, prostitutes, and celebrities, infanticide rules. Tragic, accidental infant death is just underneath the glory of a child's murder. Aiden was reduced to that one image and it almost erased every preceding memory I had of him. I couldn't think of his cute, tongue-poking-out look of concentration when reading a book without seeing the red anorak dirtied by river mud. I couldn't picture him shimmying up the tree in our garden wearing a superman cape without the newspaper headlines revolving through my mind.

The second image was pure imagination, but it was one that I could not shake away. It was Aiden, small and pale, floating in the water. Deep under the surface of the river was my child, half-eaten by fish, bloated and rotting. I dreamed of the flow of the Ouse as it met the Humber. Rushing and gushing and pouring over rocks, between built-up grassy banks, beneath stone bridges, behind houses, chasing and churning to the sea. I saw him washed away from me. Washed away from the world.

During the investigation we'd had search and rescue experts talk about the currents and the places he could have washed up. It was irregular for a body not to resurface from a river. Out at sea, you would expect a body to disappear, but in a river, they tended to be found. That was why DCI Stevenson was assigned the case. It was only when they found Aiden's coat that a kidnapping had been almost completely ruled out. There had been a flood and during that flood Aiden had wandered off, presumably towards the river. Not long after his disappearance they found his coat in the water. End of story. The thread of logic is all there, isn't it?

Except this time the thread of logic was obviously wrong, because that was my child sitting in a hospital bed wearing the same expression you see on children pulled out of a wrecked building after an earthquake, or rescued from a war-torn country. Which was why I knew my nightmares were likely to come back, and what they would be about.

With Jake by my side, I followed Dr Schaffer and DCI Stevenson into a small office. Dr Schaffer sat at a desk, I was offered a chair, and DCI Stevenson shut the door behind us. That disinfectant smell of the hospital had even seeped into this room, and the tiny window behind the desk was shut, trapping us in a heady miasma of sickness. Part of me almost opened my mouth to Dr Schaffer to open the window and let in some fresh air but I decided not to bother. It would only mean more faffing about and I was impatient to get on with things.

DCI Stevenson moved towards the desk and hovered there. Jake sat on a chair to my left, his fingers drumming against the grey wool of his trousers. I felt small beside them all, despite my distended stomach. Here I was, one pregnant woman amidst a cluster of men. A shock of femininity thrown into a testosterone-filled room. Despite the situation, I found myself straining to stay composed, self-conscious of breaking down in front of them. I was almost positive that there would be no judgement on their part even if I did, but it would only waste more time. I needed to know everything they knew about my son.

Dr Schaffer pushed a file across his desk and then pulled it back before clearing his throat. His head was bent down, looking at the file rather than at me. He seemed tall even sat there in the desk chair. With his head bent like that I could see the way his hair was thinning. I saw the pink of his scalp, slightly shining, beneath the soft greying hairs.

"This is a very difficult case," Dr Schaffer said. "Without Aiden talking to us it's difficult to make an assessment."

"Just tell me everything you know, and what you think it means," I said. I turned to DCI Stevenson. "And I mean everything."

Finally, the doctor lifted his head and I saw that he had composed himself as a professional. He rested his hands on top of the file and linked his fingers together. "Aiden is small for his age, which leads us to think that he has been malnourished. When he was found on the road, he was walking very slowly, with a limp, and was short of breath. His posture is a little crouched when he walks, perhaps to overcompensate for the limp. During our examination we found that he has underdeveloped calf and thigh muscles, and there is an indication of ankle injuries in the past, though we will need to perform more tests to discover the extent of those injuries. They are healed now.

"Aiden's teeth are quite crooked and though I'm no expert in that area, I believe that they have not been cared for particularly well, though he may have had a toothbrush. His skin is very pale, and his eyes were particularly sensitive to bright light."

It was at this point that the rushing of my blood, and the thudding of my heart, became far louder than the doctor, and I was afraid that I was about to swoon forward in the chair. I took a deep breath, stroked my stomach, and willed myself to stay conscious. The problem was, I'd already guessed what he was about to say and I didn't want to hear it. I wanted to stand up on my shaky feet and my swollen ankles, and run as fast as I could while eight months pregnant. I wanted to get out of that place—to even get away from Aiden, as sick as that sounds—and never think of any of this again. But I couldn't. Aiden had been born. He had existed. He was still here. And he had a story deep down inside that deserved to be heard and processed by his mother.

"Emma," Jake said quietly. He squeezed my hand. "Are you all right, love?"

"Do you need a break?" DCI Stevenson asked.

I shook my head. "Go on. I'm fine. Tell me everything you know."

Dr Schaffer smiled then, and it reminded me of the smile proud parents give their nervous children at sports events. But then he glanced down at his file and let out a long, deep sigh. The worst was to come. "There is evidence of damage to Aiden's gums, and there are lacerations on his body that are consistent with sexual abuse."

I leaned forward and vomited a small amount of clear liquid onto the floor of the doctor's office. Jake stroked my hair away from my forehead and helped me straighten up in the chair. DCI Stevenson quickly mopped up the sick with his handkerchief and dropped it into the waste paper bin.

"Not to worry," Dr Schaffer said. "I needed a new bin anyway." He forced a smile.

"I'm so sorry," I said.

"It's quite all right."

"I'll take this to one of the nurses," said DCI Stevenson. "And I'm getting us all some water. I think we need it."

I smiled thinly, grateful to him for pretending that we all needed water. Pretending that I wasn't the only one in the room who had lost control of her bodily functions.

I'd known it was coming. Of course I had. Little boys aren't taken away for no reason. Not long after the flood, after search and rescue had failed to find Aiden's body, I'd gone through every possible reason for a child's disappearance, from getting lost down a well to being sold into the sex trade. I went over it all. I saw men with moustaches holding my little boy's hand and leading him into murky rooms. I saw money changing hands and lascivious smiles on the faces of obese predatory men. I pictured the worst, the very worst, and I felt grimy and disgusting for even thinking it. No shower could take those images away.

And now my worst fear had been confirmed. I leaned back in my chair and closed my eyes.

"Try to stay calm, sweetheart," cooed Jake. "Think of the baby. You need to keep your stress levels down."

But I *was* thinking of the baby, the one sat in that hospital room all on his own watching cartoons. My body ached with helplessness. Whatever I did now, I could never take it away. I could never go back and stop him going to school that day. Never. I could barely breathe.

"Here we are," said DCI Stevenson as he passed a water bottle to each of us. I noticed that he gave me mine with the cap unscrewed. I realised why when my hand extended to take the bottle, only to shake so badly that I spilled some of it onto my clothes. I wrapped both of my hands around the plastic bottle and lifted it tentatively to my lips. I had to admit that the cool liquid felt good as it trickled down my throat. DCI Stevenson opened the window behind the desk and a breeze hit the sweat on my forehead.

"Thank you," I said. I tried my best to settle into my chair, preparing myself for the rest of the information to come from Dr Schaffer.

But it was Jake who broke the silence first. "Are you sure?" Hearing his voice was a surprise. Apart from asking me if I was all right, he'd remained fairly quiet since arriving at the hospital. "I mean... what you're saying is..."

"We won't be sure until Aiden is able to tell us himself, but that is what our examination suggests." Dr Schaffer's fingers tightened above the paper file until I saw his knuckles whiten. He released his hands and his shoulders relaxed slightly.

I closed my eyes, trying not to think about what the examination had involved. I should have been there holding his hand as the doctors poked and prodded him.

"Has he been in any distress?" I asked. "Has he been crying, screaming, scared?"

"No," Dr Stevenson said. "He has been very calm. He shows some discomfort when touched, but he allowed us to examine him, and to wash and clothe him, too. We were very gentle and we talked through every single procedure and why we were doing it."

"You should have waited for me." My hands clenched around the bottle. "I should've been there with him."

"I understand why you feel that way," said DCI Stevenson in the same calm voice I remembered from all those years ago. "We asked the doctors to look for evidence on Aiden's body. If we'd waited, some of that evidence would have been destroyed."

"And what *evidence* did you find?" I snapped.

DCI Stevenson pulled at the collar on his shirt.

"It was a rainy night. It seems that if there was any trace of Aiden's kidnapper left on him, it was washed away. There was no trace in his saliva either."

I didn't know what to make of that. But then my mind was swimming with so much information, I didn't know what to make of any of this. I took a long drink of water.

It was DCI Stevenson's turn to talk. He met my eyes with the patient, steady gaze of a teacher explaining a problem to a child. "The medical examination of Aiden's condition and the way he was found all suggest that Aiden has been confined somewhere for the last ten years. We think it was a small area with limited light. Dr Schaffer feels that the marks on Aiden's ankles suggest he was chained for some time."

The urge to be sick rose again, but this time I swallowed it down. *Chained. Confined.* Kept like an animal in a cage. I'd studied psychology at school; I knew what that did to a child. I knew about the wolf children and the girl raised in a chicken coop. They were feral and traumatised, virtually unable to function, and certainly unable to integrate into society.

"But that's... that's..." Jake rubbed his eyes as if in disbelief. "That's evil. Who would do that to a child?"

"That's what we hope to find out," said DCI Stevenson. "Because whoever the monster is, he belongs   in   jail."

CHAPTER SEVEN

When I was a child I had very different nightmares to the ones that plagued me as an adult. They were filled with narrow, labyrinth-like tunnels. As I walked, I'd follow a small dot of light leading the way. I really wanted to play with that dot of light because it looked appealing, all glowing and orange and sparkling. But as I walked on, the tunnel walls closed in. The bright glowing light started to dim. I'd become frantic, running for my life, no longer chasing the light, but being chased by some unknown *thing*. On and on I went, turning one corner and then the next, as the corridor became narrower and the ceiling lower. It *squeezed* closer until the walls touched my skin. Narrower and narrower it went until I was on my knees crawling through the dark.

I always woke just before I got stuck.

Being confined has been one of my greatest fears

for as long as I could remember. It's why I opened the cage for the school guinea pig to escape. It's why I made Dad return the gift of a rabbit in a hutch. It's why I leave the door open a crack when I have to wee in a public toilet.

The thought of Aiden stuck in some tiny room, *chained* like an animal... It awoke some savage maternal wildness inside me. I wanted to find whoever had done this to him and rip him apart tooth and claw, like the lioness I knew I could be.

The quote goes on about a woman scorned. *Scorned*. As if the jealousy of a lover could ever compete with the ferocity of a mother. I raked my fingers through my hair in that vomit-scented room and soaked up the rage that I would feed on to get me through the next few weeks.

"What are you doing to find this man?" I asked.

"We're searching the area Aiden was found, and we're canvassing for eyewitnesses. But... this is delicate, Emma, and you know why. We can't do much without the press finding out. We only have to call in an eyewitness from that day and they will know something is going on. You're going to need to prepare yourself for what's coming."

I let my head sink into my hands. Had I even felt joy yet? Had I allowed myself to be happy that Aiden was alive? Could I feel happy at this moment? Should I?

"Bastards," Jake grumbled. "As if they didn't do enough after the flood. Practically sent Emma's parents into an early grave."

"I need to ring Sonya and Peter," I said. "They're Aiden's grandparents. They'll need to see him, especially if this is going to turn into a shitshow of a media circus."

Stevenson nodded. "I think that's a good call. Aiden needs loving parents and grandparents around him now."

Though the detective didn't explicitly say it, I knew he was thinking it. He was hoping that Aiden would snap out of his fugue and talk to us. Solving this case would be a priority for the police right now, especially once the media started reporting on it. Beneath my growing baby, my empty stomach cramped.

"Can I see him again?" I asked.

"Of course." Dr Schaffer smiled. "But first we should talk about what we need to do to help Aiden get better. This is a highly unusual case for which there is no real precedent. Aiden has been kept away from society for ten years and will need help integrating."

"I understand," I said, balling my dress up in my left fist.

"We feel it would be best to keep Aiden in hospital for a few days for observation. When he was first admitted, we were not aware of the situation, otherwise we would have kept Aiden in quarantine to prevent him picking up a bug he might not have developed an immunity to. But he has been seen by several nurses and a few visitors and appears to be fine. Still, we will need to discuss what vaccines he was given before his abduction and whether we need to give him any more before he can go home."

I squeezed my dress, hating that my son needed this special treatment at all. "Of course."

"Social services were contacted immediately and you'll need to have a meeting with them, but I believe Aiden will need therapy... perhaps speech therapy to help him begin speaking again, and some physiotherapy for his leg. He'll need to see a dentist too. Perhaps a nutritionist—"

"That's a lot of people fussing over my son," I said. "Look, I know all of this needs to be done. I want him to get better and I want him to be able to live a normal life, but all this will be too much for him. Don't you think?"

Dr Schaffer sighed. "I do. I believe this is going to be a slow adjustment and a slow process. Not everything will happen at once. For one, I believe Aiden will need to see a specialist at York hospital physiotherapy unit, though we will need an x-ray first." He paused. "There's going to be a waiting list anyway. And maybe I can help you with his diet to begin with, and we can check on him in a few weeks. And another thing... Aiden has been declared dead. He has no identification, no passport."

"I have his birth certificate," I said.

"And a death certificate," Dr Schaffer continued. "I'm no expert in these matters but I know it might be difficult at first. All of Aiden's records show him as deceased and that will slow the whole process down. But what we'll do is test his eyesight, hearing, and vitals in hospital. Then you can arrange for your own dentist, optician, and physiotherapist when the paperwork has come through."

I let go of the balled up material. "Thank you. I appreciate it. Now, can I see him?"

I needed a few minutes with him before calling Rob's parents. Perhaps it was selfish, perhaps it was reasonable; I didn't know at the time and I didn't care. I didn't dwell on my feelings, I was protecting my son. The last thing he needed was to be bombarded by well-meaning visitors and professionals. I followed Schaffer and Stevenson through the corridor, avoiding the stares from the nurses walking up and down. For the first time I realised that there were other children on the ward. I tried not to stare into the rooms as we walked along, but through open doors I saw giggling children and fathers making silly faces. There were pots on arms and legs. Broken limbs. They were normal reasons for a child coming to hospital. And when they went back to school they'd get all the signatures and doodles of their friends. They'd have fun stories to tell—"...and then next-door's Doberman chased me over the fence but I caught my jeans and face-planted..."—and scars to show off. They would be louder and more boisterous for a while, emboldened by their escape from 'death'. But not my son.

"Hey, Aiden." I kept my voice bright and cheerful as I entered the room. Aiden sat with his back propped up against the headboard. He had a cup of juice in his hand and he sipped on it slowly. I walked over to the bed, cleared my throat as I moved the chair closer to him, and held back tears. I was determined to avoid thinking about what he had been through. I would not. I could not. "I bet you're sick of people bothering you when you're trying to watch cartoons." I let myself really look at him this time. I took it all in: the rich brown of his eyelashes, the boniness of his shoulders, the thick, straight hair. They melded with my memories of the dark-haired boy with scrapes on his knees and a grin on his face. Now there was only a neutral, placid expression on his face. Every one of his movements was slow: the turn of his head, blinking, reaching out to the table next to him for his drink.

The baby moved inside, kicking its feet. I longed to take Aiden's hand and place it on my bump for him to feel, but I only put my own hand there instead. "That's your little sister saying hello. You see, you have so many people wanting to say hello. And you know I would have come sooner, but I didn't know where you were. I'm sorry, Aiden. I'm so sorry I didn't know where you were. I'll never not know again, I promise. We're going to fix it all, you know. We're going to mend it together. You and me. We'll be a team again, like we were when we lived at Nana's house, remember? We fought crime, you and me. You were Superman, obviously, you had the cape. I was just your sidekick but you made sure we caught the baddies every time. We're going to do that again, I promise."

And that was as much as I could say without breaking down. For another five minutes I watched cartoons with my son. I rested my hand on the bed next to him, and although his eyes flickered towards the movement, he didn't flinch away. Still, I didn't try to touch him.

I found him oddly self-possessed then. I knew the doctors thought he was in shock, but he didn't seem shocked or afraid. He seemed comfortable in his own skin. He seemed quite at ease ignoring us all and casting his attention to what mattered the most to him: cartoons. And who could blame him? He'd been hurt by someone—an adult. Why would he want to interact with more adults after that happened to him? I didn't blame him for ignoring us all.

It was Jake who brought me out of the spell cast over me in that quiet room. "Emma, honey. You need to call them."

I nodded my head. What time was it? I hadn't checked the time on my phone for what felt like hours. I'd given Jake my handbag and forgotten all about it. He handed it to me now, after I crossed the room on unsteady legs. I pushed my hair away from my clammy forehead and reached for my phone inside the bag. It was almost seven. We'd been here just under three hours. Sonya and Peter would be sitting down to eat their dinner at this time. I pictured them in back of the B&B. Peter was tall and broad like Rob—a boxer's physique, which was something he used to do as a hobby in his youth. Sonya was a slip of a woman; stooped, thin shoulders on top of two matchstick legs. Her voluminous blonde bob always made her look a bit like a lollipop. The two of them dressed in Marks and Spencer cashmere sweaters and ironed jeans. They were the epitome of a nice, normal countryside couple.

The thought of telling them what I needed to say made me light-headed and nauseated. But I thought of how they had loved Aiden when he came along. We would walk to the B&B after school and Sonya would come running out with a box of Liquorice All-Sorts and a comic book. Aiden never really liked liquorice and they always got him the wrong comic book, but he was always grateful and laughed at Peter's bad jokes. They took him to the farms outside the village to see the lambs, and to the rural shows when they came around every year. They held his little hand and pointed out all the sights for him to see. They bought him candyfloss and little trinkets for him to keep. I stepped out of the room and found a quiet space to call. When I placed the phone against my ear, I started to cry.

"Bishoptown Bed and Breakfast," Sonya answered.

"Sonya, it's Emma."

"Emma, dear, you sound terrible." She sucked in a breath. "Is it about Aiden?"

"Yes."

There was a sob on the other end of the line. "Peter. Peter, it's Emma. It's about Aiden."

I imagined him hurrying through to their living space in his woollen socks. I closed my eyes and took a deep breath.

"Sonya, it isn't what you think. They haven't found a body. They've found Aiden, but he's alive."

There was silence. Eventually, I heard Rob's dad in the background. *Sonya? What's she saying Sonya? Tell me.*

"He's… alive?"

"He's alive and he's at St Michael's hospital. I can't explain much over the phone, it's difficult to… You just need to see him and he needs to see you." I decided to warn them face-to-face rather than over the phone. "And… well… you need to call Rob. He needs to come too."

"Okay. Okay… I… Are you sure?"

"I'm sure, Sonya."

"Oh… Oh my, that's…"

"I have to go. I'll see you when you get here."

I lifted the phone away from my ear and ended the call, drawing in my own deep breath. I leaned against the wall of the silent waiting room and closed my eyes for a second.

"Um, Mrs. Price-Hewitt."

My eyes opened and my shoulders slumped. Dr Schaffer stood in the doorway with his hands deep in his coat pockets.

"If you have a few moments it might be a good time to draw some blood. It's important to run the tests as soon as we can."

"Of course," I said.

"How are you feeling? Are you up to this?" he asked, meaning the blood draw.

As I followed him out of the waiting room I mulled that question over, and no matter how many times I thought about it, I still didn't have an answer.

CHAPTER EIGHT

I got a cup of tea, a sandwich, and yet more explanations of what was to come. There were more tests to be done: x-rays, scans, psychological assessments. A therapist would see him soon. There might have to be an investigation into our home to check it was 'suitable'. It was all too much.

Sonya and Peter were in tears at the sight of him, but Sonya was the first to turn to me and nod. They knew. They saw Rob in him just as I had. The phlebotomist took my blood but it wasn't necessary, not to me. The boy in that room was Aiden, and we all knew it.

I had almost fallen asleep when the social worker turned up to talk to me. Jake ended up doing most of the talking. By that point, little seemed to matter to me except for Aiden, and certainly not a cross-examination about me as a mother. By 10pm, my head was spinning but the social worker appeared happy with the interview and informed us that she would 'pop round' to the house when Aiden had been discharged from the hospital. Reluctantly, I left Aiden's room to let him rest, and slipped away from the others, picking up a bottle of water. Outside the hospital, I sat down on an uncomfortable stone bench, and let a pattering of drizzle land on my hair. It would frizz, but I didn't care.

"I've called Rob."

I flinched. Sonya moved like a panther. Her voice cut through my own suffocating thoughts, jarring me back to reality. "Thanks."

She sat down next to me, leaving adequate space between us for another person. She wrapped her arms around her body. "It's really him. I don't know whether to rejoice or cry for what he's been through."

"I know the feeling."

"I bet you do." She turned towards me. "I want to call it a blessing, but… I can't. The way he sits there, barely moving…" She covers her mouth with her hand. "He was never this quiet. Peter used to call him Chatterbox. He'd tell us all about the spiders and worms he'd collected from the garden. A real boy's boy."

I nodded. "I remember."

She shuffled uncomfortably. "Rob will be here in the morning. He's arranged a leave of absence."

"That's good. Aiden is going to need him. He'll need all of us."

Sonya nodded and bit into her thumbnail. "Where is Aiden going to stay when he leaves the hospital?"

Surprised, I turned to face her. "He'll be staying with me. I'm his mother."

Sonya lifted a hand like she was trying to placate me. "Oh, I know, it's just... Well, you don't live in your parents' home anymore. I wondered if maybe he'd want to stay somewhere he already knew, like the B&B."

I let out a cold, hard laugh. "Absolutely not. Aiden is my son and he's coming home with me."

Her lips tightened into a thin line. "Okay. As long as that's what's best for Aiden. He's all I care about now. All I'm thinking about."

"And I'm not?" My chin lifted as I regarded her through the dim glow of the hospital windows around us.

"Now, Emma, I never said that. It's just that I know you have the baby coming soon, and Aiden doesn't know Jake at all, does he? He knows us though. He knows Rob. He knows the B&B."

"But that wasn't where he grew up," I said. I hated that some of what she was saying made sense. I pushed that thought away. Aiden needed *me* more than he needed Rob, Sonya, and Peter. "He grew up with me more than anyone else. I was his constant before he..." I struggled to compose myself. "I know I'm going through some changes at the moment, but I was the one to bring him up and it won't matter where we live or who lives with me, I'm his mother and he's coming home with me." I paused to brush away a stray tear. "If that was Rob in there, would you let anyone else take him home?"

Sonya sighed. "No, I wouldn't. You're right."

But there was a note of disagreement in her voice. She didn't believe I was right at all, but I didn't know why.

*

I fell asleep in the chair in Aiden's hospital room that night. Managing that was a feat in itself, given the uncomfortable nature of the chair and the uncomfortable nature of my pregnancy. But the body takes what it wants, and I wanted sleep. It was Dr Schaffer who woke me after 11pm. Jake slipped my coat over my arms and they ushered me out. Aiden needed rest. It had been a long day for him. While I had slept, Aiden had sat up awake, either watching me or watching television.

I thought I would feel more human after a night in my own bed, a hot shower, and some real food — not hospital canteen food — but that Friday morning I woke still feeling half-conscious, like I was living in a dream world. It was only the occasional kick from Bump that reminded me everything was real. Aiden really was alive, and he really had been captured and kept like a performing bear. Every time I thought about it, the cereal churned in my stomach.

Jake took the day off school and drove me to the hospital. It was a day of x-rays and scans. I saw Aiden standing up for the first time, and my breath caught when I realised just how short he was. There was a stiffness to the way he walked, like he didn't quite know what to do with his legs. I made a joke about how I walked funny because of the bump, but Aiden didn't laugh. I even waddled as I walked, pretending I was far bigger than what I was.

"We'd like to take a better look at Aiden's ankle today," said Dr Schaffer. "We'd like to check some of his other bones, too, so we'll be sending him off for some x-rays. Then we'll draw a little blood, and afterwards a child psychologist is coming to spend some time with him."

A prickling sensation worked its way over my skin. "I don't want him to be a study. He's not some feral child brought up by wolves. He's my son, not a name in a paper."

"I agree completely," said Dr Schaffer, tilting his head down to show gravitas. "But I do think that the psychologist will help. Aiden is going to need some therapy."

That I couldn't argue with.

"Can I be with him during the x-rays?" I asked.

But before I could answer, the door to the room burst open and a small, surprised breath left my body. I was vaguely aware of Jake turning his head towards me with a frown on his face, but mostly, I stood staring at the man who'd entered. It'd been almost eight years since I'd last seen Rob. We'd spoken around the time Aiden was declared legally dead, but apart from that we rarely made contact with each other, though that didn't stop Sonya giving me updates of his progression through the army. He had joined shortly after Aiden's apparent drowning in the Ouse.

Rob stopped dead just inside the door. His gaze was focussed entirely on Aiden, and I saw a sheen of moisture over his eyes, turning them to glass. He knew, like I had, like Sonya had. He knew this was his son.

"Aiden," he whispered.

I managed to control my breathing, but my heart raced. Rob was a large man, filling the doorway with his bulk. The army had beefed him up even more than the last time I saw him. He wore boots, jeans, and a black leather jacket, well-worn and frayed at the edges. His brown hair was shorter than ever, and his deep chestnut brown eyes were all Aiden.

"It's him, Rob," I said. "It's really him."

My ex-lover's eyes finally moved from our son to me, and a shiver worked its way down my spine. In that moment I knew he understood how I'd felt as I'd walked into this very same room and seen my son back from the dead, and the intensity of that experience seemed to hit us both. When Rob's knees began to buckle, I rushed forward and wrapped my arms around his shoulders. It wasn't anything I thought about. In that moment I forgot all about Jake—who no doubt felt useless standing back watching his wife embrace another man. The problem was, Jake didn't know what I was feeling as well as Rob did, and it was Rob's arms I needed around me. Before I knew it, I was crying on Rob's shoulder, and he was crying on mine, and for the most fleeting of instants, I almost felt as though I had a family again.

"Mum told me everything before I came," he said as he pulled back.

I wiped the tears from my eyes and cleared my throat. "Everything?"

He nodded. "I'm going to tear that monster apart when I find him."

I glanced nervously back to Aiden. "Not here, Rob." I kept a sharp warning tone in my voice.

He ran his hands over his face. "You're right." Aiden had seen enough violence. We didn't need to add to it with our words. Rob bent low and opened his arms towards his son, who was hanging back next to Dr Schaffer on the other side of the room. "Hiya mate, how you doing? Remember me? You don't have to say anything, pal, it's okay. I'm your dad, okay? Sorry I wasn't here yesterday. Hey, did you know I fly helicopters now? Remember that helicopter I got for you? It got stuck in Mum's hair and then we weren't allowed to play with it inside again, remember?" He let out a little laugh at the memory. I remembered it well. Its propellers had taken a chunk out of my hair. I shook my head a little and laughed. I'd been so mad with them both, but they'd looked at me with the same puppy dog expression and my heart had melted.

"We should take Aiden to get his x-ray," said Dr Schaffer, jolting me back to the present.

"Sure," Rob said. He turned to Aiden. "Gotta get you patched up, kid. You'll be right as rain soon. Then maybe I can get you another helicopter, eh?" He glanced across at me and then cupped his mouth with his hand conspiratorially. "We'll keep it away from Mum this time, though."

I wanted Aiden to laugh or smile, or even nod. But there was nothing. His features were completely blank, like a doll's expression. I wrapped my arms around my body, then followed the doctor and Aiden into the corridor. Sonya and Peter were waiting outside, and gave Aiden a limp little wave as he passed them by. Aiden didn't seem to notice. Sonya's hand flew up to her mouth as Aiden turned his head away, and she crumpled into Peter's arms. It felt like we were walking my son to his execution, the mood was so sombre.

"I never had an opportunity to say hello," Jake said, interrupting the silence with a voice that sounded strangely upbeat, given the mood.

"Yeah, hi," Rob replied, barely even glancing at Jake.

My muscles clenched at Jake's flushed, red face and the hand he'd extended to shake as we walked awkwardly down the corridor, shoulder to shoulder.

"I think you were in one of my art classes, weren't you? The apple made of barbed wire." The corner of his mouth turned up in a sarcastic smile. "Yes, that's right."

"Yeah, that was my A-level project and you gave me a C for it. Pretty stingy if you ask me. That bastard scratched my arms to pieces."

"Well, it was a little clichéd," replied Jake, pushing his glasses further up his nose.

Rob shook his head and said nothing. I pursed my lips together. I could understand why Jake would feel put out by the way I'd hugged Rob when he entered the room, but he had to understand how difficult this situation was. Bringing up events from years ago that didn't even matter was just petty.

"We need to take Aiden into the x-ray unit now, and I think it's best that just one person comes in with him."

"I'll go," I said, stepping forward.

"Actually, I was thinking Mr Hartley would be a good choice this time. We would prefer to keep any harmful rays away from pregnant women, and it would be good for Aiden to spend a little time with his father." Dr Schaffer offered a small, half-apologetic smile.

"Is that okay, Em?" Rob said.

The familiarity of him calling me Em gave me a little jolt of surprise. "Of course." I bent down lower to talk to Aiden. "I'll be right out here, waiting for you. Dad will be with you, though.

You're going to do just fine."

I couldn't stop talking to him as if he was still six. He was a teenager. Sixteen years old. He could legally have sex; he could legally be a father and be married. The thought made me feel sick.

"He doesn't like to be touched, Rob. Stay close to him though, all right? I want you to stay close to him so he knows he's loved."

Rob nodded as he followed the doctor and my son through the double doors. I wanted to melt onto the hospital floor.

"Come on," said Jake. "We'll get a cup of tea and sit down."

I wanted to shout at Jake for what he had said to Rob, but instead I let him lead me away with his hand on the small of my back. Perhaps I was too tired to argue. Perhaps I needed someone to lead me, to tell me what to do. I didn't have the brain power to do it myself. All my thoughts were consumed by that blank expression on Aiden's face.

CHAPTER NINE

It would be easier to say that I was so focussed on Aiden coming back, and the things he had been through, that I barely noticed Rob's reintroduction into my life, but that would be a lie. Rob's presence affected me more than I was willing to admit at the time. For one thing, seeing him brought me some comfort. At one time, Rob's resemblance to Aiden had brought me nothing but pain, and it was one of the reasons why he left in the first place. But now I looked at him and saw what I hoped Aiden could one day be: confident, amiable, and overall, kind.

Yes, Rob had gone through a rebellious phase, and no, he was not the kind of boyfriend you took home to your parents, but Rob had something of the artist in him. The rest was Viking. He had a hot temper and would have been at home with the fighting and fucking of that ancient society, but deep down he had a sensitive nature and a strong sense of loyalty. He was a protective presence in my life. At least, he had been, until Aiden disappeared.

We saw Aiden in each other and it drove us both mad. I felt like half a person after I thought Aiden had drowned in the flood, and I imagine Rob felt the same. We should have made each other whole by joining our broken selves together. But for whatever reason it didn't work like that. We only reminded each other of what we had lost and eventually we had to part. Couples who lose a child often separate. We were one of those couples.

But now our child had come back. What did that mean for us?

Those were the thoughts running through my mind as I waited with Jake, my husband, for Aiden's tests to be finished. When Jake passed me a cup of weak tea, I forced myself to stop thinking about Rob and concentrate on the man before me, the man whose daughter was in my womb, who had fixed me when I was broken, rather than running away. He was the man I should be thinking about. He was the man who should make my heart skip a beat.

"I can't wait until this is all over and we can bring Aiden home," I said, sipping on my tea. I flinched as it burned my tongue, and blew softly over the liquid.

Jake had brought me to the hospital canteen. I felt guilty being so far from Aiden, but was glad to be away from those stark corridors. We sat at a wobbly table and watched as visitors bought cups of coffee for their elderly relatives. A woman desperately tried to soothe her screaming baby, red-faced from embarrassment.

"Is that wise?" Jake crossed his legs and smoothed the fabric of his trousers. "At least straight away. We don't know what kind of psychological harm Aiden has suffered. Are we really equipped to deal with it?"

I stared at Jake, unable to find the words I needed to convey how ridiculous I found that notion. I was his *mother*; I was all he needed. I must have been frowning or glaring, because Jake stuttered as he attempted to explain further.

"What I mean is… Aiden is… well, he's going to need a lot of specialist care, and we need to be careful that we give him what he requires to get better. There's a reason why he's still in shock and still won't speak about what happened to him. Let's just not rush things. Let's make sure we listen carefully to the experts. I mean, it might not even be *safe* to bring him home, especially as you'll be having the baby soon."

"You think Aiden is dangerous?" I rubbed the back of my neck, trying to piece Jake's words together in my fogged state of exhaustion. "He's not dangerous."

Jake reached across the table and took my hand. "Sweetheart. Think for a minute. You haven't seen Aiden for a decade. A *decade*, Emma. He isn't the sweet six-year-old boy you remember. He's almost a fully grown man. We know nothing about him."

Gently, I slid my hand out from his. Was there any truth in what he was saying? Could Aiden really be dangerous? When I saw him sitting there in that hospital bed, all I could think about was the boy in the red anorak who kissed me goodbye in the school carpark. Maybe Jake was right. I didn't know him, not anymore.

"Okay, we won't rush things," I said. "But I really want Aiden to come home with us. He deserves to be part of a family. He's my *son*, Jake. He's my boy. I let him down and he's lived in hell for ten years. I need to make sure he has a healthy, happy home now. And that means he's your son too and you need to act like you're his father."

Jake retracted his hand sharply and frowned. "You don't think I'm acting like that already? I'm just trying to look out for him."

"I didn't... I mean... of course—"

"You don't think I'm prepared to be a dad for him? I am, Emma, I am." His cheeks flushed and the volume of his voice started to rise, which surprised me because Jake was generally such a soft-spoken man. "I mean for God's sake, Emma, not many men would deal with this so well. Your teenage son just came back from the *dead*." As his agitation grew, I sat there with my mouth flapping open and shut. "Everything was perfect. We have the baby on the way, the house is pristine, ready for the new arrival. You have your job. I had the promotion to head of the art department.

Everything was perfect." He lifted his glasses and rubbed his eyes.

"Hey." I stood, moved towards him and wrapped my arms around his shoulders. "It's still going to be perfect. So our family is a bit bigger than we expected; that's okay, right? Aiden is going to make things even better. Bump has a big brother!" I rubbed his shoulders, finally realising that this hadn't just been a huge strain on me, it had been a huge strain on him, too. Of course it had. I couldn't begrudge him some adjustment time.

Jake's hands spread up and over my arms, pulling them around his body so I was hugging him and he was clutching me tightly. "As long as you're mine, I don't care about everything else." He kissed my hands. My belly pressed against the back of the chair, and I felt Bump move again. The pressure of her small feet made me ache, and I let out a moan of discomfort.

"Seems like Bump would agree with you," I laughed.

I had to pull myself out of Jake's grip to move away. I barely caught the expression on his face as I went back to the other side of the table. He seemed to be half-frowning, and I longed to look into his mind to know what he was thinking. I imagined his thoughts as dark, terrifying and cold, isolated from the world, like a lonely boy bracing himself against the freezing cold wind on a snowy mountain top.

"How long is Rob staying?" he asked. "He'll have to go back to the army soon, right?"

I eased myself back into my chair. "I don't know. He needs to get to know Aiden again, so… However long it takes."

Jake's fingers drummed the surface of the table. "Do you think that's a good idea?"

"What do you mean?"

"Well, Aiden has been through hell for ten years. Then he comes back, he gets to know his dad again, and then…" He lifted his arms in the air in an over-exaggerated shrug. "He's gone. Back to the army or whatever whim makes him leave again."

"Rob wouldn't leave on a whim."

"He did last time."

"That was…" I frowned. Was it more than a whim? Rob had never expressed any desire to join the army before Aiden's disappearance. Before then he'd bummed around, either working in his parents' B&B or taking up bricklaying work with local builders.

"What? Different? Yes, it was, because you had lost a son and he abandoned you when you were at your most vulnerable. You know, sometimes I think you have a short memory because you've forgotten how bad it got."

"I haven't forgotten, trust me." I couldn't help it; my eyes dropped from his gaze and I tried not to think about that time. I stared hopelessly at my tea, wishing the memories away, wishing they'd slip into a black hole.

"I picked up those pieces, Emma."

"I know."

"It's not something I regret. Having you in my life has been the best thing that has ever happened to me, and I mean it. I really do."

"But it's not just me anymore," I said. "I come with baggage. I come with a son who is back from the dead. That's just how my life is." I felt a manic giggle rise up, threatening to spill out, but I managed to keep myself under control. I glanced across at two elderly women stirring their tea. This wasn't the time or the place to lose it.

He sighed and reached across the table to take my hands. "I love you, more than anything. You, the baby, and now Aiden, are my family, and no one hurts my family."

CHAPTER TEN

Aiden stepped out of the x-ray unit with the same blank expression as before. I don't know what I'd been hoping for. Tears? A big, silly grin? Giggles? I glanced from him to Rob and saw his grim expression.

"How's my brave boy?" I asked, hating the way my voice sounded far too cheerful, far too forced. Far too patronising. I rubbed one hand with the other, alternating between the two: a nervous habit I picked up after Aiden disappeared.

"He did very well," answered Dr Schaffer.

But when Rob wouldn't meet my eyes, my stomach flipped over with nerves. There was a moment of silence as we stood in a crowd in the sterile hospital corridor. I hated this silence. I just wanted to hear my son speak, and though I was trying my best to remain patient, I could already feel the frustration bubbling up inside me, like a pan simmering away.

"We're taking him back to his room to get comfy and then we'll have another chat," said the doctor, his tone inciting a creeping sense of dread to spread over my skin.

After Aiden was settled into his room, Dr Schaffer took us back into the corridor and explained the results of the x-ray in his matter-of-fact and professional doctor's voice.

"The results confirmed what I expected. There's an old fracture line in the ankle, at the lateral malleolus. But that break has healed well. I think he may have received treatment for it, in fact."

"He was taken to a hospital?" I asked.

"It's difficult to tell without seeing the original injury. Aiden may have been treated privately by the person who took him. I wouldn't like to say for sure."

"What does that mean for him, in terms of the future?" I asked.

"He may experience some stiffness in his ankle. He might have a slight limp."

I pressed the heels of my hands into my eyes, trying not to think of Aiden trapped in some cage, chained like a dog, in pain from the break in his ankle. Did he do it trying to escape? Did his kidnapper hurt him? Did the kidnapper give him any painkillers? I wanted to disconnect the traumatised boy in the hospital room from the little baby I gave birth to and nurtured, but I couldn't.

"Was there anything else?" I asked. "Are there

any more breaks?" Did he beat him? Was my little boy raped and beaten over and over again?

"No," Dr Schaffer said. "I know that doesn't sound like good news given the circumstances but I really think it is. The ankle break seems to be the most significant evidence of injury."

So he wasn't beaten, at least not to the point of broken bones. That didn't rule out bruises. His kidnapper still could have pushed his thumbs into my son's tender flesh, hurting him until he screamed. That could still have happened, let's not forget that. I was living in a reality where news that my son only suffered *one* broken bone at the mercy of a sadistic kidnapper was good news.

Dr Schaffer informed us that the child psychologist would be meeting with us after Aiden had a rest before leaving us waiting outside the room in the corridor.

"What happened in there, Rob?" I asked as soon as the doctor was out of hearing range.

"Nothing," he said with a shrug. "Absolutely nothing. Aiden didn't say a word. He didn't react. He sort of flinched a bit when they touched him but there was nothing—no tears, no screams." He clenched his jaw and pressed his fist against the wall of the corridor. "I can't *fucking* believe all this. Someone chained up my son and left him there with his ankle busted. Fucking…"

A nurse walked past and raised her eyebrow at Rob, who was still pushing his knuckles against the wall. I flashed her a quick smile and placed my hand on Rob's shoulder.

"Hey," I said. "You can't lose it. Not here. We're all dealing with this. Stay strong for Aiden."

Rob sighed and rested his forehead against the wall. He was always someone who reacted in big, dramatic ways, though this time it didn't feel over-dramatic. There wasn't an over-dramatic way to deal with the events of the last two days.

"Sorry, I…"

"I know." I rubbed his shoulder a little, trying to ignore the way Jake was watching me. "Small steps. We're here for Aiden. He'll come round, Rob, I know he will. He won't stay like this forever." But after saying those words I tried to swallow and my throat was bone dry. My eyes stung and I was tired all over. I was too exhausted to believe it.

*

DCI Stevenson arrived at the hospital in the afternoon wearing the stone-faced expression of a man carrying bad news.

"The vultures are circling. Reporters have caught wind of the search going on through the woods. It's only a matter of time before they sniff out the witnesses' report of seeing Aiden. We've told them not to talk to anyone, but these things always come out."

"Did you find anything in the woods?" I didn't care about the press, I just wanted justice for Aiden.

Stevenson shook his head. "It was pouring

down the night Aiden stumbled out onto the road. His tracks are gone. We've tried sniffer dogs using the clothes he was wearing, but they lost the trail pretty quickly. I've got a sizeable force out combing the forest for clues. We will find something, but it might take longer than we'd hoped."

"The fucking press," Jake muttered. "If they get hold of this it'll be on every national newspaper. It's going to be a nightmare. Is there nothing you can do?"

Stevenson shook his head. "These stories always come out. Aiden's drowning was a big story ten years ago. This is going to be even bigger. I know you've been put through hell and back over the last decade, and I hate to say this, but you need to brace yourself. This is going to be tough."

No one spoke for at least thirty seconds. I think we were all contemplating—in our own ways—how our world was going to change once the press caught onto the story of Aiden's reappearance. It was probably our last day of having Aiden to ourselves without the media hounding us every hour of the day. We spent it sat in his hospital room, staying close as he impassively allowed the doctors and nurses to prod and poke him. At one point I dared to hold his hand as they drew blood, forcing myself not to flinch as the needle pierced his skin. He had been through worse, and I hadn't been there to hold his hand during those horrific times.

The child psychologist was a woman in her

forties with flowing clothes—a long, purple skirt, a shawl wrapped around her shoulders, and clumpy clog-like shoes. Though her appearance wasn't particularly professional, she did have a comforting presence, like everyone's favourite aunty. She spoke softly, clearly, and gently.

"Hello, Aiden. My name is Cathy, and I'm here to ask you a few questions and see how you're doing. Is that all right?"

Aiden remained silent.

"Did… did, um, Dr Schaffer warn you about Aiden's present state?" I asked.

Cathy—who had introduced herself to me as Dr Foster—nodded and smiled. "He did. That's okay. We'll take our time with Aiden." She turned back to him. I'd bought Aiden some new clothes that morning, so he was wearing a pair of jeans with a plain blue jumper. I had wanted to buy him something trendy, something a normal teenager would like, but I didn't know what a sixteen-year-old boy would want to wear. When I was sixteen I wore nothing but black. My dad would balk at the length of my skirt or the coating of eye-liner around my eyes, and Mum would just roll her eyes. Somehow I didn't think Aiden was interested in rebelling against me just yet.

Aiden sat quietly at a little table in the corner of his hospital room. Dr Foster joined him at the table, sitting opposite him. The psychologist reached into her bag and removed a notepad and pen. "Would you like to write or draw anything, Aiden?"

I watched eagerly as Dr Foster pushed the notepad and pen across the table. I rubbed one hand with the other, hoping and wishing he would lift the pen. If he could communicate with us in even the smallest way, that would be something. It would be wonderful.

Aiden stared down at the notepad but didn't make any move to pick up the pen. I chewed on my bottom lip, while Rob stood on my right side and Jake hovered on my left. DCI Stevenson had left us in the care of two 'family liaison officers' while he went back to the police station to work on the case. They were waiting in the corridor to give us some space. Denise and Marcus, they were called. Dr Schaffer was doing his rounds on the ward. As much as it felt like Aiden was the only child in the world, he wasn't. He wasn't even the only child in the world who had been through the same suffering.

"Perhaps you could draw us a nice picture," Dr Foster went on. "Doesn't matter what it is, anything that pops into your mind."

His gaze never moved from the pen and paper, and in my mind I imagined that he really wanted to take the pen. I rubbed my hands again, hoping and praying he would. He leaned forward and I leaned with him, almost stepping towards them. But I didn't. I hung back, giving them space. It must have been off-putting, having us all watching him like that, but there was no way I was letting the psychologist in the room with him without me there.

Then, in one quick, fluid moment, he snatched up the pen and pulled the notebook towards him. I let out a breath, only then aware that I'd been holding it. Dr Foster glanced up at me with a small, hopeful smile on her face. What if Aiden could write? He'd been proficient for a six-year-old before he was snatched, but I had no idea what he'd been taught or not taught since then. Did he have books where he'd been? Had he kept a diary of his world? I screwed my eyes shut and opened them again. Aiden was drawing in the notepad. He was drawing something.

I turned to Rob and then to Jake, my chest heaving up and down. This was good, it had to be. This was a step in the right direction. Finally. And after this, how long would it be before he started talking again? Then he'd be able to tell us what had happened to him. We'd find his kidnapper and throw him in jail, unless I murdered him first. If it weren't for prison… I shook my head, forcing the dark thoughts away, though one question remained… Could I?

While Aiden scribbled in the notebook I resisted the urge to step closer and lean over his shoulder. Aiden deserved a moment to express himself. There was a terrible tale inside him that one day he would need to tell the world. *Let him breathe*, I thought to myself.

Slowly, Aiden's hand came to a stop. I wasn't close enough to see what he had drawn, but I knew he had been scribbling rather quickly, veering his fist from one side of the page to the other as he worked the pen.

"That's wonderful, Aiden," said Dr Foster as Aiden pushed the book back to her. "And what is this a drawing of? Is it the place you were when you were away?"

My heart skipped a beat, but Aiden's face gave nothing away. He was as blank and calm as always.

"Shall we show this to your mum?" Dr Foster asked.

He didn't reply, of course, but I stepped towards the table anyway. With a face as pale as milk, Dr Foster lifted the sheet of paper. It was filled with one untidy, black scribble with ferocious pen strokes that almost completely filled the page.

CHAPTER ELEVEN

I could've kicked myself for not thinking to give Aiden a pen and some paper before the psychologist saw him. Aiden was always a visual child. He hated colouring books as a child, preferring to scribble or paint on blank sheets of paper. I bought him his first watercolour set when he was four. Bishoptown-on-Ouse has an abundance of spots perfect for the exploration of young mothers and their sons armed with a painting set. We found a huge oak tree which turned into the HQ for a badly-behaved fairy king. Aiden painted orange and red leaves on a thick brown trunk. The Ouse was the perfect spot for a tsunami, so I drew little surfers on top of his blue waves. Aiden loved to paint with colours. He copied the pictures from his favourite comic books, creating his own messy versions of Superman and Spiderman.

He'd grown up with a set of parents who loved art and who loved to paint and draw. And of course he needed that outlet now. But the picture I saw in that hospital room was not Aiden. It was spiky and harsh. It was painful to look at. Dr Foster gave me the sheet of paper to keep and even as we were driving home from the hospital I took the paper out and stared at it, following the lines with my finger.

There were no recognisable shapes within his drawing. There was nothing that could be used in the investigation. Aiden had not drawn us a pretty picture of his prison, nor had he drawn us a map of where he had come from out of the woods. There was nothing except pain and anger in his work, and I didn't need to be any kind of therapist to see that. But I did feel that it was worth visiting Dr Foster again, so we arranged some dates for over the next few weeks. She pushed things around but managed to fit Aiden in as a priority around her other clients, and I was grateful for that.

The next day, Dr Schaffer informed me that there was little reason to keep Aiden in the hospital. Aside from the old injury on his ankle, there was nothing wrong with him. His growth had been somewhat stunted, but otherwise, he was healthy. I would be taking him home tomorrow.

That Saturday disappeared in a blur as I rushed back to the house, made up the bed in the spare room, and placed the one stuffed toy I'd allowed myself to keep after I declared my son dead. It was a small, soft dragon with red scales that shimmered when the light hit them. My mum had given it to Aiden when he was a baby, representing her Welsh ancestry. I placed it on the pillow and folded the bedding around it to make it look like it had been tucked in. It was silly, but I used to do that when he was a toddler. Then I took the clothes from the shopping bags around the room and folded them into the drawers. Poor Jake had given me his credit card to use and I had gone a little wild, trying to somehow make up for Aiden's ten years of hell with expensive jeans.

At one point I dug out a couple of pieces of his artwork and tacked them to the wall. Then I thought better of it and pulled them down again. Aiden wasn't a little boy anymore. The dragon, though—that had to stay. He had never slept without it when he was little. He needed to know I remembered.

The next morning I woke with butterflies in my stomach at the thought of bringing my son home. With it being a Sunday, Jake was off from work, of course, but I suggested he give us the day to settle in. He agreed, eager to do what was best for Aiden, and, I think, a little guilty about the way he'd reacted in the hospital.

Rob picked me up to take me to the hospital, driving his dad's car. We'd decided that it would be too much for Sonya and Peter to be there. We wanted to keep this simple and quiet. There was the threat of the press looming above us. They would find out soon, we were certain of that, but how much, and when? That axe was yet to fall.

"Are you ready?" Rob asked as I pulled the seatbelt across my body.

"Are you?" I replied.

He'd rolled up the sleeves of his shirt, and I noticed the hint of a tattoo peeking out from underneath the sleeve. It was black, with a slight tail looping down.

"A dragon?" I asked.

"Like Aiden's," he replied.

"I found it and put it on his bed."

"He never slept without it," Rob said.

"I know." I pressed my finger into the corner of my eye and tried hard to stop the tears building up. "No, I'm not ready for this. But I won't let it show. I won't."

"It's all right, Em. You're doing a good job. Fuck, you're doing better than I am. And you have the…" He glanced at my belly.

"The baby? It's fine, she's not the elephant in the room. You can mention her."

"She? So Aiden will have a little sister. That's great. It'll be great for him."

"I hope so."

Rob was quiet for the rest of the journey, and I couldn't help but wonder what was going through his mind. After a few minutes I gave up and thought of Aiden. There was a nervous tickling in my stomach as we pulled into the hospital carpark. It was early October and the leaves of the old sycamore trees on the edge of the paved area were turning amber and gold. Low-hanging mist obscured the autumn colours and blurred through the parked cars. The windscreen wipers squeaked across the glass, smearing fine rain into milky streaks.

"So what's he like?" Rob asked as he unclipped his seatbelt.

I gave him a look as if to say 'Who?' With Aiden in hospital I'd spent a fair bit of time with Rob, and I was already allowing myself to relax. I remembered giving Rob that look a hundred times when we were together. He'd always tested my patience, but at one time that had felt like a good thing, an exciting thing.

"Hewitt."

"Supportive," I said. "Reliable. A good husband. He'll be a great dad."

"Better than me, then."

"Oh, for God's sake," I said in a raspy voice, struggling with the door to the Ford. "Does it matter? Fucking grow up, Rob. You weren't there, I moved on. I'm happy, all right? What's done is done and it doesn't matter anyway. None of it does. Aiden is all that matters now." I let go of the door handle and sighed. "So can you deal with this? Can you work through your pathetic issues and be a man? Be a dad? Because if you can't, then turn around and drive out of this carpark right now and never come back into Aiden's life. He needs stability and he needs love. It's not an either/or situation here. I need you to give him both."

Rob held his hands up in surrender. "All right, all right. I know, okay. I know he needs that from me. I'm going to be there for you both. I promise."

His words freed a part of me, lifting a suffocating weight from my chest. Who knew that what I'd needed the most was his reassurance that he'd help? I guess I'd been carrying too much on my own to breathe.

Outside the car, the air was full of drizzle with a strong breeze rustling the auburn leaves. Though it was a small hospital in an affluent area, St Michael's still had that faded hospital look, with a dirty-beige painted exterior and steps grimy with moss leading to the entrance. I pulled my woollen cardigan closer to my throat to stem the chill.

We walked the familiar steps towards the ward and exchanged pleasantries with Dr Schaffer. The family liaison officers from the police were already there. PC Denise Ellis was a short but sturdy woman of Afro-Caribbean descent. PC Marcus Hawthorne was tall, lanky and pasty-faced, with limp red hair. Though I preferred DCI Stevenson to keep us updated, the two of them seemed mild-mannered and professional, never raising their voices and always offering us cups of tea and coffee.

We walked into Aiden's room to find him standing at the window staring out. He was dressed in jeans and a striped jumper that I'd dropped off at the hospital. He hadn't had his hair cut, so it was still straggly and touched the tops of his shoulders. His eyes were slightly red-rimmed, though I doubted it was from crying. More likely he'd had a bad night's sleep. I hoped he didn't have any nightmares, but I was almost sure he did.

"Are you all set?" I asked, again with the bright, cheery voice that sounded forced. I kept reminding myself of annoying TV presenters on the kids' channel, bright-eyed and blonde with a permanent grin fixed to their faces.

Aiden moved away from the window and towards me, but again he didn't say a word. He didn't really look at me either, but at least he was walking towards me. That was a start. It was an acknowledgement of my presence. It was better than nothing.

"Right then, pal," Rob said. "You'd better say your goodbyes to Dr Schaffer and the others. We're taking you home, mate. Mum's got Walnut the Dragon all ready for you."

I'd almost forgotten that bit. Aiden insisted on calling his dragon Walnut because my mum loved her Walnut Whips, and I was always teasing her about the walnut addiction. Somehow, Aiden latched onto the association between his Nana and the walnuts. Hearing the familiar name hit me in the gut with a bomb of emotion. It erupted through me, fireworks extending to my fingers and toes. *That was what I used to have. That was my perfect, happy time.*

Aiden followed us silently as we made our way

back through the hospital to the carpark. His footsteps were quiet, though he still moved with a stiff gait. The jeans and jumper I'd bought for him were for a much younger child, yet they still hung loosely on his hips. Dr Schaffer had told me to cook plenty of protein-rich foods, like chicken and fish, to help build up his muscles.

I longed to take his hand but I refrained, aware of how much he disliked being touched. Instead, I matched his stride, stepping along with him, and facing the rest of the hospital with him as we walked him out of the building together. All eyes were on him. Every nurse stopped what they were doing to stare at the boy who had come back from the dead. Every room we passed, the patients and visitors peeked out through the doors. And the closer we got to the front of the hospital, the more a seeping sense of dread worked its way through my system. I glanced at Denise, and saw the tension running along her jaw. She felt it too.

Word had got out.

If the hospital staff and patients knew who Aiden was, that meant gossip of Aiden's strange arrival had started to spread. But how far had it gone?

We were only two or three paces out of the glass doors when a wiry man with a hooked nose stepped into our path.

"Matthew Grey from the Yorkshire Post. Is this Aiden Price?"

Marcus stepped forward, shielding Aiden from

the intrusive man, while Denise whispered to me, "Don't say anything."

Rob and I put our heads down and walked on, guiding Aiden gently away, but the man sidestepped Marcus and approached Aiden directly.

"Are you Aiden Price?"

"Get away from him," I said between my teeth. This time I did take Aiden's hand. I pulled him away from the reporter and hurried to the car with my heart beating hard and my chest tight.

This time it was only one. Next time, we wouldn't be so lucky.

CHAPTER TWELVE

PC Denise Ellis put the kettle on as soon as we made it into the house.

"They'll find out where you live soon," she warned. "They can't come onto the property but they'll hang around the boundaries with cameras. We'll do what we can to keep them away. It might be time to get a lawyer and maybe someone in public relations to help."

I didn't want to deal with all this. Aiden had only just taken his shoes off. I'd bought him Velcro trainers: I didn't even know if he could tie his own shoelaces, and I didn't want him to feel embarrassed by not knowing how. We were all crowded awkwardly in the kitchen. All I could think about was how PC Ellis had just left the teabag on the very expensive ash kitchen side and how it might stain, and how PC Hawthorne still had his boots on.

"Is that really necessary?" I asked. My hands were at it again, one rubbing over the other. "Won't it be expensive?"

Denise stirred milk into the tea. "Yes, but you can potentially make quite a lot of money, you know. There are newspaper interviews, TV interviews, the lot. They pay well and you get to tell your story." The stirring stopped and she looked up at me. "But don't speak to anyone until the investigation is over. When we put the kidnapper behind bars, that's when you can start talking to the press."

"No one is telling this story except Aiden."

"I know, but the press are going to hound you. What we can do, if you want, is release a statement asking for privacy at this difficult time. It never works, but then if they cross the line, you've warned them not to."

She handed me a hot cup of tea and I blew on the liquid to cool it.

"They'd better leave Aiden alone," Rob said. "They have to, don't they? He's a minor. He's just a kid."

"The problem is," Marcus said, "they already know who Aiden is. We would usually keep his name out of the newspapers, but it was reported on during the flood. Everyone knows Aiden's name."

My heart sank. More than anything I wanted Aiden to have a happy, normal home after everything he'd been through. But he was already famous, and he didn't even know it.

"We're here to help you deal with everything." Denise tried to smile reassuringly, but neither Rob nor I returned the smile.

The tea cooled on the table as we took Aiden around his new home. He followed us placidly with small, stiff steps. I found myself rambling as I walked through the house, desperately trying to fill the silence.

"Jake chose the carpets, he loves white and cream. He's lovely. You'll get to know him soon. I thought you might want to get used to the place first, though. Jake will be home soon and then you can get to know each other. He's out buying food for us and running errands. We'll have a stocked up house for you soon. A proper home."

"Is anyone allowed to spill in this house?" Rob asked with an eyebrow raised, his eyes roaming across the luxurious cream throws over the sofas.

I chose to ignore him. "And that is one of my paintings. It was Jake's idea to hang it on the wall." I gestured to the large abstract acrylic hanging up on the corridor wall. I'd painted it shortly after the flood. It represented a great deal of pain for me, with the reds swirled into blues, but Jake had insisted that we display it. He said it was his favourite artwork of all time and I couldn't resist his excited smile. Over time I grew to look at that painting and see his smile rather than Aiden's coat in the water. Perhaps now that Aiden was back, I'd find something else to see in those swirls of colour.

"It's good, Em," Rob said.

I'd never shown him the painting before, not even in the aftermath of the flood. I'd always kept it to myself. It was only when Jake found me with a knife in one hand and red coating my arms, sat on the floor next to a pile of torn canvasses, that I had finally shown someone.

"Anyway, up here on the left is the downstairs loo." I angled my face away from Rob to hide the way my cheeks had flushed.

"Downstairs loo, you say? Very la-di-da."

I rolled my eyes at Rob. It wasn't as if his parents didn't have a nice place. He was being an inverted snob. It was cute when we'd been teenagers. I liked that rebellious streak in him, and the way he railed against his middle-class upbringing, but now it just seemed immature.

"Not that there's anything wrong with that," Rob added hastily, sensing my annoyance.

"And up the stairs is where your bedroom is, and where my bedroom with Jake is. There's a bathroom there, too, with a bath and a shower." I took a couple of the stairs and glanced back to realise that Aiden wasn't following us. "It's okay, take your time."

I shared a look with Rob. Concern laid low in my belly along with a mouthful of the tea Denise had made me. I'd never thought of this. I knew that Aiden walked with a stiff gait, and that he hadn't had much opportunity to move around over the decade of captivity, but I'd not even thought of the fact he might not have walked up stairs for years and years. It was one of those moments where the extent of Aiden's trauma hit me with full force. This was what he'd been through. This was what he had been forced to endure. This. Not even able to walk upstairs. Any other sixteen-year-old would be able to run up them, taking two at a time. I saw them running up and down the stairs at school all the time. I usually chastised them for it and received a 'sorry, Miss' in return.

Aiden stood there, with his gaze fixed on the bottom step. I walked down to meet him and hesitantly placed my hand on his arm.

"Okay, so one big step and then another." Gently, I coaxed him up the first few steps. There were beads of sweat forming on his forehead. His brow was furrowed in concentration, but after the first few steps, he got the hang of it, and I let go of his arm.

Rob met us at the top with his arms folded and his mouth in a tight line. I knew what he was thinking. He was thinking about the things he'd do to the man who had taken our son.

"This way, Aiden." I was getting sick of the sound of my own voice. It was obvious that underneath the bright, cheery tone were the cracks of my own distress. I sounded sickly and weak, desperately trying not to burst into tears at any moment. Part of me wished that Aiden was still in the hospital just so I didn't have to see his haunted expression in our home. It was worse here, somehow. Hospitals are full of sad or blank faces, but a home should be happy. Aside from the odd row, it should be filled with smiling faces and laughter, not the eerie quiet of the traumatised. "This is your room. I hope you like it. I've put some clothes inside the drawers, look, and the wardrobe. There are jeans in here, and underwear here. There are towels in the cabinet in the hall outside. And look, I know it's silly, but here's Walnut." I lifted the dragon out from the covers and held it aloft as if it were some sort of precious artefact. Aiden just stared.

"Come on, mate, you remember Walnut," Rob said. "You used to sleep with him every night."

"Dad used to call him Wally sometimes, and Grandad used to call him..." I trailed off, remembering that I still hadn't told Aiden his grandparents had died.

Before I could say any more, Aiden took a step forward and took the dragon from my hand in a swift motion that seemed jarring after his stillness. He stared down at the dragon and my breath caught in my throat. Would this be the moment he broke his silence? I watched him turn the dragon over in his hands, waiting for something... anything. A squeak would suffice. A scream. One word. One letter. Anything to indicate that my Aiden was still in there somewhere, alive and kicking and waiting to tell his Mummy all the bad things that had happened to him.

But he lifted his head and looked at me with the same blank expression on his face. His chestnut eyes were exactly the same as before, without any trace of emotion.

"Okay, well, I'll show you my room next," I said, and this time my voice really did crack.

*

When my voice grew tired of filling the silences and Rob ran out of things to say, we put the television on in the living room and left Aiden watching a children's channel. I made him a cup of milky tea along with toast and Nutella, and left him sitting on the sofa gazing at the colourful pictures on the screen.

It was in the kitchen that I let myself go. I let the tears come, and I cried into Rob's t-shirt until I couldn't cry anymore. He made me a peppermint tea and sat me down on the bench next to the table. Denise hovered awkwardly around, mopping up spilled tea, washing the few plates we'd used since we'd been home. Marcus spent most of the time checking his phone or leaning awkwardly against a chair. After Rob glared at them both for a while Denise excused herself from the kitchen, and grabbed Marcus on the way out.

"What the fuck am I going to do?" I ran a hand over my stomach and thought about my pregnancy with Aiden. It was hell. I threw up, I had back pain, I had a terrible labour. I never expected to bond with Aiden, but as soon as the midwife placed him in my arms I realised I'd never known love until that moment. The pain and the sickness melted away. It had been someone else throwing up in a bin near the school hall, someone else who had been in labour for almost twenty hours. That had never happened; my beautiful little baby just arrived and was plopped into my arms and that was that for the rest of my life.

"He just needs time." Rob sipped his tea and grimaced. "What is this shit?"

"Badly steeped herbal tea. How long did you leave the bag in for?"

"I dunno, Em. You've changed. Cream carpets, herbal tea? That's not you. Remember how we celebrated Aiden's birth?"

"Half a bottle of vodka on the bench outside Rough Valley. I remember. I had to sit on a cushion because my stitches still hurt. We sat there with Aiden in a sling until it got cold and then ate mints before taking him back to my parents. It was a good job I expressed milk before we drank the vodka. But Jesus, Rob, do you think that was *good*? We were messed-up kids. Imagine if we were still sitting around drinking vodka now. Aiden needs stability."

"Yeah, I know." Rob tapped on the ceramic mug and stared down at his tea. "It's just how much you've changed. You're... I dunno..."

"What?"

"Does this really make you happy?" Rob waved his arm around the kitchen at the neat shelves and the pristine finish on the cupboard doors. "Where's the character? Where's your influence? This is all him. There's that one painting of yours, which, by the way, is the only bit of colour in this place, and everything else is just... sterile."

I hated the truth in his words and I hated him at that moment. I stood up, took his mug and emptied it into the sink. He wasn't going to drink it anyway.

"You'd better go."

"Don't forget to rinse that mug." The chair scraped as he moved away from the table. He snatched up his jacket from the back of the chair and began to yank it on over his arms. "You won't want to leave any tea stains on the perfect cream surface. And for fuck's sake don't spill any on your grey dresses in your beige house. I'll go and say goodbye to Aiden."

I put the mug down in the sink and sighed. "Don't go."

He paused. The jacket came off, and almost immediately his arms were wrapped around my waist, stretching across my back with the baby bump between us. His head leaned against my shoulder.

"I've missed you, Emma."

"No—that's not... That's not what I meant." I pulled away, removing his hands. "No. We... We need to figure out what we're going to do." I ducked around him and avoided his eyes. I felt my cheeks, felt the flushed warmth of embarrassment. "I mean, we need to figure out a plan for how we're going to deal with the press and how we're going to cope with Aiden until he's better." I finally lifted my head and found his gaze. "I'm carrying his child, Rob. I can't do this."

CHAPTER THIRTEEN

It might surprise you to know that before Aiden was taken during the flood, I never considered myself a bad mother. Not even when I was eighteen years old with a baby at my breast did I worry about whether I was a good or bad mother. I went with it. I nurtured when I wanted to nurture. I was fun when I needed to be. I was creative when I was in the mood. There were times when Aiden was crying or throwing a tantrum that I needed a deep breath and longed for more of the vodka I'd drunk with Rob on the bench outside Rough Valley Forest, but they were rare and I didn't dwell on them.

I was never the kind of mum who bought every gadget and new-fangled toy as soon as it came out to appease her little darlings. I was never the over-compensator because I felt guilty about snapping at my precious one or losing my temper after one too many glasses of Chardonnay. Not that I want to judge those people. We're all getting by in this life. I won't begrudge people their own methods for coping, but that just wasn't me. Despite my age (or maybe because of it) I always felt secure about my parenting, and Mum always helped in her own, laid back style.

But now… Well, now I was the opposite. I was an indulger. As part of Aiden's recovery programme I was required to make him meals from Dr Schaffer's suggestions, which I intended to, but I also wanted to make up for everything he'd been through. I wanted to prove to him that there were still good things in the world. I'd already racked my brain for Aiden's favourite recipes. He'd been a boy with a sweet tooth and I had allowed him a few treats every now and then. But now I poured the treats into his hands: Mars Bars and Snickers bars and Kinder Eggs with Star Wars toys inside. I stocked up on all kinds of goodies. I made him hot chocolate and buttery toast. When Jake came home that Sunday evening, I made a hot-dog casserole with thick pieces of white bread on the side and some chips because I remembered how much he loved chips. And all the time I made this food, I had a ridiculous smile on my face, occasionally catching a glimpse of myself in the shining microwave door and wondering if I'd become possessed by the Joker from the Batman films.

I found myself filled with electric nervous

energy that spilled out as I moved around the kitchen. Even washing my hands was a frantic scrubbing rather than my usual quick rinse and dry.

"Now, Aiden, I want you to know that this is your home and you're welcome here," Jake said as I busied around the two men in my life, trying not to think about the moment Rob had wrapped his arms around me in this very spot. "But there are some rules." I turned and watched. Aiden appeared to be listening intently. I had been about to tell Jake to go easy, but he certainly had Aiden's attention, and even though I didn't particularly agree with giving Aiden ground rules so soon, it was good to see my son actually *listening*. So I let him continue. "We keep a tidy house here. We wash our dishes straight after using them and we put things away. But don't worry too much, okay. Don't get stressed out about it. We'll help you out. Okay, kid?"

I couldn't help but smile. Jake really was trying his best to deal with the situation.

As I stirred my casserole, Jake directed Aiden in setting the kitchen table. They unfolded a tablecloth together and put down the placemats. My damaged old heart fleshed out just a little bit as I watched them. If only Aiden had smiled, or said something. Perhaps listening would have to do for now. But the way Aiden quietly followed Jake's instructions felt like progress, and I loved Jake all the more for the way he was handling my psychologically wounded son.

"All right, who's ready for hot dogs?"

Jake stuck his hand up like the suck-up kid in class. "I certainly am. What about you, Aiden?"

"I hope you're both hungry," I said, trying to fill the silence while Aiden ignored the question.

As I placed the hot dish onto the table, the phone began to ring.

"I'll get it." Jake started to stand, but I flapped my hands at him and shook my head.

"I'm on my feet anyway. You two get your teas while it's still hot."

I padded into the hall to pick up the landline. There were only a handful of people who bothered to call the landline, which could explain why my heart was pattering beneath my grey woollen jumper. I shook my head, trying to ignore the irrational heat of anxiety worming its way through my veins.

"Hello."

"Emma, it's DCI Stevenson; are you well?"

"I'm fine. Is everything all right?"

"Everything's fine, Emma. But I wanted to talk to you about an idea I have."

*

The next morning, I stood on the edge of Rough Valley Forest with Aiden on my right and Dr Foster on my left. We'd always called it 'going rough' when we were teenagers. We'd drink in 'Rough' as a dare. To me the forest had always been a place of silliness, of youth and irresponsibility. That day, standing next to Aiden, could not be more different than 'going rough'. I had an important job to do as a mother.

I'd agreed with DCI Stevenson to keep our intentions quiet. Jake had wanted to come with us, but I advised him to go to school instead. The less fuss the better. I hadn't called Rob, which I was trying not to think about. Would he understand? He'd want to be here, I knew that much, but I didn't want to crowd Aiden.

We all had on our waterproof coats against the rain. Aiden's was brand new, bought only a few days ago. But I hadn't thought to buy wellies, so trainers had to suffice.

It was a grey, drab day. A nothing day. A day that should barely be a blip on our own personal radars. And yet… it was a something day, because of what was about to happen. There was also a hint of beauty in the low-hanging fog. The rain pattered against the hood of my jacket. The air was very still, without even a hint of wind, which brought the rain directly overhead. Mist clung to the branches and blocked the path to the forest.

"I would have waited," said Stevenson. "But with the story beginning to spread, I thought it would be best to try it now before the press start following us around wherever we go. How's Aiden doing?"

It was a loaded question and we both knew it.

DCI Stevenson was, of course, desperate for Aiden to start talking. We all were.

"Small steps," I said. Then I added, "Still no words."

"It's going to take time, Detective," said Dr Foster. I was glad of her presence, though she had remained relatively quiet so far. It was nice to have another woman around sometimes, especially if she backed you up from time to time.

Stevenson nodded, with his thin lips even thinner due to his sombre expression. The disappointment was easy to read on his face. "You know what I'd like Aiden to do today, don't you?"

I took in the sight of the team he had gathered. There were only two other officers because he'd wanted to keep it small to try not to spook Aiden. They were here to collect any evidence they found. I clenched and unclenched my hands, trying not to rub them anymore. There was a sore rash spreading over my hands and the constant rubbing was doing them no good.

"I understand. I think it's too soon though." My gut told me that. If Aiden wasn't ready to speak to us, I doubted he was ready to show us either, though I'd continued to let him have pens and paper in case he decided to. So far he'd drawn nothing but scribbles.

"We need to try," DCI Stevenson said. "But take your time."

I glanced from the trees to the narrow road on my left. We were deliberately close to the spot where the driver had seen Aiden staggering away from the woods. This was where they had picked him up and taken him to the police station. *What if it was them*, I thought, and then dismissed it. Of course the police would have checked that avenue already. Besides, why would Aiden's kidnapper take Aiden to the police station? I berated myself for my own stupidity. I wouldn't be much help on this case if I didn't think logically.

I turned to Aiden, who was as still as always, staring into the foggy woods. There was no indication that he even recognised his surroundings, certainly no indication that he had suffered some sort of psychological break after a traumatic event. It happened right here, in this spot. Unless... unless he wasn't speaking before. The doctors had taken an MRI scan of his brain to check for brain damage; there was none. Aside from not speaking, he understood us; he walked, put his clothes on, brushed his teeth all with perfect coordination. There was no evidence to suggest that he had learning difficulties, though the doctor did tell us that autism was a possibility. In my heart, I knew it wasn't autism. At six years old before he was taken from me, Aiden hadn't shown any indication of autism. This mutism had been triggered through the years of trauma. *Years*. How could I ever get used to thinking that? Years of systematic abuse. How was he even still a person?

I wiped a sheen of sweat from my brow and pulled myself together. "Are you ready?"

Aiden had his hood pulled down so I couldn't see his eyes. The sleeves of his jacket were too long, covering his hands, but I had the impression that Aiden was clenching his fists inside the coat. He was even straighter than usual. Perhaps I was wrong. Perhaps he was reacting more to the woods than I thought.

"Aiden? Can you show us where you came from? Do you remember the night you came out of the woods? You were walking down this road. It was raining then, too, but it was night-time and it was dark. You didn't have a coat on like you do now. You just wore jeans and nothing else." DCI Stevenson had told me to try and evoke Aiden's sense of memory by mentioning as much detail as I could. "You came out of the woods from this direction." I turned my body and indicated with my hand. "And then you walked down the road, except you were struggling to walk. I don't think you'd walked that far for a long time." I stopped to catch my breath.

"You're doing well, Emma. Keep going." Dr Foster gave me an encouraging nod.

I took a deep breath. DCI Stevenson watched carefully, with his hands tucked inside his pockets. Even though he went to great measures to keep his expression neutral, I saw the tension in his body and knew how much it would mean to him for this to work. I longed for it to work, too, but I had my doubts.

"Maybe if I walk into the woods a bit? Would

you come with me, just to take a walk?" I suggested. When Aiden inevitably didn't reply I took a few tentative steps. He didn't. I reached out for him. "Come for a walk with Mummy." There was a desperate tremor in my voice. I blinked, forcing back the emotion threatening to erupt. "It would make me really happy if you came for a walk with me. I really want to know, Aiden. I want to know what happened and where you came from. Will you show me?"

He moved with his left foot first and my heart swelled. Then another step. His movements were even stiffer than ever, like a robot taking its first steps. Then another step. I nodded him forwards, smiling so hard I felt the skin crack in the corners of my mouth. My cheeks ached. Another. But there was something wrong. He was breathing heavily.

"It's okay," I coaxed. "I'm here and nothing is going to happen to you. You're safe, I promise. Look, DCI Stevenson will make sure of that. He's like a bodyguard. He's strong, like Superman." I avoided Stevenson's eyes, worried he might laugh, or, more likely, grimace. "It's okay, Aiden."

The rain continued to patter down, picking up speed, almost drowning out the sound of my voice. I moved forward a few more steps, walking between the first line of trees into the woods. It was a large forest, almost as big as a national park but never given the status. There was rumour of private land bought within the woods, and some was owned by a stately house that resided on a hill overlooking the village. I'd often gone wandering through those woods with Rob, taking our vodka and our cigarettes and worse into the depths. Though it was cold and dark, being there with Rob had always evoked a sense of ticklish danger that warmed my extremities. But now it was different. I saw nothing but pain lurking within those trees. The pain experienced by my son, and the pain I'd felt when he was taken from me.

My coaxing seemed to work. Aiden shuffled forward, finally reaching me. I took his small hand, and found that it was like a block of ice. I rubbed it between my palms, injecting heat into those cold fingers. Aiden was deathly pale. Two bruised eyes looked out at me from beneath the hood, which should have been enough to make me turn back. I didn't.

"Everything is going to be all right," I said.

I wanted this to work. I wanted it more than anything. I wanted to find Aiden's kidnapper and get justice, not just for Aiden, but for me too. How could I sleep at night knowing he was still out there? So I pulled him on. He resisted. He pulled back. I was firm. I stepped on into the woods, holding Aiden's hand, determined that he would show us what he knew. It was in there, deep down. Everything we needed was in there, locked up tight. I just needed the key and I thought it lay within the leaning beech trees of Rough.

"Come on," I said, my tone frostier than before, frustration creeping in.

But Aiden was resisting. He refused to move any further, digging his heels into the soft, muddy ground.

"Please, Aiden," I insisted. If he did this one thing, he could solve everything. I was close to tears as I thought of the monster still out there, still lurking somewhere ready to take my son for a second time. I couldn't allow that to happen. The answers were inside Aiden, I knew they were, but he refused to tell me. I was reduced to begging him. "Aiden." I brushed away a tear, aware of everyone watching us, embarrassed, frustrated, and close to the breaking point.

"Maybe we should take a break there, Emma," said Dr Foster. This time I wasn't interested in hearing her opinion. She was supposed to be backing me up, wasn't she? Sisterhood and all that?

"No." I didn't recognise my voice, it was more like a growl. There was a hint of wild animal in there, and still I gripped Aiden's arm while he squirmed away from me, no longer silent but panting heavily. "Aiden, you will show us. You *will* show us."

DCI Stevenson held up his hands. "This was a mistake. You were right, Emma. He's not ready. Let him go."

"No." My lips trembled. My voice was virtually unrecognisable. I didn't know who I was anymore. My face was wet, but whether it was from the rain or from my tears I didn't know. "Aiden, please."

"Emma, let the boy go."

"No."

"Emma, look at his face." Dr Foster was firmer this time. "Look at the distress you're causing him."

I blinked, bringing the world back into focus. Aiden, where was my Aiden? I shook my head and tried to concentrate. There he was, all grown up, a different boy than when he left. He was red-faced with wide eyes, shaking his head back and forth, leaning away from me with his heels dug firmly in the ground.

"Aiden?" I let him go, and my knees buckled.

CHAPTER FOURTEEN

I'd messed it up. I'd ruined a good shot at finding out more about what Aiden was keeping locked up inside him, and possibly ruined any trust we'd built together.

Even after sitting in the police car with a steaming cup of tea, waiting for the rain to stop, Aiden was terrified of the woods. He was wary of me, too. He flinched when I tried to hold his hand, he backed away when I walked towards him, and he turned his head away from me when I tried to talk to him. I'd made everything a hundred times worse than before.

I felt like the lowest of the low. I was a slight step up from the deranged monster who took him. I was pond scum. Nasty, grimy. I wanted to go home and take a shower to scrub the filth from my body. What kind of person behaves like that with their traumatised child?

"Here." Dr Foster handed me the plastic cup

from a thermos flask filled with milky coffee. "Don't dwell on today. We'll talk about it in the therapy session on Thursday, okay?"

I wrapped my hands around the cup, desperate for its much-needed warmth, and nodded. There was nothing more to say. She couldn't reassure or placate me. There was nothing anyone could say. I'd been in the wrong. I'd behaved in an aggressive manner towards my own son. I thought about the way I'd tried to drag him, like a farmer with a reluctant bull, and cringed into my boots.

DCI Stevenson rested next to me on the side of the police car. Aiden was in the front seat, sitting quietly. "I shouldn't have pushed this. I'm sorry."

"We had to try. It was me who fucked it all up."

Stevenson shook his head. "I don't think he would have gone in there anyway. He's just not ready. Get the two of you home, rest up, bond. We'll try this another day."

"What's going to happen next? Are you still searching the forest?"

He scratched the side of his jaw. The bags around his eyes had deepened, revealing the toll this stressful case was having on his psyche. "As much as we can. Plots of land have been sold off and it's proving to be difficult approaching the companies they belong to. We'll need warrants to search for them. We're checking out any planning permission from ten years ago that might relate to some sort of small room built in the area. There's a chance that Aiden had been walking for a long time before he was found. We can't be a hundred per cent sure that he's been kept in the forest all this time."

"Okay. You'll keep me updated, won't you?"

"I'll be in touch," he said, "but my priority is on the case now. Denise or Marcus will be with you from now on and they'll liaise between you and the police."

It made sense. DCI Stevenson's time was best spent working on the case, but part of me had come to rely on his reassuring calmness and would miss his familiar presence.

"Get Aiden home and in the warm," he said, his voice low and soothing. "I'll be in touch as soon as I know anything."

He was right: More than anything I needed to pick myself up. The stress of the last few days had culminated in this complete loss of control, and that couldn't happen again. *Stay strong for Aiden*, I thought. It would be my mantra. I was a mother first, and a mother could always be strong for her children. Surely.

Aiden removed his jacket and pulled the seatbelt across his chest without needing to be prompted when we got to the car. I didn't try to fill the silence with my own jabbering; I put the radio on to chase the silence away. Eventually, the colour returned to Aiden's cheeks. He lost the wide-eyed, glassy look, and he seemed to relax.

Until we turned onto our street.

"Fuck."

I hadn't had time to watch the news or read the papers that morning. If I had, I would have seen the front-page story about the little boy who had come wandering out of the woods ten years after he was thought to have died in the worst flood for a hundred years. I missed it all. My phone had been on silent all morning, and I hadn't thought to check it as we left Rough Valley. The reporters were lying in wait to ambush us. Their vans lined the streets. There was a television reporter and a cameraman talking to one of my neighbours.

"Shit."

I backed out of the road before they saw me, and drove in the opposite direction.

*

"Why didn't you tell me?" Josie stood in the door with her jaw hanging open, her eyes darting from me to Aiden and back to me.

"It's been a whirlwind, Jo. Can we come in?"

"Yeah, sure." She backed away, letting us in through the enormous wooden doorway. Her eyes never moved from Aiden. "He's so like Rob." She shut the door behind us, still staring at Aiden. It was only when I cleared my throat that she awoke from her trance. "I'll put the kettle on."

Josie led the way through the large, modern entrance hall to the even larger and more modern kitchen. Jake was a huge fan of this kitchen. In fact, he had quizzed Hugh, Josie's husband, about kitchen contractors for hours. He was a big admirer of the clean, white lines and the soft-close drawers. There was even a revolving wine rack that lit up with little blue LED lights.

"Hugh's in London on a business trip so it's just the two of us. I'm sure he'll call today. It's all over the news. He'll be so happy to see Aiden." Josie bustled around the kitchen flicking on the kettle, pulling white porcelain mugs out of the cupboards. "I just can't believe it. After all these years."

I sat on a stool by the breakfast bar and Aiden stood awkwardly away from me. When I pulled one of the stools towards him, he continued to stand, which I pretended didn't feel like a stab to the gut. I had amends to make.

"It's all really complicated," I said. "It's… There's a lot." I took a breath.

Josie leaned over the counter. "Hey, it's going to be okay."

I shook my head. It wasn't, but I couldn't say that while Aiden was stood right with us.

"Aiden, would you like a tea? When you were little, you used to come and stay with us, do you remember? You liked milky tea and strawberry jam on toast."

Aiden just blinked.

"He's not talking right now," I said. "But keep talking to him, I think it helps. We've just come from Rough Valley. I've messed up, Jo."

Josie sensed the mood, so she walked around the breakfast bar. "Aiden, I think I have a DVD of

The Jungle Book. I know you're all grown up now, but you loved that film whenever you stayed with us, remember? You'd sit with Uncle Hugh on the sofa and watch it together. Shall I put it on for you?"

"He'll follow you," I said. "He won't respond, but he likes watching TV so that could help."

When Josie came back she poured boiling water over the teabags. "What's happened, Em?"

I traced the pattern of the marble with my finger. "He was kidnapped. Someone took my child, chained him up in a dungeon or something awful, and they did stuff…" I couldn't say it.

Jo's arms wrapped around my shoulders, holding me tight. When she sniffed loudly I could tell she was crying too.

"I can't believe it." She pulled away, dabbed her eyes with a tissue, and distributed the tea, made strong and brown: builder's tea.

"There were reporters outside my home, waiting for me, filming my house. I have fifty missed calls, most of them from numbers I don't even recognise. I haven't called Jake back, or Rob, or Sonya. They're all expecting me to know what to do. Aiden needs me to know what to do and I just lost it."

"When, honey?"

I sniffed and tried to compose myself. Snivelling wasn't going to help anyone. "No more than an hour ago. The police wanted to see if Aiden would walk through the woods and retrace his steps back to wherever he was kept, but I lost it. I tried to drag him into the woods, Jo. I physically grabbed him and tried to force him to do something he didn't want to do. I'm as bad as the monster who took him."

"No you are not." Josie handed me a box of tissues and I wiped my eyes. "Don't ever think that. Whoever did those things to him is a monster. They're barely even human. Their brain is wired all wrong, Em. It's not the same thing at all."

Halfway through *The Jungle Book*, we stumbled out of the kitchen and into the living room where we watched Aiden watching the film. Josie nodded for me to sit down. Rather than sit right next to Aiden, I chose a spot in a comfy armchair just next to the sofa. Josie pulled a bean bag chair closer and sat next to me.

With her help I'd called Jake, Rob, and Sonya, and talked through the situation with the reporters with them. I'd listened to voicemails from DCI Stevenson warning me that the story was out, several reporters, a woman from a PR company, and Denise, our family liaison officer. The second cup of tea finally warmed up the chill I'd gained from standing out in the cold. I felt calmer. I was almost relaxed for the first time in days.

"How's the baby?" Josie asked.

I stroked my pregnant belly. "She's a wriggler. She'll be playing for Arsenal as soon as she comes out."

Josie laughed, and when I joined in, it felt good.

"How are things with Hugh?"

Josie tucked her legs underneath her body, and wrapped her hands around her mug. It was a small, insignificant movement, but it seemed to me that she was stalling answering the question. "Things are pretty much the same."

"Ahh." Josie and Hugh had been experiencing some marital problems over the last few years. While they'd been the epitome of a happy couple back when they first married seventeen years ago, that relationship that gradually disintegrated.

Josie was a little older than me. She married Hugh straight out of university in a fancy church ceremony. Hugh wasn't from Bishoptown, but they'd decided to move here to start a family. Hugh's family had been wealthy for generations. Josie's family had made money running a successful chain of furniture shops. But Josie had been unable to conceive, and their large country pad echoed from emptiness. Hugh fell into a pattern of leaving Josie alone for long periods of time while he went to conferences and business trips in London, working in his brother's corporate investment business.

"Except that every time he goes on a business trip, he contacts me less and less. He used to ring me twice a day, then it was once. Now I'm lucky if I hear from him after two or three days. He doesn't even bother to call me when he arrives safely."

"Do you call him?"

"I used to. But these days I don't even feel the

need to do that. It's like I've stopped caring."

"Jo…"

"I know. It's awful." She curled up on her bean bag, hugging her body tightly.

I sighed. "I hate to think of you all alone in this house, not even talking to Hugh on the phone. You need to pick up the phone and call, Jo. At least call me so I can come over and keep you company."

She lightly waved her hand to simulate a breezy denial, but I could tell how hard she was trying not to cry. "You've got the baby and now you have all this with Aiden. My crap doesn't even compare."

"Of course it does. Don't ever say that."

Josie had been through things she didn't talk about. Not even to me. Perhaps that was why I thought of her first. I could have taken Aiden to Rob's. He was Aiden's father, after all. Perhaps I just didn't feel like dealing with Rob's mother. Either way, it was Josie's door I'd turned up at, and it was Josie who I felt had the strongest affinity with Aiden and what he had been through. Though Josie had never really opened up to me, I knew there was something dark lurking beneath her tight smile. I'd always known. She'd dropped little hints over the years—nothing particularly concrete, but I had a feeling she might understand more about how Aiden was feeling than anyone else I knew.

CHAPTER FIFTEEN

On the way to the bathroom I found myself wandering around the Barratt house, refreshing my memories of a happier time. Josie and I went to school together, but she was a few years older than me and we never really hung out. But one day when I was struggling with Aiden in a Bishoptown café, Josie came to my rescue, standing up for me against a busybody old lady who had told me to 'shut that thing up'. Aiden was four and had dropped his ice cream on the floor. Josie swooped in with a second bowl of ice cream to give to Aiden and plonked herself on the chair next to me. We were friends from that first moment. She even helped me snag a part-time job at the accountancy firm where she worked, on the outskirts of Bishoptown. I hadn't needed the money but I had needed a life outside Aiden, and the job gave me a new sense of purpose. I had always thrived on being a mother but it didn't satisfy me in the same way a career did. I needed that extra direction in my life in order to find my own brand of happiness. Though being a mother had always been wonderful to me, having a job fulfilled me in a different way.

Josie and Hugh welcomed us into their house with open arms. Looking back, I think they may have been a little desperate. At that point they'd been trying for a baby for around a year and nothing was happening. Their house suddenly seemed empty and they needed to fill it with people. I'd always thought that Aiden was both a reminder and a distraction them from that difficult time. I walked through the corridors, remembering the time Rob, Aiden, and I all squished into one of the spare rooms. There were plenty to choose from, but we'd all decided to sleep in the same bed.

After Aiden's disappearance, both Josie and Hugh were huge helps, delivering food to the house, offering shoulders to cry on. Hugh even paid for contractors to search the river after the search and rescue team had given up. They were my best friends. My only real friends.

I stopped and stared out at Wetherington House, which stood tall on the hill above Rough Valley Forest. The Bishoptown village lay nestled in the valley of three hills, but the boundary reached up to both the hill where Josie and Hugh Barratt lived, and the larger hill where the Duke of Hardwick resided in his stately home. Between the

Barratt house and Wetherington House, part of Rough Valley Forest snaked through the valleys. Looking at it made my chest tighten. Had Aiden been held captive inside the woods, or had he staggered through part of the woods from somewhere else? No one knew how long he'd been walking. No one knew where he had come from.

My phone rang.

I swiped the bar across, recognising the number. "Hi, what's up?"

"They took my fucking picture."

"Who took your picture, Rob?"

"The fucking reporters. Who the fuck else?"

"Calm down. I'm at Josie's place. Come up here. I'm hiding from the reporters. They're all camped outside my house."

"I'm on my way."

Less than ten minutes later, a dishevelled Rob turned up at the door, red-faced and fuming. He ran his hands through his wet hair and brushed past me as he hurried into the house.

"I can't believe it, the bastard. He shoved that thing right in my face and I nearly lost it."

Josie popped her head around the door of the kitchen. "I'll put the kettle on, Rob."

He didn't even notice. Instead he paced the length of the entrance hall. "Where's Aiden?"

"He's in the living room watching *The Jungle Book*. Listen, Rob, there's something I need to tell you about this morning." I hesitated. I didn't want to tell him, not like this, but if I left it much longer, it would get worse.

"What? Did the bastards get you, too?" Rob had a wild way about him when he was agitated. He fidgeted like a junkie in need of a fix. He scratched his forearms and rubbed his bulging eyes, as if he had more energy than he could handle but felt exhausted at the same time.

"No, nothing like that. It's about me and Aiden. I did something really stupid."

He stopped pacing the hallway and moved closer to me instead. I noticed how his hands moved up, like he was contemplating reaching out to me, but then his arms dropped by his side. "What is it? It can't be that bad. You never do anything stupid, Em. I bet it wasn't as stupid as getting your mug photographed by a scummy paparazzi."

I shook my head and backed away. "It's worse."

"Anyone for a cuppa?" Josie called, saving me from blurting everything out.

"Coming," I called. "Come and sit down for a minute. You'll feel better."

"I want to know what's going on."

I chewed on my bottom lip and scratched at a patch of dry skin on my hand. The anxieties of the last few days were catching up with me. I was changing in a physical sense. The lack of sleep, the constant worrying, and the fact that I was so busy in the late stages of my pregnancy had brought nothing but dry skin and circles under my eyes. I'd even lost a little weight.

"Long time no see, Hartley." Josie placed a mug of steaming tea onto the breakfast bar as we moved into the kitchen. "Are those grey hairs I see? And crow's feet, just there?" She pointed at his eyes.

Rob swatted Josie's hand away, but failed to hide his smile. "Yeah and that's a new moustache hair, isn't it?"

"Cheeky arsehole." Josie rolled her eyes exaggeratedly when she turned to me.

I mouthed a 'thank you' for helping calm him down. But even still, when I swallowed my throat was dry. I was dreading telling him about the incident in the forest.

"They're gonna think I did it, aren't they." Rob let out a long, slow, depressed sigh. "They're going to think I somehow did this to my own son. That's what they always think."

"How could they? You've been in the army. You've got the strongest possible alibi there is," I said. I had no idea he'd been worrying about this.

"I know that, but they don't know it yet. They'll think I've been sneaking out or something, or that I have some sick accomplice. They always think it's the dad." He sipped on his tea. "Fuck all this. I don't want to think about it anymore. What did you have to tell me? Is it worse? Is it better? Have they caught the monster?"

"No, it's not better or worse, really." I set down my tea and told Rob about taking Aiden to the woods. Though I didn't look at him directly, I was aware of his weight shifting as he fidgeted on his stool, aware of his back straightening in my peripheral vision.

There was silence when I finished talking.

"I lost control." I placed my head in my hands.

"It's all right, Em," Josie soothed.

"No it's not." Rob set his mug down with an audible bang. "Why didn't you tell me you were going to do this? Why didn't you phone me? You know what a fucking phone is, Emma, right?"

"Keep your voice down. Aiden is in the next room and the last thing he needs to hear is you ranting and swearing," I said.

"Yeah, I know that, but I'm mad, aren't I? I'm fuming because you took our son to do a bloody reconstruction of the day he staggered out of his ten-year captivity."

"Everything moved so fast. They wanted to keep it as small as possible. They suggested I go by myself. I knew you'd refuse to stay away if I told you about it."

"Oh, you knew, did you? That's a pretty trick, reading someone's mind. You'll have to show it to me some day."

I shook my head. Even after all this time he was still just as infuriating as ever. "Grow up, Rob."

"Guys," Josie intervened. "Remember what's important. The kid in the other room watching a DVD. He's all that matters."

"Exactly," Rob said. "And that's why what you did was wrong, Emma. Don't you see that?"

I knew when he got to his feet that I'd made a

huge mistake choosing this particular moment to tell Rob about the events of the morning. He was too wired, too agitated. He was on the edge. I should have seen that.

"I'm sorry."

But he'd stopped listening to me.

"I think I should take him home with me. It's the best way. You're a mess, Emma. You're making terrible decisions. You tried to drag Aiden into the woods, for fuck's sake. The reporters are outside your house. It makes sense."

It was my turn to get to my feet. "Absolutely not. I'm not giving up so easily. He's my son, he's coming home—"

"And he's not mine?" Rob's eyes were wide and pleading. Little boy's eyes. His presence was an intimidating one in the Barratt's kitchen, but there was something of the child in him too. He'd always had an air of vulnerability about him.

"That's not what I mean. I'm his mother—"

"And there it is. That's what it all boils down to. The mother. I remember the first shitshow that came out in the press ten years ago, how every picture was all about you. The poor, distraught mother. Fathers aren't allowed to grieve, are they? Not in the same way. They aren't given the luxury of breaking down like a mother is. Mothers get all the rights and are still allowed to fuck up as much as they want."

"That's not fair, Rob," Josie said.

I rubbed my hands anxiously, desperately trying

to rub away the things that had happened that morning. He was right, in a way. It was expected for the mother to break down. Perhaps I had been allowed to grieve too much and for too long after Aiden's disappearance. But this time, I couldn't. There was no way I could lose control like that again.

I opened my mouth to rebuke his argument, but lost my train of thought when a strange, high-pitched sound came from the living room. I was vaguely aware of my facial muscles slackening as I hopped down from the stool and hurried out of the kitchen. Rob only stared after me with a question on his lips as I rushed through the kitchen door, colliding against the doorframe with my hip. My socks slipped on the wooden floorboards.

By the time I reached the living room, I was out of breath and panting. Aiden was sat exactly where we had left him, watching a different DVD this time, *The Aristocats*, with the sound on mute. He turned to me as I entered the room, but he didn't say a word. He didn't make a sound.

Footsteps sounded behind me and Rob entered the room. "What is it?"

"I thought… I thought I heard him singing."

CHAPTER SIXTEEN

Three hours later, I called Jake and told him I was coming home. Josie had kindly made us a few sandwiches and a couple more cuppas, though we'd all fancied a vodka and Coke after the day we'd had. Rob settled down with us and watched another Disney DVD before we agreed to keep going as we already were, with Aiden living at my house, but communicate with each other every step of the way. We were in the midst of a journey, for better or worse, and that journey was likely to be arduous. We needed each other.

And I needed Jake, in my own way. I'd already thought of fifty things I wanted to tell him, and plenty of issues I wanted his opinion about. Whether to enlist help with PR was one thing. None of us were experts when it came to the press. God knows I'd failed the first time this happened. I shuddered as I thought about the headlines from the tabloids. Rob had remembered it one way, but I recollected that time differently. "Teen Mum Let Little Aiden Go", "Young Mum Drinking 'Heavily' Night Before Flood". They'd raided my MySpace and Facebook pages, pulling every picture of me out with my friends. What they didn't show was Aiden tucked up in bed with his grandparents downstairs. They didn't show the pictures of me taking Aiden to get his vaccinations or breastfeeding in the early hours of the morning.

No, I was a 'young' mum, a 'teen' mum, even though I was twenty-four at the time of Aiden's disappearance. Being young equated to being bad. That was what they really wanted to say. I was a bad mother and it was all my fault that he wandered away from school.

And poor Amy Perry wasn't let off the hook either. They even found a picture of us both out at the local pub with pint glasses in our hands. We were the 'boozy mum and teacher' living it large while a kid drowned in a river. That was what they meant. That was what they implied. Yes, I could lose it from grief. I could break down in a way Rob couldn't, but I had been persecuted for not shutting my legs when I was a teenager, and I was dragged over hot coals for having a social life while my son was a toddler.

I hated them. I hated them almost as much as I hated the man who took Aiden from me all those years ago. I hated them as I pulled onto my street and still saw the occasional van on our road, even though I'd waited until the after sun went down to try and sneak into the house.

I held my breath as I pulled into the driveway. My heart was racing and my hand trembled as I undid my seatbelt.

"Just stay with me, Aiden, okay? Stay close to me."

I was far more agitated than he was. He didn't need any more prompting to stay calm. The events of the morning seemed to have faded away and he was at least a little more relaxed than he had been. The look of terror on his face as we stood by Rough Valley would haunt me for the rest of my life. I took a deep breath and opened the car door, crunching gravel beneath my feet.

"Mrs Price-Hewitt, Simon Gary from the News of the World. Would you be interested in telling Aiden's story?"

"No thank you."

I hurried around the car, avoiding the gaze of the short bald man following me.

"Where has Aiden been all this time?"

I kept my mouth firmly closed as I opened Aiden's door and took his hand. At least there didn't seem to be a photographer there yet.

"What's happened to him? Where did he go?"

"I think you should leave. This is private property." I fumbled in my handbag for my keys, almost spilling the contents onto the ground.

Before I could get the key in the lock, the door was snatched open and Jake ushered us both into the house. I wrapped my arms around his neck and held him tight.

"Thank you."

"I've got you," he murmured into my hair. His voice always carried a hint of the south in his huskier moments. "I've got you now."

He led me through to the kitchen and sat me down.

"Aiden, why don't you pour your mum a glass of water." Jake moved his head in the direction of the correct cupboard.

I noticed that even the kitchen curtains were closed, which we never usually bothered to do. The kitchen faced a private back garden almost completely secluded by a line of tall fir trees. Aiden moved quietly around the room, picking a glass out of the cupboard and pouring tap water into it. He placed it carefully on the table in front of me.

"Good lad. Now, why don't you go upstairs for a little bit? I left you some books on your bedside table so you can read." Jake smiled at Aiden as he gave him instructions. He was in teacher mode and something in Aiden was responding to it. Aiden followed his directions almost robotically. I watched him with interest as he stepped out of the room.

"What is it?" Jake asked.

"It's probably nothing."

Jake tilted his head to one side and gave me a questioning look.

"It's just the way Aiden responds to your

direction. There's something weird about it."

Jake let out a small laugh. "What are you talking about? He does the same for you."

"No, it's not the same. There's something… different about the way he acts around you." I shrugged and sipped my water. "Maybe it's nothing. I'm being silly."

"You're not. You're being a mother." Jake stepped around the table and rubbed the small of my back. "Maybe it's hard for you to see a man around Aiden after what's happened to him. You're just going into protective mode."

But I wasn't sure that was true. I never noticed a change in Aiden's behaviour when he was around Rob.

"How's Bump today?"

I pulled myself out of my thoughts to answer. "She's fine."

"You look tired out, Emma Hewitt. On the sofa with you. I think a foot rub is in order."

"That does sound good. What about Aiden?"

"He needs some space, Em. Let him be." Jake took my hand and led me through the kitchen into the living room. It didn't even occur to me until long much later that he'd called me Em for the very first time.

*

We became our own little world in the days that followed. We turned off the television, we ignored the newspapers. We put our phones on silent. Only Jake was brave enough to leave the house, fetching us food from the suggestions Dr Schaffer gave me. But I added comfort food: chocolate, ice cream, white bread... I couldn't help myself. We shut the curtains and unplugged the landline from the wall. Our family liaison officers would come for meetings and ask us questions that didn't seem relevant. Questions about our daily routine. After the questions stopped they tended to hover awkwardly around us during the daytime. For the most part they were useless, seeing as the police hadn't found anything.

The only people I had telephone conversations with were Rob and a far too cheerful woman from a PR company who offered to help us write a statement to the press. I decided that the generic 'please respect our privacy at this difficult time' would be enough. And when it came to offers of appearing on television, I decided silence was the best option. I couldn't stand the thought of an interview appearing on YouTube after doing its rounds on the news, free to be judged by the hordes of people following Aiden's case. Instead, after speaking to DCI Stevenson, it was agreed that he would issue a statement appealing to any witnesses from the night Aiden was found wandering along the back road.

"We're extending the search," he said. "We've started looking into houses in the area with large basements as well as anyone who might have put in planning applications for unusual builds a decade ago. It's going to take some time."

This was the countryside. There were plenty of wealthy families with extensions, outbuildings, and cellars.

"How is Aiden?" he asked. There was an edge in his voice. We both knew it was there, but neither of us acknowledged it.

"He's not talking yet," I replied.

After hanging up the telephone, I closed my eyes and tried to wish it all away. For a while, I almost did. None of it mattered because we were an island in the middle of the Indian Ocean. We were off the coast of Australia, and every morning I greeted Aiden with a 'G'day, mate'. Then we'd spread out the picnic blanket, put Netflix on, and pretend we were sat on the top of the tallest mountain, with the world below us. I chose some of my favourite films that I'd always wanted to watch with Aiden but had been waiting for him to get a little older. *The Neverending Story*, *Bugsy Malone*, *The Goonies*. More than once I almost turned off those innocuous films when any character was in peril. I reached out for the remote with my heart racing, but Aiden never reacted. He sat, and he chewed his food, and he didn't say a word.

"You can't do this forever," Jake said from the sofa. He had an art history textbook in his hand, and his glasses pushed high up his nose.

"I know." I pushed the ice cream around the

bowl. "Okay, time for a game of basketball." It was something we'd played when Aiden was little. I used to take pieces of paper, screw them up, and play at throwing them through a hoop I'd made out of a wire coat hanger. In fact, all of the games were rehashed versions of what we had done when Aiden was a toddler. Like the indoor picnics, which inevitably occurred in fictional versions of the Great Wall of China, or Kilimanjaro, or Cairo, or anywhere but Bishoptown-on-Ouse. It had been the only way to curb my wanderlust when I was a teenage mum without the same prospects as my friends.

"He's not going to want to play basketball." Jake uncrossed his legs and stared down at us. "Look at him."

"What else am I going to do?"

"For one thing, I don't think it's good for you to be on the floor on that scabby picnic blanket when you're eight months pregnant. For another, you've eaten nothing but ice cream for two days. That's not taking care of your baby. Get up, stop messing around, and face what's going on."

My cheeks flushed with heat. He thought I wasn't accepting the grim reality of the situation, but he was wrong. I knew exactly what was happening—I was just trying to shield Aiden from it. He wasn't ready. How could anyone be ready for what was going to happen? If I, a fully-grown woman, wasn't ready, how could my damaged, vulnerable son get through the ordeal?

"Basketball," I said. I clambered ungracefully to my feet, walked into Jake's study and took a few sheets of paper from the desk.

When I got back into the living room, Jake was on his knees talking to Aiden.

"What's going on?"

"We're just having a chinwag." Jake grinned and patted Aiden on the shoulder. "I was telling him it might be a good idea for him to spend some time with his dad and grandparents."

I dropped the paper. "What? Why? How dare you say that to Aiden without suggesting it to me first?"

He shrugged. "What's the problem? He hasn't seen them for days. It isn't fair, you keeping him cooped up in here."

"I'm protecting him. I've told Rob, Sonya, and Peter not to come. You know what Rob's temper is like. The last thing we need is him yelling at the press and making a scene. I know Sonya is itching to help, but what can she do? No. Aiden needs some space from this circus. He needs time with just us so that he can adjust. Wherever he was he was probably alone for a long time. Too many people will just freak him out. "

"He needs some time away from this house."

"More like you just want him out of here," I muttered under my breath.

Jake got to his feet. "What was that?"

I backed out of the room, then turned and walked into the kitchen, shaking my head at the ridiculousness of the argument. "Look, I know you've been trying to make the most of things, but it's so obvious that you don't want Aiden around. You going up to him and basically telling him to get out doesn't help."

"Emma, I don't know how I can make myself any clearer. I don't want Aiden out of my house—I just want him to get some fresh air, to see people other than me or you, and to actually begin to face his own reality. It isn't doing him any good being here with us."

"He's improving," I insisted. "I can tell. He's *listening* to me. He's taking everything in."

"You're seeing something that isn't there. Trust me, I have some perspective on this. He's not improving. He's a vegetable, Emma. He sits there without even the slightest remnant of human emotion on his face. The other day I walked out of the bathroom and he was stood in the corridor doing nothing. Just standing. Just staring."

I rubbed the dry skin on my hands and paced up and down the kitchen. "*Vegetable*? What the *fuck*, Jake. How could you?"

He removed his glasses and pinched the bridge of his nose. "That came out wrong."

But it was too late. His harsh words had a cruel edge, but that didn't mask the truth of them. When I spoke, there was a new quaver of uncertainty in my voice. "He's not a vegetable, is he? He... he's aware. Isn't he?"

Jake moved forward, took me by the shoulders

and stared deep into my eyes. "Emma, he is psychologically damaged. No matter how much you want to, you can't do this on your own."

CHAPTER SEVENTEEN

The décor in Dr Foster's office was designed to convey a bright cheerfulness that verged on the contrived. It was the kind of room I would have hated as a teenager. I sat on a bright red sofa and stared at the abstract painting hung on the wall on the other side of the room. Large, sweeping brushstrokes whirled together every shade of yellow known to the imagination. The carpet was patterned in interconnecting loops of the primary colours, like an 80s lunchbox design.

It was Thursday by the time I'd dragged us out of our withdrawal from the world, and the two of us emerged like a bear from hibernation, rubbing our eyes and squinting at the sun. I'd spent the journey to the surgery trying to stop my hands from trembling as they gripped the steering wheel, and avoiding eye-contact with the people around me. But it was important for Aiden to see a therapist. He'd had a slow adjustment to life outside hospital, and now I knew it was time to listen to Jake. Luckily, Dr Foster was prepared to see Aiden even before his status as 'deceased' had been repealed.

When the door opened, it scraped across the wooden floorboards, making a high-pitched squeaking sound. Aiden let out a sudden gasp and sat up very straight. His face paled in a way I hadn't seen since we'd tried to force him into the woods. I placed my hand on his, moving very slowly as I always did when I touched him.

"Hello again, Emma. Good morning, Aiden." Dr Foster was as cheerful as her waiting room, but she had an organic quality about her that was less contrived. Her image belonged on the box of organic muesli. She was very natural and easy; a people person. "Would you like to come in?"

Aiden followed my lead into Dr Foster's office. After Aiden's disappearance during the flood, I'd spent some time in therapy at a place in York. That had been what I would consider a typical therapist's office to be like. It was very sparse, with comfortable chairs, a bookcase, and a large, wooden desk. This was the opposite. It was filled with colour, from the baskets of toys, to the artwork on the walls, to a couple of bouquets of fresh flowers on the windowsill.

"Take a seat wherever is comfortable."

I eyed the bean bag chair but decided I would never get out of it if I sat down, so I chose a plastic upright chair and pulled one across for Aiden.

"I'm so glad you decided to come and see me. I think it will be really useful for Aiden's progression."

I didn't know what to say so I just nodded. It wasn't that I disagreed with her—I was glad we were going to therapy, but it had been an ordeal to get to the office. I'd had to throw a blanket over Aiden's head to try to keep the paparazzi from taking any photographs of him. I couldn't bear for anyone to print his photograph without my consent.

"It's lovely to see you again, Aiden. I see you've had your hair cut."

"Well, it was me with some blunt scissors over the bathroom sink," I said with a laugh that felt unnatural. "It's not the best haircut in the world."

"Oh, well, I think you look very fetching." The touch of Yorkshire in her voice helped to calm my nerves. It was like an old friend. Bishoptown residents tended to have slightly posher voices. There were some with strong Yorkshire accents, but more often than not I heard BBC English around the village.

I smiled at Aiden. "I think he likes it. I don't think he can tell me for a while, but I like to think that if he could, he would."

There was the smallest hint of a crack in Dr Foster's smile, and I wasn't sure I liked the way she regarded me then, with a slow nod of her head. "Absolutely. So, today, Aiden, I would like you to draw me some more pictures. Would you like that? Excellent." She glossed quickly over Aiden's lack of response. "How about I set you up on the desk over here. There are some coloured pencils and plenty of paper. Draw whatever pops into your head. That's it. Very good."

Once Aiden was set up, Dr Foster came across to sit with me. "Sorry if it seems like I'm talking down to him, but I think it's best to go gently with him for a while."

"I do the same. He doesn't seem like a sixteen-year-old boy." I thought of the kids at school, so cocksure and loud, full of themselves and full of the belief that they ruled the world.

"No, but that will come in time," she said. "What can you tell me about his progress?"

"He hasn't said anything. Not a thing. But..."

"Go on," she prompted.

"I think I heard him sing."

When Dr Foster leaned forward, I didn't like the little glint of excitement in her eyes. I could see the pound signs dancing around in her imagination for when she turned in an article entitled 'The Feral Child of Yorkshire'. "Really? What led up to this development?"

I pushed my hands between my thighs to stop myself rubbing the dry patches of skin, which were now red and angry from my constant niggling. "There was an argument." I glanced up, expecting to see disapproval in Dr Foster's expression.

"I'm not here to judge. Your family has been put

in an extremely stressful situation over the last week. Arguments are to be expected."

"Aiden was in the other room. It was the day we met at the woods. I was... not in a good place. I tried to go home and the reporters were there so I went to my best friend's house. Rob came to meet us. He was agitated. Some reporter had taken his picture and he was obsessed with the idea that they'd accuse him of the kidnap. They always go after the dads, he said. I told him about the thing with the police and he lost his temper."

"In a violent way?"

"No. Just raised voices. Then there was a slight pause, and I heard this high-pitched singing coming from the living room. I think it was Aiden. We'd left him in there watching Disney films."

"You're sure it was Aiden? It couldn't have been the film?"

I shrugged. "It didn't sound like anything from the film. He had the sound muted when I walked in."

"Did you recognise the words or the tune from what Aiden was singing?"

I shook my head. "I didn't hear words, just a small voice. It was... kind of haunting. You know those creepy songs they use in horror films when a child is possessed by a ghost or a doll comes to life?"

A half-smile spread across her lips. "My husband watches those films, so yes."

"It was a little bit like that. Like a nursery

rhyme." I shivered. I hadn't thought much about the song since we'd come back from Josie's. I'd had the reporters to deal with, and then I had tried to block out the world. Maybe I tried too hard. Maybe Jake was right.

"And since that moment?" she prompted.

I shook my head. "Nothing. Absolutely nothing. Barely a whimper."

"On the day you heard the singing, did anyone else hear his voice?"

"No, actually. It was just me. Do you think I imagined it?"

"No," she said, with a voice that suggested that perhaps she did. "Not necessarily, but we can't rule it out as an explanation. Now, tell me about how Aiden is sleeping since he came home from the hospital."

"He goes to bed at 8pm every night and I check on him at 9pm. He's always laid with his eyes shut but I'm not sure if he's asleep or not. Sometimes I think he's pretending."

"What makes you think that?"

"Just the way he lies on his back with his arms on either side. It doesn't look comfortable. Sometimes when I check on him later in the night he'll have rolled onto his side, and that seems more normal."

"Any night terrors?"

"He sleeps with the door open. Always. I've never closed the door to a room he's in. I think that might help him, because he's been sleeping well since he came home. There was one time I saw him tossing and turning. I didn't want to wake him, because I know he doesn't like to be touched too much. After about thirty seconds he drifted into a deeper sleep and seemed fine."

Dr Foster tapped her pen on top of her open notebook. "That's a very good sign. He's getting rest. He's clearly putting on some weight. These are all good things, Mrs. Price-Hewitt. You're doing just fine."

"You'd say that even after what you saw the other day in the woods?" I let out a hollow laugh.

"Yes. I would. You're only human, Emma. Try not to beat yourself up about the incident in the forest. Everyone was under intense stress. It was a little too soon for Aiden, that's all." She leaned back in her chair. "Now, tell me how you're doing. Would you like me to refer you to a therapist? You've been through an extraordinary event. Talking about it might help."

"No, thank you. I had some therapy after I thought Aiden had drowned. It helped in some ways, but not in others. I'm okay. I thought Aiden had died. I've already been through the worst pain a human being can deal with. Everything that comes after that pales in significance. I'm going to be fine."

"There's a big difference between being fine and being well, Emma." Dr Foster leaned her chin on her fist and spoke softly. "Everyone wants you to be well, happy, and healthy, just remember that.

Especially Aiden." She got to her feet with a deep groan, rubbing her knees. "These old bones. The cold sets in these days. Just you wait." She winked at me. "And how are we getting on over here, Aiden? What have you drawn for me?"

Aiden lifted his picture and I broke out into a smile. Just the fact that my son had held up his own artwork was enough to make me feel joy. But Dr Foster wasn't smiling at all. I got up from my seat, cradling my belly, and made my way over to the other side of the room. It was there that I saw what Aiden had drawn.

Like his first piece of art, there was no shape, only chaos. This time he'd chosen two red crayons to complete his piece. The red crayon lines spread from one side of the page to the other, like his first drawing in the hospital. But there was one difference to this piece. In the centre of the picture, Aiden had drawn a set of white, sharp teeth. They were open wide, ready to chomp down on its prey. My first instinct was to snatch the drawing out of his hands, screw it up and throw it away. But I didn't. I nodded and I smiled, but all the time I felt as though ants were crawling over my skin.

CHAPTER EIGHTEEN

I left Aiden's distressing art with Dr Foster, uneasy about letting anything that sinister into my home. But, as she'd informed me on the way out of her office, Aiden needed some way to express himself. While he was unable to do so verbally, he needed another outlet. Drawing would be excellent therapy for him. Back in the car, before we set off, I leaned against the steering wheel to compose myself. I knew what I had to do, but I wasn't sure I wanted to do it.

"Okay, Aiden. Let's get you home."

We managed to avoid the reporters on our way into the house, and after we'd had a lunch of ham salad sandwiches—I was taking Jake's advice about eating healthily—I sucked in a deep breath and opened the garage door.

There was a reason why our car was always parked outside the house on the drive. It wasn't that we didn't use the garage, it was that the car wouldn't fit. Rob was right about the house being absent of colour, and that was because all the colour had been left in the garage. This was where we created. This was our artistic home.

I flicked on the switch and it all came to life.

"It's okay, Aiden, you can come in. It's all safe." I wanted to open the front to the garage to let in the sunlight, but I was all too aware of the reporters still hanging around our house. We had to make do with the light from the kitchen doorway. "I want to show you something."

The walls were lined with canvasses. Most of the paintings were mine, created after the flood and spanning up to a few years ago when I finally let go and accepted Aiden's 'death'. After a deep breath, I held Aiden's hand and walked him around the garage. It was strange to hold his hand now. It was so much bigger than the hand I'd held ten years ago. Though he appeared so much younger than the young men at school, I had to remember that he was a teenager now. He was almost an adult.

"This is you and me," I said, pointing to a portrait of a young girl with big eyes holding a tiny baby in her arms. "I was scared when you arrived, but I loved you so much that it didn't matter. This is you in your Superman cape." I grinned. I'd painted it from memory six months after Aiden's disappearance. There was something painful in the reds and the aggressive brush strokes, but I'd captured Aiden's cheeky face perfectly. Then, I moved onto another portrait and the smile faded. "This is a difficult one. I was in a bad place back then. I missed you so much that I didn't know what to do with myself. I felt useless." It was a zoomed in portrait of my own face. I was snarling. My eyes were sunken. My skin was red and patchy. There were dark, bruised marks above my cheekbones. This was from a year after the flood. I was angry.

I squeezed Aiden's hand and moved on. At least he was getting used to me touching him. Slow steps. The next series of paintings were all the same. "You see these?" I pointed to each one in turn. "These are the birthday cakes I made for you every year. I never forgot. The third of April. This was the first year. I made you a Superbatironman cake. See? He had a cape, an iron suit, and bat ears. You would have loved it. It was sunny that year. Then, this one was a winged Ferrari. You always said you wanted a flying car for every birthday. Then I made you a dragon cake, just like Walnut. It was a walnut cake, too, with vanilla buttercream." I cleared my throat, forcing away the emotion. "Do you see what I was trying to do? I painted my feelings out. That was what I did when I lost you. I painted all of these." My eyes trailed along the wall of paintings, reaching the very last one. The one that had been torn all down one side. I didn't look at that one for very long. "It's okay if you want to paint out your feelings, too. I'm going to set up a canvas for you. There are some paints here. I want you to paint like you used to when you were little."

I moved an easel into the centre of the garage and lowered it to Aiden's height, then pulled across a small table to set beside it, and put a chair in front. Then I brought in jam jars of water and arranged all the paints and paintbrushes next to the water.

Part of me itched to join him, and I wondered whether it would help him start, to see someone else working with him. But in the end, I decided this was all about Aiden. He deserved to be left alone. So once I had set him up, I went into the kitchen to make a cup of tea. When I leaned my head around the door into the garage, Aiden was sat leaning over the canvass, moving his paintbrush in an arc. I smiled, and took a sip of my tea.

*

There were times I believed Aiden almost wanted to talk to me, and after he finished his painting was one of them. He walked up to the kitchen door and stood there in the space where the kitchen and garage connected.

"Have you finished?" I asked.

This time I waited. I sensed that he wanted to speak. He wanted to tell me that he was done. He was proud, I realised. Instead, all I got was the slightest of nods, almost imperceptible. That was enough to get my heart soaring. Progress, at last.

I followed him into the garage where he proudly

displayed another terrifying piece of art, and I tried my best to not seem horrified by it. This time he'd painted in blues and greens. They'd been mixed together into a spiral, which narrowed to a dark point in the centre. It reminded me of the tunnels in my nightmares.

"It's beautiful, sweetheart," I said.

Later that afternoon, while Jake was still at the school—he'd taken time off for the first few days as we'd dealt with the issues with the reporters, but I could tell he was itching to go back so I let him—I took Aiden to see his dad and grandma, not just to get Aiden out of the house, but also to get away from Denise, who came to our house every day with a forced smile that made me itch.

In the living room of the B&B, Rob spread the newspapers across the table. Aiden was listening to Sonya read him *The Hobbit*.

"Look at what those scum have been saying." Rob indicated the newspapers.

"I don't really want to, Rob. I've been trying to keep all this away from Aiden, to be honest. I don't think it'll do him any good." Bump kicked on my bladder and I shifted my weight, stroking the top of my stomach.

"I'm not going to show him, Em. What kind of a bloke do you think I am?"

"Okay, well, he's only in the other room."

Rob fixed me with his intense, brown eyes. "I'm aware. I just wanted to show you."

I got it. Rob was a talker. When something

bothered him he needed to talk it out. He needed to share the burden with another person. I was always the opposite. I kept things buried inside until they threatened to burst out of me. I tried not to think about the time I'd allowed everything to erupt out of me. It had only happened once in my life, and it hadn't been a pretty sight.

"Look, there's that photo of me. 'Ex-officer Robert Hartley,' they're calling me. I'm not an ex-officer. They want to make it sound like I've lost my job. While you're some sort of saint this time around. They all feel sorry for you."

"Oh, I don't care, Rob."

"And look at this, they've even printed a copy of the thing Aiden drew in the hospital."

I snatched the newspaper from his hand. "What? How did they get that?"

"Probably one of those nurses. I bet they sold it for hundreds. People'll do anything to earn a quick buck, won't they? God, I need a drink. They think he's a nutter. They're calling our son a nutter. And have you seen what they're writing about Jake?"

Even though I was still staring at the full-page print of Aiden's disturbing artwork from the hospital, I still noticed the slight change in Rob's tone. It was quieter. Less agitated. It made me wonder if this was what he had wanted to show me all along.

"What are they writing about Jake?"

Rob licked his finger and flicked through the newspaper to find the right page. The first thing I saw was a photograph of Jake when he was younger, with an arm around an even younger girl's shoulder.

"Who is that?" I whispered, trying my hardest to keep the tremulous note from my voice, but failing miserably.

"One of his students, apparently. They say he left his job in Bournemouth rather abruptly after the headteacher found out he chatted with several of the students on MSN Messenger and Emailed them, too. They say they became Facebook friends."

The blood drained from my face. I closed the newspaper, not wanting to look at that picture any longer. I felt lightheaded. Jake didn't talk about his time in Bournemouth very often. In fact, he didn't talk about his life outside of Bishoptown hardly at all. I knew he'd studied his PGCE in Bournemouth, and I knew he had worked at a school there, but that was about it. His family were from that part of the country too, but his parents had only visited us one Christmas, and I hadn't thought much of it.

Though I had to admit, they'd seemed like odd people. They'd rolled up in their Land Rover dressed in the kind of attire that was more suited to a spot of pheasant shooting up at Wetherington House. But even though they were dressed in Wellington boots and Barbour jackets, each item of clothing was pristine, as if it were brand new. Even the Land Rover was gleaming.

Jake's mother, Christine, had brought her own

port to drink with the meal and not offered a drop to anyone else. She'd also pushed her turkey to the edge of her plate, and asked if there was any goose as an alternative. Jake's father barely spoke all evening, except when he offered Jake a brandy in the lounge while the 'ladies' tidied away the plates. Christine had then asked whether I'd made the trifle for dessert or bought it from Tesco or 'one of those places', as if she didn't even know what a supermarket was.

I'd known that Jake's parents were rich, but I hadn't expected them to be quite so snooty. Just like I'd known about Jake's background in Bournemouth, but hadn't known anything about why he had decided to move so far north. I'd always thought it was just that the opportunity arose, but it seemed odd that he'd moved quite so far away from home. Was he running from something?

What else didn't I know about my husband?

"You didn't know, did you?" Rob said. "He's never mentioned any of this."

"Of course I knew," I snapped. "It's all a load of rubbish."

But Rob's eyes narrowed. "What else has he lied to you about?"

I shook my head. "Nothing. He's not a liar. Not like you."

Rob's cheeks flushed. "Don't, Em, don't bring that up. Not now."

"I think it's time to take Aiden home. You can

stop by and visit him when you like." I tucked the newspaper under my arm and waved through the door to the lounge for Aiden to leave.

"Are you sure, Em?" Rob moved towards the front door of the kitchen. We were in the private area of the B&B, behind reception.

"We've got to go."

"Em, listen to me. Just hear me out. If you notice anything weird about him you have to say something. I know you'll dismiss this as jealousy or whatever but it isn't. I don't trust that man, Emma. I never have."

CHAPTER NINETEEN

I stopped at the Sainsbury's on the way back from Rob's and bought every newspaper I could find, avoiding familiar faces as I hurried from aisle to checkout. But as I ducked down and hurried out of the shop, I couldn't resist looking back to see if any of the people milling around were talking about me. I spotted two people I knew—Carol, a barmaid at the Queen's Head, whispering to Barbara, who lived on the hill down from the school. There they were, whispering behind cupped hands, nodding in my direction.

I fumbled with my car keys, remembering the exact same thing happening after the flood. It was all the same: the desperate rushes away from the shops, almost dropping my car keys or my house keys while trying to keep away from the whispering masses, the pitying looks. That was why I'd ignored every phone call from my colleagues at work. I'd listened to all the voicemails. Their bunch of flowers was still in its cellophane, dumped into a vase by Jake. I hadn't thought to arrange it.

Since the story had broken we'd received a multitude of cards and presents, but I couldn't deal with any of them. Instead, I asked Denise to take care of it, which suited me since it gave her a job to do that kept her from under my feet. She was the one who opened the cards and placed the ones that wished us well on the mantelpiece, and the crazy ones filled with death threats and other nastiness in the recycling. She was the one who stood by the bins before the bin men arrived to stop the press going through our rubbish to find a new angle to their story. That much I was grateful for. It allowed me to ignore it as much as I could.

But that was how I coped. I blocked the outside world away. When the flood hit Bishoptown and I thought Aiden had drowned, I'd learned that I couldn't trust anyone. I lost friends over it. I'd mention a tiny detail to someone and the next day it'd be in the newspapers. It was better that I didn't talk to anyone except immediate family. There was no way of knowing who would go to the media and sell our secrets.

I pulled into the drive and let Aiden out of the car. His steps were lighter since those precious moments of painting. Even the stiffness in his gait was improving. Though he still didn't talk to me, I got the sense that he was starting to relax around me, which was real progress after what had happened with the police. When he walked, his shoulders were down, instead of hunched up. He was loosening up. He seemed taller, too, even though it had been barely a week since I'd first found out he was still alive. And, though there was little change in his demeanour, I had a feeling that he was beginning to relax around me, or maybe I was beginning to relax around him..

I waved to Denise, who was standing patiently outside the house for me to let her in. "Thought we could have a catch-up," she said.

"Sure," I replied. "Any news from the police station?"

"No," she answered in what I felt was a clipped, sharp tone. Perhaps she was getting fed up of that question, or at least fed up of having to relay the same response.

After the bustle of Rob's B&B, my house was quiet and still, so silent that when the floorboards creaked, I flinched. I took Aiden's coat and hung it on the rack, shutting out the chill from the October wind. I had the newspapers tucked under one arm, and my handbag looped over the other. Once in the kitchen, I spread all the newspapers out over the table and opened them.

Denise pulled a stuffed bear out of a bag. "Do we want to keep this teddy?" she asked. "It came in with a bunch of fan mail. What do you reckon, Aiden?"

I glanced at my son, but he didn't react to the

stuffed bear with the glass eyes. It was a sweet toy, but far too young for him now that he'd grown up.

"Charity bag," I said.

"Gotcha," Denise replied.

"Where's Marcus today?"

"He's working at the station today. We felt you didn't need us both around all the time anymore."

"Ahh, I see. Aiden, why don't you go watch some TV with Denise for a while." I shifted my gaze to Denise. "Unless there was anything else you wanted to talk to me about?"

"Well…" she started.

"Nope, good then. Off you go!" I smiled as if there was nothing wrong as Aiden made his way out of the room and into the lounge.

"Everything all right?" Denise asked.

"Yes," I lied.

She glanced at the newspapers but didn't say anything more.

"I'll leave you to your reading then." The pointed look she gave me as she left the kitchen made me think that what she had really come to the house to do was deliver the bad news that my husband was not all he seemed. Or rather, to spy on us as a family to see if Jake was acting suspiciously since the news broke of his friendship with a student on Facebook.

As soon as the door was closed I began reading. And I didn't stop reading until I heard Jake's key in the door. During that time I read about all the supposed things that had happened to my son, things they didn't even know for certain. He'd been taken as a 'sex slave' by a 'sadistic paedophile' and chained up in some sort of dungeon while I was out gadding about with a glass of Chardonnay in my hand. There was even a photograph of Jake and me on our honeymoon with fat grins on our faces. Then there were photographs of Rob, who had been branded a 'thug' by some local source. Jake was portrayed as the sketchy teacher with a dark past, who disappeared from his last school under a cloud of suspicion. They hinted at illicit affairs with underage schoolgirls.

The papers were careful not to accuse, but they knew what they were doing. They knew what they were suggesting. If my husband could stick his dick in a teenage girl, what else was he capable of? And my judgement was awful. I was pregnant again, remember? With a man whom they all considered some sort of sick paedo without any evidence to back it up, along with the fact my first boyfriend was apparently a thug, and I was out partying all the time anyway because I was 'young'.

I slammed the papers shut as soon as I heard the door open.

"Anyone home? It's quiet in here. Oh, hello, Aiden. Denise. You can turn the sound up you know. Go on, that's it. Where's your mum? Don't worry, I'll find her." Jake gave me a limp wave as he stepped into the kitchen and set his briefcase on the table. "Sam Sutton finally handed in that homework I was telling you about. A week late, and he expects me to mark it. It's ridiculous. I might go to the head. What's going on, are you…?" Jake glanced down at the papers spread out on the table. "Ah."

"Ah? Is that all you have to say?" I demanded. I opened and closed my fists by my side.

"I told you that you needed to read them," he said, chastising me like a child. "You need to know what's going on. You need to see the lies they're spreading."

There was the sound of a throat being cleared and Denise appeared in the doorway with her coat in her arms. "I'm going to head off for the day. Call if you need anything."

My heart was pumping as I watched Denise leave the kitchen. I was waiting for that door to close so I could direct my attention back to Jake. "Lies like this?" I held up a picture of my husband with his arm around a teenage girl. "That's not a lie, Jake. That's an actual picture of you fondling some girl."

"Fondling? Are you mad, woman? It was the end of the school year. She wanted a picture of us together before she left to do her A-Levels at college. They're finding malice where there is none. And quite honestly, I thought my fucking wife would be on my side."

The sound of his raised voice caused a jolt of anxiety to spread up my spine. Perhaps it was because he was always so soft-spoken, but it was frightening to hear the ferocity in his voice. I felt sick.

"Jake, reading those things was a shock. Why didn't you warn me?"

"I tried, but you were so stuck in your little bubble with Aiden. You're so naïve, Emma, and you'd think you would have learned after everything that happened the first time. They called you a slut. They branded you a little whore for getting pregnant when you were eighteen."

"It wasn't that bad," I pointed out. "They made out like I was a bad mother for being so young." And I had hated them for it. But I never remembered them calling me anything derogatory like a slut. Was Jake making it up? Did he read more into the papers than what I remembered? I wasn't sure.

"No, no, no, you're remembering it all wrong. They made you into a little whore and it wasn't right. You were a good girl at school. It wasn't right." Jake paced up and down the kitchen. Beads of sweat gathered just above his brow, even though it was a particularly chilly day. Why was he so warm? He'd already taken his boots and coat off.

"Jake, have you been drinking?"

He spun to face me, wobbling slightly and clutching the top of the chair as he moved. "No."

"Don't lie to me."

"I had one on the way home from school."

I shook my head. "A few more than one, I think. Maybe you should go to bed and sleep it off. We'll talk about all this in the morning."

But Jake wasn't listening anymore. He was pulling old bottles of whiskey from the kitchen cupboards. Most hadn't even been opened. They were neglected Christmas presents, the kind you allowed to gather dust at the back of an old liquor cabinet.

"I never laid a finger on that girl. Not in that way, anyway. The newspapers, they twist things. They make them dirty. You know what I mean? I was congratulating her, that's all."

"Jake," I said, with a warning in my voice. "I don't think the whiskey is going to help anything, is it? Sit down and I'll make you a coffee."

"Not a chance. You're the pregnant one. You sit down and I'll do it." He banged the cupboard door shut. "I'm the man of the house. I'm the one who helps his wife. Need to look after my pregnant wife, carrying *my* child."

"You don't sound well. You sound stressed out and drunk. Sit down, just for a minute. Then you can give me a foot rub. How does that sound?" I tried to coax him into a chair, but just as I thought it had worked, he stood up again and began pacing the length of kitchen.

"I provide for you, don't I? I had this kitchen built especially. I bought the house for you, you know, because I imagined what it would be like to live here and raise our kids. It was always for you."

"I know, I know." I put my head in my hands. This wasn't supposed to happen. Not now. My rock had cracked. He'd been busted open like an egg.

"We were so close. So fucking close. And then…"

"Don't say it," I begged. "Don't tell me you resent my child. If you say it now, you can never unsay it."

I raised my head and our eyes locked. He didn't need to say the words because they were written all over his face. He was ashen, with clammy skin and a red flush working its way up from his shirt collar. His hands were clenched by his side. His eyes were wide and wild. When he breathed, spittle flew from his clenched teeth.

"You hate him. You've hated him since we first brought him home," I said miserably, feeling a chill work its way up my arms and legs.

"Just shut up, I can't think. I need to think." He took off his glasses, pinched the bridge of his nose, and commenced pacing again. "I need to think."

"What do you need to think about?" I was on my feet, anger and frustration bubbling to the surface. He was supposed to be the man who had saved me. But here he was, with these secrets and badly hidden animosity towards my own son. Here he was, and I couldn't stand the sight of him.

He spun to face me. "Don't you remember that day?"

I lifted a hand to cut him off. "Of course I do. I don't want to talk about it though."

"There were two knives. One you had stuck

through the painting, and the other was slitting your wrist. Remember that? Remember how I found you in your mother's house? That was what you were before I saved you. I *saved* you. If it wasn't for me you'd be dead. You wouldn't even be with Aiden right now."

CHAPTER TWENTY

My most shameful day had started with a glass of Pinot Grigio. Back then, I'd thought that if I drank wine, it wasn't like being an alcoholic. Vodka or whiskey was the drink of choice for alcoholics, not wine. Not white wine. That was civilised. You don't put a bottle of Sauvignon Blanc in a brown paper bag and sit in the park.

I was at home on my own. My parents had been dead six months. I sat on the floor in the living room of Mum and Dad's cottage with a smorgasbord of disgusting items littering the floor. Leftover cartons of Chinese food that had barely been touched, crusted over with congealed grease along the rim. Bowls of cereal strewn across the carpet heavy with clotted milk. Half-eaten sandwiches attracting flies. I sat in the middle of the mess and I drank my wine. Who was I kidding? I knew what I was. I saw the mess and I knew that I was at rock bottom; despite the Pinot I'd bought from the Bishoptown newsagent with a pair of sunglasses over my smudged, shadowed eyes, I was an alcoholic. A depressed mess.

After draining the last of the wine, I wandered into Aiden's room. It was untouched. Every now and then I'd come in and dust away the cobwebs. I'd sit on his bed, lift up Walnut and still smell the faintest scent of my son. But I hadn't cleaned his room for a long time and there was a thick layer of dust along the windowsill. Worse still, a large, fat spider sat on top of his pillow. The sight of it was so wrong, so jarring, that I lunged forward, punching the pillow. The spider scuttled away before my fist connected, probably running under the bed. But I kept going. I punched the stuffing out of Aiden's pillow, and then I threw back the duvet cover and threw the mattress to the side. A roar built up from my chest as I ran my arm along the window sill, knocking away his trophy from sports day—third in the egg-and-spoon race—and a framed photograph of when he'd met his favourite footballer.

I ripped down his poster of Iron Man. I threw his clothes out from the wardrobe. I tore the covers from his books. And then I stopped. I wiped my eyes. A sense of calm washed over me and I knew what I needed to do.

There was a second bottle of wine in the fridge so I opened that and took a long swig. There was no need for glasses anymore. Who did I need to impress? Who would care? There wasn't anyone left. On my way through the house, I picked up a picture of us all together. Aiden was at the front wearing his Superman cape. I was behind him with my hands on his shoulders. And on either side of me were my parents. Dad on my left, Mum on my right. I didn't cry, I just smiled and cradled the photograph to my chest.

I'd already turned my bedroom into something of a studio. There were a dozen or more paintings stacked up along the walls. I picked one up. It was a self-portrait. I hated this portrait. It was angry and torn-up. I'd used reds and blacks. My teeth were bared. I was ugly and ill in this painting, with booze-soaked eyes because I'd painted it while wasted, barely able to see the canvas with my blurred vision. I hated it. Setting down the wine bottle, I picked up the box-cutter knife I used to trim my canvasses and stabbed the knife into the canvas. Slowly, I dragged the knife down.

A great fire burned inside of me and I knew it was time to extinguish it. What was the point of life if it was just pain? I felt like I was standing inside a burning building and my only choices were to jump or let the fire consume me.

I was sick to death of the fire.

I collapsed onto the ground, dropping the torn-up canvas next to me, before taking out a second knife and placing it on my lap. Then I swigged from the bottle of wine. I was so numb from the alcohol, I figured it wouldn't hurt at all. I thought of the fire roaring within me. I thought of all the shit I'd been through. I thought of Aiden's coat pulled from the river and how the river continued on, rushing and gushing through the country while my son was rotting somewhere. I didn't even get to *bury* him. I didn't even get that much.

I cried out before I plunged the knife into my wrist. I screamed before it even hurt. The pain wasn't from the gushing wound, it was from the fire.

Burning. Burning. My skin on fire. I screamed and I screamed until the flames finally died down. When I looked down, the blood poured out of the wound and I began to feel deliciously woozy. This was it. This was how I stopped the fire. If only I'd known sooner that it would be so simple. I started to fall back onto my bed, smiling. Finally, I had stopped the pain and finally I had found the inner strength to jump from the burning building.

But in my woozy state I didn't hear the banging at the door, or the frantic voice calling my name. The door must have been open because Jake managed to get in within seconds. There were clattering footsteps and then my door was open. A face blurred before my eyes as he hooked his arms underneath my body, calling my name over and over again. There was pressure on my wrist and I was vaguely aware of the blood oozing between his fingers. I was vaguely aware of him saying 'no, no, no, this wasn't supposed to happen' and then I woke up in a hospital bed.

It took me a long time to find gratitude for what Jake did for me that day. When I first woke up in that hospital room I hated him more than I've ever hated anyone. Hate was an emotion I'd never discovered before Aiden was taken from me in the flood. If you get to live your life without ever experiencing hatred, then count yourself lucky. Count your blessings. Hate isn't something to crave or wish for. Never say you hate someone or something unless you really mean it, because hate is not finding a presenter on the telly annoying, or losing your temper with a sibling—it's an all-consuming living thing that starts in your bowels and infects your blood until it blackens your heart.

And I hated myself. That's the worst kind of hate.

I cried for a while. I went through shivers and shakes as the alcohol worked its way out of my body. I scratched at my bandages and refused to talk to Jake as he sat at my bedside reading from his art history books. He came day after day, reading to me as I sat sullenly with my head turned away. He read about the Renaissance, about Caravaggio and his brutish tendencies and murderous temper. He read about Picasso and his painting of Guernica. He read to me every day and soon enough I started to listen.

Instead of picking at my food I began to eat it. I requested water and orange juice rather than sipping on whatever was available when my throat went dry. When it was quiet in the hospital I turned on the television and watched a few daytime soaps. I even started replying to the nurses when they asked me how I was feeling.

When they released me, I found Mum and Dad's cottage cleaned up and sparkling. Jake had sorted it all. He'd cleaned up my mess, removed all the alcohol from the house, hoovered, swept up the broken items and thrown them away. He'd even fixed up a few photograph frames I'd destroyed in my rage.

On the coffee table was a stack of books about Picasso, Caravaggio, Monet and more. John Singer-Sargent, Rembrandt, Da Vinci. There were brand new DVDs on the same subjects piled up next to the DVD player. I thumbed through the books, flicking past the text to get to the beautiful portraits, some of which I'd never seen before. Then I found a new set of paints on the dining room table with a get-well-soon card standing next to it. On the other side of the paints was an application form for a part time administration job at the school. I sat down and completed it.

I know some people might have been put off by the extraordinary lengths Jake went to, to aid my recovery. There are some women who might have found him creepy or overbearing, but it was everything I needed. Without even a hint of anything more than a platonic relationship, this man had taken his time to see me through the worst possible point of my life. I wasn't capable of love at that moment—I was too dried out by all the hate that had burned inside me—but I was close to loving him. There was a strong sense of affection blossoming in my blackened shell.

Which is why I allowed myself to become swept up into his life so suddenly. It's why I failed to see what he really was.

CHAPTER TWENTY-ONE

It was Friday and there were still no leads about what had happened to Aiden. Marcus, the family liaison officer, informed me that fingerprints and DNA were being collected from various men in the area. Jake and Rob were to be included. I wasn't sure why they were bothering, since nothing had been found on Aiden the night he was found. Both Jake and Rob were questioned about the day Aiden went missing. Jake had been teaching at the secondary school on the day Aiden was taken. He'd been walking around the school checking the leaking roof. Various members of staff had seen him at that time. Rob had been making his way home from the building site, stuck in traffic outside Bishoptown. I didn't suspect either of them, but I understood that the men closest to Aiden were likely to be the first suspects.

But watching them go into questioning made me think about the case differently. It had to be someone local. And that meant it might be someone I know.

Aiden was taken from somewhere between Bishoptown school and the river Ouse between 1:15pm and 2:10pm. I had crossed the bridge at around 2:10pm. That was how close I was to my own son being snatched from my life. Sometimes I still lie awake at night and wonder—if I'd just reached out, I might have found him, grabbed him, and kept him close to me. But I could never go back and relive that day. I could never turn back the clock, run to the river, and stop the monster who stole my son. It's the helplessness that gets to you in the middle of the night, the fact that no matter how safe you think your child is at any given time, there is always someone out there who wants to hurt them.

In the days that followed, in between battling with bureaucracy to get Aiden an identity, I began forming a list of possible suspects. There were five male teachers at the local school, two of whom I'd always found a bit creepy: Simon, the IT teacher, a man in his fifties with a potbelly and dirty fingernails, and Chris, a young PE teacher who made crude, un-PC jokes in the staffroom. Then there was Gail's weird son, Derek, who ran the local bakery with her. He'd never moved away from home, even at the age of forty, and never had a relationship with either a woman or a man.

They were horrible thoughts, toxic and prejudiced, but I couldn't help it. Once I pulled at that thread it went even further. I spent the weekend cooped up in the house, still fuming with Jake over his apparent betrayal, passing all the names of those I suspected to Denise and Marcus, telling them in guilty whispers that perhaps this man was capable of such a crime, or that one. Denise was the one who spent most of her time with us, and she became my main confidante when I had a light-bulb moment about yet another local man. Her response was always, "It could be anyone. We're doing the best we can." Once she said, "We don't even know for sure that the suspect is male." Of course I'd presumed that it was a man, but she had a point. Though there was evidence of sexual assault, the police hadn't found any traces of semen on Aiden's clothes or in his body, and without knowing where he had been confined, it was impossible to know if he really had been abused by a man. Though the thought made me feel physically sick, there was a chance that the kidnapper could be a woman. It might even explain how Aiden was able to escape. He would have had more chance of overpowering a woman than a man.

In those days I rarely left the house, but there were times when it was needed. On Monday, I took Aiden to his second therapy session, and all the way there I couldn't stop myself from making mental notes of yet more suspects as we drove through the village.

Dr Foster met us with a bright smile, but her

gaze lingered on me for a little longer than usual. She could tell I was wired. She sat me down and let Aiden draw. When he was settled, I took more of his artwork out of my bag and showed it to her. She spread the paintings out over one of the tables, but seemed more distracted by me.

"Has something happened, Emma?" she asked. "You seem a little on edge."

I rubbed one hand over the other. "I read the newspapers. I've been reading them all. The stories are insane. They keep insinuating that it's my husband, Jake, who took Aiden." I swallowed but my mouth was dry. "It can't be. I know him."

"Take your time, Emma. No judgement here, remember. If you need to talk you can."

I shook my head. "It's not just about whether I think it's true; it can't be true. He had an alibi. He was working in the school at the time. It's not possible, but they keep pointing the finger and dragging up some stupid business from his old school."

"What business is that?" Dr Foster asked.

"Some stupid photograph of him with his arm around a student. He chatted to her on the internet if you believe the newspapers. They were Facebook friends. But that doesn't mean anything, does it?"

"Do you think it means something?" Dr Foster asked patiently.

"No. I'm letting myself get caught up in the game. The one played by the press. They're spinning tales that will sell newspapers, finding culprits who don't deserve to be accused. They're printing lies about my family." I took a deep breath and stroked the bump. My back ached, my legs ached, and I was tired.

"I know this is hard. But you need to try and relax. Those stress levels are not good for the baby. Have you been to see your GP recently?"

I shook my head.

"You should go. Just for a check-up."

I nodded my head and rubbed my eyes, realising she was right. With everything that was going on I hadn't concentrated on looking after myself or the baby. I was letting down my unborn child. I hadn't even thought to concentrate on how often the baby was kicking.

"Now, about Aiden's art." Dr Foster stared down at the paintings. "I'm seeing more expression here. He's forming more shapes and pictures than before. I think this is a door."

I peered down at the picture she was pointing to. I'd had it the wrong way around before, horizontal instead of vertical. I turned the picture around and examined it properly for the first time. She was right. There was no handle, but it did look like a door. Aiden had used light grey paint to almost completely fill the page, but there was some shading on the sides that indicated hinges. Wherever this door led to, it was almost certainly made from some sort of smooth metal, like a large fridge in a restaurant kitchen.

*

The next morning I managed to get to the doctor's before 10am to get an impromptu appointment. Aiden sat next to me on the chair, quietly looking at a magazine for women. Next to us was a mother with three children, all of them climbing up over the seats like monkeys and throwing the toys from the play area onto the floor. It began with the mother glancing up at me every now and then, as if trying to figure out where she knew me from. Then there was a longer stare, and her eyes widened in recognition. I squirmed in my seat, adjusting my weight and trying to ignore the way she watched me from the other side of the room.

"'Oribble what happened to you," she said.

Though I didn't owe her anything, I found myself offering her a thin-lipped smile in response.

"Is this 'im then?" She indicated with her chin, moving her acne-scarred face in Aiden's direction. When Aiden didn't react she waved her arm in the general direction of her kids and ushered them closer to her. "Sick what happened to 'im."

The blood whooshed in my ears as I tried to remain calm. What right did this woman have to bring up the things that had happened to Aiden? Who did she think she was? I tried to ignore her, but found myself rubbing my hands more frantically than before. I gritted my teeth, clenching my jaw harder and harder.

"Kieran, come 'ere," she said, gathering her

brood, clearly wanting them away from Aiden. Every now and then her eyes flicked over to Aiden and I saw fear in them. Perhaps she thought Aiden had been turned into a monster by what he had been through. Maybe she thought he was going to harm her children, in some sort of by-proxy paedophilia.

While she manoeuvred her children away from us, I found that I couldn't stop staring at her. She had a greasy ponytail pulled back so tightly it gave her skin a stretched, glossy appearance. She openly swore at her children when they misbehaved.

"What makes you so special?"

The room went very quiet. An elderly man placed his newspaper back down on his lap and turned towards me. I hadn't meant to say the words out loud, and certainly not with as much venom as I'd uttered them. But looking at that woman I couldn't believe she'd been given the gift of normal, healthy children, when my child had been to hell and back.

"Excuse me, love?" she said, in her rasping, ugly voice.

"I said, what makes you so special? Why do you get to have everything?"

"What the fuck's that s'posed to mean, eh?"

I turned my head away, scowling at the health pamphlets and a poster about heart disease. The doctor called my name and I stood. With Aiden following me, I walked straight past the woman and tried my best not to look at her again.

"I only tried to be nice to you, miserable cow," she muttered, which I figured was typical of the British public. They want gratitude for caring. A little boy was kidnapped and tortured for a decade and they feel sad about it. Good for them. So after feeling all this sadness they see the boy in question out with his mother and they just have to tell them the obvious—they feel sad. Wasn't it awful? Yes, yes, it's very sad and it's very awful, thank you for feeling like that. But if you don't placate them then fuck you and your son. Fuck right off, you deserve it.

No one is as fickle as the public, and the reason they're that fickle is that the media tell them how to think and how to feel. Why else are talent shows packed full of sweeping emotional music edited just right to make you *feel* the pain and heartbreak when a hopeful doesn't get through? Why else are shots of tearful audience members shown during a sad rendition of a song or a tragic backstory retelling? It's all *manufactured* to make you buy things. Whether it's a car or a lifestyle or a newspaper, you're buying it because you're buying the *story* and that is the truth of it all. When I lost my cool at that woman, I shattered the story she'd bought into. I made her reconsider what she thought was true.

But I didn't resent people for buying into Aiden's story. I didn't begrudge them their sadness over his tragic life. What I hated was the idea that I had to be perfect and if I wasn't perfect, then they weren't sad for me anymore. I hated and resented that. I was in pain and I was allowed to snap or make mistakes or do whatever the hell I wanted. I was a human being, not a story, and the world forgot that.

As I passed that woman on the way to my GP's office, I thought all of that and more. A heavy tiredness seeped into my bones, and I wondered when—or if—this would all be over and I could get into a normal life.

"Hi, Emma, how are you today? Hello, Aiden." She didn't miss a beat and I was glad for it. I'd had the same doctor since I was a baby—Dr Fiona Watson—and over that time she'd been a constant, albeit in a professional capacity. They hadn't been friends, Mum and Fiona, but they'd respected each other, and Mum would have been pleased that Fiona had taken over the running of the surgery after she died.

"As well as to be expected."

"I'm sorry for what you've been through, but it's a pleasure to see Aiden again." She smiled at Aiden but he didn't react. Her eyes dropped, and I was glad she didn't bring any of it up again.

After some poking and prodding Dr Watson sighed. "Your blood pressure is high. Now, you had some high blood pressure after Aiden... after the flood. I think it's stress again. I'm going to prescribe you the same tablets you took back then. They're safe for pregnant women to use. The little one been giving you any gip?"

"She's a kicker," I said. "But apart from that she seems fine."

"Have you been to see your midwife recently? Have you got anything set up for the birth?"

"I had some blood taken a few months back and we discussed it then. This last week has been a whirlwind."

She nodded. "You did the right thing coming to me." She scribbled on a pad of paper and tore the top sheet away. "Try and get your feet up if you can. I know it's hard given everything that's happened, but it's important. Is Jake looking after you?"

I smiled. "Yeah, of course he is. He's been great."

She nodded. "I'm really sorry about what's happened. If…" she paused, and I could see she was struggling with the desire to maintain professionalism and seeing a person before her whom she had known for over thirty years. "If you need anything, I'm here."

I thanked her and hurried out of the office, afraid I might begin to cry again. I was sick of crying.

When I left the surgery, the woman and her kids were gone. But when I reached my Focus in the carpark, there was a scratch running all along the length of the car.

CHAPTER TWENTY-TWO

I held off from driving like a maniac on the way to the pharmacy, even though the adrenaline running through my veins begged for speed. I'd never been a careless driver, but when my stress levels were high, I wanted nothing more than to put my foot down on the accelerator and drive as far and as fast as I could. But I wouldn't do that with Aiden in the car.

As I made my way down the steepest hill in Bishoptown, I glanced in the rear-view mirror and noticed a black transit van behind me. After turning right to drive over the bridge, I checked again and there it was—the same black transit van. Even when I turned left onto the main shopping street in the village the van was there. I frowned and wondered whether it was a reporter.

Bishoptown was a small place so it was just as reasonable that it could be someone following the same route through the village.

When I parked up outside the pharmacy, the black van slowed down for a heartbeat before continuing on down the street. My suspicions were raised, but it could be just as possible that the driver had been looking for a parking space and hadn't found anything.

"Wait for me to get out first," I said to Aiden as I checked for oncoming traffic. I was still spooked from the van, but also, Aiden's confinement had resulted in him missing out on the kind of 'street smarts' that most sixteen-year-old boys would possess. I didn't feel comfortable even allowing him to get out of the car onto the pavement without me there. Not yet.

Aiden was silent as I exited the car and hurried around to his side. He opened the door himself and I took his hand to lead him down the street. With my free hand, I clutched my cardigan more tightly around me. It was a cool day, but the heavy knitwear and the anger coursing through my body made me feel sweaty and unkempt. My heart was still pounding from the unfortunate incident with the woman at the doctor's office, and from the strange van following me along the street. I almost walked past the pharmacy, I was so distracted. I couldn't stop my eyes roaming the faces of those walking around the village. No doubt they were tourists, but I couldn't stop thinking about who had taken Aiden. What if Aiden had already been face-to-face with his attacker but hadn't been able to tell me? What if the kidnapper came back and took him again?

The pharmacy was like every other shop in Bishoptown, in a small, limestone terraced building that looked more like a house than a business. Most of the shops had quaint hanging-baskets of busy-lizzies and marigolds, but the pharmacy had only one window and a wooden door with a bell.

As I was paying for the prescription, the bell on the door jingled, indicating someone else had walked in. Eager to leave, I hurried to put the change from my purchase into my wallet so I could get out of the small shop.

"Emma?"

High on adrenaline, I spun around too fast, almost knocking into Aiden. "Oh, hi, Amy. Didn't expect to see you here." It was a Tuesday. Teachers never had time off in the week. "How are..." I trailed off. Amy wasn't listening to me at all, she was staring transfixed at my son.

"It's break time," she mumbled. "I came to pick up my prescription." She didn't even look at me once. She was staring at my son in such an intense manner that I almost pulled him back towards me and away from her. "Aiden, oh my... oh my God, it's really you." She took a step forward with her hand outstretched, but he ducked away from her, moving behind me. Amy's eyes raised to meet mine and she blinked away a few tears before composing herself. "I didn't… I mean, I heard what happened on the news and I wanted to call you but…"

My spine straightened. This was the woman whose negligence had led to my child being stolen from me. No wonder Aiden was cowering behind me. "It wouldn't have been appropriate, Amy." My fingers tingled. After all these years I thought I'd forgiven her, but I was wrong. I'd only managed to push those feelings aside in favour of getting on with my life. Now that Aiden had come back, those old feelings had resurfaced. Perhaps it was the unfortunate incident with the woman in the surgery, or perhaps it was the strange black van following me around the village, but I was in no mood to coddle the woman who had turned her back and allowed my son to disappear from school.

Her face fell. "You're right. Sorry. I'm so stupid. I'm just so… I'm so glad Aiden is alive. I mean, I know he's been through…"

"Hell," I finished for her. "He's been through hell." As I stood there on the street looking at Amy, our years of working together melted away, leaving only my bitterness for the woman. I forgot all about the doll she'd bought for my unborn child, and the friendship we'd tentatively garnered over the last few years. I'd been desperate for someone to blame and suddenly here she was.

"I'm so sorry, Emma," she said. From the red flush working up her neck, and the way her bottom lip trembled I could tell she was about to cry.

I turned away. "I should go."

"Wait," she said. "I don't want... Emma, we've been friends for a long time now. I thought we'd got past what happened."

I shook my head. "Everything is different now. I grieved for him and I let him go; that was the only way I could look past what you did. But now he's here and he's in pain and I can't help but..." I paused. For the first time I really looked at her. Why was she so emotional? Why was there a single tear running down her cheek? It all seemed... contrived. How could I trust anything she said?

I pulled Aiden away, hurrying to my car. Thinking back to the reports and eyewitnesses on the day of Aiden's disappearance, I wondered if there was anything inconsistent about Amy. I remembered that, after she'd noticed Aiden was missing, she had asked another teacher to take care of the class while she'd gone looking for Aiden herself. She was on her own for a number of minutes. What if...? I opened the car door and let Aiden inside. DCI Stevenson had admitted that the kidnapper didn't have to be a man, though it was most likely that it *was* a man. I put the key into the ignition. Aiden would do something if he was face-to-face with his attacker. Wouldn't he? He'd recognise them.

So why was I suspecting everyone? Why was I suddenly believing that Amy, a petite and shy woman, could have stolen my son away and kept him locked up? Because I was beginning to believe that people were capable of anything. People are multi-layered. Anyone can have a private side that verges on the dark and dangerous. Your doctor could be a sadist. Your primary school teacher could be a paedophile. Your beauty therapist could be a murderer. It could be anything.

I watched Aiden put on his seatbelt and wondered if he remembered anything from his time as a captive. He was frightened of Rough Valley Forest, that much I knew, and I understood. But would he remember his kidnapper, and how would he act if he came face-to-face with them?

As I pulled quickly out of the parking space, a black Renault Clio had to brake suddenly to avoid my car. I fumbled with the gear stick and waved sheepishly as the driver of the Clio honked his horn at me. My fingers trembled as I guided the car out of the space and onto the main street.

"Shall we listen to the radio?" I said, too brightly.

Aiden didn't respond. He gazed straight ahead in that same uninterested way. I clicked on the radio and tried to stop myself wondering what was in his mind. All the knowledge was there but he refused to let it out. That was when I realised I was angry with him. I couldn't help it. I was angry with Aiden for not communicating with me. And I was suspicious. I was suspicious of everything.

"Why don't you talk?" I said, banging the steering wheel. "Why won't you tell me?"

I ran a red light. If Jake had been there he would

have forced me to pull over and driven the rest of the way home. He would have hated to see me in this state. But he wasn't there. It was only Aiden, who didn't seem perturbed by my unhinged state in the least. All he did was stare out through the windscreen—staring and thinking and not reacting to anything around him. Maybe Jake was right. Maybe he was a vegetable.

No, I wouldn't believe it. A vegetable doesn't paint. A vegetable doesn't acknowledge my words. There was the time he nodded at me, and the time where I thought I heard him singing—unless it had been a figment of my imagination…

As the streets faded one into another I took deep breaths and eased my foot off the accelerator. The paper bag from the pharmacy sat on Aiden's lap. My heart was pounding all the way home. When I checked the rearview mirror, the black transit van was back. I pulled in to my drive and swore. Even more reporters were clustered all around the house.

The transit van stopped a little way down the street. I was right—they'd been following me around as I went about my day-to-day chores, hanging around in a transit van like the mob following a target.

The front door burst open and Denise stepped out. She rushed over to the door and opened Aiden's side, as a swarm of people with cameras and microphones gathered around us.

"What's going on?" I shouted. "How did you

get in the house?"

"Jake let me in earlier."

"Where is he now?" I asked.

"We need to get inside. There's been a development," she whispered.

"It must be a big one."

She nodded. "It is."

"Aiden, what's it like being in the real world? Aiden, do you still have an attachment to your kidnapper?" yelled a reporter.

I turned away from Denise and Aiden, stepped down the path towards the reporters at the end of the drive, and clenched both of my fists. I was hot all over despite the chill in the air. "Fuck off and leave us alone! This is fucking private property and you're trespassing. I mean it. Leave us alone. LEAVE US ALONE!"

I was shaking as Denise wrapped an arm around my shoulder and guided me back up the path to the door.

CHAPTER TWENTY-THREE

"I'm putting the kettle on," said Denise. "Why don't you sit down for a minute and try to calm down."

I was pacing the length of the kitchen, rubbing my belly in circular motions. It was less than two weeks to my due date and I was supposed to be nesting, not yelling at reporters. I was supposed to be making the house pretty, buying pink booties and hanging a mobile above the crib like a pregnancy montage in an 80s romantic comedy.

"What's happened? Why are the reporters like rabid dogs again?"

"Sit down for a moment, Emma." Denise flicked the switch to turn the kettle on.

In the interest of getting the information faster, I sank my backside down onto a dining chair. Then I opened my hands and shrugged to prompt her to continue.

"The police have asked Jake to go to the station for questioning."

"What?" I could feel my blood pressure rising. "Why?"

She spoke slowly, in the same way I'd seen teachers talking to agitated students. "I don't know all the details. I think they want to go over Jake's statement for the day Aiden went missing."

"It can't be Jake. Aiden has lived here with him for days now. Don't you think Aiden would have reacted? It can't be. I know him. He's my husband. This is his baby. Anyway, how would Jake have had the time to keep a boy locked away for ten years?"

"Now, I'm not saying that it is Jake. I'm not saying that at all. But, wives have been lied to in the past and husbands have found ways to conduct all kinds of heinous and time-consuming activities." She poured water into two mugs. "But I'm not saying that Jake did it, okay? All I know is that he's been asked to answer a few questions to help the investigation. It could be nothing."

"Fat lot of good you are." My brain-to-mouth filter had stopped working due to the intense stress of the day. "If you can't even tell me why they're questioning Jake."

Denise was very quiet as she stirred the milk into the tea.

"Or maybe you won't tell me. That's more likely."

"My job is to aid you through this difficult

process. Doing that is my priority, which is why my colleagues might feel it necessary to hold back information at times like this. I'm here to help, okay? I know this is hard. Now, have a cuppa and try to relax. You have the baby to think about."

"Oh yes, I forgot I'm a walking incubator," I snapped as I took the tea from her. Then I shrugged and sighed. "Sorry. Difficult day. I'm getting fed up with everyone expecting me to put the baby first. I am, of course, but I matter too, you know."

"Of course you do. Sorry, I didn't mean to imply that you didn't."

I smiled thinly. "You probably didn't. I'm just sensitive."

"I'm not surprised. You're a strong woman to be getting through all this. Don't let anyone tell you otherwise."

"I screamed at those reporters."

She sipped her tea and chuckled. "They've heard worse."

"Oh God, poor Jake. Alone at the station. I should go, but I can't take Aiden there. Not with all those reporters out there." I chewed on my bottom lip and wondered whether I could send someone else to meet him. We had a solicitor, but maybe that would send the wrong signal. I could ask Sonya or Josie, but Jake had never been as close with Josie as I had, and Sonya was Rob's mother so that could be uncomfortable. Jake didn't really have any male friends. He hadn't even bothered with a stag do before the wedding. "Can you call and ask how long he'll be there for? Can I talk to him over the phone?"

Before Denise could answer, my mobile phone started to ring. I dug it out of the bottom of my bag and frowned in disappointment. I had been hoping it would be Jake calling from the police station but it was Rob.

"Hi."

"Emma, I heard they took Jake in for questioning. What's going on?" he said.

"They just want to ask him some more questions about the day Aiden was taken. It's nothing, Rob. I mean, they've had you in for questioning too. They've had half the town in."

"No, this is different." I heard him moving around as he spoke. There was a breathlessness to his voice, as though he couldn't stand still. I imagined his energy seeping out in nervous tics. I could see him pacing in my mind's eye. "The press has caught onto this like it's a big deal. They've not done this before."

"They'll latch onto anything, Rob," I argued.

There was a pause.

"You don't really believe that Jake took Aiden, do you? And then fooled me for ten years. How would he do that, Rob? How? How would he have my son locked away all these years while romancing me and marrying me and getting me pregnant? Don't you think I would know?"

"Em—"

"Don't you trust me to know?"

"Emma." His voice was calmer now. The deep tone caught my attention and my body reacted in a physical way. I shook my head, passing it off as leftover feelings from when we were teenagers. I'd always loved Rob's deep, velvety voice. "I do trust you. You're one of the few people in this world I'd trust with my life."

"Why do I sense a 'but' coming on?"

"I don't think you see him the way others see him. Don't you remember how at school some of the girls called him 'perv' because of the way he looked at them?"

"What? No! And how would that—"

"Emma, listen to me. This isn't coming from a place of jealousy. I swear it. God knows I hate him because you love him, but this is me thinking rationally for a change. It's possible. I know you don't want to accept that, but if he doesn't have a watertight alibi for the time Aiden disappeared it's possible that he did this. Do you know where he is twenty-four hours a day?"

"No, but—"

"Then it's possible."

"You're forgetting one thing, Rob."

"What's that?"

"Aiden. He was afraid when we went to Rough, which means he's afraid of the place he was held captive, right?"

"I guess so."

"With that logic, he must also be afraid of the person who kidnapped him."

Rob sighed.

"Aiden and Jake have lived in the house for days now. He's never shown *any* fear towards Jake. The first night here they set the table together. In fact, Aiden seems to really like Jake. He'll follow him around doing everything he says."

"Emma, don't you see how that's strange? If Aiden has more of an attachment to Jake than anyone else then that's fucking weird on its own. Look, this is really hard to say but I'm just going to say it."

"What?"

"Aiden was with this person for ten years. We don't know what happened between the two of them. I've been reading up about Stockholm syndrome and all that stuff. Abusers and victims have a complicated relationship—"

"No. This isn't like that. No." I shook my head. I was on my feet now, clenching and unclenching one hand. Denise watched me carefully so I turned my back on her.

"There's a chance that Aiden hasn't seen *anyone* apart from the person who took him. Like that girl in Germany or wherever. There's a chance that the only person Aiden remembers from his childhood is the monster who took him, and there's a chance that Aiden has developed a fondness for his attacker."

"Fuck off, Rob. I can't—"

"I think you should come and stay with me."

"No. It's not him." I was crying now. Fat tears

rolled down my cheeks.

"I don't think the two of you are safe there. Stay with me. Please, Emma."

"It's not him."

"You don't know that. What if it is?"

"Rob, he's my husband. I know him."

"Those are the famous last words, aren't they? 'I know him. I love him.' Don't be that woman."

I took in a deep, shaky breath. "And who's to say you're any better than him? You could be a monster too, for all I know. Everyone could be."

I hung up.

"Are you okay, Emma?" Denise asked.

I wiped my eyes and nodded. Then I walked over to the window and opened the curtains an inch. The reporters were still there, waiting on the pavement outside the house. I hated them. They made me feel trapped inside my own home. With a flick of my wrist, the curtain was closed and I backed away. What was I going to do? Aiden sat on the sofa in our living room with his hands on his lap, watching the television. It was only when I turned around that I noticed the television was off. He'd been sat in silence watching nothing.

Though the heating was controlled by a thermostat, I still felt a chill creep up my spine, and I shivered. I thought of Rob's words, not only about Jake, but also about Aiden and what he'd said about the kidnapper. Up until that moment I had been so sure Aiden would be terrified of the person who had stolen him from me. We knew Aiden had been chained, and we knew he had been abused. But what we didn't know was what the abuser had said to him. Had he played mind games with my son? Had he spent the last ten years convincing Aiden that *he* was only person who loved him? What had they done to my little boy?

I couldn't stand to be in the same room as my son. Not at that moment. I rushed out of the living room and hurried upstairs to lie down. But as I went into my bedroom and looked at the bed I shared with my husband, I couldn't stop thinking about what Rob had said. I'd let him into my head, and a seed of doubt had been planted. Of course I'd seen wives in the press talking about how they'd had no idea their husband was a serial rapist, or a child molester, and, yes, there had been occasions when men had locked young girls or women up in a basement and sound-proofed it, living one life upstairs and another downstairs. But this was different. *Ten years.* How would that be possible? And wherever Aiden had been kept it was nowhere near Jake's house. Jake would need to go to this hypothetical place every day, or at least every couple of days. But the only time Jake and I were apart was the adult learning art class he ran in York twice a week. He'd have no time.

The baby kicked me again and I rubbed my belly as I sank down onto the bed. My head was spinning with disparate thoughts. My ankles ached. My legs were tired. I knew that if I leaned back I would fall straight to sleep despite the stress of the day so far. But I didn't do any of that. I picked up my phone and called the adult learning centre in York. I asked to book onto the Introduction to Art History course on Tuesdays and Thursdays.

"Absolutely. What name is it, please?"

"Amy Perry," I lied.

"I should let you know that the usual tutor has taken some time off so we have a support tutor in place at the moment."

"That's okay. Who is the usual tutor?" I asked.

"Oh, sorry dear, I'm new and I don't have that information to hand at the moment. We're in the middle of changing our computer system and it's all a little hectic here. But if you like I can arrange for a prospectus to be sent to you. It has the course information and contact details for your tutor."

I agreed to have the prospectus sent straight away.

CHAPTER TWENTY-FOUR

Jake tumbled into the house after hurrying away from the reporters. I watched him pull into the drive through a crack in the curtains, and he slammed the door so hard that I thought the glass panel might shatter. Aiden barely processed the loud noise, but Denise came hurrying through from the kitchen. I noticed she'd stayed later than usual. It was dark out and I had expected her to be on her way home by now.

"Fucking arseholes," Jake exclaimed. "It's bad enough I'm hounded by the police but now I have to be hounded by *them*, too."

I bit my thumbnail as he came striding into the living room. His hair was dishevelled and his shirt was unbuttoned at the collar. His skin was flushed and his eyes were wide.

"Jake," I said. "Not in front of Aiden."

His eyes narrowed, but he glanced at Aiden before nodding.

"Are you all right?" I asked, aware of how stiff my voice sounded.

"Did you say anything to the reporters?" Denise asked.

Jake shook his head. "The fuckers wanted me to, but I didn't give them the satisfaction. And, yes, I am all right, thanks for asking."

I found myself rubbing my hands again. Then I started scratching at the sore skin on the fold next to my thumb. I shoved my hands deep into my jeans. "I couldn't come with them all out there. A black transit van kept following me around all day today."

"It's all right," Jake said. "I know you couldn't come." He pulled me into a tight embrace and whispered into my hair, "I'm so glad you're here. I've needed you all day." Then he took my hand and led me over to the sofa and sat me down next to him. "Emma, it was awful. They kept going over my statement, picking it apart. It was ten years ago, how am I supposed to remember? Everything was so blurry with the flood happening. I just don't understand why they keep asking me these things."

"It's okay," I said. I pulled him closer to me, but some of the adrenaline from earlier was still rushing through me. There was a part of me that wanted to push him away, not bring him closer. My skin prickled where he touched me. "It's over now. They didn't charge you with anything so you must have cleared up whatever issue they had."

"They have nothing because I've done nothing." Jake glared at Denise. "Maybe you can tell that to your mates down the station."

Denise shuffled awkwardly from one foot to the other. "I think it's probably time I headed home. I'm glad that everything has been sorted out, Mr. Hewitt."

I noticed that Denise never called him Jake. Perhaps it was because Jake still carried the air of a teacher even when he was outside the classroom. Or perhaps it was because Denise didn't feel completely comfortable around him. Or maybe it was more indicative of the patronising way she tried to pal up to me. Always calling me Emma and 'popping the kettle on'. On the other hand, Marcus struck up the occasional conversation about cars or football—probably in the hope that it would ignite Jake's attention and get him onside. It could be sickening at times.

The door closed behind her and I heard a few reporters speak to her as she made her way to her car down the street.

"They'll get bored soon," I said. "They'll stop hanging around after dark soon anyway."

Jake pulled me closer. "I'm so glad you're here."

I tried not to allow my body to stiffen, but all I could think about was Aiden sitting across the room from us. I tried to disentangle myself from Jake's arms. "Hey, Aiden's here, you know."

Jake gave him the barest of glances. "Oh yeah."

"Maybe we could stick the telly on for a while."

"What, and watch more Disney? What is it this time? *Aladdin*? *Sleeping Beauty*? The boy's sixteen. He doesn't need to be subjected to more of that claptrap."

"What happened at the police station?" I asked. "You're far more agitated than I would be after being asked to clarify something simple."

Spittle flew from his mouth when he answered. "How do you think it went? I knew what they were meaning when they asked me those questions. They were insinuating I did it. They think I could take a six-year-old boy. It's disgusting."

"What questions did they ask you?"

"What didn't they ask me?" He sighed. "It was a breakdown, basically. They wanted to know every second of my whereabouts for the entire day. Of course it was impossible to answer. It was ten years ago and everyone was rushing around like a blue-arsed fly trying to find a dry classroom in that leaking cesspool of a school. I thought I'd been with Simon from IT for most of the day but apparently he says he wasn't. I distinctly remember us going into E6 to check on the roof there. It's all ridiculous. As if I would have even had *time* to do such a thing. Ten years!"

"That's what I said."

He pulled me closer and kissed me on the mouth. "My Emma. My beautiful wife. To think our little daughter will be here to meet us soon."

I pushed him back. "Jake. Aiden's here."

"Aiden, dear boy," he said, imitating a

stereotypical public school teacher. "Perhaps it's time for you to go to bed now. I have some things to discuss with your mum."

"Actually, it is getting a bit late," I said. "Maybe we should all go to bed."

"Has he eaten?"

"Denise made him a sandwich."

Aiden made his way out of the room, closing the door behind him. My heart sank to see the way he plodded along the floor with his stiff, cumbersome gait. It was getting a little better each day, but I wondered whether he would ever stride or run in the same way as the other young men and women.

"Where were we, Mrs. Price-Hewitt? Hmm, maybe one day we can ditch the Price." He landed a few small kisses down my neck.

"Jake, come on. It's been a horrible day. Can we just sit and chill for a bit?"

He pulled away and crossed one leg over the other in a fluid motion. From the way he held his body I could tell he was annoyed.

"It's just... I'm so stressed out. And... look, we'll have some sandwiches and watch an hour of TV and then see how we're feeling, okay? I just need to decompress." I started rubbing my hands again. "Someone keyed my car. I was at the doctor's and this woman was talking to me—"

"Who keyed your car? Why were you at the doctor's?"

"When I took Aiden to his therapy session yesterday, Dr Foster suggested I might need a check-up. When I was in the surgery, this woman started talking to me about Aiden and... I dunno... I think I snapped at her. She must have keyed the car on the way out. And then there was a transit van following me. I guess it was reporters. I lost my temper with them coming into the house." By this point I was scratching the skin on my hands. Jake leaned forward and took them in his own.

"What about the doctor? What did she say? Are you all right? The baby?"

"I'm fine. Just a little bit of high blood pressure so I have some tablets to take."

He kissed both hands and then let them go. "You need to rest. Why don't you ask Rob to take Aiden for a few days? He can take on some of the responsibilities for a change."

Mentioning Rob only made me think about the things he'd said over the phone. I couldn't stand to think about Aiden somehow still connected to his kidnapper. But what if it was true? What if Aiden was even in touch with his kidnapper? Did Aiden know how to use a phone? Could he speak when I wasn't around? I rubbed my eyes before letting my fingers run through my hair. Jake reached forward and took my arms, pulling me towards him.

When he kissed me, I kissed him back, but my body reacted on its own. My mind was elsewhere. I was considering everything I knew so far. I knew that Jake had been called in for questioning. I knew that the adult learning centre could not confirm that he worked there, but they did offer up a story in line with Jake's personal life. He hadn't been working at the centre since Aiden was found. He had been going to work at the school part-time but that was all. And I couldn't stop thinking about how things had been with Jake before all this started. In fact, before I found out I was pregnant.

We'd been married for a year. Though we'd discussed the idea of a child, Jake had always said that there was no rush. He wanted to make sure I was ready after everything that had happened with Aiden. I thought it was sweet, and I'd agreed. I wasn't even sure I wanted another child. It felt too much like replacing Aiden.

But after the honeymoon period a lot of things changed. After we'd filed the wedding pictures in an album and found ourselves lost in the routine of day-to-day living, something changed between us. Jake was very particular about how the house should look, and whenever I tried to buy a new ornament or rearrange the furniture to accommodate my own belongings, Jake didn't like it. For a time I could see that he was trying to put up with these changes, but I saw the long hard look he gave the old pine desk I'd brought from my parents' house. He made plenty of offhand comments about the paint marks and the coffee rings on the lid, and more than once jokingly suggested we put it in the garage.

Then one day I came home and in the place of my beloved childhood desk stood a brand new glass-topped monstrosity.

"Ta-da!" he had announced, standing next to the desk with his arms out wide.

I remember that it was a Saturday and I'd spent the morning with Josie in York. In fact, it had been Jake's idea for me to go. Clearly, he'd wanted me out of the way so he could replace the desk. I had stood there, thin-lipped and tense, digging my thumbnail into the palm of my hand.

"Where's my desk?" I asked.

"I bought you a new one. It has—"

"Where's *my* desk."

It was probably the worst fight we've ever had. Jake had not thrown the desk out, as I had first feared. Instead, he'd created an art studio in the garage with the desk, my paints, my easel, and a bunch of my paintings. Once I had cooled down, I decided that it was nice to have my own space, even if it was relegated to the garage. In summer, the garage is the perfect place to paint. The sun streams in through the open shutter door.

But after the desk incident it was plain to see that the honeymoon period was over. Though Jake had always had a voracious appetite when it came to the bedroom, our night-time activities became a desperate way to convince ourselves that despite the constant bickering about who should do the washing up or whose turn it was to take the bin out, there was love at the core of our relationship.

I fell pregnant with Bump a few months after that, despite taking my birth control pills daily. And after I fell pregnant—which we called kismet because it was a happy accident—Jake rarely touched me. There was something about me being pregnant that turned him off. Even when the pregnancy hormones made me rage with sexual frustration he completely ignored me. He even slept in the spare bedroom half a dozen times, saying that I "clearly needed some space" which I decided was code for "satisfy yourself tonight, honey, I'm not in the mood".

Jake did not like the way I looked as a pregnant woman. He was supportive. He rubbed my feet and made me cups of tea. He asked after the baby and checked that I was feeling okay. But he never touched my bump. Not ever. He never felt the baby kick. He was delighted to know that she was kicking, but he could not touch my bump. He said it made him feel nauseous but wouldn't go into any further detail when I pressed the matter. Of course I found it a bit weird, but I had been creeped out about pregnancy at one point, and he was so supportive about everything else. He came to all the scans. He held my hand. He listened to the birth plan and took an interest in how to make it as safe and comfortable as we could. He could be quite protective about what I carried and how much I moved around. I used to jog three times a week, but once my belly began to get bigger, he found the thought of me tripping and landing on my stomach too much to bear. In the end I gave up the running in favour of yoga.

Jake was, is, and has always been a complicated

man. That evening when he came home from the police station and wanted me more than ever... well, it made me realise that I was also a complicated woman, because I wanted him too.

CHAPTER TWENTY-FIVE

The next day—Wednesday—I learned that women have to pay a price if they allow themselves to be shrill. I was a YouTube phenomenon. The clip of me screaming at the reporters went viral, and the comments were toxic.

Women can never be shrill. It does something to a man. It hits them square in the testicles and shrivels them right up. I've seen Jake physically wince if my voice rises a few notes. I've seen the reaction of internet users to popular TV shows where the man is a murdering anti-hero with a wife who, on occasion, dares to yell at him. Guess who they hate.

The time of societal pity towards my tragic circumstance was over. The media had taken their gloves off.

Headlines took a punch at my mental health: *Back-From-Dead Mother in Banshee Screech, Aiden's Mum Loses It, She's Lost her Marbles!, Is This the Face of a Good Mother?* They dug out every unflattering photo they could find on social media and plastered them between poorly written paragraphs in online news articles. In nearly every single one I was holding an alcoholic drink. They even found a picture of me drunk off my face in the background of someone else's photo. My bleary eyes weren't even looking at the camera. It had been taken not long after my parents had died and I was ill, but of course no one cared about that.

It was clear that the reporters thought Jake was the kidnapper and they'd found a new angle: I was an accomplice. For some reason it made sense to them that I would have my 'lover' kidnap my own son and imprison him for a decade, only to release him and claim him back.

The house phone did not stop ringing that morning until I unplugged it. The only call I answered on my mobile phone was one from Josie.

"I'm so sorry," she said. It was the third time she'd said it. "You haven't done anything wrong, you know. Those fuckers deserved to be yelled at. Why shouldn't you scream at them?"

"It's okay. I don't care about what they think anymore. There's nothing they can do or say that will change my mind."

"Just stay safe, all right? Do you want me to bring food around to the house? Stay at home so they leave you alone."

"I'm okay, Jo. Honestly. We have tons of food in. We're staying holed up with Denise and Marcus."

"Who are they?"

I rolled my eyes. "Our family liaison officers."

Josie knew me so well that I could tell she knew I'd just rolled my eyes. "Aha. Annoying busybodies, are they?"

I glanced over my shoulder. "I'm pretty sure they're only hanging around to see if I know anything. I think Denise suspects Jake."

There was a pause.

"You can ask me if you want," I said.

"Okay. But I'm only asking because I'm worried about you."

"I don't suspect him. I really don't. I honestly don't think he would even have the time. I know women say 'but I knew him' all the time, and I feel like that too, but practically, he just wouldn't be able to do it."

She let out a long sigh. "I get it. I think you're right, too. Jake isn't… like that. I'm sure of it."

"Have you heard from Hugh?"

Josie paused. Then I heard the sound of a sob.

"Jo? Jo, what's happened?"

Her voice came out strangled. She was crying — sobbing, in fact. "I didn't want to tell you because of everything you're going through, but I think Hugh's left me."

"What? Oh my God, Jo! When did this happen?"

"I tried to get hold of him to tell him about Aiden, but I couldn't. He was supposed to be working with his brother in London for at least four weeks, which is normal for him. He used to come back and see me once a week but that fizzled out long ago. Nowadays he doesn't even call and he's a nightmare to get hold of. So I called his brother and Steven told me that Hugh hadn't even been at the office for a week."

"What?"

"Hugh told Steven he was coming home for a few days so Steven figured he was spending some time with me."

"What do you think has happened, Jo?"

"He's having an affair, I know it. I've known it for a long time. A friend of mine saw him with a woman in London. Bitch had blonde hair, apparently. Anyway, I checked our joint account and there's hardly any money in it at all. I think about ten grand is gone."

"Fuck."

"I know," she said. I heard her sniff and then take a deep breath. "I've got enough money in my personal account. I've been savvy, Emma, don't worry. I would never let myself end up destitute. I can afford the mortgage, though I'd probably sell this fucking house. I never liked it."

I knew that was a lie, but I didn't point it out.

"I wish I could come over and see you. There are so many reporters around the house—"

"Don't be ridiculous, Em. It's fine. You stay with Aiden. Jesus, you've got enough to be going on with without getting involved in this shit with me and Hugh. Listen, he's a waste of space, it isn't even worth discussing. I hope he never does come home. He probably will, though. Steven will kill him if he fucks up the family business by clearing off with some tarty blonde."

"Jo. Christ. I don't know what to say."

"There's nothing to say."

"I know. Will you do me one huge favour?"

"Course, Em, anything."

"No matter how shitty you feel, get up, get showered, and go to work. Don't let that arsehole bring you down. God, I was such a mess after my parents died. Don't end up like me."

"Emma, I'm so sorry about back then. If I'd known you were struggling so much—"

"Hey, it's not your fault."

"I was working too hard. I got too involved in work and I forgot about my friends."

"You're doing it again," I said with a smile. "You're telling yourself off. You always do that. Stop blaming yourself for other people fucking up."

She laughed. "You're right. He's the arsehole. I'm awesome."

"Better."

*

It wasn't like the first time we holed up, where we played games and watched DVDs. This time there was an uncomfortable atmosphere throughout the house. Denise flapped around making tea and sandwiches. She was much more present than she had been near the beginning of the investigation. Marcus came and went, constantly going for meetings at the police station. When he was here he had private conversations with Denise. Jake stayed off work for a day, but then went back to school on Thursday morning. While he was at home he was like a bear with a thorn in its paw. He kept opening cupboards and then closing them. I often caught him staring at Aiden with narrowed eyes. More than once he suggested that Aiden should go to Rob's parents' B&B for the week, but when Jake's lawyer heard of that plan, he told us not to do it. Apparently if we did that it would raise suspicion.

But Rob did come to visit, which frankly was a huge help. He sat and drew with Aiden, not even balking at the strange jangle of black spirals that Aiden liked to scrawl. He brought DVDs we'd watched as teens. Nothing too violent or scary. Things like *The Breakfast Club* and *Home Alone*. He brought pizza and told stupid jokes. *Why do bananas have to put on sunscreen before they go to the beach? Because they might peel!*

"You look better," he said. It was Thursday afternoon, a mere few days since the 'shrill' video had gone viral. "You've got more colour about you. I reckon you need to get out of this house though."

"I'm taking Aiden for another therapy session tomorrow."

"Good," he said with a nod. "Just be careful, okay? Did you think about what I said? About Jake?"

I nodded. "It's not him, Rob. I'd know."

He took my hands and smiled. "All right. I won't mention it again. But if there's anything you need, and I mean *anything*, you call me. I'm talking 'Wispa bar in the middle of the night' shit. Remember when you were pregnant with Aiden and you sent me out for a jar of Nutella at 3am?"

"Oh yes, I remember that," I said. "I didn't even spread it on toast, I got a spoon."

"That spread did not stand a chance."

It had been a while since I'd laughed. I'd barely cracked a smile for days. We stood in the kitchen watching Aiden through the hallway sat on the sofa. The television was on but I got the feeling he wasn't watching it at all, and that made goose bumps appear along my arms.

"Do you think he'll ever speak?" Rob asked.

"He will when he wants to tell us his story," I said. It was what I always said when I answered that question. "But I want to hear his voice. I want to know what he sounds like. He won't be like the little boy who disappeared all those years ago. I know that. He'll have a deeper voice, like a man's, I suppose. Right now he's more like a shell than a person."

"Aiden is in there. I'm sure of it." Rob set down his mug to hook an arm around my waist. It felt natural. I was being comforted by the father of my child and it felt right. "It's just going to take some time."

"I'm so sick of time." I shook my head. "Time is

what I've been robbed of already. Time with my son. Buying him football boots when he grows out of his old ones. Arguing with him about tidying his room. Watching him awkwardly try to flirt with girls."

Rob laughed through his nose. "You'll still get to see him try to flirt with girls."

"Will I? Rob, is he ever going to be normal? I know it's early days, but can you ever imagine him at school or at university? I can't imagine him interacting with anyone at the moment." Though the words felt good to let out, they left a sour taste in my mouth because deep down I knew them to be true. Aiden was damaged. He would never be like the other kids.

Rob's arm tightened around my waist. He leaned into me and rested his head against mine. "We'll figure it out, Em."

And as we were stood there in the door of Jake's kitchen, linked arm in arm, I genuinely believed it would be me and Rob who figured out the best path for Aiden. We were his parents and we would know what was best for him. At that moment I didn't even think about Jake, though later I would look back and feel shame for not doing so.

The spell was broken when the door opened and Denise stepped in. "It's chilly out there. The autumn is really setting in now. How's Aiden doing?"

We'd stepped away from each other as Denise had walked in. It was a move we'd made countless times when we were young teens in love—every time my mum popped into my bedroom to deliver laundry. Well, we were like silly teenagers again.

"He's fine," I replied. "Any news from DCI Stevenson?" I idly let one hand stroke my belly.

"You'd better give him a call and speak to him yourself," Denise said.

CHAPTER TWENTY-SIX

"Try again," Rob insisted.

"I've called three times," I replied.

"He's bound to be in important meetings," Denise chipped in.

"Can't you just tell us?" I demanded.

Denise only shook her head. "It's best it comes from him. Try again in a while. Shall I—"

"—pop the kettle on?" I mimicked. "No, I've had quite enough bloody tea, thank you."

Rob smirked. I rubbed my hands and tried not to think of my high blood pressure. I picked up my mobile phone from the kitchen table and clicked through to my recent calls for DCI Stevenson's number.

When he answered, I almost dropped the phone from shock. It was my fifth attempt and I'd already come to the conclusion that he wouldn't answer.

"Emma, now isn't a good time."

"Denise says there's been a development," I

said. "What's happened?"

"We've made an arrest that may or may not be relevant to the investigation. Now, Emma, this is confidential, and it's important that you don't look too much into it at this stage. We don't know if it's relevant to the case or not, okay?"

"Stop patronising me and tell me," I snapped.

"You're right, I'm sorry. We have arrested James Graham-Lennox for possession of child pornography."

"*What?*"

"An IT consultant found images on his personal computer and informed the police."

"The Duke of Hardwick?"

"Yes."

"Shit." Then a disgusting thought popped into my mind. "Is... Is Aiden on—"

"We've not found any pictures of Aiden on his computer."

I let out a long, deep sigh.

"This is very sensitive information. Do not repeat it to anyone outside the family. Is that clear? We need to tread carefully."

"Of course. Shit. He'd have the money to do it. He'd have the opportunity. Oh God."

"Emma, I need you to stay focussed. There's no evidence linking the duke to Aiden. Not yet anyway."

When I hung up the phone, I could tell by Rob's expression that I'd paled to a deathly white.

"What is it?" he asked. "They've made an

arrest?"

I could feel Denise hovering over us. I wanted to talk to Rob but I hated her listening in on every conversation. I didn't trust her. She was police, not family. Her loyalties were with the police and that was a barrier I could not climb.

"Denise, would you mind checking on Aiden?" I asked.

"Is everything okay?" she replied with a bright smile.

"Sure."

She hesitated for half a heartbeat before making her way out of the kitchen and through to the living room. But she did it.

"They've arrested someone with child pornography on their computer. But there were no pictures of Aiden."

Rob gripped the kitchen table so hard that I could see his knuckles whitening. "And it was that duke, was it? The one who lives up in the big house lording it over us? Was it him, Emma?"

"Yes," I confirmed.

His eyes widened and his jaw dropped and I knew his mind was racing through exactly the same thoughts that had raced through mine when DCI Stevenson had told me. He staggered away from the table and raked his hands through his hair.

"Fuck."

"There's no connection to Aiden yet."

"He's a paedo living in the area. What else do

they need?"

"They need a lot more than that, Rob. They need to find where he was kept. They need *proof*."

"It's him," Rob said. "I know it. It's him."

"Emma!"

Denise's urgent call sent a jolt up my spine. I clutched hold of my bump as I rushed through the hallway into the living room. Aiden stood on one side of the room with Denise on the other. He had a pair of scissors in his hand and was holding them up high in a gesture that could be perceived as threatening. Behind him, the curtains had been chopped to pieces.

"I'm so sorry, I was setting up a DVD for him on the television. I didn't see what he was doing and then when I did, I tried to get him to stop," Denise said. "But he kept ignoring me."

"Aiden, honey, put down the scissors." It was only now that I realised how much he had grown since he had been living with us. He was still shorter than the average sixteen-year-old boy, but he had filled out. His pigeon chest wasn't as prominent. His shoulders appeared broader. He cut a far more intimidating figure than he had a week ago.

"Mate, it's all right. You're not in any trouble. Just put the scissors down, okay pal?" Rob coaxed.

But Aiden ignored us. He turned around and resumed his haphazard chopping of the curtains, letting the world see into our home.

*

The media were spoiled for stories. I'm not sure they knew quite what to report on first. There was the arrest of the Duke of Hardwick and the warrant to search Wetherington House. There were pictures of Aiden cutting our curtains to shreds with Rob and myself standing like idiots behind him, clearly afraid. There was the aftermath of 'screech-gate' going on, with the YouTube clip still trending on Facebook. And in the midst of this toxic melting pot, I managed to get Aiden to the therapist, along with Marcus providing a police escort.

"What do you think brought on this new development?" Dr Foster asked. "Aiden hasn't shown any other signs of disruptive behaviour. What has changed?"

"Perhaps he heard me telling Rob about the arrest. That could have triggered something. Or maybe it was all the reporters waiting outside the house. I tried asking him but..." I shrugged.

Today, Aiden scrawled red and black against a grey background. Then he drew what appeared to be solid steel bars in front of a dark background.

"This could be his cage," I said, showing Dr Foster.

"It's a shame there isn't more detail for the police."

I agreed. Aiden's pictures never had an awful lot of detail. When we asked him to draw more, he clammed up and pushed the pens aside.

"What about at night?" Dr Foster asked. "Any changes?"

"The same. I'll check on him at nine and he seems to be sleeping. When I go into his room at around 7 or 8am, he's usually awake but still in bed. Then he'll have a shower, though the bathroom door stays open. After his shower we eat breakfast. Then he'll often sit and watch television. He'll watch whatever's on and remains impassive to it all. I've stopped trying to fill his days with children's TV. He sits and watches daytime TV just as easily though."

"The routine to his day is interesting. When inmates are released from prison they often live in the same routine that was forced upon them in prison. That means wherever Aiden was, he had a routine. He woke at a certain time, ate at a certain time and went to bed at a certain time."

"So the kidnapper enforced this?"

Dr Foster shrugged. "Perhaps it was Aiden filling the days in the best way he could to stay sane. Or perhaps the kidnapper did it as a form of discipline."

"Rob said that Aiden could be suffering from Stockholm syndrome, that maybe he is sympathetic to his kidnapper. Maybe... maybe he's working *with* the kidnapper and against us. Is that possible?"

Dr Foster paused, a hint of uncertainty in her demeanour. She cleared her throat slightly and released her hand from a fist. To me it seemed she was stalling. She didn't want to answer. When she did, she lifted a stuffed toy from the desk and poked at its eye with a thumb. "I think it is possible. It's not a pleasant thought, I'll admit. But the fact is that Aiden spent ten years in the company of this person and we don't know what happened between them. We know there was abuse and neglect, but many children—I'm sorry to say—are abused and neglected by their own parents. Those children grow up to have a very complicated relationship with their parents."

I glanced across at Aiden, now working on another piece of art. His head was bent so that I saw the circular swirl of his hair. "Does that mean I can't trust him?"

"Honestly, I don't know what it means. Aiden's case is unique." She leaned forward. "If you don't feel safe, it isn't your fault, and you should call me or DCI Stevenson right away."

*

Her words echoed around the empty shell of my mind. *If you don't feel safe.* What if I can't trust my own son? I was tired that day. The effort of growing a human being in my uterus, coupled with the stress and strain of Aiden's case, made me want to do little more than curl up in bed and pull the duvet over my head. I was running on adrenaline and sheer force of will. Instead of nesting for the arrival of my second child, I was driving my son to a therapy session for traumatised children, and dwelling on the fact that a paedophile who may have kidnapped my child was in police custody. All the time there was a sickly feeling in the pit of my stomach. I felt constantly nauseated by the world. I hated everything, and there was a part of me that didn't even want to bring this baby into the world. How could I tell my daughter what had happened to her brother?

Next, I took Aiden to the dentist. I'd finally found one willing to give him a check-up without him needing identification. Though I abhorred the word 'luck' when it came to my son, he had been lucky that his teeth had formed without being too crooked, and there wasn't too much damage to them.

But today he needed fillings.

It took three of us to hold him down as the dentist injected anaesthetic into his gums.

Afterwards I was shaking, and Aiden, though as quiet as always, walked briskly away from the dentist with arms held stiffly at his side. He let himself into the car and pulled the seatbelt across his chest. Though there was nothing I could put my finger on, I was certain he was angry.

"I'm really sorry, sweetheart," I said for the fiftieth time since setting foot in the dentist's office. "It was to make you better."

But Aiden didn't look at me. He turned his head away and gazed out of the window as a blurry Bishoptown whizzed past.

"I'm sorry," I said again, with the distinct feeling that it was falling on deaf ears. "I don't want to be afraid of you. If only you'd talk. I need to hear your thoughts." I'd taken to doing this while we were alone. My brain to mouth filter turned off and I rambled at him. "Was it the duke? Was it him? If I showed you a picture would you react? Of course not. Maybe you're in contact with him. Do you sneak onto the house phone and dial his number? Do I need to get an itemised bill just to check that you aren't plotting against me? Why did you cut up the curtains? Now everyone can see into our home. Why would you do that?" I banged my palms against the steering wheel. "Why would you do that?"

A car pulled out in front of me and I swerved into the right hand lane, almost directly into oncoming traffic. After swerving back into the left lane I sucked in a long, deep breath before wiping the sweat from my forehead.

"I'm sorry we had to hold you down at the dentist's. That must have been very frightening for you. But Aiden, you can't hold a grudge with me about things like that. Promise me?" I sighed. "I have to make horrible decisions for you sometimes. But you know I love you and I will always keep you safe. No matter what. I'd die to keep you safe, I really would."

CHAPTER TWENTY-SEVEN

It's hard to remember what it was like when I was a *regular* teenager. Back when I was sixteen I had a future. I had *options*, and there is nothing so delicious as having options in life. My parents were not rich, but they were comfortable, which meant I could go to whatever university I wanted to go to. My grades were As, Bs, and Cs. But instead of the future I thought only of *now*. I wanted fun, laughter, friendship, and love. Who doesn't? I didn't know what a consequence was—at least not really. I just wanted to be in Rob's arms, discovering the world through our senses.

Life became more complicated after Aiden was born but I still managed to live in the moment. We lived like that together. That was how I got to know him and he got to know me, by playing and pulling silly faces and running through the park. My life stopped in one sense and started in another.

But I didn't just live in the moment with my son. Aiden was the most important part of my life, but I'd had a life before he came along. I'd had a wonderful, vibrant social life with my friends.

There were a bunch of us. Rob, me, half a dozen other guys who ended up going away to university and never coming back, and then, Amy. She was never a best friend, but she was always part of the group. She was quiet, kind of mousy back then. I think she had a crush on Rob but she never really said anything. She was an inoffensive presence, sometimes overlooked for being so shy, but sweet enough to spend an evening in the pub with. Her connection with Aiden's disappearance was always highlighted by the press. They often dragged out photographs of us both sipping bottles of lager in the Bishoptown local, our hair badly straightened and highlighted.

And I'd always thought she hated that attention.

But I was wrong.

The day after I took Aiden to the dentist—while the police were still searching Wetherington House on a drab Saturday—I opened the newspapers to find Amy's story in black and white. Perhaps the way I snapped at her on the street had affected her more than I realised. Perhaps Amy wasn't quite the mousy girl I thought she was. Perhaps that doll she gave me at my baby shower wasn't a sign of remorse, but of unhealthy obsession. Why else would she sell a story to the tabloids?

According to her, Aiden had been a problem

child. He was a troublemaker at school, always winding up the other students and acting the class clown. He was obstinate and unaware of danger. That was the part that upset me the most. She suggested I never taught my son to be afraid.

"Aiden possessed a kind of blind indifference to danger. On school trips, I always had one eye on him. I didn't like crossing the road with Aiden because he was likely to run straight into traffic," so went the article. "But worse was how he'd encourage others to follow him blindly. He once convinced a young girl of five to climb the tallest tree at the bottom of the playground. Luckily, through a joint effort with other teachers, we managed to get her down again, but she could have hurt herself. Aiden was standing at the bottom of the tree when it happened."

Jake walked into the kitchen as I was holding my head in my hands, leaning over the kitchen table with the papers spread out over the surface. It was 7:30am and Denise was already pottering around us with fresh pastries, making coffee. I wanted her gone. I was sick of her. There was no reason for a police officer to see my husband in his dressing gown, but she'd brought the pastries as a gift, knowing full well that I'd be awake. I was up well before the sun these days.

"What's happened?" he asked.

I pushed the open newspaper towards him and jabbed at Amy's face with my finger.

Jake rubbed his eyes and donned his glasses

before reading the article. "That fucking bitch!"

I glanced guiltily towards Denise. "Jake."

"Why is she saying these things?"

"Money, probably," I answered. My blood was boiling but I refused to let Denise see the ugly side of my temper again. "I wonder how much they paid her."

"All this stuff about Aiden, is it true?"

In the background, Denise continued to faff around with plates for breakfast. I was aware of her presence but I didn't want to seem like I had anything to hide.

"I remember the tree incident, but it hardly appeared sinister at the time. Aiden told me he was telling her to come down." It had been precocious child Rosie Daniels who had clambered up the high branches of the tree. I'd always thought that she was sweet on Aiden and had decided to do it to impress him. Aiden was certainly a little monkey when he was five, there was no argument there. He did enjoy climbing trees and he was adventurous, but he wasn't reckless. He wasn't flippant about crossing the road. I always made sure that he held my hand.

Jake's frown deepened as he finished the article and closed the newspaper. "This is the last thing we need."

"Why are they even talking about Aiden? They should be going after the duke, not my son. He's the one who broke the law. He's the one who took my son. He's the monster." I heard the rushing of blood in my ears as my heart sped up to double time. The baby moved inside me and I leaned forward. With the baby pressing on my bladder I'd already been up two or three times in the night and I was exhausted.

"Decaf?" Denise offered brightly.

I shook my head and tried my best not to glare at her. "Have you heard anything about the duke?"

"Not yet, sorry."

Whenever I thought about Wetherington House looming over Bishoptown, the rage inside me was so strong I felt capable of tearing the mansion down brick by brick. The Graham-Lennoxes were rich, there was no doubt about that. We never really saw them in the town, and Wetherington House was partly open to the public, with some private wings cordoned off for their living quarters. The duke had the money to do whatever he wanted. He could have a dungeon filled with children for all anyone knew.

"Emma? Emma, are you all right?" Denise asked.

Jake rushed to my side as my knees buckled slightly. "Sit down."

"I'm fine. I'm just tired."

"Have a croissant." Denise proffered a golden brown croissant on a plate Jake usually reserved for special occasions. I glanced at Jake before I took the plate. He was most likely torn between making sure I was okay and wanting to tell Denise to put that plate back and use one of the daily ones from the front of the cupboard.

"You're taking it easy today," Jake said. "I've got a staff meeting I'm supposed to attend but I'll call the school and tell them I can't make it."

"No, don't do that. The press will think it's because of Amy and I don't want them to think she's got to us."

"I don't want to leave you alone today," Jake said.

"Then I'll get Rob to come watch Aiden while I have a lie-down."

"What about Josie?" he suggested.

"Jo has her own shit going on at the moment. Stuff with Hugh."

Jake raised an eyebrow but he didn't question anything. "All right. But make sure you have a nap today. Denise, will you keep an eye on her?"

"Absolutely." And off she went to put the kettle on again.

*

There was no reason for me to leave the house that day, and I admit, I didn't want to. Amy's article referenced people in the village, people who knew me and vice versa. Rosie Daniel's mum certainly wouldn't be pleased to have her child dragged into this, though Amy was at least careful not to use her name.

About an hour after Jake left for the school I got a phone call from him. Amy had been suspended and sent home. It brought me no pleasure, but it did bring me some relief. I'd been dreading Jake getting into an argument with Amy over the article.

Rob turned up with a football. "Thought me and Aiden could have a kick about in the garden."

"Good idea." And I meant it. Why hadn't I thought of trying exercise with Aiden? The doctor had suggested that some light exercise would be good for him. I had wanted to take him for walks, but the pressure from the media had grown too intense.

It was a blustery day. There were leaves scattered over the lawn. Aiden had on a blue puffa jacket I'd bought for him when I kitted out his room with new clothes. It felt good to be outside, and it felt even better when Denise brought me a chair to sit on.

"This whole mess is tearing the village apart," Rob said, shaking his head sadly. "I was in the village shop earlier and heard someone calling out Amy as a traitor. They said she and that duke needed to be strung up. Then I overheard other people on the street arguing about whether we were good parents or not. Some of my mates called to see if I was all right when Aiden first came back, but now they cross the road to avoid me. I'm…" he lowered his voice. "I'm reaching the end of my rope, Em. I just want this to end."

Rob dropped the ball onto the dewy grass and kicked it gently over to Aiden. My heart was in my mouth as I waited. What would Aiden do, confronted with this alien object? Would he shun the game altogether and shuffle inside to sit himself down in front of the telly? Or would he break into a grin, and kick the ball back to his dad, laughing when Rob got hit in the crotch? The latter was the old Aiden. He loved to be cheeky and he loved playing football with Rob. That was one part of parenting that we always did well. We were young and energetic. There was so much running and jumping and messing around that I missed it so much I physically ached.

I hardly breathed waiting for Aiden to do something. Anything. At first he stood and stared down at the ball like it was from another planet. Then, he took a step forward and nudged it with the toe of his trainers.

"That's it, mate. Kick it over to me," Rob encouraged.

This time Aiden retracted his leg and full on kicked the ball towards Rob. It was nowhere near as enthusiastic as he used to be, but it was a start. I found myself leaning forward and applauding like a ridiculous 'pushy mother' on sports day.

"Nice one!" Rob exclaimed, dodging forward to stop the ball with the side of his trainer before aiming it back to Aiden.

Though my son barely cracked a smile, there was a moment when it felt like a little of the old life had creeped in. It was a shame the old me wasn't there to jump up and join in. With the stress of the two weeks, as well as my pregnancy, I couldn't play at all that day. I'd exhausted myself to the point where keeping my eyes open was a challenge. I had to sit and watch, with my pregnant belly a constant reminder that in little more than a week my next challenge would arrive.

And it was awful but that was how I saw my new baby. A challenge. I was beginning to think that life was set out to test me, and I was getting mightily sick of being tested. When the little one moved inside me, I winced and stroked the bulge of my bump.

"Everything all right?" Denise asked.

I hadn't heard her approach, and her voice was something of a shock. "Just the baby moving."

"Not long now," she said.

"No."

There was an awkward pause. What do you say to a woman barely a week away from her due date whose son had recently come back from the dead? There was no standard reply for that situation.

"I'm sorry it's such a stressful time for you," she said eventually. "But at least Aiden will have a little sister soon. I'm sure it will help a lot with his... development."

I watched as Aiden kicked the ball back to Rob. Each kick was the same. There was no enthusiasm or energy about what he was doing. I tried to remind myself that Aiden was weaker than most sixteen-year-olds but it was still painful to see him in a situation that should have been normal for a boy his age, behaving like it was the strangest thing in the world. The more he kicked the ball, the more that fleeting moment of hope ebbed away. He moved like a robot, drawing his foot back and kicking the ball in a slow, repetitive motion. The smile slowly faded from my face as I sat there and watched them.

The thing is, I should have been excited about having the baby and getting Aiden back. And I should have been encouraged by the fact that Aiden had chosen to *join in* with the game. But I wasn't any of those things. Looking at the dull blankness of Aiden's expression, I felt nothing but fear.

CHAPTER TWENTY-EIGHT

The Duke of Hardwick was pictured in *The Sun*, red-faced and blotchy on his way out of York police station. Alongside it were pictures of him on holiday with his children. The media raked him through the coals, too, dragging up an old allegation of sexual assault, and photos of him attending parties with women in bikinis flanking him on either side. I couldn't stand to see their grinning faces. The photos of him with the scantily clad women came from the 70s, and there was something about his leering grin that turned my stomach. It was like looking at photos of radio DJs in the 70s and feeling the grime of rape accusations coating your skin. Looking at those old perverts makes you want to take a shower.

But looking at a picture of the duke's blotchy red face showed me one important point: He was old. He walked with a cane and his hair was snow white. Now, I didn't know what kind of physical condition he was in ten years ago, but I did know that he would have needed to be fairly fit to abduct a child. Unless he had received some sort of assistance throughout the decade of my son's incarceration. My mind wandered into the murky depths of paedophile rings. There could be more of these men. I was almost sure of it. I reached out to the photograph of the duke and clawed away his face with my nails.

He was on bail.

The Wetherington House search had proved fruitless. Aside from the duke's computer there was nothing else incriminating. There was no hidden dungeon. There were no secret passages or rooms that had not been scoured by the police. Or so they said. I was dubious. Surely a man with so much wealth and so many connections could afford to pay a builder to work in secrecy. But then again, as DCI Stevenson had told me during a brief telephone conversation informing me of the duke's release, any change to Wetherington House was a ball-ache for the duke and duchess. They had to jump through more hoops than the rest of us, and it would take an awful lot of effort to build any kind of addition to the house. There was, of course, the possibility that he had used his money and influence to pay someone off, but even then he would have had to hide the whole thing from his family.

I was beginning to have doubts. The duke was a

sick man. He had broken the law, perhaps multiple times, but I was no longer sure that he had taken and abused my Aiden.

I told Jake my thoughts over breakfast. We had a rare morning without any family liaison officers, as they had been called into the station for some sort of meeting. I was sure that it was to report back about us. They were spies.

"It has to be him." Jake pushed his glasses up his nose, as he tended to do when he was anxious. "He had all those pictures on his laptop. I bet he's so rich he can pay people off."

I cringed. "Don't say that."

"Why not? It's true."

"I can't stand the thought of Aiden's kidnapper out there being allowed to live his life. Free to do whatever he wants."

"Well, if Aiden would man up and open his gob, none of this would be going on."

I quietly seethed as I buttered my toast.

"It's true though, isn't it?" Jake said, clearly not understanding when to shut his own gob. "All Aiden has to do is talk."

"I think he's blocking it all out. I'm not sure how much he remembers at this point," I said. "And I'm not convinced that it was the duke. He's too old. If he did do it, he had a lot of help. Maybe someone worse used his money to set the whole thing up. Maybe it was someone in the village." My stomach churned. I set my toast back down on the plate.

"You need to eat something," Jake said. "The

baby needs you to be healthy."

"I know." I picked off a corner of the crust and ate it. It tasted of nothing.

"Is the nursery all set up?" Jake asked.

"We set up most of it before... before Aiden came home. But we haven't got all the toys and clothes out of the packaging."

"Maybe you can do that today," Jake suggested. "I've got to take the car in for its MOT so I'll be out and about most of the day. Besides, It'll be a nice reminder that you have two children, not one."

My face flushed with a mix of shame and anger. It was true that my thoughts were mostly concerned with Aiden, but it was unfair of him to actually say it out loud. The last thing I needed was to be reminded that I was already a bad mother to the little girl growing in my womb.

When I flashed Jake a stern glance he only shrugged his shoulders and went, "What? Sorry, love, you know I speak my mind, and I have to say that it's all true. What's happened is truly awful, but for how long are we going to put our lives on hold?" He stood up and cleared away his cereal bowl.

"Are you serious?" I ripped another crust from my toast and angrily threw it back on the plate.

"Yes, I'm serious. Look, I understand that Aiden's investigation comes first but... but you're hardly even the woman I married. You're a mess, Emma. You're strung out, agitated. Irritable. In fact, your temper is downright awful. The way you screamed at those reporters, well—"

"You watched the video."

"The whole world watched the video. They all think you're unhinged, for fuck's sake. And the way you don't even *see* that Aiden is not just a traumatised kid—"

"What's that supposed to mean?"

"Come on. You read Amy's article. I know I didn't know you and Aiden all that well before the abduction, but you already admitted how a lot of what she said was true. Aiden was a badly behaved child—"

"No!"

"You've ignored all the bad bits and built him up to be some sort of angel. But it's not true, is it? He was out of control."

"Shut up!"

"I would, honey, but you have to hear this. You have to wake up and realise that our house is not going to be safe while Aiden is in it. We can't bring a newborn home with him living here! He could be working *with* the kidnapper for all we know. Teenagers build some weird fucking alliances."

"Jake!"

"I'm sorry. I hate to say these things but they need to be said."

I let out a gasp. My hands were gripping the table so hard that my nail had bent back. I placed the finger in my mouth and sucked it while Jake finished rinsing his cereal bowl and moved back to the kitchen table.

I removed my finger. "How long have you thought these things?"

He took my injured nail in his hand, gentle as always. "Since we brought Aiden home. I had hoped he would snap out of this fugue, but, honestly, Emma, I don't think he ever will. I think he has something wrong with him that you can't fix. Maybe no one can. But don't you think he should get help from professionals? Don't you think you're being selfish by keeping him here in your house?"

Though my finger smarted from the bent nail, that wasn't the pain that brought tears to my eyes. Jake went to fetch me a plaster while I sat and stewed in the sourness of his words. Was he right?

Aiden stepped into the kitchen and silently moved around. He took bread from the cupboard and placed it in the toaster. He took the butter out of the fridge and a knife from the drawer, and he waited by the toaster staring out of the kitchen window as casually and as eerily as a sleepwalker.

"I hurt my finger," I said. "Jake's getting me a plaster. Are you having toast for breakfast?" I began to ramble again, and the more I talked, the more my voice started to crack. "It's weird without Denise or Marcus here making us cups of tea, isn't it? They've gone to the police station for a meeting. They're working really hard to figure out who took you. I wish you could tell me. You'd save a lot of people a lot of time and effort if you would talk to us. I know it's hard, sweetheart, but you have to try."

The toaster popped up and Aiden calmly removed the toast with his fingers. If the bread was hot, he didn't show it. He buttered the bread and placed the knife in the sink. I watched, with tears streaming down my face, as my mechanical son ate his toast without even acknowledging I was there.

Was Jake right? Was I being selfish keeping him at home?

CHAPTER TWENTY-NINE

Jake's words continued to play on my mind throughout the day. I ended up doing as he asked. I went into the nursery and I opened cardboard boxes of stuffed toys, and plastic wrappers filled with brand new baby grows. Carefully, I folded the tiny items and placed them in the shelves of the little wardrobe Jake had put together a month ago. It was only as I was collecting all the empty wrappers and boxes that I saw the doll Amy had given me.

There it was with its perfect porcelain skin, mocking me through the plastic. The worst thing about seeing that doll was that it brought all the emotions rushing back to me. I had been so grateful to Amy for buying that present, and I'd felt so strong and so ready to have this baby. Now all those feelings were absent, leaving me with confused rage that I didn't know how to direct. I wasn't excited to meet my new child, I was terrified. With Aiden here the balance had tipped. What was I supposed to do? How was I supposed to find enough love in my withered heart?

In a fit of rage, I drove my heel down onto the plastic and smashed through the porcelain. The crack was so sickening that I gasped and retracted my foot as quickly as I'd stamped it. When I backed away there was a tiny shard of the porcelain still stuck in the bottom of my foot. I hopped backwards and tripped, landing on my backside with a jolt. Instinctively, I reached around and cradled my bump with both hands. That was when I saw Aiden standing in the doorway watching me.

"Help Mummy up," I said. I don't know why I said it like that. I'd stopped thinking of him as a small boy a few days ago when I realised he was filling out after eating decent food and getting more exercise. But the way I laid sprawled out on the ground made a sense of desperation wash over me and I guess I couldn't help but try to endear myself to him by calling myself 'Mummy'.

He stared while I reached out. He stood five feet away in the doorway, watching, with the same impassive expression as always. Blank, like a doll. And yet... was there part of him that was mocking me? That empty expression with the slow-blinking eyelids. That straight line he kept his mouth in at all times. The way his hands fell at his sides, never gesturing, hardly ever moving. It was all designed to mock me. He was testing my patience. For some reason I was so sure that he was doing all this on purpose. Why did I think it? Why? It was an awful thought. Aiden had been through hell and yet here I was considering that it was all a guise to mock me.

"Aiden," I said. My voice deepened and took on a stern note. "Help me up. Take my hand, and help me up."

I already had a plaster on my finger and now my foot was bleeding from where I had cut it on that stupid doll. If Jake was here he'd admonish my clumsiness, telling me how I made him worry and how he hated to leave me alone, especially with Aiden in the house.

"Help me onto my feet," I pleaded. "I've fallen and I can't get up. Do you understand me? Do you understand what I'm saying?"

I growled under my breath in frustration as I rolled myself forward, trying to manoeuvre myself with an injured foot. First, I had to get the shard out of my foot. I needed both feet to get me back up. So I struggled to reach my own toes in order to pull the shard of porcelain out. By now the nursery felt more like a sauna than it did my house. Stringy, damp hairs clustered on my forehead. The maternity dress I was wearing clung to my back.

"If you'd just help me this would be a lot fucking easier!" I blurted out. Why wasn't he helping me? He understood other orders. He knew to shut the kitchen cupboard doors and to put his plate in the sink after dinner. He did anything Jake asked him to. He always listened to *him*. Why wouldn't he help me now?

Aiden took a step back as I finally reached the soles of my feet. Gritting my teeth, I gripped the shard with my thumb and forefinger and yanked it out, letting out a breath of both relief and pain. Then I threw the offending article away and lay down on the carpet to catch my breath.

He was still there a moment later when I examined the wound and determined it wasn't too bad. There was blood, but it would be fine with a rinse and a plaster. Some of it had got on the carpet, which was unfortunate. I'd need to clean that up before Jake came home.

I winced as I put the injured foot on the floor to help push myself back up. I huffed and puffed as I struggled, and all the time my son stood and watched. By the time I was on my feet I was fuming.

"Get out of my sight," I hissed.

That he obeyed. He scuttled down the hallway like a frightened spider. I shook my head. None of it made sense. Why wouldn't Aiden help me? After the frightening conversation I'd had with Jake there was a part of me wondering about whether Aiden actually intended to hurt me. Or at least to watch me suffer. Why else would he ignore my one request for help? I threw the thought away. Surely if he wanted to hurt me he'd just missed a perfect opportunity. I'd been helpless. Yes, he stood and watched me struggling without attempting to help, but he hadn't actively attempted to cause harm to my wellbeing.

I sighed. That sounded so messed up. I was actually pleased that my son hadn't attempted to harm me while I was vulnerable. Was this what my life had come to? Gratitude for not being strangled to death while I struggled on the floor like an upturned beetle?

I limped into the bathroom and rinsed my foot in the bath before finding a plaster to apply to the cut. Though I wasn't a medical expert I felt fairly certain that it didn't need stitches and hoped that the bleeding would stop when the plaster was affixed. Then I went downstairs to collect cleaning products to wash the carpet. I was alone with Aiden that day. With the media finally beginning to leave us alone, and the police more interested in the duke than Jake, the need for the family liaison officers being around us throughout the day wasn't as great. I was glad of it, and I believed they probably were too.

When I went back upstairs, Aiden was in his room. I paused for a moment, but then I decided to pop my head in and see what he was doing.

Nothing.

That's what he was doing. Nothing. Not watching a film on the small flat-screen TV we bought for him. Not drawing using the nice pens and pencils that cost me a fortune in the arts and crafts shop in the village. He certainly wasn't reading any of the books Jake gave him, or even throwing the ball Rob had brought him. He was sitting and staring out of the window.

"What do you see out there, Aiden?" I asked. "Is it him? Is it the man who took you? Do you see him now? Tell me what he looks like. Tell me, please. Draw his face." I limped into the room, picked up a drawing pad from his desk and grabbed a pencil. I hurried across the room to where Aiden sat and took hold of his hand, forcing his fingers out of their tight fist to make him hold the pencil. "Draw him. I know you can. Ten years, Aiden. Ten years. You know his face. You know who it is. Draw him."

With a force I didn't know he had, Aiden ripped the paper from my hand, and threw the pad and pencil down onto the carpet. Then, silently, he stood up and walked away from me.

*

It took a good hour on my knees to get the stains out of the carpet. Afterwards, I collected up the broken doll, as well as all the empty wrappers from the many packages for the new baby, and tidied up the nursery. It was perfect. We'd gone for striped yellow wallpaper with a border of farm animals. The cot was made of pine, and nestled inside was a tiny mattress and a soft white blanket. Above the cot hung a mobile of colourful stars made out of glittering metallic fabric. Before Aiden had returned, Jake and I had spent a fortune on matching the nursery curtains with the wallpaper and carpet, as well as setting up the perfect wardrobe and a high-quality changing table.

I stood in the same spot Aiden had watched me struggle to get up from the floor and I breathed a sigh of relief. It was done. The room was ready for the new arrival. I stroked my stomach and breathed in the smell of the new room. The cleaning product had lingered, but underneath I could smell the plastic scent of new furniture. It was a pleasant and fresh smell. The room was airy and bright with a large window letting in the sun. I closed the door and started on that night's dinner. We'd been living on convenience food for the week: fish fingers and breaded chicken cooked from frozen, with oven chips and ketchup. Today I decided to make a stew with some beef Jake had brought home from the butcher's the day before.

The air was fragrant with rich stock and bay leaves by the time Jake came home.

"Well, isn't this a sight. My wife barefoot and pregnant in the kitchen," he teased.

"Don't get used to it," I chastised, though it was nice to do something special for him for a change. I'd been so confused by Rob's return to Bishoptown that it was nice to feel like a wife again. Though I would never conform to social stereotypes — especially not sexist ones — it was reassuring to have a role again. Wife. Better than 'failed mother'.

"Did you get the nursery sorted?" he asked.

"Oh, Jake, it looks so pretty. I'd forgotten how

beautiful the wallpaper was."

"Yeah, and it should be. It cost a fortune! I'm going to nip up and have a look before tea's ready."

Like an excited puppy, Jake bounded out of the kitchen and up the stairs. I smiled to myself as his heavy footsteps hit each board. It was nice to see him excited about the baby again. There was a time I had worried that he'd changed his mind about having kids, especially when he became so freaked out about my pregnant body. But here he was, bouncing around, hardly able to wait to see the finished nursery. It was nice. It reminded me why I loved him.

"Emma!"

The urgency of his voice made me drop the wooden spoon into the stew. Beef gravy splattered across my chest.

"Emma, come here!"

My stomach lurched. What was wrong? Jake sounded upset. No, he sounded angry and… what? Afraid? I hurried away from the oven with my heart pounding. What was happening? My breath came out in ragged gasps as I limped up the stairs. I struggled on my injured foot down the hall and into the nursery.

"What the fuck happened?" Jake said, pointing down at the cot.

"I… I…" There were no words.

"Still think it's safe to bring a newborn baby back to the house with *that boy* living here?"

"I…" Why couldn't I speak?

Jake stormed out of the room, leaving me to stare down at the destroyed mobile. It had been cut up with scissors and strewn across the brand new blanket. And across the white blanket was a spray of red paint that mimicked blood all too well.

CHAPTER THIRTY

The day of the flood was the day I had realised that my life was not under my own control. So you would think that no matter what happened, I would be able to cope with the idea that I can't control the world around me, only myself. But I don't think that anyone can deal with that. Maybe after hours of meditation you might be able to convince yourself that you're at peace, but I'm not sure I can believe it. Staring down at the red paint splattered all over the brand new crib for my unborn child, I realised once again that I was not in control of anything, especially not my son.

It took some convincing to get Jake to go to work on Monday morning. The truth is that I wanted him out of the house. He'd spent the night tossing and turning, pulling the duvet angrily around him, sighing and leaving his unspoken words dangling between us. There was no way I wanted him around Aiden in that mood. It'd be like pouring water on a chip-fat fire.

Despite everything Jake had said, I still didn't want to send Aiden away. His accusation of my selfishness hit me hard, but the more pressing issue was of control, again. If Aiden was with some psychiatric care facility, I wasn't able to control what happened to him. In my mind, I pictured him in a room with psychologists, going through test after test, pointing at their silly cards, ignoring repetitive questions, taking their numbing pills, and worse—becoming the subject of their latest book. No, I couldn't let that happen to Aiden, but I didn't want him to hurt the baby either.

After breakfast, I leaned across the kitchen table and took his hands in mine. Aiden still wasn't particularly keen on being touched, but he had learned to tolerate it better. He didn't squirm or flinch like he used to, and he was more allowing of me touching him than anyone else. If Jake or Rob touched his shoulder, no matter how lightly, he would move away from them.

"Aiden, I know you understand that in one week I'll give birth to your sister. I don't know what happened in the nursery. Did my fall frighten you?" I shook my head. "It doesn't matter. Look, I want you to know that your little sister is going to love you very much. We all love you very much. Me, your dad, Jake, Grandma and Grandad, we're all one big family. I want to show you something." Obediently, Aiden followed me up the stairs, moving with his usual stiffness. I kept glancing behind me to read his facial expression, but there was nothing.

More than once I imagined him grabbing my shoulder and pulling me back. More than once I picked up my pace, desperate to get to the top of the stairs to the corridor where I felt less vulnerable. I hated myself for thinking those thoughts.

"Remember yesterday, Aiden?" I asked, leading him into the nursery. "I fell over and you wouldn't help me up. Well, that's not very nice for one person to do to another person. We should always try to help each other. So if you fell down, I'd help you back up. If I fall, you should help me. Especially seeing as I'm pregnant at the moment." I smiled down at my bump, but Aiden's gaze didn't follow mine. I cleared my throat and continued. "This is difficult to talk about, Aiden, because I don't know why you did it. Why did you destroy the mobile and throw paint into the crib?" I moved away from the offending area so that he could view his handiwork. "That's not a very nice thing to do at all. That's not welcoming your baby sister to the home. Are you listening, Aiden? I can't tell if you're listening..."

I stopped speaking. For the first time since he had arrived back from the hospital, Aiden was frowning. There was a line forming between his eyebrows and his face was angled down at the crib. Slowly, he shook his head and backed away.

"Aiden?" I whispered.

He ignored me as usual, but this was different. He was absorbed by the sight of the broken mobile and red paint. He seemed frightened of them. A tingling sensation snaked up my spine and the blood drained from my face. Why was he so afraid of what was in that crib? He'd done it. So why did it frighten him?

And then it dawned on me: He didn't remember doing it.

*

Spooked by Aiden's reaction to the red paint (although I didn't want to admit it at the time) I called Rob and asked him to come over. He brought his parents with him and they sat with Aiden watching a silly comedy film in the living room while I shared a pot of tea with my ex. He seemed tired today. Rob was generally an attractive man, but a little tiredness actually worked in his favour. Some stubble and eye-bags made him sexier, though I tried my hardest not to remember.

"Did you read Amy's article?" I asked. We'd already discussed Aiden's progress, though I decided not to tell him about the crib, and we'd exchanged pleasantries in the presence of his parents. *The weather has turned quite mild for this time of year, hasn't it? Unseasonably warm. Makes you wonder if there's going to be a storm to clear it all away.*

"I did." His uncharacteristically laconic response

made me wonder if he was holding back.

"And? Tell me what you thought."

Hunched over his tea, Rob had to lift his chin to look at me. "You're not going to like it."

"Just say it."

"I think she was right."

I exhaled in a rush. "What?"

"Hear me out, okay? Don't go jumping to any conclusions. I know you'll take that to think I'm calling you a bad mother."

"I didn't think that until you just said it."

"Oh. Well, anyway, I don't think that." His face flushed pink. He took to staring at his tea again. "It's just… some of it rang true. Aiden was a little wild. We both thought that was a cool thing. He was a brave kid, an active kid. I loved the fact that Aiden could climb a tree and played in the garden all day collecting spiders. I dunno if it's some stupid macho thing but it made me feel good that he was a boy's boy, you know?"

"Yes," I answered. "And it is a stupid macho thing."

His eyelashes flitted apart so he could roll his eyes at me. "What Amy said was mean-spirited and nasty. She was implying we'd let Aiden down and I don't think we had."

I bit my lip because there was a question I wanted to ask, but every time I thought it, tears pricked at my eyes and I was afraid that my voice would crack. "Was Aiden a bad kid?" The weight of the question lifted from my shoulders and I let out a long, slow breath.

"No, Emma, no. He wasn't a bad kid. He was a little bugger when he wanted to be. I don't think it was ever malicious, though, do you?"

I shrugged my shoulders, trying to ignore the way I'd begun to tremble. My entire body worked on stopping myself from bursting into tears. The pressure of taking care of my damaged son was getting to me. The exhaustion had seeped into every one of my muscles, but I wouldn't admit it at the time. Looking back now, I know I should have asked for more help, but I was stubborn, and I was determined to try and keep in control. The problem was that in trying so desperately to stay in control, I couldn't see that I was destined to lose it.

"Do you remember that camping trip to Brittany?" Rob asked.

I nodded, still gripping my tea to stop my hands from shaking. I was only half listening to him at this point.

"We went with Josie and Hugh. Oh boy, the hours of driving with Aiden cooped up in the car. I thought my eardrums were going to burst. Hugh had brought that huge tent with the little windows and the open porch bit at the front, and we ate nothing but sausages and beans for the week. Anyway, do you remember that prank Aiden pulled on the German couple two tents down?"

I shook my head. The entire week was a blur. Josie and Hugh were beginning their rocky descent into a bad marriage, and Josie and I spent the week chugging Chardonnay. No matter how many times I tried to extricate myself from Josie's binging, she managed to pull me back in. Needless to say, Rob and Hugh were the responsible adults that week.

What I did remember was laughing. Aiden would stay up late with us at night and we'd sit around the campfire chatting about everything and nothing. Hugh liked to entertain the group, telling stories of his early years in an all-boy's public school. I'd put my hands over Aiden's ears as he told us about walking in on the other boys' improprieties. He had us in stitches telling us stories with funny posh accents and silly faces.

"Do you remember how the campsite had that stupid little flagpole with the French flag on it? The thing was about half the size of a normal pole. Well, Aiden stole a couple of bras from the German woman's tent and shimmied up the thing to tie them onto the pole. The poor woman was so large that those bras just started flapping in the wind."

"Why don't I remember this? Jesus, how old was he then?"

"Just over five," Rob said. "He was definitely a monkey."

Though Rob appeared to be delighted by his son's naughtiness, I didn't feel the same way. Why didn't I remember him acting like that? I had a highlights reel in my mind of Aiden being a sweet, intelligent little boy. But there was more to him. He could be naughty. He used to steal things when he was three. He'd grab chocolates from the supermarket aisles. But he didn't put them in our trolley. I once caught him sneaking them into a stranger's trolley when they weren't looking. I caught him at it, told him off, and forgot all about it until Amy's article brought some of Aiden's naughtier acts back to me. Was that normal behaviour for a three year old? I couldn't help but wonder if I was now actively trying to find examples of him being bad.

"Is everything okay?" Rob asked.

"Fine," I lied.

"How's Josie doing? Any news from Hugh?"

"I haven't called her." I finally let go of the mug to run my warm hands over my face. It was shameful that I hadn't been in touch with my best friend after her messy break-up.

"Why don't we look after Aiden for a few hours so you can go and see her," Rob suggested. "You've had Aiden 24/7 since his release. You need a break."

At that moment, a few hours away from Aiden sounded like pure bliss. As much as I wanted complete control over everything around my damaged son, I *needed* some time away from him. I needed room to breathe.

"Are you sure?"

"Absolutely."

I was already off my chair and searching for my car keys.

CHAPTER THIRTY-ONE

After a quick phone call, Josie told me she was in, and that she hadn't been at work for a number of days. Even though I'd asked her to promise me she'd go to work, I'd expected as much. In all honesty, if Jake left me without a word I wouldn't bother with work either. So I hopped into my car and drove across the village and up the winding hill towards the Barratts' home. It was warm enough to leave the house without a jacket, which was unusual for mid-October, and the blue sky above seemed almost superficial, or at the very least, fleeting. I was waiting for dark clouds to plunge us into darkness. While I'd been going through hell, the weather had mostly been fair and mild, belying my own stormy disposition.

Yet another way the world decided to betray me.

I took it steady around the narrow roads,

pulling in warily when meeting other cars.

The Barratt home seemed eerily serene when I parked the car. The mild weather meant Josie's yellow pansies were still in bloom in pretty pots around the front door. But my gaze did not linger on them. I found it difficult to look at anything beautiful during those weeks.

Josie answered the door after the first knock. Her large blue eyes were red-rimmed and I noticed that she clutched her mobile phone in one hand. She was wearing leggings and an oversized jumper.

"I'm so sorry I didn't come earlier," I said.

"Are you kidding?" she replied. "I'm ashamed for not coming to *you*. I mean, I know you said you wanted space and that you were fine, but still. With everything you're dealing with, my problem is tiny."

"Have you heard from him?"

Josie sighed and led the way through her house to the kitchen. Her messy bun bobbed up and down as she dragged her feet over the carpet. Her body was loose and lazy, but it almost seemed like an act, as though deep down she was in real turmoil. I knew her well enough to know that she dealt with stress by trying to pretend it wasn't happening, or at the very least pretending she was fine with it all. Josie was a 'fake it 'til you make it' person. She wanted to see the bright side, but I wondered whether, when she was on her own at night, it really worked.

"Nothing. Not even a text. But guess what? He posted something on Facebook."

"What?"

She nodded, gesturing to an open laptop on the breakfast bar. Hugh's profile was on the screen. For the first time I realised that he'd updated his profile picture. It used to be a photograph of him and Josie on a skiing holiday, but now it was a solo picture of him smiling on top of a jet ski. Next to his profile picture was a status where he had 'checked in' to the McCarran airport in Las Vegas.

"What?" I said again. "What on earth is he doing there?"

"I spoke to Steven again. Apparently he's not replying to any messages from the family. Steven admitted that he knew about the affair but not the extent of it all. I bet they're gambling through our money as we speak. Damn it, Emma, why did you have to be pregnant right now? I need a stiff drink."

"Hey, I won't judge you." I smiled. It felt good to talk about any other topic than the investigation with Aiden. "This all seems so out of character, though. Has he taken off like this before?"

"That's the thing," Josie said. Her eyes lit up with the glitter of anger. "Steven said that he *has* done this before, not that I knew about it. He took some receptionist to Cornwall for a dirty weekend." She uncorked a bottle of Malbec and began to pour.

"Fuck." I glanced around the kitchen searching

for evidence with how Josie was coping. Most people would be relieved that there weren't any Chinese takeaway cartons or dirty dishes in the sink. The place was pristine, which was somewhat disconcerting. Had the weight of her husband's activities truly hit her? "I'm so sorry, Jo."

She shrugged. "I knew it was coming. Deep down, I honestly think I'm relieved." She took a gulp of the Malbec. "Don't look at me with those big puppy-dog eyes. I know you think I'm going to go off the rails, but there's nothing to worry about."

"Are you sure, because—"

"It's all in the past." Josie set her wine glass down on the kitchen side with a finality that warned me not to delve into the murky past I was about to bring up. "Now, what can I get you? Herbal tea? Sparkling water?"

I groaned. "What I'd give for a nice gin and tonic. Or a measure of whisky." I lifted my fingers and pinched them together. "I was this close to opening a bottle of vodka the day Aiden came home. And then this week has got worse and worse. Did you see they'd arrested the duke?"

"Arsehole," she said with real venom. "Do you think he…" She swallowed, uncertain whether to say it or leave the implication hanging.

"I honestly don't know, and that's the worst of it. I just want the person who hurt Aiden to be behind bars. I want all of this to be over."

She nodded. "Well, I always thought he was a shifty fucker. Don't worry, Em. If he did it, the police will find the evidence and they'll put him away. What are they doing for the investigation now?"

"Well, apparently they're searching the surrounding area for any suspicious outbuildings or old shelters that could have been converted into a prison. But DCI Stevenson told me that there aren't always records for some of these old buildings, and the woods are really dense so it's hard going. Most of their resources have been taken up looking into the duke. It took them ages to search Wetherington and they're going through all the images on his computer." What I didn't say was that they were looking for images of Aiden on his computer. I didn't say it because it made me feel ill.

"They'll find him, Emma. I know they will." Josie reached across and took hold of my hand. She squeezed my hand and then leaned away, frowning. "Is there something else wrong? You seem a bit peaky."

"It's going to sound really stupid."

She laughed. "I bet it won't. Remember that time I thought Argentina was in Europe?"

"Oh yeah, *that* was pretty stupid."

"Can't be worse than that, can it?" she offered.

"It's Aiden. He's been acting really strangely recently and I'm worried."

"How do you mean?"

I settled into the stool at Josie's breakfast bar. "Well, I never expected him to be fine after everything he's been through. Of course he will have been affected by the trauma of what he's been through, but I'm starting to wonder whether I'm going to need help with him. Whether I can't cope. His behaviour has gotten a little... out of hand. First he decided to cut up the curtains with scissors. Then he cut up the mobile for the new baby and threw red paint into the crib."

"Oh shit, Emma. That's scary."

"I know. Jake thinks it isn't safe to bring a newborn home with Aiden here, but I just can't bring myself to send him away."

"Well, that's understandable. He was taken away from you."

"But I'm beginning to think that maybe Jake is right. Maybe I can't cope with Aiden and maybe I'm being selfish by pretending I can."

"Being selfish about what? Emma, you are the least selfish person I know."

"If I'm putting Jake and my unborn child in danger because I can't let go of my son, then that's selfish, isn't it?"

Josie swallowed another mouthful of wine. "I wouldn't say it's selfish. But if you're afraid of Aiden, you need to get some help. Jake might be right about it not being safe for your newborn with Aiden around. It isn't Aiden's fault and it isn't your fault. It's the bastard who took him's fault."

"Do you remember him having behavioural problems when he was little? I can only remember the good things, but maybe that's because of what happened to him. I think I'm blanking on anything bad because I can't stand to think about it."

Josie sighed. "Honestly? Hugh had more patience with him than I did. Don't get me wrong, he was a lot of fun, but he was a bit... tiring."

"And?" I prompted, sensing that there was something she wasn't saying.

"He was a bit moody, Em. He used to have tantrums quite a bit."

I frowned. I remembered him throwing a wobbly in a supermarket once but he was never *that* bad. I was getting to the point where I couldn't trust my own mind. Why did I keep pruning away the bad times?

An hour later I left Josie's house and made my way down the gravel drive to my car. The wind had whipped up, and it howled through the Rough Valley Forest below. I turned my head towards the second hill overlooking Bishoptown. There it was: Wetherington House, standing tall and proud above the village. At one time the village was owned by the Duke of Hardwick, though the family had sold much of the land since those days. The house had been closed to the public since the police inquiry, but I knew there was a good entrance at the rear of the property because I'd once snuck in with Rob. It was a dare we'd had while drinking Lambrini on the grounds of the house.

I got in the car and started the ignition. Butterflies tickled at my stomach, but I knew I needed to get some answers. Though I was filled with nerves, I tried my best to back out of Josie's drive carefully, and warned myself not to let my adrenaline take over like it had the day I went to the GP surgery. No, I needed to keep a cool head.

It was a short drive to Wetherington. The scene of Bishoptown spread beneath the hill in a patchwork of green fields and forest dotted with small cottages and local pubs. Who would think that a monster lived in this beautiful place? No one had suspected a thing, and that was the most dangerous aspect of this entire sorry story. No one had even an inkling until the day Aiden stumbled out of the woods. He had brought his own abuse to our attention, but he held the full story locked up tight inside.

If Aiden wouldn't tell me what had happened, maybe someone else would.

I navigated the twists and turns down the driveway towards the stately home. In order for this to work, I needed to make sure I knocked on the door of the private wing of Wetherington. I had no idea if the duke and duchess were even living in the mansion at the moment. Perhaps they had nipped up to a private residence in the Highlands, or a summer cottage in Devon. DCI Stevenson hadn't gone into much detail about the conditions of his bail.

I hesitated for a moment after lifting the handbrake. What was I doing? What if I was arrested? I scratched at the angry red rash between my thumb and forefinger as I worked up enough courage to open the door. This was for Aiden, but it was also for me. I needed to talk to *someone* who might have some answers.

Before I left the car, I pulled off my thick cardigan. I was already sweating. I didn't need the extra layer, even with the winds. The gravel of the back drive was difficult to walk on, especially when carrying extra weight at the front of my body. I was completely off balance and forced to stumble my way to the back door. But I got there without anyone telling me to clear off and I knocked on the old oak wood. Three raps.

I'd expected Wetherington to be something like Downton Abbey, with a butler ready to answer the door. That wasn't the case at all. A small, stooped woman with greying but neatly set hair opened the door. She looked me up and down, no doubt taking in my shocked expression, and her lips thinned to a tight line.

"Do you know who I am?" I asked. The words were strange coming from my mouth, especially given who I was facing, but then I wanted her to know. I wanted her to know who she was looking at.

"I do," she said. "You'd best come in."

CHAPTER THIRTY-TWO

As I followed the back of her tasteful cream cashmere cardigan, it struck me that I had absolutely no idea what to call this woman. Would I call her Duchess? Or would I call her Mrs Graham-Lennox? Or what about Maeve, her actual name?

"He isn't here," she said. "In case you were wondering."

The thought had entered my mind. As soon as I stepped foot over the threshold I'd wondered whether the man who took my son shared the same breathing space as I did. That was, if he *had* taken my son.

"I asked him to leave," she said, stepping through an ornate doorway into a small but beautiful little sitting room adorned with antique dressers and racehorse paintings. "I couldn't have him here in this house with me. Not after the things the police found on his computer. I'd shared a bed with that man for over fifty years, but not for another night. Would you like a cup of tea?"

"No, thank you," I said. Since entering the house I had found myself feeling more and more like the teenager who snuck onto the property as a dare with her boyfriend. I clutched hold of my bag and stared at the beautiful antiques like a child in a posh department store. I certainly didn't want to spill anything.

"Make yourself comfortable," she said, gesturing to a floral sofa with mahogany legs.

"Thank you for letting me come inside. I didn't expect you to."

She laughed as she settled into a red velvet armchair across from the sofa. "I bet you didn't." Her make-up was perfectly applied, with pink lipstick and a little rouge on her wrinkled skin. She sat with her legs crossed, and cut the figure of a woman holding everything together. "I wanted to meet you. I've wanted to meet you ever since my husband was arrested. I feel somewhat responsible, you see. Though I had no idea about the lengths of my husband's… obsession, I did have a suspicion that I constantly ignored." She moved her hand in a vague, swatting motion. "I never knew for certain, and I never knew *what* was wrong, but I always suspected that my husband had a dark side. This may sound extremely trifling after what you've been through, but you have no idea how much pressure I have been under to maintain certain standards throughout my marriage. Divorce was not an option for me fifty years ago. So even when I realised I'd married a dud, there was no going back."

"But if you thought he was a *monster*—"

"What is a monster?" she asked. "Is it a scary ghoul hiding behind the bedroom door? Is it some sort of beast with sharp fangs? No. Those things don't exist. Monsters are men and women just like us, and they have the ability to hide their true face. No, I didn't think I'd married a monster, I thought I'd married a homosexual. I never caught Edward looking at children in *that* way, I only knew that he wasn't particularly interested in me. We managed to continue the family line, but that was about it."

"And your kids?"

She shuffled uncomfortably and removed her glasses like she was stalling for time. "I've broached the subject with them. Neither remember him doing... anything." She closed her eyes and I realised that she had removed her glasses in an attempt to distract me from the fact that she was trying not to cry.

"If you didn't know, it isn't your fault," I said.

The duchess leaned back into the chair and let out a soft laugh. "And is that what the newspapers say about you? Oh, the mother is always at fault. So is the wife, really. Women are supposed to *control* men, isn't that how it goes? What's that saying again: 'Behind every great man is a great woman'. We're supposed to be the ones holding them up, or holding them back. Forget having our own lives. Forget our own careers and loves and losses. We're the matriarchs." She narrowed her eyes and clenched her hands as she said the word 'matriarchs'. Her body slumped forward, suddenly appearing exhausted. "For what it's worth, I don't think James ever touched your boy. He hasn't been particularly active for the last decade, riddled with gout and in remission from bowel cancer. My husband has not been a well man. If he ever has abused children—and I'm not certain that he has—then I would say it happened long ago. Long before your boy went missing." She had crumpled into herself, leaning over like a wizened old crone. The woman had aged a decade just speaking to me.

"Thank you for your time." I stood and collected my bag. For a brief moment I hesitated, searching for some words of comfort. I grasped at nothing.

The duchess did not watch as I turned around and left her crumpled up on the antique armchair in the middle of that vast, stately house.

*

Since meeting the duchess, there have been times when I see the shape of her body wilted forwards on that armchair in my dreams. She haunted me. After the investigation settled down, the Duchess of Hardwick would die less than three years after I met her on that mild October day. I attended her funeral, accompanied by Aiden. It was a quiet affair with a surprisingly small number of attendees. They talked about her strength as a mother and a wife, and how efficiently she had run the day-to-day workings of Wetherington House.

Her children decided to sell the house and the last I heard it was to be converted into a museum, with many of the antiques auctioned off at Wetherby's.

Her husband outlived her.

*

I'd left Aiden with Rob and his parents for longer than I'd intended to, though I didn't rush back. I needed time to contemplate Maeve Graham-Lennox's words. I pitied her and what she had been through. Families like hers weren't designed to deal with such gritty issues. For them this was *scandal* and it meant their high reputation ended up dragged through shit. Their reputation was everything. Would people still pay to enter Wetherington House? Perhaps they would, but there would be an air of morbid curiosity. 'This, ladies and gentleman, is the computer where the duke stashed his kiddie porn.' The more I thought about it, the more I realised that we *are* all monsters. Yes. Us. We're monsters. We enjoy reading about these stories. We're the voyeurs of human suffering.

As soon as I pulled into the drive at home, I had the tickling feeling in my gut that I get when something feels wrong. The front door was open, for a start. I parked the car, unclipped my seatbelt and hurried out of the car. I was almost knocked over by a blonde woman half-dragging a boy of about ten, who was crying and holding a bandaged hand. Rob hurried out after her.

"I'm so sorry about what happened," he said. He had to jog to keep up with the woman, and had his hands out in placation.

It was only after I'd had a moment to take in the chaos that I realised I recognised the woman as Siobhan Michaels. Her son, Billy, attended the Bishoptown Primary School, and she happened to work as a manager for Sonya and Peter's holiday cottage business.

"I hate to say it, Rob, but the papers are right. He's a menace."

"Who's a menace?" I snapped, moving into the turmoil.

Siobhan stepped around me. "I'm sorry, Emma. I think what has happened to Aiden is awful, but I don't think he's safe to be around children."

"Well, not right now, no," I said. "He's still healing after what happened to him. Rob, what the hell have you done?"

Rob's face was pale and sweaty. He was grimacing and his jaw was clenched. I noticed his eyes flitting around the yard, as if searching for reporters. "It wasn't my idea. I got ambushed, all right?"

As Siobhan climbed into her car with the crying

child, I grabbed Rob by the arm and forced him to look at me. "What did your parents do?"

"I think they were trying to help. They thought if Aiden had someone to play with, it might help his... development."

"What happened?" I asked, my stomach already sinking down to my knees.

"He stabbed the kid in the hand with the scissors."

I let go of Rob's arm and staggered back. "Fuck."

"Billy kept playing with the remote control for the television. He'd keep snatching the thing out of Aiden's hand. I told him to stop it, but it seems Siobhan has spoilt that little shit rotten because he wouldn't listen to me. The next thing I know, the kid is pulling on Aiden's hair. So Aiden picked up these scissors from the coffee table and stabs him in the hand. They were kids' scissors so they didn't do much. Just broke the skin a little." He rolled his eyes. "You'd think the kid had been shot from his reaction."

"Jesus, Rob. How could you think this would be a good idea?"

"I'm really sorry."

"Just get your parents and get out," I snapped.

"What?"

"I'm serious. You've done a shit job, here. It's time for you to go." I turned my back on him and stormed into the house.

CHAPTER THIRTY-THREE

After that incident I wasn't sure if Sonya was malicious or just an idiot. Somewhere in that thick-skulled head of hers she'd thought that inviting Siobhan over to *my* house would kill two birds with one stone. For one thing, it set up Rob with a woman who wasn't me. For another thing, it introduced Aiden to another kid, which I genuinely believe she thought was going to go down well and get her some brownie points as the perfect caregiver. Sonya's endgame was Rob and Aiden under one roof, with me free to be with my 'other family'. I was sure of it.

I didn't tell Jake about the incident with the scissors, and I especially didn't tell him about meeting Maeve Graham-Lennox. That, as far as I know, remained a secret between me and the duchess herself.

The next day—a grey October Tuesday—I had a

call from DCI Stevenson confirming what I already knew. The duke hadn't taken Aiden. The duke had been in hospital for long periods of time during the last ten years, there was no evidence of any kind of room that could have been used to keep Aiden captive, and he had an alibi for the day Aiden was taken. He'd been attending a shoot at a different stately home in Yorkshire with a lord who could corroborate his whereabouts. It all brought me back to the beginning. Who took my son? Who did this to him? Who broke him?

I no longer made picnics and pretended that we were eating on Mount Kilimanjaro. I didn't show him my favourite children's films and television shows, nor did I hold his hand if we crossed the street in the village. I certainly didn't talk to him like he was still the little Aiden I'd known ten years ago, if that boy had even existed. I was pulling away, though I didn't realise it at the time. Yes, the thought of Aiden's kidnapper still out there made me feel sick, and I wanted little more than for that man to be put behind bars—if it was a man. I remember being on the phone to DCI Stevenson, begging him to look harder. Who could it be? Who was it?

I was withdrawing from them all: From Jake, from Aiden, from Rob, and from everyone else. My dreams drifted between nightmares about Aiden's attacker, to nightmares about my parents' car accident, to disturbing but erotic dreams about Rob and Jake. Sometimes Jake wrapped his hands around my throat and squeezed until I couldn't breathe. I called DCI Stevenson over five times that Tuesday, leaving strange messages with some assistant at the police station: "Look into Brian who runs the White Hart", "Have you spoken to Jeff from the farm outside Bishoptown?" There had to be something in the farms. They were sprawling with outbuildings. It seemed like a genius idea; why hadn't I thought about the farms before? I even drove Aiden around the village to see if he reacted strangely to the buildings. Of course, looking back now it didn't make much sense. Jeff's farm was miles away from the woods so unless the farmer had driven Aiden to the woods and dumped him there, chances were he wasn't the kidnapper.

I started writing to Aiden as I sat in silence and watched him from the kitchen table. I angled myself so I saw him staring at the television set, watching people on daytime TV discuss matters they were unqualified to discuss, and I wrote to him to save myself talking to him. "When you were little you used to make cakes out of mud and throw them at Nana. She didn't find it as hilarious as you did though. Do you remember? And when you were four I read *The Call of the Wild* to you. A few chapters every night before you went to sleep. When you were a baby you were afraid of your own nappies! You'd cry *after* I took the nappies off, not before. A little older than three and you were obsessed with hugging everyone and everything even if they didn't want to be hugged: the leg of a random man in Costa; a tree in the park; the feral cat that roamed the village. You hugged them all and you didn't care who they were or where they came from. These are all the things I know." That was how I signed every letter, as a reminder to myself that I did remember his childhood.

"I know you," I whispered to myself.

But it was a lie, because I didn't know Aiden at all. He was an alien to me now. His abuse had made him a completely different person and I couldn't forgive myself for being so afraid of him, because it's victim-blaming, isn't it? Victims shouldn't have to explain their bizarre actions after trauma, but it's so difficult for the rest of us to understand why they behave in that way. If a grown woman is raped and she doesn't scream for help, why didn't she scream? That's what the jury can't get their head around. Why didn't she scream? Why won't Aiden tell us who took him? Why won't he talk at all?

The house was filled with unspoken words. My conversations with Jake had turned to pleasantries to stop us arguing about Aiden's presence in our house. He welcomed Sonya's offer to take Aiden with gusto, but I put my foot down. As afraid as I was of my son, I couldn't stand the thought of not seeing him every day. Besides, he was my responsibility, for better or worse. Mothers don't get to take back a child like it's a toy that isn't working properly. I needed to look after him to make sure he didn't hurt anyone. That rested on my shoulders.

And then, to top everything off, as I was sat at the kitchen table writing another of my manic letters to a son who was sitting a mere few feet away from me, I heard a voice I recognised. Amy.

The chair scraped against the kitchen tiles as I abruptly rose from my seat. I hurried into the living room and dropped onto the sofa next to Aiden. By this point I had virtually given up trying to protect Aiden from the media. He wasn't stupid; he knew what was going on anyway, or so I thought. Though he barely reacted to anything, I noticed the way his eyes scanned the headlines. Once I caught him flipping open a newspaper to a page plastered with his face. He didn't point or gasp or in any other way react, but I could tell that he understood what was going on.

I turned up the television. Amy sat with her legs pulled together and her hands resting on her knees like a prim little girl waiting to have her picture taken. While her expression was relatively impassive, there was a haughtiness to her chin that I recognised for what it was: anger. This Amy was nothing like the meek, mousy girl I had worked with for years, nor the girl I remembered from school. I thought about the way she had sobbed as she'd begged me for forgiveness after we thought Aiden had drowned. I remember the way her eyeliner had smudged all the way down her face. It was all phoney. This girl, this woman, in her two-piece skirt suit and deep blue blouse—an obvious choice to highlight her eyes—was an attention-seeking jealous bitch.

"Now, we've all been talking about the shocking case of Aiden Price," said the grey-haired male presenter. "Not only was Aiden declared dead three years ago, he was found walking the streets in a disorientated fashion, and police believe he has been held hostage for a *decade*. It truly is the most shocking crime, well, certainly that I've ever heard of, and possibly the most tragic, too. It's been hard to make sense of the nature of this crime, and it's sometimes difficult to quite understand the behaviour of both Aiden and his mother. We're joined here today by Amy Perry, a friend of Emma Price-Hewitt, and schoolteacher of Aiden Price. Thank you for joining us today."

"Thank you for having me, though I wish it was under less tragic circumstances." She beamed at the camera, revealing her white teeth. It was at that moment I realised she'd had work done. She'd had her teeth bleached before this interview.

"You've known Emma Price-Hewitt for many years, haven't you?"

"I have. We actually went to school together."

"And you were friendly?"

"We were, mostly," Amy said, glancing slightly at the camera. "Emma was a lot more popular than I was. We hung out in some of the same circles. Bishoptown-on-Ouse is a very small village, so everyone knows everyone."

"We know that Emma fell pregnant when she was eighteen. That must have been very difficult for her."

"Oh, it was," said Amy, as if she had any insight into what I was thinking and feeling at the time. "She would come to school with red eyes and smudged make-up. She was having a really tough time, I think."

"Do you think the stress of having a child so young impacted on Aiden as a baby?"

"I would say so," Amy replied, nodding along to the questions. "Aiden was a fussy baby. He would cry a lot whenever she walked him around the village."

Lying cow.

"And you were actually Aiden's schoolteacher, weren't you?" asked the presenter.

"That's right. I taught Aiden at ages five and six."

"Was he a well-behaved little boy?"

Amy paused. "Well, I wouldn't go that far. I would say he had a few behavioural problems. He was a very... energetic little boy with a great curiosity for life."

"In the article you wrote for *The Mail*, you mentioned that Aiden was quite a reckless little boy and that you didn't think he had been taught to stay safe."

"Yes, I believe strongly that he hadn't been taught how to protect himself. It's sad, really. I mean, I love Emma like a sister, and I would never accuse her of negligence, but you have to wonder… If she hadn't allowed Aiden to get so feral, maybe he wouldn't have wandered off that day, and maybe he wouldn't have gone with a stranger."

I stood up and walked around the room, squeezing my fists closed and unclosed. My pulse was racing and Amy's smug face had a huge target on her forehead. I wanted to smash that television screen, but I didn't. I needed to see what else she had to say.

"So our phone-in today is on the subject of making sure our children are safe. That's why we have child behavioural expert Raj Patel with us on the sofa. Please call on…"

I was dialling. I couldn't help it. I was dialling in to the show. I spoke to some runner for the show first. They told me to turn off the television before I went live on-air. I didn't tell them who I was. I lied and said I was Emily from Yorkshire. I waited for a few moments as my blood pumped so hard and fast I felt the pulse in my fingertips. Before I knew it, the presenter was introducing me.

"Emily from Yorkshire, what is your question?"

"My question is for Amy. Who do you think you are? Where do you get off blaming Emma Price when you're the one who was supposed to be watching Aiden when he was taken? He walked away on *your* watch, Amy, not his mother's. When children go to school, parents expect them to be taken care of—"

"—But teachers *aren't* parents. Children need to

be taught—" she started.

"Shut up, Amy. You lying cow. You sat there and you gave me that doll and you pretended to be my friend—"

"Um, who is this?"

"—Do you remember turning up to my house two months after Aiden was taken? Do you remember getting on your knees and begging my forgiveness? I wrapped my arms around you and I told you it was all forgiven, when I should have been driving a knife through your back like the one you've driven through mine."

CHAPTER THIRTY-FOUR

Maeve Graham-Lennox had talked to me about how normal men and women can wear a mask. Beneath that mask is the potential for any one of us to become a monster. I'd seen Amy's mask slip, and I knew she was as much a monster as anyone else. I hated her then. I hated her freshly dry-cleaned silk blouse and her newly whitened teeth. I hated her TV hair and proper pose. And I was absolutely convinced that she was the one who took Aiden.

I called Denise and DCI Stevenson, and I begged them to look at her again, but they told me she had been dismissed from the investigation. She had been accounted for during the storm. There was only a five-minute period while she was on her own, and it wasn't enough time to take Aiden to wherever his enclosure was. But still, I couldn't let it go. That woman had *transformed* into another person before my eyes. How long had that other person existed? How long had she been planning to go to the press with her story?

Jake thought I was crazy. "No one who took a boy and kept him locked up for ten years," he lowered his voice, "and did all that *stuff* to him, would ever go on TV and draw attention to themselves." Even Rob agreed, and he was generally suspicious of everything.

In the midst of all that angst, I still took Aiden to his therapy session with Dr Foster on Wednesday.

"How's Aiden getting on?" she asked.

"He's the same, really. No change."

"And you?" she asked.

"It's my due date in a week," I said. "So I have a lot to think about."

"But you're so small!" she noted. "When I was nine months pregnant I looked more like a cow or a beached whale. You're..." she trailed off and smiled—to cover up her mistake?

"Lucky?" I finished. "In some ways, I suppose."

"So. Are you all set?" she asked, changing the subject.

I frowned. "We've just got to put the crib together and then we'll be done."

"How has Aiden been handling the changes going on around the house?"

This was my moment to tell Dr Foster about the incident with the crib. But my maternal instinct held back. While I actually liked Dr Foster, I did not completely trust her. I certainly didn't want her to recommend that my son be taken away from me.

"He's doing okay. He's been in the nursery and he knows what's happening, but he still isn't talking so there's not much to report."

"And his drawings?"

Violent, I thought. So much more violent than before. He drew blood on steel, blood on leaves, blood in the crib... He had worn his red colouring pencil right down and his tube of red paint was down to the last drop.

"Same as usual." I glanced nervously across to where Aiden sat colouring on his own. Away from us. That was who Aiden was now—he was an outsider looking in.

"I have been thinking about Aiden, and I believe it's now time to look at some other options."

I sat up straighter. I hadn't been told about any *other options*.

Dr Foster lifted her hands in a calming gesture. "Don't worry, it's nothing too taxing, but it is important. I want Aiden to start seeing a speech therapist to help him. Now that he's settled into his environment, I think it's time for us to actively help him speak."

"Okay."

"It's been over two weeks and this level of mutism is unheard of. DCI Stevenson and I thought it was best that we push Aiden a little harder. Now, I don't want to push too hard, which is why I've suggested a speech therapist."

"I understand," I said.

"Good. I'll get my diary and give you some recommendations."

I scratched the rash on my hand and pondered over what Dr Foster hadn't said during our conversation. It was time for Aiden to talk, because otherwise we would never find out who took him ten years ago.

*

Bump was active that day. When your baby is kicking, the last thing you want to be doing is driving. I couldn't wait to get us home. When we arrived, Aiden disappeared into the garage and I sloped into the kitchen for a glass of water and a biscuit.

My phone buzzed. When I checked the screen I saw Rob's number. "Hello?"

"Emma, they've taken Dad in for questioning."

"What?"

He spoke quickly, in a breathless, panicked voice. I heard movement in the background of the call and imagined Rob pacing up and down, unsure what to do with his anxious energy. "The police asked him to go down to the station for questioning. They say they've been reviewing CCTV footage from the day Aiden was taken and they've seen him walking near the bridge ten minutes before the abduction."

"Are they serious?"

"I don't know what's going on. Maybe they

think he saw something, but it seemed... formal, like he was a suspect. Mum's going mad. It's so stupid, he only went down there to take some pictures of the flood. And how the hell would he keep Aiden locked away for ten years without any of us knowing?"

"Rob, try to stay calm."

"I'm so fucking angry, Emma."

"I know, but that isn't going to help anything."

"I need to go. Mum needs me."

I slumped into the chair at the kitchen table. Of all the possible suspects, I'd never thought to distrust Aiden's grandfather. The man was a walking bore. But... he was a birdwatcher and a carpenter. He spent quite a lot of his time outdoors in silly sheds staring at birds. If he could build a shed, what else could he build? A cage? I shook the thoughts out of my head. No. I knew Peter. He wasn't... But then I thought about how I'd known Amy. I'd seen how her mask had slipped, and now I knew her true face. What if the same were true for Peter?

I sipped the cool water and wished for something stronger. The baby moved, reminding me that it wouldn't be a good idea to open the bottle of brandy we had stashed somewhere. Another unwanted Christmas present we hadn't got round to throwing out.

Instead, I put my head in my hands, and tried to work it all out in my mind. I knew that Aiden had gone missing between 1:15 and 1:20pm. That was when Amy said she got distracted by the flood and left the classroom for five minutes. Only one of Aiden's classmates said they saw him leave, and that was Jamie, a little boy whose father worked in the GP surgery with my late mother. Apparently Jamie had asked Aiden where he was going, and Aiden hadn't answered.

At that time, Amy had been placing buckets under streams of water leaking through the roof along the school corridor. The head-teacher and the janitor were walking around the school building assessing each classroom. Jake was with Simon from IT looking for dry classrooms to relocate their students. According to those statements, none of them had time to take a child and hide him somewhere. I highly doubted they would have had time to take him deep into Rough Valley Forest either—though I didn't know for certain that was where Aiden had been kept captive.

If Peter had been alone for the longest amount of time out of all of them, maybe I couldn't trust my son's grandfather after all. I felt sick. I'd felt sick all throughout this process, but especially now. I ran my finger along the rim of the glass and tried to piece everything together. After a few minutes I called Rob, but there was no answer; then I tried Jake but was sent straight to his answering machine.

I got up from the chair and paced around the kitchen. My hands were red-raw from where I'd continued to rub them; hand lotion was doing nothing for me now.

This was all going on far too long. There's only so much pressure the human mind can take. I was reaching breaking point. I had been ever since that woman keyed my car. I'd been walking along a razor-sharp edge, barely keeping my balance. I just needed to hold on for Aiden. It was strength he needed, not weakness.

I decided to make something. Perhaps using my hands would help. So I went to the kitchen cupboards to take out a loaf of bread and make us both some sandwiches. I highly doubted either of us were hungry, but at least I'd be doing something. That was when I noticed the stack of letters on the end of the kitchen work surface.

We had a letter organiser, but with everything going on, the mail had ended up piling on the edge. Denise and Marcus hadn't been around as much, so Aiden's fan mail was going neglected. There were letters from all over the world telling me how sorry they were for what had happened to Aiden—though I also got letters from all over the world telling me I was a terrible mother and that I deserved to go to hell.

What caught my eye was the card from the post office. It was one of those cards that informed you that the incorrect postage had been placed on the letter. I would have ignored it—I didn't particularly want to pay for postage for another letter of abuse—but the card had the postcode of the sender written on the card. It was local. I put the post code into Google and it came up with the York College of Lifelong Learning. That was where Jake taught art history every Tuesday and Thursday. It was also where I'd requested a prospectus from, to check that Jake actually worked there. The woman on the phone hadn't known the instructor's name, only that he'd taken some leave, and the website had only listed the courses, not the names of the tutors.

I'd forgotten all about requesting the brochure, and now it seemed the incompetent woman on reception had underpaid the postage when sending it to me. I snatched up my bag and car keys and hurried through to the next room.

"Get your coat on, Aiden. We're going to the post office."

CHAPTER THIRTY-FIVE

Though there were dark clouds hovering above, the temperature remained unseasonably warm for October. As I drove through the narrow streets of Bishoptown village, I sweated in the thick jumper I'd worn over elasticated jeans. Aiden sat quietly next to me with his hands on his lap. Between us, 90s pop blasted out of the radio. I didn't ramble to Aiden like I used to. There was a pile of letters addressed to him in the drawer of the desk in the bedroom, but as far as us chatting went... it didn't.

When I think about this part of the ordeal, this moment in the crazy weeks that led up to my second child's birth, I wonder whether I'd lost hope. I think about it like that in a way to challenge myself and who I believe I am. Did I give up on Aiden? Perhaps I did, however briefly. Sometimes I think that giving up on a victim is unforgivable. Other times I consider the term 'lost cause' with more weight than I used to.

Since Aiden's reappearance, I'd avoided the post office. It was run, as all post offices seem to be, by middle-aged women and men so camp they'd fill the stereotype quota on a sitcom. In Bishoptown, though, I knew the names of all the post office workers. There was Sandra, with a son at Cambridge University. Everyone in the whole village knew Sandra's son was at Cambridge, bless her proud mother's heart. And Sam—a young guy in his twenties—who once gave me a recommendation for a good beautician to sort my eyebrows out. I hadn't experienced that level of passive-aggressive criticism since my mother was alive, but I took the damn number anyway. The two of them called themselves collectively 'San-Sam' as though they were two celebrities who had married and thus merged their personas into one behemoth of infamy.

Though San-Sam were kind at heart and generally pleasant, up until this point I had always sent Denise to the post office to sort out the mail, partly because the police were worried about any unpleasant hate mail, and partly because I knew they'd fuss over me and I wasn't sure if I could cope with that. However, I soon realised that I couldn't have been more wrong. When I stepped into the post office with Aiden next to me, the place went deathly silent.

I joined the back of the queue and tried to pretend that I hadn't noticed how the usual chatter of the shop had ceased as soon as I'd walked in.

The stuffiness of the small shop made me sweat even more, and I felt a trickle run down my temple. I wiped it away with the sleeve of my jumper and hoped I wouldn't have to wait too long. San-Sam were both at the counter, serving a customer each. I was third in the queue behind two OAPs I didn't recognise. If there was ever a group of people who were forgotten about in Bishoptown, it was the elderly. They rarely left the house, but when they did, it was as a pack. Strength in numbers. Unfortunately for them, we tended not to really *see* them unless they were in the way, like they were today. It was sad, and it was something I was aware of, but I had too much on my plate to worry about it any further at that time.

It was Sandra who was free first. I flashed her a wan smile, and led Aiden over to the counter. I couldn't bring myself to leave him in the car alone.

"I… umm… need to pay this postage." As I passed the card through the gap underneath the glass screen, I felt like everyone in the post office was watching me. I wiped my forehead again.

"Sure." Sandra took the card, glancing at Aiden as she scanned a barcode on the front of the card. "One pound eighty, please."

I had the change ready. I slid it through the gap.

"I'll just get the letter."

As Sandra walked away, Sam glanced over and gave a small half-smile. He opened his mouth to speak but then stopped. His gaze dropped to his hands and he drummed on the counter like he was trying to fill the silence. I was the only customer left in the shop, and awkwardness reached a new height. Luckily, Sandra bustled back to the front of the post office.

"Here you are."

"Thanks."

The envelope was thick, A4-sized, and slightly battered at the corners. I rammed it into my bag and began to leave with Aiden.

"Emma."

I turned back to face Sandra. Her mouth was flapping open and shut and I averted my eyes so as not to make the moment even more awkward.

"I'm really sorry about Aiden," she said.

"Me too," Sam joined in.

"Thanks," I mumbled, hurrying to leave the shop before the tears emerged from my eyes. My shrivelled heart twanged a little, like someone had plucked a taut string. That was something I never got used to: the overwhelming feeling you get with genuine concern or well-wishes. Most people are utterly fake. They don't care about you and they barely manage to hide it. Then you get people like San-Sam, who knock you over with a sudden burst of kindness, and it's so stupid because they only said 'sorry'.

I managed to pull myself together back in the car. I took the letter and ripped open the flap while Aiden sat watching me. At least he seemed vaguely aware of his surroundings for a change. There were times when he ignored whatever was going on around him.

The prospectus was thick, which surprised me for such a small college. How many courses did they offer? I flicked through to the arts and humanities section and found the page for art history. My eyes scanned down the page, searching for Jake's name. But when I found the course—art history on Tuesday and Thursday evenings—the name next to the module was not Jake Hewitt. It was David Brown.

I frowned and searched again. Had I got the wrong course? This time I trailed every single name with my finger, making sure that I hadn't somehow read the wrong name alongside the wrong course. No. There was no mistake, Jake Hewitt was not listed in the prospectus. I removed my phone from my bag and dialled the number for the college.

"York Lifelong Learning Centre, how can I help you?" It wasn't the same person; this time, it was a younger woman.

"Hi, I'm really sorry but I have an essay due in tomorrow and I've forgotten the name of my tutor. It's for art history on Tuesdays and Thursdays."

"Oh, that'll be David Brown."

"I could have sworn he was called Jake something. I must be going crazy, unless David is new?"

"No," she said. "He's been working here for eight years now. Same evenings, too. But there's a Jack Hawthorne who teaches Business Studies. Maybe you're thinking of him?"

"I must be. Thanks so much for your help."

"No problem."

I hung up with my heart pounding against my ribs. I dabbed at the sweat on my forehead and leaned back against the car seat. How was this possible? When I'd first rung the college, I hadn't truly believed it was possible Jake had lied to me about working those evenings. Why would I think that? It had just been to make sure. I'd ordered the prospectus just to double check. If I'd believed Jake was lying I would have called back, but I didn't. I didn't call back. Instead I'd forgotten all about it.

In a fit of rage I punched the steering wheel and let out a slow, deep growl of frustration. How could he lie to me? And why?

Aiden let out a tiny whimper and I quickly twisted my body in order to face him.

"Aiden, it's all right," I soothed. "I'm sorry. Mum is really sorry about that. She's just… I'm just…" I deflated forwards and placed my head on the steering wheel. "I got some news that shocked me. I didn't mean to frighten you."

I noticed that Aiden's hands had balled up, so I gently unclenched them by working his stiff fingers out with my own. Then I stroked his hair and let out a long sigh.

"Everything is going to be all right. I promise."

As I put the key in the ignition, I wondered whether that was a promise I could keep.

*

I went back to the house because I needed answers. Jake had been lying to me for years. He'd been lying since the very first day I met him. He'd *always* had that job. This wasn't something that had happened a few months ago; it was right from the very start. Every Tuesday and Thursday he worked at the college.

Aiden was happy enough to potter into the garage to work on his painting while I paced the kitchen, switching from biting my thumbnail to scratching the rash on my hands. The rash had spread out from my thumb across the back of my hand and down my wrist, and it was on both hands now. I raked my fingers through my hair and tried to calm the heat of anger as it spread over my body.

Without the television or the radio playing, the house stood silent, with only the sound of my own movements filtering through the rooms. The loaf of bread was still on the kitchen side where I'd left it. The butter was next to it. I put it away instinctively without really thinking about what I was doing. My mind was too busy trying to process the knowledge that my husband had lied to me.

My scratching spread from my hands to my neck, and then my forearms. Every part of me itched when I thought about the lies. I stroked my pregnant belly, trying to sooth the gurgling in my stomach. I felt sick.

Suddenly, I burst to life. This was crazy. I couldn't stay in this house. Moving as fast as I could, I hurried up the stairs and began packing. What the hell was I going to do? My husband was a liar and I was about to have his baby. I stopped and stared at the clothes in the suitcase. I'd made no plans for this situation. The only thing I could do was to go to Josie's house with Aiden and then think about what to do with Jake. Perhaps he could move out and I could take a little time to figure out where to go next. I knew Josie would tell me that there was no way I should move out of the house after he'd lied to me, but it wasn't my house to begin with, and honestly I didn't particularly like it.

It was his house.

The door opened and I froze. Jake was back.

I slammed the suitcase shut and stared at my trembling hands. At this point I knew there was no innocent explanation for him lying to me. Either he had been having an affair this whole time, or he'd been hiding a second life from me. The one thing I didn't know was whether that second life included kidnapping and abusing my own child.

I ran my hands over my hair and tried to remain calm as Jake shouted hello upstairs. I'd been so *sure* that Jake was innocent when the police took him in for questioning. They'd found nothing. He'd had a decent alibi. The police had questioned several men, so I'd thought nothing of it except that I was certain I knew my husband and that he wasn't capable of hurting a child like that. I was *certain*. But now... this lie. It was different. It changed everything and threw my entire home-life into question.

I didn't know what to believe. All I knew was that my son was downstairs with a man I could no longer trust. I gritted my teeth, hefted the suitcase, and began to drag it downstairs.

CHAPTER THIRTY-SIX

I lugged the suitcase down the stairs and left it by the front door. Then I hesitated, wondering whether to put my shoes on now or to see what happened when I talked to Jake. I scratched my wrists and tried to collect myself. This was going to be incredibly tough and I needed to be strong and calm. The baby kicked as I moved through the hallway into the kitchen, and I bit my lip to deal with the pain. Jake must have seen the strain on my face because he was next to me in an instant.

"What's wrong? Is it the baby?"

I shook my head, biting harder on my lip. I couldn't look at him, and I think he sensed that right away.

"Emma, you're white as a sheet. Tell me now. Have the police made an arrest?"

"You'd like that, wouldn't you," I said. "It'd get you off the hook." I clenched and unclenched my fists, still itching all over my body. I felt a flush of heat work its way up my neck. My entire body was hot and itchy and I wanted nothing more than to scratch every inch of my skin until it all came off.

"What the hell?" Jake took a step away from me and tried to get me to meet his gaze. I noticed that behind him on the kitchen counter was a new bottle of Scotch.

"Is that what you drink to numb the guilt?"

"What the hell are you talking about, Emma?"

I lifted the prospectus from the kitchen table and slapped it down on the counter in front of his Scotch. The glass rattled against the bottle as I flipped the page to the art history course. The spine was already bent in the appropriate place, meaning it took only a few moments to find the evidence of his lies.

"I'm talking about this, Jake. You've been lying to me since we very first met. All these years. Where did you keep him? Where was he?" I flew at him, with my claws out, my nails reaching for his neck. But Jake was quicker. He grasped me by the wrists and pushed me away.

I backed away from him, wide-eyed and shaking, while Jake snatched up the brochure and read the page. When he realised what I was talking about, the blood drained from his face and his jaw slackened.

"It's a typo," he said. But he also reached for the bottle of Scotch and began to unscrew the cap.

"No it isn't. I rang them. Twice. The college has never heard of you. Unless David Brown is some alter-ego you've dreamt up, you don't go to York every Tuesday and Thursday. You go somewhere else."

He poured a large measure of Scotch into a tumbler and drank it quickly. "You don't understand."

"Then enlighten me, because my son has been missing for ten years and I've defended you against people who suspected you. Now I find out you've been lying to me all these years and—"

"You think I took Aiden?" He shook his head and poured another large measure. "Fucking hell, Emma. Of all the… You actually think I'm capable of *that*? You think I'm a paedophile, do you? You're my *wife*, Emma. You're supposed to know me."

"I thought I did. But then I found out that you've been lying to me all these years. What am I supposed to think?"

Jake necked his drink and leaned over the kitchen counter, gripping the sideboard with his fingers. His knuckles turned white as I waited for him to answer me. I couldn't stand still, yet I barely moved. I found myself sort of rocking back and forth onto the balls of my feet like a runner psyching themselves up for a sprint. Anything to rid myself of the energy coursing through me.

"It's not what you think," he said.

"Then what is it?"

"I love you. I really do." He sucked in a deep breath, but still he didn't face me. Instead he stared down at his hands gripping onto the kitchen counter like he was holding onto a cliff ledge. "But I have other… needs."

Part of me didn't want to ask, but of course I needed to know. "What kind of needs?" I scratched at the hot, itchy skin on my wrists and waited.

"You're the only woman I've ever wanted to share my life with. To me, you are *the* woman. You are everything. You're so much kinder than anyone I've ever met. You're just *beautiful.* I fell in love with you the moment I saw you, but there is something inside me that craves a different… a different connection." He licked his lips and hesitated. "It isn't your fault. I'm… I'm dirty. I have an affliction."

My knees felt like they were going to buckle. Jake tried to help me into a chair, but I swatted his hand away and leaned against the kitchen counter instead.

"I think I'm addicted to sex." He pulled his hair forward over his face and dragged his fingers over his eyes and down past his stubble to his neck. "I have to meet with women and have sex with them. I've always had to do it." He began to cry. "I made up the excuse about the part-time job because I thought if I kept it to twice a week I would be able to, I don't know, manage it, I guess. I couldn't stop myself before I met you. When I helped you recover from that dark time, you helped me recover too. You were… everything to me." He tried to reach out but I backed away.

"Don't touch me." I snapped.

"I'd never hurt Aiden." His eyes were glistening from the tears, and his skin shone under the kitchen lights. "I'm a… fucking idiot, I know that. But I would never hurt him."

"How can I believe that?"

He covered the ground between us in an instant. "By looking in my eyes and knowing it's true!" He grabbed me by the shoulders. "How have we got here, Emma? We love each other. You love me. How can you even think these things?"

"Because people hide their faces. They hide them for years and years, even to the people who are closest to them. You've hidden this from me for years. How can I trust anything you say or do anymore?" I yanked myself free from the tight grip he had on my shoulders. "You're not the person I married, are you? You're someone else, and as far as I'm concerned that someone else could be anyone."

He took a step back and fingered the empty glass of Scotch on the kitchen side. "I have an alibi for the time Aiden was kidnapped. The other teachers saw me walking around the school."

"I know," I said. "Simon from IT, apparently, who got a little *confused* a few weeks ago until you went into the station and sorted it out. What did you do? Pay him off? The guy is a slimy shit, Jake, so I'm not surprised."

He rolled his eyes. "You still don't believe me."

I turned away. "I don't know what to believe anymore."

"Oh, come on, Emma. Do you really believe Aiden would live in this house if I really was the kidnapper?"

I faltered. "I don't know. He's not... I'm not sure he remembers."

"All the shit I've had to put up with. Teenage sons coming back from the dead. Ex-boyfriends taking up all your time. And I know you go gallivanting around town while I'm at work. You couldn't give a shit about me. I mean, come on. I'm the first person you blame when things get tough, and even when I tell you the truth you don't listen to me."

"I am listening. I just don't know what to believe or who to trust. You must see why, Jake. My life has been turned upside down over the last few weeks. I've been driven almost to insanity by the things that have happened. It's just... too much. I don't know where to turn."

"That's why I'm here." Gently, he spun me around to face him. "I'm here to help you get through all this. And I will be, I swear. I'm so sorry I've let you down. I never meant for any of this to happen."

"Is it true?" I whispered. "Have you really been sleeping with other women? Why? I'm not enough for you?"

His eyes welled with tears and his arms dropped down to his sides. He was hunched over like a broken toy. "You're everything for me. You really are. But... it's an affliction. I should have got help for it… I… I think I'm addicted to casual sex."

"My heart fucking bleeds."

Fresh anger worked through me and I needed to do something to use up all the pent-up energy. I paced back and forth in front of the kitchen table, pulling on my hair until it hurt. Why did all this have to happen now?

"I'm sorry, Emma," he whined. He was full-on crying now, with snot dripping from his nose. "I swear it. I'll never do it again. I'll go through therapy. I'll do whatever you want me to do."

"I want you to leave. No… forget it. I hate living in this house anyway. I'll go. I'll take Aiden and we'll go to Josie's for a few days. Then we can sort out what we're going to do going forwards. For fuck's sake, my due date is in a week. I'm having your child and you're fucking other women." As heat spread through my veins, I found a coffee mug on the kitchen table, snatched it up, and hurled it across the room. Jake ducked, and the mug hit the extractor fan above the stove, smashing into pieces.

"Jesus… if that had hit me…."

"It didn't."

"Emma, I don't want you to leave." The smashing of the mug had sobered us. Jake's crying had stopped and he spoke at a regular, low level. "I love you *so* much. You mean the world to me. I would never hurt Aiden. I'd never hurt a *child*, Emma. You believe that, right?"

I let out a long sigh and nodded. "I believe that

much, yes. I think, anyway. But I can't stay here, Jake. You've betrayed my trust. I can't have Aiden around someone I don't trust. Not right now."

"But we're having a baby. The crib is all set up. Our little girl is coming into the world soon. You can't just up and leave a few days before your due date. What about the baby, Emma? Doesn't she deserve to come into this world with all the comforts she needs?"

"I… I could have some stuff taken to Josie's," I said uncertainly.

"And what is Josie going to think of all that? The woman is infertile and you're going to bring a newborn baby into her home just a few weeks after her husband left her? That's pretty low, Emma."

"Fine, then I'll find my own place."

"Don't leave," he pleaded. "Don't break up this family. I know you love me. I can change. I will change for you."

"I can't trust you anymore," I whimpered. I was tired. So tired. I sank down into one of the kitchen chairs.

"I can't live without you." Jake poured another glass of Scotch and drank half in one go. His eyes and nose were wet from crying. His skin was pale and there were red rims around his eyes. He seemed older. "I just can't. You're everything to me, Emma."

I flinched. "Don't say that."

"Face it, without each other we both have nothing. Neither of us have any family, not that count any—"

"I have Aiden."

"I'm sorry, love, but he doesn't even speak to you."

"Stop it, Jake."

"You have to face the fact that he isn't the boy you thought died all those years ago. Aiden isn't that boy anymore and I'm not sure you'll ever connect with him again."

My chin began to tremble. "Don't say that."

"Emma, we need each other. We need to stay together for the baby."

I was so tired. I didn't want to fight anymore. I just wanted it all to stop.

"Don't leave me, Emma. I'll go to counselling. I'll get help. This will all work out. You'll see. I promise."

CHAPTER THIRTY-SEVEN

No one wants to believe they are weak, but we all have weakness inside us. We have strength, too, but there are times when the circumstances in our lives are so overwhelming that we easily succumb to that weakness. Jake wore me down that day. I was so tired I couldn't fight anymore, and yes, I felt trapped. What he said about Josie did hit me hard. She was my best friend and I hadn't thought about what it would do to her to have a newborn baby in her home. My parents were dead. I didn't have my own home. I was one week away from the due date for the birth of *our* child. I was emotionally drained, physically weak, and easily swayed by what seemed like the easier option at the time. I stayed in the house with the compromise that Jake slept on the sofa. The next morning, I waited in the bedroom pretending to be asleep until he left for work.

I wiped my eyes, took a shower, dried my hair,

and dressed. I plugged in my phone, which had died while Jake and I had been arguing until late into the night. Then I checked on Aiden. He was up, making himself some toast.

"Morning," I said, attempting to inject some brightness into my voice. "I hope we didn't frighten you last night. Jake and I had some things to discuss and it got a little heated. I know you were working hard on your painting so I don't know what you heard, but we should probably talk about it. Jake and I are having some problems. He's made some mistakes and I said some horrible things, but we're both adults and we're going to work through them. We might even have therapy, like you do, Aiden. We want to move forward as a family."

The more I spoke, the more I worried I was trying to convince myself rather than him. I shook cereal out of the packet and ignored my trembling hands. I swallowed two of my blood pressure pills with a glass of water and sat at the table with my silent son. If he was in the slightest way perturbed by what had been going on, he didn't show it.

When breakfast was over, I went upstairs to make a start on putting the blankets inside the new crib. After Aiden's paint incident we'd bought an entirely new crib. We could probably have washed most of it away, but there was something about seeing the red paint splattered across the baby's blanket like that. It made me want to buy a new one just to rid my mind of that image. So we did.

And I decided to keep Aiden out of the baby's room.

That was as far as I'd allow myself to think that morning. Though my due date was looming, there was so much going on that I decided to block out my worries about Aiden around the baby. Did I trust my son? Did I believe that he was dangerous? Those were the kind of questions that played on my mind when I allowed myself to think for too long. If I admitted those things then it led down a road I didn't want to tread. It meant giving Aiden up. I couldn't do that. I had to believe that everything would turn out okay somehow, but that belief waned by the day.

After spreading out a soft baby blanket I went back to the bedroom to straighten up the bed and sort out some washing for the machine. While I was there, I checked on my mobile phone charging up next to the bed. I had five missed calls and a two voicemail messages.

The first was from DCI Stevenson asking whether Aiden had made any progress. He usually made that call once every couple of days to 'check in', or, when the family liaison officers were with us all day every day he'd check in with them. I felt bad for DCI Stevenson. He was a good man trying to do his job under extraordinary pressure. But the fact was that after two and a half weeks of investigation, he had come up with nothing.

The second voicemail was from Rob. I sat upright when I listened to the message. Then I quickly unplugged my phone from the charger and made my way downstairs. The message said: "Emma, it's Rob. Dad has just been released. They didn't find any evidence. They searched the house and there was nothing. He didn't do it, I know that and you do too, probably. That's not the main reason I'm calling you. Look, I didn't want to say this over a voicemail, but you're not answering and you need to know. I don't trust Jake, you know that. Well, I've been following him for a while. He keeps going to some garage outside Bishoptown near the A59. There's something dodgy about it all. I'm not saying that he's hurt Aiden, I'm not saying that... yet. But I think we should go and see this garage and figure out what's going on. No police. Just you and me. Drop Aiden off at my parents' place and come meet me."

*

It was Peter who answered the door, though I'd been hoping it wouldn't be. I offered him a thin smile. "I'm so sorry you were questioned by the police like that."

"It's all right," he said, ushering me in. "They've questioned everyone else. I'm just sorry I never saw Aiden. I had no idea I was so close to where he was taken. If only I'd seen something. Anyway, they've cleared me from the investigation now. Apparently the CCTV footage went on to show me taking pictures at the time they suspect Aiden was taken.

Why they couldn't check all that before holding me for hours I don't know. It's that duke they should be questioning. I don't like the look of that fella."

"Me neither," I said. "Is Rob around? He thought it might be a good idea for you guys to watch Aiden while we check something out."

"Yes, and he was just as vague. I hope you're not getting yourselves into any trouble?" Peter walked beside me as we made our way through the front of the B&B to the living quarters behind the main reception.

"No, nothing like that." I hesitated outside the door into their personal rooms. "Listen, Peter. This is hard to say, but I need to say it. Can you make sure that Sonya doesn't do anything without getting my okay? She had another child visit Aiden last time and it didn't go so well. He isn't up to playing with other children just yet. It's all a delicate balance and I need to be sure that Sonya isn't going to—"

"Upset the apple cart?"

I let out a sigh of relief. "Exactly."

"I'll keep her reined in, don't worry," he said.

"Thanks, I appreciate it." I paused. For a moment I was going to tell him that I never suspected he could have hurt Aiden, but that would have been a lie. There had been a moment where I'd sat down and thought about whether Peter could be capable of kidnapping, imprisoning, raping, and torturing my own son. The truth is, I had thought that it might be possible, just as I had thought about virtually everyone in my life being capable of such an act. As we walked into the back rooms of the B&B, I felt sick to my stomach with the realisation that I presumed everyone guilty.

Whoever did take Aiden had won. He'd broken Aiden to the point where he was an empty shell, and he'd turned me into a suspicious, anxious woman. I attempted to rearrange my face to hide these thoughts from the others, but Rob was the first to frown at my fixed grin.

Nevertheless, we settled Aiden and left the B&B. I was on edge, scratching my hands and my temples. I didn't want to leave Aiden with them, but I knew we couldn't take him with us. We made our way back out of the B&B and headed to Rob's truck.

"Are you all right?" he asked as I climbed into the passenger's seat.

"I've been better."

"What's happened?"

I pulled the seatbelt across my body and clipped it in place. "There's something you need to know. Whatever Jake has at this garage it might not be what you think. I found out yesterday that he's been lying to me. He's been meeting women and having sex with them."

"What?"

"I know. I'm… I'm in shock, too. I… Look, can we just get on with this? Why aren't we going to the police anyway?"

"Because they already think I'm an idiot. I'm

aware that this whole thing might be nothing and that's why I wanted to bring you along. I'm not wasting their time if he has some secret motorbike in there or whatever. And I want you to see it too so I have someone to back me up. Besides, they'd need to get a warrant or whatever, and God knows how long that would take."

"It's probably some awful sex room." I shuddered. "Full of porn and sex toys. He says he's an addict."

"Fucking hell."

"Don't say anything more. Just drive. I can't… I don't want to think about it, and I need to know what's in that garage."

Rob started the engine and the radio came on, blaring out Katy Perry. He apologised and turned the volume down as he pulled out of the B&B carpark. He had the radio tuned into a local station as we made our way out of the village and out towards the A59. Neither of us spoke, and we barely heard the radio, but there was some sort of talk about a storm hitting the Bishoptown area.

The baby was unsettled that day. I rubbed my pregnant belly and tried to calm myself down. Stressed mothers produce stressed babies, or so they say. With my due date approaching, I needed to think about my own wellbeing more than I had been. That wasn't an easy task given what was going on around me.

Rob's old truck thrummed with the sound of rain as it began to spill down from the dark clouds above. There wasn't a single part of the sky that wasn't grey or dark. There was no blue whatsoever. No sun. No light. I pulled the collar of my coat higher and tried not to think about the threatening sky.

We pulled into the storage centre in grim silence. Before clambering out of the truck, I pulled the hood from my coat down low over my face. Rob used a baseball cap to protect himself from the rain. We hurried along a long line of garage doors until Rob stopped.

"It's this one. Number 29."

"How are we going to get in?" I asked. "We can't break in."

"I have a mate who works here. Remember Fletcher?"

I groaned. "You mean your weed dealer?"

"The very same. Anyway, he owed me, so he's left the door open for me. Look, if anyone finds out, we say that we heard something inside and the thing was open anyway, so…"

"Just get it open, Rob. Careful of fingerprints, though."

Rob pulled on a pair of leather gloves. "Way ahead of you."

The garage door opened with a rumbling rattle that sounded uncannily like thunder. The pouring rain was cold, leaving a chill on my skin so that I was glad to duck under the doors and into the garage.

"What the hell?" Rob said.

I pulled my hood away to glimpse the filled garage. What I saw took my breath away. It wasn't anything at all like I had expected, and I admit, I had already considered the worst. I had thought of a terrible soundproofed dungeon for nefarious activities. I'd thought of a place dedicated to a sex addict, covered in pornography with a dirty mattress pushed against a wall. I'd thought of it all, and yet I was still surprised.

There was one element that I had guessed correctly: The garage was filled with pictures, but they were not pornographic—at least, not all of them. Most of the pictures were paintings. There were dozens hanging from the walls, and in between the portraits were small photographs all with the same subject... me. In the middle of the garage was an easel with a desk stacked with paints. There was also a tall filing cabinet shoved against the wall.

I walked across the garage and stood close to the wall, taking in all the photographs of my face. There were pictures of me walking through Bishoptown, sitting on a park bench feeding the ducks, carrying shopping bags home, getting off the bus. None of them appeared to be in chronological order, they were all jumbled up along the walls. In some I had Aiden's small hand in mine. Here we were throwing pebbles over the bridge into the Ouse. There we were sitting in the park eating sandwiches. Me stood at the bottom of a tree gazing into the branches at my monkey-like child. Me wandering through the streets of Bishoptown with my make-up spread halfway down my face, bags filled with bottles of Pinot Grigio. And then, the most disturbing of all: me getting on the school bus. Me dressed for the school prom, with Rob on my arm (though Rob's face had been scratched out).

"Look." Rob pointed to a large portrait in the centre of the back wall. "You're wearing the school tie. That was before sixth form. We didn't have a uniform in sixth form."

And then it hit me. Partway through our argument the night before, Jake had admitted that he had fallen in love with me *the first time he had seen me*. I was in school the first time he'd seen me. He was a teacher.

"Oh Jesus."

"Emma, I'm so sorry. I didn't expect any of this."

"What did you expect?" I whispered.

Rob didn't answer, and I was too distracted by the pictures to listen anyway. It was the paintings that disturbed me the most. He'd mostly painted my face. They were intricate portraits, almost photo-realist in style, with my features captured perfectly. In one of the paintings I was clearly sleeping, with my hair flowing out behind me. On its own I would have considered it a beautiful and flattering surprise, but as it was part of this disgusting invasion of my privacy, it was creepy and made my skin crawl.

"Don't scratch your hands," Rob said. He reached into his pocket and pulled out a pair of thin plastic gloves, the same sort that surgeons wear. "Put these on. We can't leave any DNA. This is a crime scene."

I was about to ask why, but of course, I was the crime. He stalked me. He took pictures of me when I was a minor. Some of them were definitely provocative. I might not be naked, but I was bending over wearing a short skirt, or spilling out of my school shirt. I wanted to run away from that garage and immerse myself in scalding water to get the stink off me. I'd been violated.

"Let's see what's in the filing cabinet," Rob said.

He was gentle now. It wasn't like Rob to keep from erupting in a stressful situation, so I knew it was for my benefit. He knew that things were more complicated than Jake being a 'bad guy'. I was carrying his baby. We were linked, however disgusting that felt.

"I don't understand any of this," I said in a quiet voice. "If he was so obsessed with me why was he sleeping around with all those women?"

"I'm not sure he was, Em," Rob said. "I think he came here instead."

"But why? He had me. I was married to him."

Rob didn't answer so I began to look through the stacks of paintings piled along the floor, while Rob opened the filing cabinet. I gasped. These paintings were even worse than the ones on the wall. Jake had painted me in sadistic ways. In most of them I was naked or scantily clad, with my hands tied up and a ball gag in my mouth. There wasn't any hint of desire in my eyes. He'd painted me afraid. His fantasies saw me as a reluctant slave; an unwilling participant in his games. This was all about dominating me. But he hadn't been like that in our relationship at all. He was... controlling, yes, I can look back on that and recognise it for what it was. He found me the job at the same school where he worked. He owned the house and the car. He was finicky about what was in our home. But he was never sadistic. He never hit me or even tried anything daring in the bedroom. Why did he need these bizarre pictures?

I was beginning to understand Jake's true addiction. It wasn't sex, it was fantasy. It was ownership. What was better than putting a child inside me? I thought back to the day I'd found out I was pregnant. I'd blamed it on a cold making my birth control pill less effective, but what if... what if Jake had tampered with it?

A cold stone of dread sank to the pit of my stomach.

"Emma, come and look at these."

I left the paintings the same way I'd found them and walked over to the other side of the garage to see what Rob was looking at. He'd found a large binder inside the filing cabinet. He lowered it so I could see what was inside. At first I didn't want to look, but then I forced myself to.

"It's another girl," said Rob. "Remember when

the press got hold of that photo of Jake with a student? That's the student. There are a ton of pictures of her in here." He flipped the page and I gasped. The girl—pretty and dark-haired—was naked on the next page. "Fuck. He lied. He did have a relationship with her." The pages flipped, showing more and more photographs of this young girl in shockingly vulnerable poses. I knew then that her slightly bemused expression would haunt me forever. The poses were brash and confident, but her expression was one of complete insecurity. "He took advantage of her. Fucking arsehole. Look, he has two or more copies of some of these. He kept them as leverage, I bet. To make sure she didn't tell anyone. I bet the bastard threatened to show people." Rob slammed the file shut and a USB stick fell onto the floor.

I picked it up. "I don't even want to know what's on it."

Rob shook his head, then dug out a bunch of letters held together with a rubber band. He pulled the top one out and began reading. "'I miss you so much. Please call me back, Jake. I want to see you. I'm so frightened that people will find out what happened and we'll get in trouble…' Shit. It's from the girl. And this is post-marked a week ago. He's still in touch with her. I bet he keeps her as his little pet, hanging onto every word he says."

I wanted to collapse onto the ground. I wanted to stop and let the weight of the world push me down until I was nothing. But I didn't do any of that. I searched through the filing cabinet with Rob looking for more incriminating evidence against the man I had sworn to love in sickness and in health, until death do us part. Did this count as sickness? Was I supposed to remain in love with this man forever?

I straightened myself and took a deep breath. No, I wouldn't collapse, and I wouldn't throw up. I wouldn't do any of the things I would do if this were a movie I would keep my head, and I would find out exactly what was going on.

"Emma." There was a warning in Rob's voice that tickled at my stomach and made the hairs on the back of my neck stand on end. "There are newspaper clippings in here... about your parents."

"What?"

I took the scrapbook that Rob was holding and read through the pages. Every article about my parents' death was documented within the book. He had meticulously cut out each page and glued it into the book, taking care not to fold over or crumple the corners.

"Why would he have this?"

"Emma, he was obsessed with you. Don't you think he would have wanted your parents out of his way? Aiden was gone, I was gone—that left just two people in your life."

My eyes burned with withheld tears. My arms lost all strength and I almost dropped the scrapbook. It was Rob who caught it before it fell.

"You think he killed them," I whispered.

Of all the horrible things that had happened to me, this was the most unexpected moment since I'd walked through the hospital doors and seen my son alive. This I had not anticipated at all.

"I do," Rob said. "I'm sorry. And there's more. Clippings of articles from when we thought Aiden had drowned."

I closed my eyes and tried to steady my breathing. "Do you think he took Aiden?"

Rob frowned. "He's obsessed with you. I dunno whether it fits the pattern but I think he's capable of anything. I'm sorry, Em."

"But… I saw Amy on that TV show and I was sure it was her. She's evil, she's…" I trailed off, thinking about the masks people wear. I'd seen Amy for who she was during that interview, and now I had seen Jake for who he was, too. He was clearly unhinged, and that meant I had to assume he was capable of anything.

I thought back to the moment I was told about my parents' accident. Mum and Dad had been on their way to London for a weekend away when their brakes failed on the motorway. They told me it was because of water in the brake fluid. An easy problem to miss when you're not good with cars. It was all so feasible. But what if it was Jake tampering with the engine?

I thought back to that time. Who had I told? Who knew? Most of the village, probably. Mum was the GP and she treated most of the town. I would have mentioned it to anyone while doing my chores, shopping in the newsagents, or sending a parcel in the post office. It would only have taken Jake to overhear, or have a conversation with Mum herself. Or maybe someone mentioned it at school. Gossip was rife amongst the Bishoptown residents and not a lot happens, so a short trip to London might make itself into the daily chatter. *Did you know Gina Price is going to London for the weekend? Well, she must be still trying to get over the death of her grandson. I wonder if they'll see a show…*

Yes, he could easily have heard about my parents' trip down to London.

"Rob, I can't bear this," I whispered. "I'm trying to be strong. The air in here…"

"Take a step outside," he said. He wrapped his arm around my waist. "Just for a moment. Breathe."

CHAPTER THIRTY-EIGHT

The rain was soothing, and I didn't care about the cold. I was freezing to the bones of me anyway, and it had nothing to do with the October weather. I leaned against the slick exterior of the garage and let the rain wash over me. The place smelled like wet cement and mould. That would be the smell I would most associate with Jake as time wore on. Wet cement and mould. That was him, slippery and foul, a man with two sides. How had I fallen for him?

He had manufactured it. All of it. He'd seen the way I'd fallen apart after Aiden and he'd seized the opportunity while he had the chance. With my parents out of the picture he knew I had no one to take care of me, and he knew I would fail to take care of myself. So there he was, swooping in like a knight in shining armour, becoming my protector and my healer. He introduced me to paints again. He helped me find a job. He set me back on my feet, always with an arm behind my back propping me up.

Rob emerged from the garage with his head held low. When he came closer, he pulled me into a hug. "I never should have left. I'm so sorry, Emma. I shouldn't have left you grieving for Aiden by yourself. I was fucking selfish and I'm sorry."

Though I hugged him back, I felt like a shell. Now I understood how Aiden could sleepwalk through his life without uttering a single syllable. I got it. My heart shrivelled up inside my rib cage, barely fluttering. I was hollowed out.

He shut the garage door and led us to the truck. Once inside he removed his cap and rubbed the rain water from his skin.

"Aside from the pictures of you as a minor and the girl, there's nothing. At least, there's nothing that might prove whether he killed your parents," he said. "He didn't keep any souvenirs if he did do it, just those clippings, and I guess you could say it was his obsession with you that made him keep them. I think he did it, though. It makes sense. It fits in with all these lies."

"Does it?" I spluttered. My throat was so choked that I could hardly get my words out. "Are we jumping to conclusions, here? He's... he's my husband and I'm accusing him of murder."

"Emma, I really think he did it. And I think you believe it too."

The sick part was that I did believe it. I wanted to be wrong, but I believed it.

"It's not your fault, Em. He took advantage of you like he did that girl. That's what he does."

"I know… I just…" I stared down at my stomach. Was I carrying the child of a murderer? "How could I have fallen in love with him?"

"Did you though? Wasn't it just the security he offered that you fell in love with? If you were really in love with him, would there have been this spark between us?"

I waved a dismissive hand. "That… that's because of Aiden coming back. Our emotions were all over the place." I tried to ignore the hurt look in his eyes. "Why didn't the police find any foul play when they investigated Mum and Dad's deaths?"

"Probably because they weren't expecting any. Your parents didn't have any enemies. No one would expect them to be murdered."

"We should call the police," I said.

He nodded. "And we need to figure out what to do next. It's lunchtime now. He'll still be at the school, right?"

"Yes."

"We'll go to your place and get some stuff. You can stay with us in the B&B."

I shook my head. As much as I hated to do this to my best friend, it was now necessary. "I want to go to Josie's. Your mum is too much of a wildcard, Rob. She makes decisions without consulting me and she's too stubborn. She thinks she knows what's best for Aiden all the time and I don't want to be fighting with her. Besides, I'm due to give birth in days and your parents haven't got the room." The thought of my impending arrival weighed so heavy on my shoulders that I let them sag. I rested my head against the window of Rob's truck. "What am I going to do?"

His warm fingers caressed my hand before squeezing it tight. The way my hand fit right into his injected a little warmth into my bones. It wasn't much, but it was something.

"I'm not going anywhere this time, Emma. I'm going to help you."

Yes, but for how long? I thought. "You've said that before."

Rob sighed. "I mean it this time."

"How do I know you're not lying to me again? You lied last time, didn't you? You told me, in the weeks after the flood, that you wouldn't leave my side, that no matter what we would be together. You lied."

"It's not a lie if you believe it to be true. I thought we would be."

I wiped a tear from my eye. "Sorry. I... I'm just upset. We should go."

Rob started the engine and we finally left the storage yard. When we arrived at Jake's house— not my home, not anymore—Rob phoned the police and left an anonymous tip that Jake Price had stashed drugs in a storage garage outside Bishoptown. I forced myself into the shower and let the hot water wash away the smell of mould from the wet garage walls. Then I dressed, collected my suitcase, and repacked some of the things I'd packed from the night before, along with more of Aiden's clothes. Rob loaded his truck with as much baby paraphernalia as he could, while I tried to get in touch with Josie.

"Still no answer?" Rob wiped rain and sweat away from his forehead with the back of his hand and straightened up. His face was red from the effort of carrying heavy suitcases into the truck.

I shook my head. "I thought she'd still be off work. She's taken some time off to deal with Hugh's disappearance."

"Do you want to stay with my mum and dad?"

I chewed on my bottom lip. "No. I have a key for Josie's. We'll go pick up Aiden and then I'll call Josie when I get there. I've left a voicemail for now."

"Are you sure she's going to be okay with this?"

A sudden cramp rippled through my abdomen and I creased over.

"Emma?"

I straightened up as the pain dissipated. "I'm okay. Josie will be fine. I'd do the same for her given the circumstances, so she won't have a problem with it."

Rob nodded to indicate it was good enough for him, but he frowned at the same time. "Are you sure you're all right?"

"Just the baby kicking."

But I was quivering down to my toes. The pain had felt a lot worse than the baby kicking and I had no idea whether Josie would take me in. All I knew was that I didn't want to be around Rob's parents. Not after the trick his mum pulled that upset Aiden, and not after his dad had been questioned by the police. No. I needed to be somewhere that would be safe for Aiden. Though things were a mess with Hugh gone, I knew that Josie's was the best option. It sounded as though Hugh wasn't coming back, at least not for the foreseeable future, so I got to live with Josie alone for a week or two until I'd had the baby and could look for a flat in the village.

I couldn't believe I was even at this junction in my life, but that's what happens when all the control is taken from you. The worst part was how I'd let Jake take even more control from me. I'd let him persuade me to sell my parents' house. I'd put my money into a joint account. I'd taken a job where I worked with him. I'd done all those stupid things because I loved and trusted him. Though I regretted it as I climbed back into Rob's truck and watched the rain blur Bishoptown into an abstract painting, there came a time when I stopped regretting my decisions. No one should regret loving and trusting another human being. Yes, sometimes we direct our love and trust to the wrong person, but that doesn't mean we shouldn't have done it at all. Hearts should be protected, but they shouldn't be forced to close. The withered piece of coal hidden deep in my chest had once been full of love. But as we picked up Aiden and drove on to Josie's house, it was full of nothing but hate.

CHAPTER THIRTY-NINE

It was late afternoon by the time we reached Josie's house. The sun wouldn't set for hours, but dark clouds had descended, preventing sunlight from penetrating the murky sky. I opened the door to the truck and climbed out, holding my protruding pregnant belly. The rain fell over us in one great torrent, and instantly I was transported back to that fateful day ten years ago when I lost my son. But this time, he was by my side. I held onto his arm with one hand and readjusted the hood on his raincoat with the other. Beneath the hood he was there, quiet as a church mouse, pale as a raw potato, and lifeless as a mannequin. My son. The boy whose only reactions since coming back to me had been destructive and violent. I wrapped a protective arm around his shoulder and walked him up to the house.

"Do you think the police have been to the garage yet?" I asked, raising my voice above the wind. "Stevenson's not called."

"He'll ring you when they've put two and two together. At least you're safe here away from him. They'll have arrested him by the end of the day."

I bent down to retrieve the spare key from the bottom of a pile of decorative rocks placed around a potted plant. The thing about Bishoptown is that nothing really happens. No one gets burgled, so no one thinks to keep their house safe. I dug the key out from the bottom of the fake rock.

"They'll have him for the relationship with that girl in Bournemouth. I put it all front and centre so they'd find it right away," Rob said. He carried the heaviest of my suitcases. "Then we need to figure out if Jake really took Aiden and why." Rob glanced back at Aiden and lowered his voice. "Aiden hasn't told us it was Jake."

His words made me feel exhausted. There was too much to consider. Too many thoughts swirling around my mind in a whirlpool of words like *kidnap* and *murder*. I shut my eyes and forced the thoughts away.

"Are you all right?" Rob asked. "Do you want me to open the door?"

I nodded and handed him the key, stroking my stomach with one hand.

Though the rain was soaking us through and the wind was howling above the forest that sat in the valley beneath us, I still didn't rush to get into the house. The place reminded me of a happier time. Seeing just this door brought back memories of

Hugh and Josie's parties when Aiden was little. The five of us—me, Rob, Aiden, Josie, and Hugh— would light the fire in the living room and watch films before putting Aiden to bed and breaking out the wine and cheese. This was supposed to be a house filled with laughter, not a refuge for two wronged women. Hugh, the surprise philanderer, disappearing with another woman, and Jake, the surprise stalker, spending hours locked away in his garage painting bizarre portraits of me. Another cramp tore through my lower body and I leaned into it, biting my lip against the pain. Rob placed a hand on my back.

"Are you in labour?"

I shook my head. "I don't think so. I had these pains with Aiden; they were Braxton-Hicks."

"Let's get you inside and sat down. You need to get your feet up and relax." He gave me a smile that was half-pitying and stiff with concern.

"Relax." I laughed.

Rob shook his head with a hollow chuckle. He pushed the key into the door and twisted it. The suitcase was cumbersome so he had to shove it forward with his knees as he opened the door. He bent down to lift it up as the door swung open.

At first I was looking down at Rob, but when I lifted my eyes, I screamed. A large, heavy object swung down, hitting Rob's skull with a crack, and above that heavy object stood a man with a toothy grin, his cheeks stretched wide from the manic smile, and blood splattered across his face.

"Hello, darling," he said.

I spun around and pushed Aiden forwards. "Get in the car!"

But Jake reached out and grasped my hair from behind, yanking me back with such force that I lost balance and fell into him. His fingernails scratched my scalp and his fist pulled painfully on my hair as I tripped over Rob's lifeless body. But I didn't care about the searing pain—all I cared about was Aiden, standing in the driveway, still as a statue.

"Get in the car and lock the doors!" I screamed. Rob had the car keys in his pocket, which I tried to convey with my eyes, but Aiden could only stare at me.

"He's not going anywhere. Are you, Aiden?" Jake said. His voice was so calm and collected that a shiver ran down my spine.

I pulled away from Jake, desperately trying to release myself from his grip, but my feet couldn't find purchase on Josie's tiled floor. I kept slipping on something wet. When I looked down, I saw that I was slipping on Rob's blood. His red blood seeped into the material of my shoes and for a brief instant they appeared as mundane as feet covered in red paint. I suppressed a retch, trying to stay focussed on everything going on.

"Let him go, Jake. It's me you want."

Jake's free hand wrapped around my neck. "That's what you'd like to think, isn't it?" His hot breath tickled my ears. I smelled the sourness of stale Scotch on his breath. "Come on, Aiden. You, me, and your mum have got a lot to talk about."

"Please," I begged. "Please, Aiden. Run away. Get help." I cried out as my hair was yanked back even harder, and Jake started to drag me back, away from Rob, and away from my son. I tried to scream as loud as I could, but the hand around my throat worked its way up and clamped over my mouth. I struggled as Jake pulled me further into the house, and all the time, Aiden stood there watching it happen.

Time seemed to stood still. I was kicking and screaming in Jake's grasp, while Aiden stood in the doorway with his eyes wide and his face slack. Was he afraid? Did he care? I didn't know. I couldn't tell. I started to cry.

Aiden stepped into the house. He had to lift his knees to step over his father's lifeless body.

"Good boy, Aiden," Jake said. "Now pull the arsehole further into the house, will you?" Aiden bent down and dragged Rob further into the house. I felt sick. I'd stopped struggling. I was just watching as my son obeyed the monster I'd married. "Take the phone out of his pocket, and then lock the door and bring me the key." Aiden did everything Jake said as if in a stupor. I could only watch as my son handed the key over to Jake, who had to let go of my mouth to take the key and put it in his pocket.

"What are you doing, Aiden?" I said. "Why did you do that?"

But he didn't answer.

CHAPTER FORTY

"What have you done with Josie?"

Jake finally allowed me to stand, but he pushed me through the hallway by the crook of my elbow. I didn't struggle, because I knew he was stronger and that if I tried anything, he'd have the upper hand. My mind was sharper than it had ever been, brought into focus from the adrenaline and anger coursing through me. If I was going to do anything about Jake's attack, I would need to wait for the perfect moment, as hard as that would be while Rob was injured on the ground and Josie was nowhere to be seen.

"She's a little tied up at the moment." The corner of his mouth lifted in amusement.

"What are you going to do with me?" I asked.

Jake pushed me into the living room and gestured towards the sofa. "We're going to talk. Aiden, why don't you sit down next to your mother? And why don't you make yourselves comfortable? Take off those coats, and while you're at it, Emma, hand me your phone."

I reluctantly did what he wanted. Jake threw my phone and Rob's onto the Barratts' carpet and stamped hard on the screens. Then he kicked them away into the corner of the room.

It sickened me to see the way Aiden obeyed him. Since my son had come back from the dead he'd had this strange way of doing whatever Jake asked of him. I'd never really understood it, but I'd put it down as some strange residual aftereffect of spending ten years of confinement at the hands of another man. But now? He had the choice to leave and he didn't.

"You took Aiden," I said.

Jake frowned. "That's not what I want to talk about."

"I loved you."

"And I loved you, but look how you repaid me. You snuck around looking into my private things. You accused me of kidnapping your son." Jake paced up and down the living room. I could see that he was wearing the same outfit he left for work in, but he'd removed his tweed jacket and rolled up the sleeves of his check shirt. There were droplets of blood on the collar of his shirt, up his neck, and splashed across his cheek.

"I don't understand, Jake. I wasn't... We were going to give it another go. Weren't we? We'd talked and sorted it all out."

"Don't lie to me," he spat. "You've been to my

private space. You've seen the garage."

My jaw dropped. "How do you know that?"

"Remember that phone I bought you for Christmas last year?"

I nodded. "My iPhone. Yeah."

"It has a 'Find My Phone' app on it. I use it to watch your every move, Emma. I know how much you've been coming here, too. What's that for? To complain about me? To talk about me behind my back?"

"No, Jake. I wouldn't do that." I heard the pulse of my blood thumping in my ears. I was short of breath and trying hard not to panic. Next to me, Aiden sat very still. I tried to keep calm. If I was calm, maybe I could calm Jake down. "I'm sorry if I betrayed your trust. I swear I never meant to, I just wanted to find out what happened to Aiden. Jake, why don't you call an ambulance for Rob? We can say it was an accident. He fell and hit his head. We can sort all this out later, but Rob is bleeding to death in the hallway and he needs—"

"That's all you care about, isn't it? Ever since he's come back to Bishoptown you've been lusting after him like a wide-eyed schoolgirl. It's sick." He paused and rubbed his temples. For one fleeting moment I thought about rushing him and knocking him down, but then he was back to pacing, and the determination on his face gave me caution. "There's no way the waster survived that blow. I hit him with Hugh's African warrior statue. The thing is made of stone." Jake snatched the large stone figure and lifted it above his head. I flinched at the sight of Rob's blood and hair smeared across the face of the African man.

"Hugh could come home at any time," I said, forcing myself to keep my voice level and calm.

But Jake just laughed. "Hugh knows how to live. He takes whatever he wants, no matter what. He'll be fucking some nineteen-year-old in Vegas or something. I like a man who takes what he wants."

"You think that making a mockery of marriage vows is something to be proud of? You think that lying and cheating is admirable?"

"We do what we have to do to stay in *polite society*," he said, sneering at the term. "But we all have desires, don't we? We all have secrets deep down. I bet you didn't know Hugh was screwing Amy Perry, did you?"

I frowned. "No, I didn't know that."

"She was wild in the sack, according to him. Into some real hard-core stuff. Not like you, my beautiful wife. But I didn't marry you for your abilities between the sheets. You were broken, and I liked that. And no, I don't mean when you jammed that knife into your wrist—I mean before then. Before Aiden, before everything. Even at school. I saw who you were before you knew it yourself. You needed guidance. You were like a baby deer walking on ice. Without someone by your side telling you where to step, you'd slip and slide around until you fell through the surface." He had stopped pacing now. He seemed calmer, but that was even more unnerving than his agitated state. "You needed *me*, but you turned to that idiot in the hallway."

"Please, Jake. If you love me even a little, call an ambulance for Rob. Let Josie and Aiden go so we can talk on our own."

Jake laughed. "Don't you think I know you're trying to manipulate me? Do you think I'm stupid? Do you?"

"N-no," I stuttered. Though the adrenaline still pumped through my veins, I was twice as frightened as I was angry. I'd never seen this side to Jake and it was terrifying. He was dangerous. All this time I had been sharing my bed with a dangerous man and I never knew it. My eyes roamed around the room searching out potential weapons. There was nothing within reach.

He sighed. "I really thought you were everything I ever wanted and ever needed, but now I look at you and I see very little at all, Emma."

"I'm carrying your child." My throat rasped as I tried to speak without letting myself cry. "Our baby girl."

"Yes, I know," he snapped. "But do you even care? All you do is whinge and whine about *Aiden*, who, by the way, is nothing but pathetic and messed up in the head, until you put our baby at risk. You prioritise everything else apart from me and our baby. I thought once we were married you'd finally put all that behind you. The drowned son. The lover who abandoned you. The parents who died. I thought you'd actually moved on and would finally, finally notice *me*. But you could never leave it alone, could you? It was always about them and never about me, even though I'm the best thing that's ever happened to you. Just look at what I've given you—a job with people you like, a home that you love, a lifestyle most women would kill for, and still you can't find it in yourself to be grateful."

I opened my mouth to speak. I wanted to yell at him, to show him there was more to me that he could possibly understand, that he could never break me down in the way he thought he could, but all that came out of my mouth was a whimper. I crumpled forward, clutching my abdomen. Another cramp seized my uterus. My body grew hot from the pain and I felt sweat forming along my hairline. It started from my back and radiated around me, turning my bump hard as a rock.

"Jake," I said. "You need to call an ambulance. I think I'm in labour."

For the first time, there was a slight twitch of doubt in Jake's expression as his jaw clenched and his eyes narrowed. "It's still a few days until your due date."

"What do babies care about a due date? Call an ambulance!"

He shook his head. "Your waters haven't broken yet. Besides, we haven't finished talking."

I rubbed my stomach and tried not to think

about what would happen if I went into labour here in this room with my ex-boyfriend dying in the corridor and my husband emotionally torturing me, with my son sat still and traumatised to my right and my best friend tied up in one of the rooms upstairs. What had I done to arrive at this lowest point in my life? What mistake had I made to not see this coming?

"What is it you want to say to me?" I said bitterly. "Are you going to tell me about how you took my son and abused him for a decade? Is that what you want to say? Why did you do it, Jake? Was it some sort of sick, controlling fantasy where you took everything away from me to see what would happen? Am I just a doll to you? A plaything you can experiment with? Or did you want to turn Aiden into some robotic slave to do your bidding for this precise moment, so you could reveal to me what an evil fucking man you are? And what about my parents? What did they ever do to you?"

"You were alone after they died," he said with a smirk. "That was useful."

My blood was hot with rage. "I hate you. You stalked me. You murdered my parents." I refused to cry. I would not give him the satisfaction of seeing me cry. "That day, when I tried to kill myself, where were you? How did you know?"

"Recording device," he said, the smile spreading across his face. He relished the fact that he had fooled me.

"You're evil," I repeated.

"I'm not evil, Emma. I'm just free. I do what I want."

"And what you want is to be an art teacher in a comprehensive school? What the hell *are* you? You're just pathetic."

"I don't really care about being a teacher. That's just an easy way to get people to like me. Teachers are warm and cuddly. Art teachers who wear tweed are even cuddlier."

"You messed up with that girl in Bournemouth though, didn't you? You might have manipulated her into not talking about your little affair, but her photo of you both was a slip up."

"Katie was young and made mistakes. She was almost as broken as you. She loved to be led. She liked to be controlled. Most women like it."

"What have you done with Josie, Jake? Have you hurt her?" My bottom lip trembled. Why didn't I see his disregard for other people? Why had I never noticed how much he hated the world? This was all so hidden from me. He kept it in that garage along with his true face. That was where he hid his obsession.

Slowly, he walked across the room towards the fireplace and retrieved a shining object from the mantel. I gasped. It was a long, sharp knife, wider than a chef's knife, with a smooth handle made from some sort of ivory-coloured material. My stomach twisted into a knot when I realised it was bone.

"Hugh gave me this as a present," he said. "It's a hunting knife. He told me you probably wouldn't approve, so I decided to keep it hidden. It seems appropriate to use it now, in his home."

"Jake," I whispered. "What are you going to do with that thing?"

"Finish what I started ten years ago," he hissed.

CHAPTER FORTY-ONE

My muscles felt like stretched elastic. The hairs stood up on the backs of my arms as Jake tilted and examined the knife in his hand. I tried to ignore a third cramp as it took hold of my womb, squeezing and twisting up my insides. My fists clenched, pressing my fingernails deep into the palms of my hands.

"I've wanted to tell you this for a long time, Emma." He smiled, revealing those white teeth I had once found so attractive. Handsome Hewitt. "It's a confession, really. An event that I wasn't proud of at the time, but it grew to be an accomplishment I praised myself for after the dust settled. The thing is, I got away with it. At least, I thought I had. The problem is, your son came back, and it's only a matter of time before he starts talking, I'm sure of it."

My fingernails dug harder into my skin. I felt warm liquid pool there.

"Despite all my best efforts to get rid of him again, you seem determined to keep the little brat around, so I suppose I may as well spill the beans." He laughed. "Not even the little incident in the crib with the paint changed your mind."

"That was you?" I said. Why was I even surprised? He was clearly capable of anything.

"Yes, darling. It was. But going back to the past… I wasn't ever going to tell you, but then you went to my garage and you snooped in places you shouldn't be snooping. You made it so that I've got nothing to lose." The knife blade glinted as he held out his arms and grinned at me. "You've only got yourself to blame, now. This all would have been swept under the rug and we could have lived a happy life if you hadn't kept digging. Somewhere down the line, preferably before Aiden grows a pair and starts talking, I'd have ensured Aiden had a little accident. So tragic, but these things happen."

Heat washed over me. My chest was tight, making it hard to breathe, but I forced myself to concentrate. I could see how Jake was loving the captive audience, drinking in the way I hung on his every word, waiting for the moment I would finally get some answers. He wasn't going to make this easy for me. He wasn't going to make this quick. He was going to enjoy it.

"Let me tell you a story about a feral child. You see, feral children usually have terrible mothers. Those mothers are often too young to *be* mothers and let their children run riot wherever they feel like it." He paused to see if his words got a reaction from me but I didn't give him the satisfaction. "When all the other, normal children are behaving themselves, feral children do the opposite. Normal children know how to behave when there's a natural disaster like a flood, but fucked-up children like Aiden wander off on their own and decide to play in the river."

I kept my mouth firmly closed, waiting for him to tell me. There was an infuriating grin on his face that made my blood boil. He knew he was in control and he was milking every single second of it.

"I saw Aiden walk away from the classroom. I saw him slip through the corridors and out of the school." He paused to push his hair back away from his face. Hair that I'd caressed. A face I'd kissed. A body I'd touched. A man I'd made love to over and over again. "I'd been watching you for years. I remember the first day I saw you at school, with your dark hair long and luxurious. You were more hesitant than the other girls. You didn't wear those slutty skirts or thongs pulled up above your waistline. You had something about you. You had paint under your fingernails and lowered eyelashes. You blushed when boys tried to talk to you and were oblivious when they were clearly besotted with you." He sighed. "You used to be so beautiful, and now you're old, fat, and covered in that disgusting rash."

Instinctively, I hid my hands beneath my legs,

ashamed. Then I realised that I was looking at a murderer. I pulled my hands back out and scratched them in front of him.

"I'd been biding my time with you. The incident with Katie had been rushed and I didn't want that to happen again. Besides, Katie was the appetiser. You were the main course, and I wanted to make sure I was ready to devour you." I retched but nothing came out of me. Jake seemed oblivious, and carried on with his story. "But that lump of clay, that walking black hole, *Rob*, got there first. You needed to be led, and I was going to show you the way, but he was the one who got to you first and for that I will never forgive him. That's the reason why he's bleeding onto the Barratts' hallway tiles. That's what happens to people who cross me."

"Get to the point," I snapped, unable to cope with this for much longer. I scratched at my itching skin, feeling dirty just from listening to him. Next to me, Aiden sat quietly, still and impassive as always. He could be watching cartoons again, not listening to the ramblings of a psychopath.

"You were tainted when you had Aiden, but I knew I could salvage you. It would just take some breaking to get you where I wanted you. When I saw Aiden slip out of school that day I followed him at first to see what he was doing. I realised that I might never get him alone like this again. I might never have a chance to do what I'd wanted to do for years." He licked his lips as he relayed the memory. "I was already soaked through from checking the outside of the school with Simon. I followed your son's red coat through the pouring rain all the way down to the river. There he was, just standing and staring at the gushing water."

I thought of my nightmares after Aiden was taken. I thought of that image forever haunting me: Aiden floating beneath the tumultuous waters. Aiden in the still, calm part of the river with his lips blue and his skin white.

Jake's fingers gripped the knife even tighter. He lifted his arms in animation as his excitement grew. "This was my *chance*. I knew what it would do to you, and I knew I had to do it. The slate had to be wiped clean, Emma. I needed you to be that broken girl again, the one I fell in love with. You'd become too assured in your role as a mother. I saw how you played with Aiden in the park, and I saw you slowly becoming a family with Rob. You even had the friends I saw us having, Josie and Hugh. It wasn't *fair*. It was all supposed to be for *us*."

"What did you do?" I whispered.

"I pushed him," he said.

"You did what?"

"I pushed him into the river."

I turned to my son. He was blank faced and staring right at me. There were no answers in that face, only more questions. I reached out to touch him, before retracting my hand. Then I moved to face my husband.

"What happened after you pushed him into the

river?" I asked.

Jake shrugged. "I went back to the school."

"I don't understand."

"That's because you're stupid. You've accused me of kidnapping your son, but why would I do that? I never wanted *him*, I wanted *you*. Aiden just gets in the way. With him around you have no time for me, or the baby growing inside you. He's an obstacle to me."

"Who took him? Tell me. I need to know," I begged.

Jake just laughed. "I don't know. Some chancer who was nearby and saw a kid drowning in the river. They must have fished him out and thanked God because it meant they could keep him in their sick little dungeon or whatever." He was so casual and callous that my stomach lurched and I tasted bile at the back of my throat.

"It wasn't you," I whispered.

"Of course not," he said. "I wanted him out of the way, like I wanted your parents out of the way."

I threw my head into my hands. I'd slept in the same bed as the man who had tried to kill my son, and who had also succeeded in killing my parents. My skin was full of ants. My body was cold, down to the core. I shivered, but I had to keep my head. I had to try and stay in control. I had to put all of that aside and focus on saving the lives of the people in the house.

"You said you were going to finish what you

started ten years ago," I said, lifting my face to meet his gaze. "What did that mean?"

The laughter faded from Jake's face and instead his eyes glassed over like marbles. Without his usual amiable grin, he was frightening. He angled his chin down, and dark shadows flooded his eyes, turning him into the cliché movie villain. But this wasn't your average bad guy. He was my husband and the father of my child. He was the man who rubbed my feet at the end of the day and brought me a hot chocolate when I had my period. He was the man who laughed at my jokes and teased me when I mispronounced a word. He held my hand through horror movies and chatted to my friends. He listened to me when I talked about my past and he was a shoulder to cry on when it was the anniversary of my parents' death. He had been everything to me, but all of it had been a complete and utter lie.

"You've ruined it all, Emma." The cold edge of his voice was like a razor blade running down my spine. "I can't fix it anymore. I can't break you into the woman I need you to be. It's too late for us all. I'm going to finish what I started ten years ago, and then I'm going to move on to you." He took a step forward with the knife gripped in his hand.

CHAPTER FORTY-TWO

There's a kind of strength in weakness that comes from hitting the absolute lowest you can go. There have been many moments in my life where I've hit such depths that I thought I would never claw my way out of them. Jake talked about owning the darkness within him and taking what he wanted, but he wasn't the only one in that room experienced with dealing with darkness. When I look back on my time in that room, I realise that Jake had made the same mistake over and over in his life, and that was underestimating me.

Because he was wrong about me.

I wasn't a broken bird always coming back for a beating. I wasn't someone he could break over and over again without a fight. I'd never fought because he'd never given me anything to fight. He'd taken the best of my life and tossed it away but he'd never shown me what I needed to be shown. He'd never revealed himself for the person he really was. But now that he had, I could fight him. I finally had a physical manifestation of all the pain I'd suffered for the last decade.

When he rushed at Aiden with the knife, I knew what I had to do.

As Aiden cowered away from Jake, I threw myself between them, holding my hands up to shield my son. Jake's knife caught the palm of my hand and I screamed as it tore through my skin. But I didn't give up. I pushed against the knife with one hand, my skin sliced open by the blade, and reached up to hit Jake on the nose with the other.

The blow caught Jake off guard and he staggered back, giving me a slight reprieve. My injured hand was covered in blood but I couldn't let my eyes linger on the wound, because Jake was readying himself for another attack.

"I was going to kill you last," Jake said. "But this works too."

The sparkling glint of anger in his eyes had changed to a dull, grim determination. I knew he was stronger and bigger than me, but I also knew I wanted to live—for both of my children. I quickly checked around me for weapons, but there wasn't anything, only a TV remote and a magazine. Even the lamp was on the other side of the room with Jake blocking my way. He came at me again, throwing his force against me and pushing me back, colliding with my pregnant belly in a way that made me gasp for breath. But I managed to throw my weight to my right side, duck beneath his armpit, and then push him full force with both hands, hissing with pain as my injured hand made contact with his side.

Jake tumbled to the floor but he still had hold of the knife. I knelt down on his chest and pressed on his wrist with my full weight, but my fingers were slippery with blood. Jake hit me across the face with his free hand, a blow so hard I felt a crunch in my nose. I ignored it, and sank my teeth into his wrist. Jake beat the back of my head and roared with pain. My mouth filled with the rusting taste of warm blood. I sank my teeth deeper and deeper until I felt his grip loosen on the knife.

He finally managed to throw me back, but I took a chunk of his wrist with me and a spray of blood hit me in the face. My bloody fingers couldn't grip the knife and it flew from my hand to the back of the room. Jake, face sweaty and contorted, lifted his leg and I recognised that he meant to kick me in the stomach. I rolled to the right and struggled up onto my feet.

"Aiden, we need to go!"

My son was sat on the sofa, his eyes wide and his face set in horror. I quickly wiped away some of the blood from my mouth as Jake climbed to his feet, holding his wrist.

"Just let us go, Jake," I pleaded. I was prepared to do anything to keep myself and my children alive.

"I can't do that, Emma."

As he ran towards me, I saw the bloodied statue

that Jake had used on Rob. I ducked down and scooped it up as Jake's punch missed my face by inches and connected with my shoulder instead. The force almost knocked me off my feet, but Jake was sporting a deep injury on his wrist and that had slowed him down, so I was able to lift the statue and throw it at him. Jake's expression was filled with surprise as the heavy, stone figure hit him squarely on the chin before falling onto his foot. He was still screaming from the pain as I threw myself sideways at him. We tumbled to the carpet, Jake pushing my face up to the ceiling away from him, groping for my neck. I managed to find the warrior statue and took it in both hands as Jake's fingers wrapped around my throat.

I lifted the stone figure and a pop of anger exploded inside me. I wanted him dead. This was the man who had lied to me every day. He'd violated my trust. He'd stalked me when I was a vulnerable young woman. He'd murdered my parents and tried to murder my son, all so he could break me and mould me into whatever he wanted. He had controlled me and hunted me. There was a lot of hate inside me and a lot of anger, and the taste of his blood in my mouth wasn't enough. I wanted to see him suffer.

I brought the statue down onto his head and his hands loosened. I lifted it and did it again. This time, Jake's hands fell from my throat. A trickle of blood rolled down his forehead until it pooled on the carpet and in his ear. I lifted the bust again.

And then I stopped.

Aiden was singing.

It was the same song I'd heard while I was arguing with Rob. His voice was soft. He sang high notes with ease, rising and falling with the melody. He had a beautiful voice, like a choir boy's voice, and it made me cry. I dropped the statue and climbed off Jake whilst holding my pregnant bump. Jake was still. I'd killed him. I clenched and unclenched my fists, trying to calm myself, before I bent down and searched for Jake's mobile phone. It wasn't there. I glanced across at the house phone on the corner table of the room. The wire had been cut.

"Aiden," I said. "We need to go now."

But Aiden wasn't on the sofa anymore. He was standing by the door of the room staring at me. His mouth opened and closed to sing the quiet song, and tears trickled down his face. I stepped towards him, holding out my hands for him to take.

"Aiden."

He backed away from me. That was when I realised that Aiden wasn't scared of Jake anymore—he was scared of me. His eyes flicked from me to the corridor and back to me in rapid motion, and I realised he was thinking of a way to escape.

"We'll go together, Aiden," I said. "I'm going to find a phone and call an ambulance and the police, then I'm going to see if your dad and Josie are okay. Then we're going to go and wait in the car for the police to come. Is that okay with you, Aiden?" I didn't want to spend a second longer in this house.

But his song only grew louder. His body was trembling and he shook his head. He glanced back to the corridor.

"You can't go out that way," I said. "The door is locked."

Aiden clenched his fists and ran at me. His sudden movement took me completely by surprise, which was why he managed to knock me off my feet. My stomach cramped with another contraction, which gave Aiden time to search through Jake's pockets and retrieve the key for Josie's front door. By the time I'd managed to sit up, Aiden had disappeared from the room and I could hear the key in the lock.

"No!" I called, but it was no use, the door was open.

I hurried over to the corner where Jake had kicked my broken phone. The screen was smashed, but I could still scroll through the options. I pulled myself up onto my feet and hurried through the corridor where Rob was laid out on the carpet. I bent low to check his pulse.

When Rob lifted his head I almost cried out. "Follow… him…" he croaked.

I nodded. "I'm calling an ambulance."

It hurt my heart to leave him there, but I had to follow Aiden. I hurried out of Josie's house as fast as I could, dialling 999 on the phone. Luckily Aiden hadn't thought to lock me in the house.

"I've been attacked at my friend's house," I said after the operator took my call. "My husband attacked my ex-boyfriend. I think he's badly hurt, I don't know. He's hurt my friend... I think she's tied up upstairs but I haven't seen her. He could have killed her. I think I killed him, my husband. I hit him with a statue but it was because he was going to kill my son. He had a knife. We need an ambulance. I have to go. My son has run away." I relayed the address and hung up, not even bothering to give my name.

As I hurried down the gravel path, I could just make out Aiden's form moving through the dark. He was heading down towards the road. I rushed along as fast as I could whilst scrolling through my phone. I had to call DCI Stevenson. He was the only one who knew the case.

He answered on the first call.

"It's Emma. Jake attacked me, Rob, and Aiden. I think I killed him. He's at Josie Barratt's house. Aiden has gone running off. I'm following him."

"No. Emma, stay where you are. I'm on my way."

"I have to follow him." I stopped as another contraction rippled through me. I had no idea how often they were coming. Every five minutes? I couldn't tell.

"Emma? Are you all right?"

"I'm in labour."

"Shit. Stay where you are. We'll have an ambulance—"

"I've already called it." Up ahead, barely visible in the pouring rain, Aiden took a sharp turn away from the road. I staggered down the steep hill to see better. "I think Aiden is heading into the woods."

"Rough Valley?" Stevenson asked.

"Yeah. I think he's going to go in."

"I'm on my way."

"Did you find the garage?" I asked.

"Yes," he said.

"Good," I replied, and hung up. I couldn't keep up the pace while I was distracted by talking.

I saw Aiden slow down as he entered the boundary into Rough Valley. He seemed to be trying to figure out which direction to take. That suggested that there was somewhere he wanted to go. There was a purpose to him entering the woods.

My shoes slipped down a grassy bank as I followed him towards the dark, thick trees. It was muddy underfoot. My clothes were soaked, but at least the downpour had washed away most of the blood from my face. My head was throbbing from Jake's fists, my hand was sore and bleeding from the deep cut across my palm, but I was determined to keep my boy within eyeshot. He had been taken from me ten years ago, and I was not going to allow that to happen again. I never wanted to let him out of my sight ever again.

I hurried into the trees. The wet grass stuck to my jeans. I was moving as fast as I possibly could, given the circumstances, and I couldn't help but wonder if any woman had been through anything like this while being in labour. Then I realised, of course they had. Of course. Women gave birth in war-torn countries. Women were forced to run for their lives. Children survived the most horrific of circumstances. Humans are strong, resilient, and determined creatures. I gritted my teeth and staggered on, determined that my baby would wait for me. I could hang on and hang on until I was sure Aiden was going to be safe, too.

The sun was beginning to set. Rain hammered down onto the fallen leaves, turning the ground into mulch. Despite the freezing rain, I was warm. The effort of moving faster than my pregnant body was accustomed to had taken its toll, and my muscles ached, but I was resolute in my purpose. I would find my son. I would take him to safety.

He moved swiftly, and that made it difficult to follow the back of his red jumper. I kept thinking about the day they pulled his red coat from the river. That wouldn't happen today. It would never happen again, I'd make sure of it.

Aiden slowed down and made three jagged turns in opposite directions. I could see that he was trying to figure out where to go.

"Aiden!" I called. "Please don't be scared, just let me walk with you."

He turned to stare at me. Ghoul-like in the dark forest, his pale face contrasted against the almost pitch-black background of the close thicket of trees.

"Talk to me," I said. "I know you can. Please talk to me and tell me what you're trying to do. I want to help you."

But he didn't speak. He went back to moving through the trees. Slipping through them like a spectre.

A contraction tore through me and I doubled over in pain, trying my best to ignore it so I could follow Aiden through the forest. To my surprise, after the pain had faded, I looked up to see Aiden had stopped. He was facing me. When I was recovered, he started moving again.

He wanted me to follow him.

CHAPTER FORTY-THREE

Sometimes, when I hold Aiden close, I imagine that I can smell the scent of the forest from that night. It's not a completely pleasant smell. There's the fresh scent of pine and rainwater, but along with it comes the must of wet leaves, the mildewed earthiness of mud, and the metallic hint of blood. A shivers runs down my spine every time I remember that night, and how my clothes were sodden from the rain. My feet ache from the memory of slipping through wet leaves and mud. I'm reminded, by the constriction in my chest, of how short of breath I was. My abdomen clenches as I remember the pain of my contractions.

Would I prefer to be able to hold my son and not think of these things? Of course. As much as I'd like to close my eyes without seeing Rob's blood on Josie's corridor tiles or Jake's dull, determined gaze as he approached me with Hugh's hunting knife.

As I followed my son through the forest, I knew

that whatever it was Aiden wanted to show me, it would change everything. Part of me was dreading that change. Part of me ached for it. I needed answers, and Aiden was the key to those answers, as he had always been.

But it seemed right that the journey was as arduous as it had been. This was Aiden's story, not mine, and it had been long and harrowing for him, so to live through even the smallest iota of the kind of pain he had endured made me feel closer to him. I slowly began to close the gap between us, and I longed to slip my hand into his and feed from the warmth of him, but I knew not to.

I was in labour. There was no doubt about that. The contractions were frequent, but my labour with Aiden had been stretched out over many hours, so I could only hope that Aiden had time to show me what he needed to show me before we found the police.

But the pain was worsening as I continued on through the woods. I had to stop and clutch a tree as another contraction pulsed through me. "I... can't... keep... up. Aiden."

I felt my phone buzz from the pocket of my soaked jeans, but I ignored it. No doubt DCI Stevenson was hoping to get me to stop what I was doing and turn back. But there was no going back now. I wouldn't be able to find my way out of this place even if I wanted to. All I could do was follow my son as the forest grew ever darker.

Aiden stopped. His head turned left, then right,

and I sensed that he had seen something that he recognised. There was a very tall birch to my right, set up on a slight mound. Aiden regarded that tree long enough to make me wonder if he had seen it before. I took a moment to stop and catch my breath as my son collected himself. I examined the wound on my hand. It would need stitches, but the bleeding had slowed down. I felt light-headed and tired, but I wanted to press on.

He stepped onto a narrow path next to a shallow drop. After passing a row of half a dozen trees, the path widened out into a clearing. Rough Valley forest was a tangled heap of trees and roots, which is why the clearing was surprising. Most of the land was owned by the National Trust, but the Trust had sold off pieces of land to property developers hoping to create more homes in Bishoptown. There'd been a mediocre protest about the plans but most people didn't really care about the forest. It wasn't a pretty place. It was dark and overgrown, and walking through it sent a shiver up your spine. It wasn't a place for dog-walkers and hikers.

Aiden carried on through the clearing and I followed, almost tripping on a smooth and slippery patch underfoot. I turned around to see what it was. It looked like a few trees had been felled around here. I'd slipped on the stump left over. I pressed on, trying to catch up with Aiden. He seemed to know exactly where he was heading now. Whatever this place was, he knew it, and he traversed it with ease.

I held onto my bump as I continued into the centre of the clearing, silently willing the child inside me to stay put for a while longer. I'd already put that child through hell, but I had to push those thoughts from my mind as I watched Aiden. He was acting strangely. He seemed to be kicking leaves, which was not something I was expecting him to do after the struggle back at the Barratts' house. I was beginning to wonder if he had finally cracked. Then my paranoid mind conjured up the idea that it was some sort of signal, and that Aiden's kidnapper was about to stride out from the trees with a machete to cut the baby out of my belly. But it was none of those things. Aiden was clearing the leaves away from some sort of door built into the ground. I could see it poking out of the earth now. It was perhaps three or four feet high, and built into a natural slope. I moved over to help Aiden clear leaves, branches, and mud away from the opening.

"Didn't want anyone to see."

I staggered back. My hands were trembling. It was the first time I had heard my son speak. It was the first time I'd heard his voice, his *speaking* voice, and not the strange, high-pitched singing voice.

He sounded like a teenager and that brought me almost to my knees. Yes, I'd come to see Aiden as older than the little boy taken from me ten years ago, but with his diminished size I still hadn't thought of him as sixteen years old. Then he spoke and suddenly he was almost a *man*. It wasn't a deep voice, but it wasn't a child's voice either.

I stood stupidly next to the strange door with my mouth opening and closing. I wanted him to do it again, but I didn't want to frighten him. He was in some sort of trance and I was concerned that if I spoke, I would break the spell that had been cast over the still forest that night. The only sound was the rustling of leaves as Aiden cleared the leaves away. When he was done, he clutched the handle and pushed.

"Still open."

This time I pounced on his words and committed them to memory. Joy flooded through my veins and my heart swelled. I'd waited so long to hear his voice.

He had to push the door hard, and the hinges squeaked as it opened, but I could see that it had been used often. The moonlight glinted on the dark metallic surface. This was it. This was what Aiden had been painting in therapy. This was the dark grey from his nightmares. On the other side of the door was where Aiden had been held captive for ten years. I tried to steady my breathing.

There was a step down, cut out of the slope of the hill. Once I stepped down, the door wasn't quite so small, and I was able to follow Aiden through that small, metal door, by ducking my head down. I was careful not to touch the handle. This was important, now. This was the part where all the pieces would come together and I would finally get justice for Aiden.

"Don't shut."

Of course not, I thought. That door would never shut again.

The door opened into a narrow passageway that descended down several cement steps. I resisted the urge to place my hand on the cement wall of the passageway to steady myself in the dark. I had to be careful not to contaminate any evidence. At the bottom of the steps was a second door. This one hung open, leaving the doorway exposed like a missing tooth, obviously vacated in a hurry. It was when I reached this door that the foul stench hit my nostrils.

Aiden hit a switch but nothing happened. He groped around the hallway before lifting something from a hook. I heard the clunk of a switch and a bright light flickered on. I winced at the sudden brightness. Aiden walked into the room and pressed on a lantern. He moved around the room turning on several small lanterns, the torchlight bobbing around as he made his way around the place. With more light I could see my surroundings. I was in a small room—about the size of a large living room—that had been partitioned into two areas. One of those areas was sectioned off with what looked like a heavy metal barred fence that had been welded in place. Someone had cut into the bars to create a door that was hanging open. On the ground near to the open door was a heavy chain and a padlock. Inside the cage was a small mattress with a crumpled duvet on top, a pile of books, a small desk with a plastic chair next to it, a sink, a tiny fridge, and a toilet. They were the kind of sinks and toilets you would find in a caravan, with pumps instead of regular taps.

"This is where I sleep," Aiden said, pointing to the bed.

Every hair on my arms and scalp prickled. I had thought I couldn't get any colder, but I was wrong. Looking at this room, and hearing my son say those words, brought the severity of his ordeal home, and I wondered whether I would ever be warm again. Would a hot bath or shower ever take away the chilling sensation of knowing and understanding exactly how cruel a human being could be? I'd pictured something like this in my mind. I'd actually pictured worse. I'd had nightmares about cages and chains and stained mattresses, but somehow, the reality of seeing my son's cage was worse than anything I had imagined.

I couldn't move my body, but I forced myself to look around the room. My eyes trailed the length of the place as Aiden's torch roamed from corner to corner. I watched as the torch moved from the barred area, to the things that were around the rest of the room. I followed the beam of light as it moved towards the misshapen lump in the corner, and then quickly looked away. I didn't want to see that yet, not properly, and instead took in the fan, the ventilation grates on the ceiling, the leaking freezer, the small armchair, the shabby toys, the dirty clothes, the unplugged heater, the wall of crayon drawings that I never got to receive from my own child. Of all the disgusting facts I knew about what had happened to my son, the part that disturbed me more than anything was that this had been a home. This was where my son had grown up. My knees weakened, but I forced myself to stay upright.

"This is Beaver the Bear. I got too old for him though. I drew that picture. It's the Great Wall of China. I had my picnic there. This one is a mountain, see? That's the heater. I'm allowed it on for thirty minutes in the morning and thirty minutes at night. I can't use it more or the generator will run out."

No one knew. Ten years and no one knew this place existed. I never knew.

How did he do it?

My eyes moved across the room to the lump in the corner. "Aiden, who is that?"

But Aiden was distracted by trying to pull one of the pictures off the wall. "This one is you. I drew a lot of you at the start. You don't look the same now."

"Aiden, who is it? Who brought you here?"

The walls were too close. I couldn't breathe. Every part of my body felt heavy with the knowledge that I knew who it was, and I should have guessed earlier. I'd been so stupid. Why hadn't I figured it out?

"Oh, yeah, him." Aiden sounded sad. "I watched his thoughts go. Didn't want to, but I wanted to leave."

My voice shook as I asked the question. "What's his name, sweetheart?"

But Aiden looked down at my feet instead. "Did you wee, Mummy?"

I'd barely noticed the warm water spread over my jeans and down my legs. Now that I glanced down I saw that my waters had broken all over my shoes, leaving a puddle of murky fluid spreading across the floor.

CHAPTER FORTY-FOUR

AIDEN

He should be here by now. I check the clock. It's 9pm. He said 7pm. Wednesday, champ. Seven on the dot. You can cope 'til then. You've got food in your fridge. The generator is all charged up. It's only three days, mate, okay? You've managed that long before.

It's worse when he doesn't come. Then he comes and it's worse again. But when I'm alone for days I'm scared. When I was little I just felt cold and lonely. I thought of Mum and Dad and Nana and all the kids in my class. Even annoying little Rosie, the one who used to steal my red crayon. I wished they were all here.

Then I got older and I started thinking other thoughts. What if the generator broke? What if the electricity goes out and I'm stuck in the dark? What if the ventilator clogs up and I suffocate to death?

But the worst that had happened so far was the toilet flush breaking or the time I got a stomach bug. Both those times he threw the cleaning products into the cage and watched me clean up from the other side of the bunker, holding a scarf over his mouth and nose.

At least it gave me something to do. There's never anything to do and that makes me crazy. Sometimes he brings me books. I ask for pens and pencils but one time I jabbed the pencil in my arm and he only brought me crayons after that. I draw pictures with them but I want to learn to get better. I can't do that with wax crayons.

Sometimes he cuts my hair. Sometimes he brings down a tub and pours hot water into it so I can have a bath. He tells me he loves me and sometimes I believe it.

But I don't want to stay here and I never have. That's why he makes sure I'm locked in the cage every night. Then he locks me in from the main door. I hear him walk up the steps before there's a clunk. I think there are two doors.

I'll spend hours wondering where I am. I draw pictures of what I think it looks like. When he comes into the room, I see the mud on his boots and so I know we're outside somewhere. Maybe it's a field. Maybe I'm on a farm. I don't remember much about the day I was taken. One minute I was looking at the river, the next I woke up on a bed surrounded by metal bars.

I didn't understand anything.

I cried and cried for Mum but she never came. I guess she doesn't know where I am because I think she'd come if she did.

I asked for a map once, but he didn't bring it. I guess he forgot. I wanted him to show me where we were on the map. Mum used to show me maps all the time. She'd show me pictures on the computer of different places in the world and I always said that I wanted to go there.

I used to try and think of ways to get out. He used to let me out of the cage sometimes, but he was big and strong and if I tried anything I got a smack round the mouth. I've been trying stuff a lot recently. I dunno why. I'm changing, I guess. I'm getting bigger and I don't like it down here anymore. I'm sick of it. I'm sick of him.

He keeps the keys in his pocket. Two weeks ago I tried to hit him with a plate, but he saw what I was going to do and pulled the plate from my hands. After that he gave me paper plates. I'm not allowed knives or anything sharp. I'm not allowed shoes with shoelaces. I have to eat cereal and bread and fruit all the time, nothing that needs knives and forks. Unless I'm supervised by him.

He's changed too. He looks at me differently. He doesn't do the stuff he used to. He says I'm getting big and that I look all wrong. He mumbles to himself about being tired when he thinks I'm not listening. He looks tired. I don't think he likes keeping me a secret anymore. Sometimes I wonder if he'll just never come back. Then I'll run out of food, water, electricity, water... I'll die.

There were times when I thought it might be nice to die. At least then I might get to go somewhere else. But I don't know for sure, so I decided not to. I might one day get out of my cage, but I might not go anywhere when I die, so it seemed too risky.

It's 9:15. This is it. He's never coming back. I've almost run out of food and I'm cold. My shirts and jumpers are all too small for me. The nights are colder lately. Maybe that means winter. I remember winter outside the bunker. I remember making a snowman and throwing snowballs. Sometimes he shows me movies on his phone. I like the Christmas movies the best. I like watching the happy families making snowmen and snow angels. But they make me cold so I only watch them when it's warm in the bunker.

I walk back and forth in my cage trying to keep warm. I press the button on my LED light. On. Off. On. Off.

Thu-thunk.

The first door.

A scrape.

The key.

The door opens.

He's here.

"Hiya, mate. Sorry I'm late."

He's always friendly like that. I don't talk back.

"I brought you a treat. Pizza." He grins at me.

I don't want it to, but my mouth waters. I'm so

hungry my tummy hurts.

"It's a bit cold. It's a walk from the car to get to here. Should've built this place closer."

He always complains. Especially when he has to fill up the water tank.

"How you doing, mate? You look cold. You should wrap up in the duvet when you're cold."

There's something wrong. He's avoiding my eye and I don't know why. He's never brought pizza to the cage before. Why is he doing this? I stare hungrily at the pizza. I cross my arms and try to figure out why something feels wrong.

"Want to come out here and eat?" he asks.

I nod.

He puts the pizza box on the table and reaches into his pocket for the key. His fingers are shaking. Why is he trembling like he's scared? He never has been before. Not even right at the beginning. It always frightens me that he's so calm and in control. I never liked that. It used to make me think about what else he could do. What was he capable of? I decided he was capable of anything very early on and that was why I did everything he told me to do, no matter what.

It takes him a few attempts to unlock the cage door. He's fumbling with his keys. He keeps his head angled away from me. I stand away like I always do. I'm not allowed near the door to my cage. I have to keep my hands out in front of me where he can see them, otherwise he's forced to hurt me like he did the time he stamped on my ankle. Or he tells me he'll put me back in the shackles like at the beginning.

"Stay there, Aiden," he says in a croaky voice. "Wait at the back for a moment."

It doesn't feel right. He's different today. I've been wondering for a while whether he's trying to figure something out, like he's been struggling to make a decision. Now, watching him, it seems to me that he's made a decision and it isn't a good one. It isn't a decision like whether to eat pizza or Chinese takeaway, it's something horrible. I can feel it. My insides are all squirmy, like they're moving. I'm not hungry anymore. I just want to throw up.

The door swings open and he stands there looking at me. There are tears in his eyes.

"You're a good boy, Aiden. You've always been a good boy. We've loved each other, haven't we? You've loved me? I love you?"

I don't answer. I'm not sure I know what love is anymore. I don't think it's this, though. I don't think love should make you feel dirty like I do now.

He takes a step back, with his eyes all shiny and wet. He's looking at me now. He won't stop looking at me. His arm reaches back behind him and his fingers fumble with the pizza box.

I don't think there's pizza in there.

The lid flips open and he grabs the wooden bat inside, like the kind I used to play sports with. Rounders. That's what it was called. We ran to bases after hitting the ball with the bat. I was always good, I got picked first. I cower away from him. That squirming feeling in my tummy is gone, instead I feel like a large, cold hand is gripping my stomach, squeezing tighter and tighter.

"I'm sorry, mate," he says. "But I have to finish it. I can't go on like this anymore. You're too old now. It's time to stop. I want to let you go, but I can't. I just can't, I'm sorry. I wanted to get a gun, you know, to make it quicker, but I don't know how to shoot one. I tried to learn about pills and poisons but they can go so wrong and I didn't want to do that to you, mate. So I'm going to do it like this. One quick blow. I can do this. I can end it this way. I know you want to die. You tried that time with the pencil. You could've hurt me but you did it to yourself instead. This way we both get what we want. Don't we?"

I lift my hands to my face and realise that I'm crying. My throat is raw.

"You don't really want me to die," I say.

He shakes his head. "No, I don't. But this is the way it has to end."

"I still miss the times before. I miss the camping holiday."

He lets out a sob. "I know you do, but I don't. This has been everything... You've made it so I could live."

"You took my life," I reply. "I don't love you."

Snot trickles out of his nose. "Don't say that, mate." His head lowers and he pushes his blond hair away from his eyes. He wipes his nose with the back of his hand. He's in his smart clothes today. A soft maroon jumper and trousers with the crease down the middle. He looks like someone from the telly. Someone who belongs inside the movies on his tiny phone screen. A person with their life all sorted. Doctors. Lawyers. Businessmen. He's one of those. Outside here, he probably looks like everyone else. He's normal.

"I still hate you, Hugh," I say. "I always have."

He begins singing that song, the one he sang to me when I stayed over at his house. The one he sings to me at night when he's telling me about Josie and Mum and Dad. Dad's in the army now. He's a soldier. Sometimes I think about how he could shoot Hugh down with his machine gun.

He grips the bat with both hands, widens his legs and squares his shoulders. I take another step back. My legs feel like jelly and I'm either going to be sick or wee my pants. I don't want to die, I don't want to. But he's bigger than me. If I fight him, would I win? I have to try. I have to.

"You should hate me, Aiden," he says. "I thought I wanted to kill you. I was so sure." He lowers his head and pauses. It feels like the moment is all stretched out, like it'll go on forever. But then he says, "It has to end all the same."

He lifts the bat like he's going to hit me, but just as I'm bracing myself to fly towards him, to hit him first, he swings the bat upwards. He screams loudly as he hits himself in the face, smashing his nose. I scream with him, afraid of the blood spurting from his nose. Afraid of him swinging the bat again, hitting himself in the head.

Hugh falls down. He drops the bat on the ground. I run over to him and bend down.

"F-f-in-ish-it." Bloody spit dribbles from his mouth.

I shake my head.

Hugh reaches out and pushes the bat towards me. "H-it-m-me."

There are tears running down my face. Snot comes out of my nose. I'm scared. I don't know what to do. I almost trip over the bat as I step away. Hugh lies there with his face all broken and bruised, with his eye all swollen. If I took the keys and left, he'd lie there in pain for hours and hours. I don't know how hurt he is. He could die on his own. Or I could go and get help. My mind feels all weird, like it can't cope, like it doesn't want to make the choice.

I don't want to make the choice.

I want it to all go away.

I bend down and pick up the bat.

I lift it over my head.

When it's done, Hugh twitches two or three times and then he goes still. His eyes aren't the same as they were before. They don't glitter or sparkle like eyes should.

And then I think about how lucky he is because he doesn't have to remember anymore. All his thoughts are gone and he doesn't have to think about the cage anymore.

There's some blood on my shirt too. I take it off and mop up the blood on the floor. I pull Hugh into a corner and put my t-shirt over him because I don't want to see his face anymore. I pull the keys from his pocket and unlock the door. I switch off the light and hurry out of the door up the steps. The further up the steps I go, the more afraid I feel. I drop the keys before I reach the top. The air is fresh and I take two big gulps of it, but I feel shaky.

It's dark and I don't know where I'm going but I keep walking. There are leaves on the ground and lots of trees. It's raining. I fall over twice.

I sing Hugh's song.

Then I decide that I don't want to remember anymore. Someone finds me. I know who I am, but I don't want to tell them. I don't want to talk to anyone, and I don't want to remember. I want all my thoughts to go away like Hugh's thoughts all went away.

I don't want to remember.

CHAPTER FORTY-FIVE

I called her Gina after my mother. She had my eyes and Jake's mouth, but we won't talk about how she looks like Jake. The nurse brought Aiden in to see me and his new sister after the labour was over. I took my small, squirming little baby, swaddled in a soft blanket, and I gave her to my son to hold. The son who had frightened me, and who I'd thought was dangerous. The son the media called 'feral' and insinuated was uncivilised after his incarceration away from society. Aiden cradled her gently in his arms as though she was precious, delicate cargo. And she was. She was as perfect as Aiden had been when he was born. She was a fighter. We both were. We'd been through hell together and now we were both rewarded by her being here. She was alive and perfect and I was glad I'd fought for our future.

"Is it too soon for visitors?" DCI Stevenson poked his head around the corner.

"No. It's fine," I replied.

The last two hours felt like a lifetime ago. After Aiden had pointed out the fluid pooling on the ground, we'd struggled back up the steps and out into Rough Valley forest. The contractions were worse than before, which meant Aiden had to prop me up as we struggled through the trees. I shouted. I screamed. I yelled.

The police weren't far away. They'd been coming for me, just as Stevenson had promised. He was the first to reach me. He hooked my arm over his shoulder and guided me through the dark wood, the light from his torch bouncing up and down like a scene from *The Blair Witch Project*. As we stumbled through the forest I told him about the underground bunker and the cage.

"I think it's Hugh," I whispered. "Aiden won't say but the... body has the same blond hair. I think it's Hugh and he's been dead this whole time."

Stevenson had only nodded.

He didn't understand. Hugh being dead this whole time meant that I had been afraid of a ghost. Aiden's kidnapper was a monster. A spectre. Though once very real, even in death Hugh had turned my life upside down to the point where I'd even suspected my own son of siding with his kidnapper. I'd become my own worst enemy, my paranoia seeking out danger in every corner whilst blinding me to the true threat: my husband.

Now, with the bright hospital lights overhead, Stevenson bobbed his head up and down and cooed at my baby. The smile on his face was genuine, and I was pleased with us all for surviving this long, arduous journey.

"How's Rob?" I asked.

"Stable, they say," he answered. "We got to him in the nick of time, I reckon."

"And Josie?"

"She was tied up to her bed with a gag over her mouth. She's shaken up, but she's given us a statement about Jake. He dragged her up there and tied her up, but aside from a few bruises she hasn't been hurt."

I nodded. Aiden carried Gina to the other side of the room and sat down in the visitor's chair.

"Jake?"

"Deceased."

I nodded. I wasn't happy about it. I wouldn't be dancing over his grave or breaking out the champagne, but I was relieved, and that relief lifted a heavy weight from my heart. It was over. Or, at least, it was almost over.

"And the bunker?"

"There's not much we can do at night. Forensics will go in first thing in the morning. We'll need Aiden to make a statement. Is he… is he talking?"

"A little."

DCI Stevenson rocked back on his heels, awkwardly. "That's good."

"There's one other thing," I said.

"What is it?" Stevenson asked, frowning.

*

I knew that one day Aiden would want to tell his story. Some stories are told from the beginning and they don't stop until the final word. Some stories start at the end or the middle and they show you the beginning. I knew that Aiden's story would take a lifetime to tell, but we had the rest of our lives to explore it. In the week that followed Gina's birth (not Jake's death, not the discovery of Hugh or Rob's assault; it was Gina's birth, the start of life) Aiden revealed a tiny island in the midst of an ocean. The glimpse he showed me was enough for the time being. I knew he would show me the rest when he was ready.

Why was I so confident that Aiden would tell me his story? Because we tell stories to heal. Aiden has a lot of healing to do. We both do. We'll both be healing together.

Forensics found Hugh's DNA all over the bunker. They found the paperwork detailing the purchase of land in Rough Valley Forest. No one had been suspicious because of Hugh's dealings with various property developers. A few companies had bought small plots of Rough Valley but no one had built on the land. Hardly anyone ever went into Rough Valley Forest, a fact that Hugh had exploited.

After an appeal for information a builder came forward to admit he'd been hired to adapt an old World War II bunker as a living space. Hugh had told the man that he was thinking of turning it into some sort of 'glamping' spot. The place was decked out like a caravan, with a portable water tank and a generator for electricity. Hugh would need to replace them on a regular basis so Aiden could survive on his own in the woods. Because the part of the woods Hugh bought was private property, none of the public paths went even close to the bunker where my son was kept. No one heard the generator. No one. When Aiden escaped, he told me he was afraid he'd be in trouble for killing Hugh. He had turned the generator off and hid it beneath a pile of leaves.

There was no record of the bunker on any plans or included in any maps. Hugh had thought this endeavour through from the beginning to the very end. Aiden told me about Hugh's intentions to end it by killing him, but how he had been unable to do it in the end. I didn't like to think about what had happened the day Aiden escaped from the bunker.

I had a hard time putting together the idea of the Hugh who invited me into his home, who made us delicious roast dinners and served us fine wine, with the Hugh who snuck away from home and work to visit my kidnapped son in his private bunker. But I learned a lot about Hugh from Aiden.

Josie came to see me in hospital after Gina was born. She was in tears. Her shirt was on inside out. I gently told her to turn it the right way and she stared at me open-mouthed.

"Tell me," I said. "Tell me you didn't know."

"I thought it was affairs," she said. "That's what everyone told me. They saw him with women. I just…"

"The day of the flood. You were there. Were you stalling me?" I asked.

She shook her head so quickly that she seemed almost manic. "No. I couldn't. I wouldn't. I…"

"It's all right," I said. "I know you didn't know. He went to extreme lengths to hide this side of himself. I don't blame you." I reached out and took her hand.

"I should have seen it." She wiped tears away with the back of her hand. "I should have known the signs. After things with my dad… I thought I'd recognise it if it ever happened again."

"I keep thinking about one night when Aiden was, I don't know, maybe two or three, and we stayed at your place for the night. Hugh took Aiden to bed, all wrapped up in his arms. I followed them up the stairs a few minutes later and watched him tuck Aiden into bed. He was singing this lullaby really softly. I remember thinking about what a good dad he'd make. I went into the bathroom and I cried for you both because you couldn't have children and you so deserved them." I shook my head. "I was so wrong. And I should have known that day when Aiden sang that little song to himself. It was the same song. I should have known. Instead, all these weeks I've been afraid of a ghost while my own husband…"

Josie touched my hand lightly. Tentatively.

"They wore masks."

Hugh had made Josie feel safe in the same way Jake had made me feel safe. They'd done it by hiding behind their masks. Why should either I or Josie feel guilty for that? Why should we feel weak? People who prey on the vulnerable aren't strong—they're cheaters. While the rest of us are working hard to keep our lives in control, these cheaters are taking our lives away from us. They steal and they lie because they can't connect with people, they don't know love, and they don't know what it feels like to be loved.

I almost feel sorry for them. But not quite.

When Josie left I felt very hollow and empty, but she wasn't part of Aiden's story, and that was my priority until everything was over. Aiden had to come first.

The media had not let us out of its greedy fist just yet. The remarkable story of the baby born just hours after the discovery of the grisly body in the bunker was splashed all over the papers. We sold millions of copies for them. But I was fiercely protective of Aiden. I ignored every phone call and every offer that came my way. I kept my cool and I learned not to scream at the reporters.

After Josie left my hospital room, I got out of the bed and took Aiden's hand. Gina was nestled in the crook of my free arm. We walked together through the wards to bright white room filled with six beds. Three on either side. It wasn't visiting hours and I knew I shouldn't really be there, but I didn't care.

"Here she is. The miracle." Rob was propped up with pillows, smiling at us, his eyes twinkling. The same eyes as Aiden.

"Do you want to hold her?" I asked.

He nodded. His head was still bandaged, and I could see by the way he moved that he was still in some pain, but I passed Gina across to him, making sure he cradled her head, which he did with great care.

"She looks like you," he said. Then he smiled across at Aiden. "How you doing, buddy?"

Aiden fidgeted next to me, looking down at his feet. "Okay."

Rob turned to me with tears in his eyes and I met his gaze while heat radiated through my chest and into my veins. I nodded and mouthed the words 'he's back'. Then I placed my hand on top of Rob's and squeezed it. We remained like that for at least five minutes, none of us quite believing we were there, alive, and—mostly—in one piece.

*

After being discharged from the hospital I went back to Jake's house because I didn't have anywhere else to go. The first thing I did was take down every photograph, strip the beds, and throw his clothes into a bin bag. I would never take pleasure in his death, but that didn't mean I wanted to be surrounded by his belongings.

Once all of that was done, I had only one more

task, and it was to do with Aiden's story. Hugh had planned his kidnapping down to the letter but I never believed he'd set out to take Aiden. It didn't make sense to kidnap a child to whom he was so close. As soon as Aiden went missing, every person in my life would be under scrutiny. But Hugh got lucky. Aiden decided to wander off to the river in the middle of a flood. Not only that, Jake *pushed* Aiden into the river. Hugh came across Aiden floating in the river, fished him out, and took him to his bunker while the rest of the world assumed that Aiden had drowned. Then all he had to do was come up with good excuses to everyone for disappearing so often (business trips and long hours to Josie; affairs to his brother and colleagues). I found out that Hugh would live in the bunker with Aiden for days, staying overnight. Then, when he actually did have to go on business trips, Hugh would drive back from York or London to check on Aiden, put more petrol in the generator, and replace the water. Keeping him alive was a lot of work, but taking him had been convenient. Too convenient.

There was one missing element, and I knew exactly what it was. I also knew what I was going to do about it after forensics finished examining the scene of the crime, because there wasn't any other DNA evidence inside the bunker aside from Aiden and Hugh. That left me with one choice.

I dropped Aiden and Gina off at Sonya and Peter's house. Then I got in my car and drove towards Bishoptown school. I took a turn off the main road and instead headed down Singer Lane to the third house on the left. When I got out of the car I checked my pocket, locked the car, and knocked on the door. Mrs White from across the street waved through the window and I waved back.

The door opened and I stepped through, not even bothering to wait to be invited in. I reached into my pocket, retrieved the knife, and pressed the point against her throat.

"Are you alone?"

She hesitated but she answered. "Yes."

"Shut your curtains in the living room."

I hid the knife behind my back and followed her into the living room. She did as I'd asked.

I'd been in Amy's living room about a year ago when we met for takeaway and movie night with a couple of the women from school. It had been tidier then. Amy had left a few mugs on the coffee table, as well as a stack of newspapers. One of them was spread open, with her face shown in a little bubble above a picture of me getting into a car with Aiden.

"You're not on the front page anymore," I noted. "That has to hurt."

"What are you doing here, Emma?" Amy asked. She backed away from me with her hands behind her back. Her eyes were wide, like a frightened puppy. I could tell she was attempting to back up to the vase on the bookcase behind her. I strode across the room and she yelped as I placed the knife edge against her cheek.

"They're not going to be able to prove it. That's why I'm here. Aiden told me you put the idea of him going down to the river in his head. You kept telling him how pretty it would be and how brave he would be if he went. You told him the bridge was going to sink and that he should go and watch. You told him I'd be proud of him for sneaking out of school. Then you deliberately turned your back as he wandered out of the classroom. You knew the school would be too distracted with the flood to notice. Then you sent a text to your boyfriend Hugh to tell him where Aiden was. You knew what Hugh was and you *helped* him. You're sick."

Amy took another step back but I saved her the trouble by knocking the vase onto the carpet. I pressed the knife so close to her skin that it drew blood.

"And then, when Aiden came back, you logged into Hugh's Facebook account and you checked him in at a Las Vegas airport. That... *that*, the police might be able to trace back to you—"

"They won't," she snapped. "I covered my tracks. Hugh showed me how. He learned all kinds of tricks on the internet when he was feeding his *habit*."

"Then I suppose I'll have to serve out my own justice," I said.

"I didn't hurt any kids," she said. "It was... I..."

"What?" I snapped. "Spit it out. Tell me your justifications for doing what you did."

"We took drugs together, all right? We took drugs and we experimented. It all got a bit out of hand. He used to strangle me sometimes and we'd talk about things in bed. We told each other the darkest parts of us." Her eyes glittered and she smiled at me. I was tempted to cut the smile from her face but I couldn't. Not yet, anyway. "I bet you don't know what that's like, to crave that kind of darkness. You're so... normal. Boring. You never deserved Rob." She sneered, her frightened puppy act slipping. "You're so... vanilla. You don't understand what it's like to live on the edge. I wanted to help Hugh because he was... free. Knowing that I'd helped him was enough for me. I got to go to work every day with the knowledge that I knew what had really happened to your son. I knew every day. Hugh even let me go down there once, while Aiden was sleeping."

"Why the fuck did Hugh trust you?"

"Because he knew me!" she exploded. "He was the only one who did. That's why I protected him when Aiden came back. I knew the police would sniff around his house if I didn't do something to account for his disappearance. That's why I logged into his Facebook. Everyone thought he was having an affair, but I figured out what must have happened."

"You weren't protecting him, you were protecting yourself," I said. "You thought the affair you had with Hugh might come out and lead back to you. But you're an idiot, Amy. You're not good at this at all, not like Hugh. You craved your fifteen minutes of fame when you should've been keeping quiet. Didn't you realise that Aiden would start talking eventually?"

"I thought he'd come back wrong," she said. "I figured he was retarded and would never say a peep." She shrugged. "He is your son, after all."

I ignored the dig. "You're weak. Hugh was controlling you and you can't even see it," I said. "He was controlling everyone. You. Me. Josie. Aiden. That's what he wanted. Complete control."

"No," she said. "I allowed him to."

"You're pathetic."

"Whatever," she replied. "You're a bitch. You never noticed me. None of you. I was nothing to you all. A follower. The dirt on your shoe. You never deserved Rob. He's better than you."

"You're sick," I said, pressing the knife harder against her skin. When a red bead trickled down her face she started to cry.

"Don't hurt me! Please!"

I let out a long, hot breath right into her face. "Do you know what it felt like to kill Jake? I saw the life fade from his eyes. I tasted his blood when I ripped his wrist open with my teeth. I could rip out your throat right now." She whimpered and closed her eyes. "The only reason I won't do that is because I'm not an idiot like you. I'm not about to waste my life over a cretin like you. I have a life now. I have my son back and I have Rob back. I have a daughter. What do you have? A stack of newspapers with your name in them. You're not worth going to prison over. So I'm going to tell you exactly what you're going to do. You're going to sell this house. You're going to quit your job. You're going to take the blood money you received from the lies you told and you're going to move far away from here. You're never going to show your face again, because if I see you, I will plunge this knife into your belly and I'm going to keep cutting until I reach your lying mouth. Do you understand?"

She nodded.

*

It was a steep climb. My legs ached and my back was sweaty, but the view was beautiful. I lifted Gina's hand and waved to the tiny, scurrying people below. She was strapped to my chest, nuzzled against my skin.

"Do you remember this place?" I asked.

Aiden nodded. "We used to come for picnics."

Bit by bit, day by day, I was learning what Aiden remembered and what he didn't. He remembered my mum and dad, he remembered the school, but he didn't remember his favourite food or the football team he'd supported.

I spread out the blanket and placed the picnic basket down. It was cold, and the grass was wet, but I'd brought a waterproof blanket and we were all covered in thick layers to keep us warm. I removed the baby halter from my front and sat down on the blanket, putting Gina on my knee. She looked funny in her little ski suit, all red nose and cheeks.

"Isn't it lovely down there?" I said.

Aiden rested his hands on his knees. He was learning things too, like how to interact with his surroundings. He didn't stand around looking like a sore thumb like he used to. He relaxed into seats. He rested against tables. He drummed his fingers on the armrest of the car when the radio was on.

He nodded. "Thought I wouldn't see it again."

I couldn't get used to the sound of his voice. He spoke in short, abrupt sentences. Sometimes it took him a while to get his words out. He would work his jaw as if feeling the words move around his mouth before he spoke. But I was proud of him for the way he was developing.

We sat there for a while, looking at the river Ouse snaking through the tiny village. It was morning, and the winter sun gave everything a sharp, bright look. The trees were so orange they hurt your eyes to look at. The sky was so blue it was more like the sea, and the air was so fresh it left your lungs with that rasping, raw feeling you get from exercising on a cold day.

The events of the last decade would rest heavy on my soul until the day I died, but I had a glimpse of the happiness that lay before me. A road to be travelled.

"Next time we have a picnic," I said. "It's going

to be on the Great Wall of China." I opened the basket and removed the sandwiches.

"Okay," he replied.

I paused, and turned to look at my son. There was colour on his cheeks, and his eyes were bright. I reached towards him and gently brushed his cheek with my hand. Aiden slid down to the left so that he rested his head against my shoulder. It was awkward at first, but after a moment or two he settled in. For the first time in over a decade I breathed in the scent of my son. I placed my nose against the top of his head and I breathed in the notes that lay below shampoo and shower gel to smell his skin, like I had done the day he was born. As my nostrils filled with that slightly sickly, sweet scent of skin, my heart was finally full.

THE END

A note from the author

I truly hope you enjoyed the book. If you would like to leave a review, please do. Even a few lines of your honest opinion is worth so much to me and to other readers who might want to read this book.

If you would like to hear about my new releases and any free books I might have on offer, please sign up to my newsletter on my website Sarahdenzil.com.

Aiden's story is never devoid of hope. He had a mother who loved him and who fought for him, risking everything she had.
There is a lot of light and a lot of hope out there, but if you are feeling as though you have lost that light, then please consider the following:
http://www.samaritans.org/
http://www.mind.org.uk/

Thank you for reading this story.

ABOUT THE AUTHOR

Sarah A. Denzil is a British suspense writer from Derbyshire. In her alternative life—AKA YA author Sarah Dalton—she writes speculative fiction for teenagers, including *The Blemished*, *Mary Hades* and *White Hart*.

Sarah lives in Yorkshire with her partner, enjoying the scenic countryside and rather unpredictable weather.

Saving April, Sarah's debut suspense thriller, is a psychological look into the minds of the people around us who we rarely even consider—our neighbours. What do we really know about them, and what goes on when the doors are closed?

https://www.facebook.com/sarahadenzil/
https://twitter.com/sarahdenzil
http://www.sarahdenzil.com/

Writing as Sarah Dalton -
http://www.sarahdaltonbooks.com/

CPSIA information can be obtained
at www.ICGtesting.com
Printed in the USA
FSOW01n1517140417
33127FS